Night Song *makes you wish that every historic story from WWII could be told. It shares the challenge of sacrifice, courage, faith, love and friendship. I cannot wait for the next one.*

—Annie von Trapp, member of the von Trapp family, as popularized in the movie, *The Sound of Music*

Tricia Goyer takes time to craft her novels with all the right ingredients. Readers easily connect with her characters and find themselves thinking about them long after the final note has been sung. A powerful historical story of darkness overcome by love.

—Robin Jones Gunn, best-selling author of the Glenbrooke series and the Sisterchicks™ novels

After nearly 60 years, I was transported back to Mauthausen, remembering the days when I delivered the daily ration of bread to the dying. The author has the uncanny knack of recreation, and I found myself remembering everything, including the smell.

—Charlie White, 11th Armored Division Veteran

Night Song *is filled with many details that are exactly how they were during my military career. Though I am a compulsive reader of WWII, I learned things I did not know!*

—Wilfred "Mac" McCarty, 11th Armored Division Veteran

Tricia Goyer has very cleverly combined fact and fiction to create a well written and wonderfully emotional novel set during World War II.

—Bert Heinold, U.S. Army veteran 11th Armored Division

Night Song

A STORY OF SACRIFICE

TRICIA GOYER

MOODY PUBLISHERS
CHICAGO

© 2004 by
TRICIA GOYER

All Scripture quotations, unless otherwise indicated, are taken from the King James Version.

Scripture quotations marked NIV are taken from the *Holy Bible, New International Version*®. NIV®. Copyright © 1973, 1978, 1984 by International Bible Society. Used by permission of Zondervan Publishing House. All rights reserved.

Library of Congress Cataloging-in-Publication Data

Goyer, Tricia.
  Night song : a story of sacrifice / by Tricia Goyer.
     p. cm.
  ISBN 0-8024-1555-5
     1. World War, 1939-1945—Underground movements—Fiction.
2. Mauthausen (Concentration camp)—Fiction. 3. Concentration camp inmates—Fiction. 4. Americans—Austria—Fiction. 5. Orchestral musicians—Fiction. 6. Musicians—Fiction. 7. Austria—Fiction. I. Title.

PS3607.O94N54 2004
813'.6—dc22

                                                                2004010480

1 3 5 7 9 10 8 6 4 2

Printed in the United States of America

For John, my wonderful husband
You believe in my dreams and urged me to follow.
This book is one of those dreams brought to life . . .

PART ONE

Yet the Lord will command his lovingkindness in the daytime,
and in the night his song shall be with me,
and my prayer unto the God of my life.

Psalm 42:8

Prologue

It smelled the same—cold stone and quarry dust. He had told himself he would never return to this place of death, yet here he was, to play again the music that was never more than a heartbeat away.

Jakub Hanauer perched on the edge of a metal folding chair on the platform and stared out at the crowd waiting in the open air. The striped prisoner caps and colorful scarves worn by the attendees were once the distinguishing marks of inmate status and nationality. Now they were marks of survival. The banner of what they had overcome.

This was a yearly trek for some. For those with no family graves to visit, no weathered headstones marking a loved one's rest, this fortress of stone and iron, built to serve a thousand-year Reich, remained as testimony.

The Vienna Philharmonic sat ready in a half circle behind him, instruments tuned. Beyond the makeshift stage towered the Mauthausen quarry itself. A mountain of rock scarred by those who'd mined it.

At this place where prisoners—skeletal waifs—had once chipped away at the stone, new generations joined the old. In the faded footprints of dying men who had carried forty-pound boulders up 186 stone steps, a world-renowned orchestra prepared to play. And where Nazi dogs had once ripped flesh from those too weak to work, a crowd gathered to remember.

Jakub watched as Dr. Thomas Klestil, president of the Republic of Austria, rose and strode to the podium. The president cleared his throat. "For seven years, two hundred thousand people were incarcerated by the Nazis in Mauthausen concentration camp and compelled to perform the heaviest of labor under inhumane conditions. More than half of them did not survive these agonies. . . ."

As the president's voice trailed on, Jakub saw the endless sea of marching prisoners in his memory. He heard their cries. He smelled their burning flesh. A cloud of death had once hung over this place the way spring's white clouds did today.

The president's voice interrupted his thoughts. "May every visitor to today's celebration of the liberation understand and pass on the message that without remembrance, there can be no future."

Jakub stirred as the audience exploded with applause. Other important men spoke, but he could not wipe from his mind the faces of the past. *Jakub,* they called out in his mind. *Play. It is in you; let it out. Play for us.*

"Jakub Hanauer and the Vienna Philharmonic Orchestra."

All eyes followed as Jakub adjusted his own striped cap, then lifted his instrument from his lap. He rose from the creaky metal chair and stepped to his place. Glancing over the crowd, Jakub again saw *their* faces. He nodded at the conductor, lifted his bow, and began to play.

Many years ago, when his life had depended on it, his fingers had fumbled. They'd been stiff and unyielding. Now, through the music that flowed from his instrument, Jakub told about that time. The melody spoke of bondage and fear. And he hoped his listeners understood.

The orchestra joined in on cue, stirring goose bumps on Jakub's neck. A warm wind caressed his cheek. For a moment, it seemed he could feel Alexi's work-toughened hands engulfing his own, pressing the strings, humming the melody . . . saving Jakub's life.

The wind passed, the orchestra ceased its playing, but the song of Jakub's violin continued. Tears trailed down his cheeks, and again he hoped his listeners heard. He hoped they understood what love can do even to those condemned to die.

One

For better or for worse, Nick Fletcher knew his life would change tonight. He touched the small box in his coat pocket for the hundredth time as the credits to *Mrs. Miniver* rolled. He was sure he hadn't absorbed ten minutes of the film; he'd been too busy watching Evie. The way she cried at the latest newsreel of the bombing of Pearl Harbor. The way she laughed, and then cried some more, with the Miniver family on the big screen as they faced life after the Blitz in Britain.

Her fingers had dug into the palm of his hand during an especially sad scene. Later, a smile replaced the tears when the stationmaster, Mr. Ballard, showed Mrs. Miniver a rose he had cultivated and asked her permission to name it after her.

I don't have a rose, but perhaps you'll call yourself by my name. Nick lifted her hand to his lips.

The houselights came up, and Evie turned to Nick, dabbing her eyes. "That was such a good movie." She let out a low breath. "Look at me; I'm a mess."

Nick stroked her cheek and gazed into her dark brown eyes. "I'm looking. I'm looking, Evie Kreig, and I can't get enough, lady."

Her cheeks reddened slightly, and she rose from the velvet chair. Her straight, silky brown hair cascaded over her shoulders, and she brushed it aside as she slipped on her blue jacket and buttoned it at the waist.

"So, you ready to get something to eat? I know the perfect place." *This is it. The moment I've waited for.*

Evie shrugged. "I don't know, Nick. It's awfully late, and I don't want Papa to worry. He was acting sort of funny today." She grabbed her clutch and leaned close. "And we still have tomorrow, and the next day . . . and . . ."

Nick attempted to hold his smile. He offered his arm, then led Evie up the aisle. "The thing is, I found a wonderful restaurant and made reservations. They promised to stay open just for us." He looked down at her. "Seeing that it's late, we'd better hurry. What can I say to convince you?"

Evie squeezed his arm tighter. "Okay. You know I can't say no to you."

Nick kissed the top of her head. *That's what I'm hoping for. . . .*

14

Nick's hand engulfed Evie's, and it took her two quick steps to keep up with his one as he pulled her through the city. The signs in the square buzzed past her peripheral vision like a neon dream. Above, a fluorescent billboard broke through the fog: *Lena Horne. Live Tonight.*

Where is he taking me? She wished she'd left a note for her parents. Papa liked Nick, but he always scowled, his dark eyebrows meeting in the middle, when she arrived home after ten.

"Nick, hold on. You're leaving me in the dust," she panted.

Nick slowed slightly, glancing back with a grin. "I love your Viennese accent when you're all worked up. But we have to hurry now before they close."

He rounded the corner, and Evie followed, full skirt swishing around her legs and high heels clicking across the littered sidewalk. While most of the businesses on 42nd Street were closed, a single warm glow beckoned from a small café.

At the door Nick released her hand, adjusted his Davenport jacket, and flashed his best smile. "Well, what do ya' think, my little chickadee?"

Evie laughed. "Oh, please, Nick. You are more Jimmy Stewart than W. C. Fields any day." She glanced at the sign. "Danube! Like my river! How did you find it?"

"A friend told me about it. It's new. An Austrian

chef, just immigrated." He took a step back, jutting out his elbow. Evie entwined her arm in his.

The door opened with a jingle of bells against glass. Small tables were lit only by candlelight. A waiter dressed in Austrian lederhosen and an embroidered shirt hurried toward them.

"I feel like I'm back in Vienna," Evie said.

"I checked the menu a few days back." Nick helped her out of her coat. "*Wienerschnitzel* and beef goulash. Even braised pike in hazelnut sauce."

"I would give anything for a good goulash. Americans never get it quite right." Evie's eyes feasted on the rich velvet draperies and Klimt reproductions.

"Mr. Fletcher, sir?" The waiter smiled. "This way, please."

He led them to a candlelit table in a corner of the room. Nick pulled out the chair for Evie.

"Thank you." She watched him as he took a seat across from her. There was definitely something on his mind. He kept looking at her as if he were about to speak.

The waiter handed them menus.

"Oh, look, Nick, they have Sacher torte. My favorite!"

Nick didn't respond, and he hardly glanced at his menu. Instead, he ran his fingers through his hair, then took a sip of water.

"Nick, are you with me?"

His eyes locked with hers. "Of course, yes."

She reached for his hand. "So, when are you going to tell me your secret?"

He leaned close, wrapping her fingers completely inside his. He tried to hide his smile, but one corner of his mouth refused to submit. "I don't know what you're talking about."

"Oh yes, you do, Nick Fletcher. We've been together almost every day for a year. I know when something's up."

"Okay, you got me."

He leaned close and lifted her hand to his cheek. She felt the slightest hint of stubble on his chin.

"I think you're the most beautiful, caring, talented . . ."

Evie laughed and pulled her hand away. "There's more to it than that, mister." She crossed her arms and raised an eyebrow. "Fine. We will just sit here until you tell."

A childlike grin formed on Nick's lips.

She laughed. "Okay, if you're not going to tell me, will you at least order so we can eat?"

Nick's finger's tapped against the menu as he pretended to read it. "What are you having?"

"Goulash and Sacher torte for dessert. I told you that." Evie placed her menu on the table and rested her chin on her hands. "Okay, really. What's going on? Do you have news? Did Dr. Erikson put you on the surgery schedule?"

Nick put down the menu. "No, not that. I still haven't heard. The residency schedule will be up next week." He sighed. "But if you won't let it go, I guess now is as good a time as any." His face broke into a huge grin. The candlelight danced against his dark hair and eyes. He rose and reached into his jacket pocket.

Evie placed one hand over her heart, then without warning the bell on the front door jingled and a cold wind struck her.

Nick turned, and the color drained from his face. A man in a dark coat and hat hurried in. He lifted his head, eyes full of sorrow. Evie jumped to her feet, the chair toppling to the floor behind her.

The waiter rushed forward. "I'm sorry, sir. The restaurant is closed."

Nick waved him away. "It's okay. He's with us."

"Papa?" Evie rushed over. "How did you find us? What's wrong?"

Her father approached Nick. "I am sorry, Nicholas. If there were any other way—"

Evie grasped his hands. "Tell me, please."

"We must go home."

"Has something happened to Mother?"

"No. Home to Vienna. All of us. Our passports have been revoked, my job as ambassador nullified. Our ship leaves in the morning."

Nick's hands tightened on Evie's shoulders. She felt his breath against her ear.

"No," he whispered.

Evie grasped Nick's hand on her shoulder. "This can't be."

Her father turned to Nick. "I'm sorry, son. I can't let your plans happen now."

"I don't understand."

The older man shook his head. "They're closing the embassy. All Austrians must return to Europe."

"Congress declared war on Germany, not us!" Evie said.

"Austria is Germany's ally." Her father shrugged wearily. "They see us as the enemy too."

"We've been kicked out? A man in your position? It isn't as though Austria had a choice. The Germans annexed us!"

"I'm sorry." Her father placed his hat upon his head and turned toward Nick. "I told you this might happen, son. I had hoped you would have more time—" He walked to the door. "A cab is waiting. Really, I am very sorry, but you only have a few minutes."

The bell jingled again as the door closed behind him.

Evie turned to Nick. "I can't do it. I can't leave you. And your surprise—"

Nick smiled ruefully. He opened his suit jacket and tenderly removed a small velvet box, then placed it on the white linen tablecloth and opened it. An antique diamond ring sparkled in the candlelight. "Evie, this was meant for you."

🐾   🐾   🐾

Evie pushed aside the porthole curtain and took in the Manhattan skyline. The ship's engines purred from somewhere below, vibrating the floor. The sound made Evie think of the rumble of German tanks spreading over Europe. *War.* This war would soon be more than images in print or newsreels. It would be as real to her as New York had been for the past five years.

19

She rubbed her puffy eyes, then quickly pulled the pins from her chignon, dropped them into the night-stand drawer, and shook out her hair. She wished she could unbind her life as easily. From the first word of *Anschluss,* Evie had a hard time believing Austria was a sovereign land no longer. As a diplomat's daughter, she had spent nearly as much time in New York City as she had in Vienna. She'd sampled American freedoms and had flourished in lived-out democracy. The culture appealed to her taste. Only Nick understood these things, loved these things, about her.

A quick knock sounded at the door, and Evie jumped. It must be Mother reminding her to air out a dress for dinner in the captain's quarters, or Papa checking to make sure she'd acquired suitable accommodations.

She rebuttoned her jacket and opened the door.

A tall, broad-shouldered man leaned against the doorjamb, wearing the common gray cap and wool vest of a cabbie. The cap's bill was pulled over the man's face, and his gaze was turned downward to a small satchel in his hand.

Evie squared her shoulders. "I'm sorry, but you must have the wrong room."

"Wait a minute, ma'am. Dis cabin here is where I was told ta go."

"Sir, you have the wrong room," she repeated, moving to close the door.

The man jabbed his foot in the doorway. "No, ma'am, I don't believes I do." The scruffy cab driver lifted his head. Dark brown eyes glanced down at her.

Evie gasped—then socked him in the stomach with a soft fist. "Nick Fletcher!" She grabbed his free hand, pulling him into the room. "What on earth are you doing? How did you get on board? And where did you get those clothes?"

A familiar grin lit up Nick's handsome features, displaying a hint of a dimple on his left cheek. He dropped both the satchel and his cap to the floor, then swooped Evie into his arms.

"First off, I told the porter a pretty little lady left a satchel in my cab. And second, would ya hate me if I told you I traded my fancy threads for these?"

Evie caught a whiff of roasted wieners at the same instant that she noticed a smudge of ketchup on the white shirt collar. "You're not talking about the hot dog vendor on the docks, are you? I recognize these clothes. What am I going to do with you, Nicholas? You are going to get both of us in awful trouble. The boat is set to disembark in just a few moments."

"Disembark, eh?" Nick's cultured speech slid into a New York cadence. "Dis here could be a problem. I wish I could go wit' ya. Bein' as how I'd follow ya to da ends of de earth." His face grew somber as he caressed the scar on her jawline.

Evie's skin sparked under his touch.

"Seriously now." His voice was low. "Do you know how hard it was sitting in church, realizing this ship was still anchored? I know our official parting was last night, but I remembered a few more gifts." He opened

21

the clasp of his satchel and plunked down on the red cushioned chair.

"You're not talking about the ring, are you? Honestly, as much as I love it, I don't feel it's safe taking your grandmother's keepsake with me. And you've already given me so much." Her hand reached to her collar and the French cameo pendant hanging around her neck.

"No. Nothing like that. Just some little things to remember me by." He reached into the satchel. "First, a little lady for the lady." Nick's fingers opened to reveal a miniature model of the Statue of Liberty. He placed it on her palm. "This is to help you remember that day when we gazed up at *her* and you gave that wonderful diatribe on just how lucky I was to be born under the lady's torch.

"Next . . ." Nick placed a foot-long hot dog—piled with kraut and relish—in her other hand.

Evie took a big whiff.

"This is to remember our many fine dinners together.

"And finally." He reached into the bag and pulled out a small book.

Evie recognized the burgundy cover worn from the touch of a hundred hands. "Nick, you didn't!"

"But I did."

"You stole a hymnal from church?"

He laughed. "No. I asked Pastor Simons if I could buy one. When I told him who it was for, he gave it to me."

Evie placed the hot dog and tiny statue on the small

table, and then she grasped the book. The pages were soft from use, and she could barely make out the gold words on the cover. "Songs of Praise," she whispered.

Nick placed his hands over hers. "This is to remind you of all the services when we sang side by side."

Evie pressed the hymnal to her chest and reached her other arm around his neck. "Thank you. I will remember and will pray that we'll be together soon."

Nick's eyes studied hers. "Did you talk to your father? Does he know of a way we can communicate?"

Evie sighed. "He says that receiving and sending letters from the States will draw too much attention. He promised to think of a way, though. Maybe we should just write anyway, then when we're able, mail them all at once."

Nick pulled Evie close and whispered in her ear, but his words were lost amid the loud shrill of the ship's whistle.

She took a step back and looked into his dark eyes. "What did you say?"

"I said, sounds like a good idea. I'll be thinking about you, loving you, no matter how far apart we are." He replaced his cap and pulled it low over his brow. "Now, I better get outta here before I end up on the other side of the world—although that doesn't sound too bad, if I could be with you. I love you, Evie."

He kissed her again, whispered "Be safe" in her ear, and disappeared out the door.

"I wish I could promise such a thing," Evie murmured as she moved to the doorway and watched him jog down the narrow hall. Her chest tightened, and she imprinted the blurry image of Nick into her mind . . . one last time.

~   ~   ~

VIENNA, AUSTRIA
DECEMBER 12, 1941

From the shadowed doorway, SS *Sturmmann* Otto Akeman observed three Reich officials gathering around a small wooden table. Apprehension stirred in the pit of Otto's stomach over the privilege of guarding these men tonight. He'd heard rumors about the mystical events that often took place inside this bunker but had a hard time believing them. Now was his chance to know for sure.

A few years ago, Otto would have never guessed that he'd be safeguarding important men in Hitler's regime. He'd been a performer, not a soldier. Wielding a violin, not a weapon. But music mattered little now.

A low moan rose in the room, vibrating off the walls. The sound hummed in Otto's ears like a dog's injured cry. He scanned the dark recesses before realizing the laments came from the leader. Like a dark magician of old, the officer's hands punched the air as low, guttural chants rose from deep in his throat. Otto blinked and was sure his eyes deceived him.

The voices of the other men joined in. The three sounds merged, spinning around the room, increasing with speed and intensity. They uttered chains of meaningless words and scraps of sentences. Ice came over Otto's limbs, followed by a great heat, as if an unseen presence had suddenly entered the bunker. Otto longed to run, to escape the hungry presence that desired to consume him, yet he stood straighter and refused to budge.

Then, just as quickly as fear had overtaken him, curiosity replaced it. Who were these men? And who, or what, were they summoning? *Focus on the men. Learn their secrets,* he told himself.

Then he spotted it. On the table before them, a bloodred swastika had been carved into the wood. For a thousand years the swastika had been symbolic of life force, solar power, and regeneration—yet wasn't it simply a symbol? Heat moved through Otto as if energy radiated from the swastika's crooked rays. He blinked again and dared to lean closer, partially into the light.

Then the three walked to a large, rectangular table in a far corner. Scattered over its scarred, wooden surface, maps, charts, and diagrams waited.

Otto strained to listen to the men's words. They spoke of dates and times, of places and people, and of deportment. Words like "death squad," "transports," and "key supporters" caused Otto's ears to tingle.

One officer plotted his plan with a simple graph. The jagged, black line plunged sharply, like a lightning bolt rune striking the earth. For the Reich. For *der Führer.*

Just yesterday, Otto had joined hundreds of soldiers

in an official parade as they'd goose-stepped in rhythm, carrying banners bearing swastikas. Yet even as he'd marched, with the uniform rhythm of hobnailed boots pounding, Otto had not sensed the same presence as in this room. *Ultimate power.* His curiosity birthed into longing.

Here's where the power lies, Otto thought an hour later as he escorted the three men into the frigid night. And with each step, perception filled his mind, until suddenly he understood. *What the world sees in parades of men is just a distraction . . . what I've seen here is where the real power lies.*

The four quickly strode through the fenced-in compound. Otto's precisioned steps led the way. He cocked his head as a sound emerged, cutting through the silence. In contrast to the Celtic-like chanting of the bunker, a dreamy cello melody drifted through the midnight air as if someone were trying to lull the city to sleep.

Otto straightened his shoulders and tightened his grip on the handle of his Lugar, considering the player. *I pity you, poor man. While you birth notes and tempos, I have seen the birthing of power.*

And at that moment, walking amongst these men of influence, Otto vowed to acquire the knowledge of this secret power. No matter what it took.

Two

Nick scrubbed for surgery, allowing the warm water to thaw his hands chilled by the frigid New York air. He'd awakened to find Morningside Heights under a frosting of new snow. Pretty to look at, not so fun to tromp through as he'd walked to Columbia University Medical Center.

A pang of sadness had hit Nick when he noted the halted construction on St. John the Divine. *Evie'll be so disappointed.* He pictured her face as he hustled across campus, remembering how she'd tilt her head to view the stained glass windows of the cathedral whenever they passed—he on his way to the medical center and she to the foreign language department where she'd worked. *The war disrupts even the plans of the godly,*

Nick had thought as he hurried with the other pedestrians along 112th Street.

Plans. If only I had some. Since Evie left, everything that had once seemed simple now whirred around his mind in muddled confusion. Should he sign up for the army and finish his medical training there, or wait for the draft? He wished he could talk to her about it.

He'd been up late last night debating the decision when he finally decided to put his words on paper. He wrote Evie about his indecisiveness and about his jitters over his first solo surgery in the morning. He could imagine her response.

"God will be with you, Nick. He hasn't abandoned you yet." She'd said it a hundred times, and he wished he could hear it once more.

Her words replayed in his mind as he finished scrubbing up to his elbows. He dried his hands, then turned to Dr. Erikson—the best teacher he'd ever had *and* a skilled surgeon. Dr. Erickson was equal in height to Nick, with gray hair, a beard, and a gentle gaze that put his patients and students at ease. A knowing glance passed between them, then they moved into the operating room where Nick alone gloved up. They'd joked last week that Dr. Erikson had scheduled the surgery as a birthday present to Nick.

"Son, you get to start your second quarter century knowing you're a capable surgeon."

Nick wasn't so sure about the capable part—that was still to be seen. And even though "solo" meant Dr. Erikson was still there to observe, sweat beaded on his brow as he looked through the large window and saw the young patient being prepared for surgery. The young girl clung to her mother's neck. Her thin shoulders trembled as she cried. Nick forced himself to look away, turning to Dr. Erikson for assurance. Just then the door opened, and a fellow student, Jack Simmons, burst in—his curly hair still damp from melting snow.

Jack was a year ahead of Nick in the residency program. Only the two of them remained this semester—the rest had been drafted by the military months ago.

Jack's dead meat, Nick thought, knowing no one was allowed into the operating room unauthorized. Dr. Erikson's brow furrowed.

Jack approached the professor, undaunted. "Nick's received a telegram. Looks important. Can I read it to him?"

Nick noticed the slip of yellow paper in his friend's hand.

Raised eyebrows of concern replaced the professor's scowl. "Yes, please do."

Jack cleared his throat. "PROCEED JANUARY SIXTH CARLISLE BARRACKS PENNSYLVANIA REPORT COMMANDANT MEDICAL FIELD SERVICE SCHOOL FOR TEMPORARY DUTY FORMAL ORDERS AWAIT YOU AT DUTY STATION."

Nick felt his heart skip a beat. *I guess that solves my dilemma.* He turned to the professor.

Dr. Erikson shrugged his shoulders. "Hate to lose such a fine student." He glanced to the young patient, then placed a hand on Nick's shoulder. "As skilled as you are, Mr. Fletcher, you might have a hard time keeping focused with such urgent news. Besides, you have things to do. People to inform. Jack here will take over for you. Just make sure you stop by for a final good-bye before you ship out."

Nick's shoulders sank as he glanced over at the young girl who was now being wheeled into the room. *Now I'll never know if I have what it takes.* Not knowing what to say, he nodded to his professor and Jack. Then he pulled off his sterile gloves and hurried out the door.

The white halls echoed with familiar sounds. Nick glanced at the uniformed nurses and a huddle of students getting a tour of the surgery ward and realized this might be the last time he'd walk these halls. He turned into the residents' changing room and put on his civilian clothes. *Could I have done it?* He zipped his heavy jacket and slipped on his shoes. *Now what?*

Nick knew he couldn't go home yet. His mom would be baking a cake for his surprise birthday party tonight—the one she threw every year. He strode to the wall phone and dialed the operator.

"Can you connect me to the Manhattan Duty Station, please."

He tapped his foot as he waited for the connection. *I'm sure Jack will do fine. What will my mom say? Maybe Dr. Erikson should have given me a chance. What will Evie think? Maybe this is God's way of getting me over to her after all.*

Nick jogged up the three flights of stairs. His arms felt light after carrying his new duffel bag all over Manhattan. After leaving the college hospital, he'd made his way to the duty station. In the hours he should have been in school, he had visited the transportation office, booked a train to Pennsylvania, and gone to the PX for service uniforms.

He left the duffel bag filled with his army regulations downstairs with Oscar the bellhop until he could break the news. Now he paused at #312 and tucked the telegram into his pocket.

I'll tell them after dinner, he decided. *Probably after dessert too. It might just be one of the last good meals I get for a while.*

He inserted his key into the keyhole, but instead of feeling the click of the lock, the door gently swung open.

"Surprise!" A chorus of voices rang out. Nick jumped back, pretending to catch his breath.

His mother, father, and two sisters and their families hovered around him, their faces flushed from excitement. "Happy birt-day, Unca Nick." His niece Linda stretched out her arms to him.

Nick swept the little girl up into his embrace, gave her a quick nuzzle, then plopped her down. She scurried across the room to join his other nieces and nephews, six in all, pounding out their "unique" melodies on his father's piano.

Nick found his mother placing a large chocolate cake on a table already filled with his favorites: pork chops, scalloped potatoes, and lime Jell-O.

She looked at him, her eyebrows pointing downward. "I know it's not the same without dear Evie. But—"

"Mom, you didn't have to." He placed a big kiss on her black curls.

She patted his cheek, then turned to the others. "Dig in, everyone. You first, Nicky."

Nick took a seat next to his father, who said a prayer over the meal. Nick filled a plate until the china pattern disappeared under mounds of food. He listened as the men's conversation turned to the construction downtown coming to a halt and the effects rationing might have on the city. Then he watched his sisters brood over their children, thinking about the last time Evie had been with them. She'd looked at the curly headed Linda and whispered, "I'd love to have a little girl just like that someday." Nick's stomach ached at the thought of it.

In the midst of the small talk, Nick noticed his sister's intent gaze. "What, Peg? Do I have food on my chin?"

"You play a good part, you know, but I helped you find a box for Grandma's ring."

His mother's gelatin-laden fork stopped halfway to her mouth. "We all miss her, Nicky. When do you think you'll hear something?"

"For goodness' sake, Luisa, there's a war going on," his dad bristled. "She can't just drop a note."

"Daddy's right," Peg said. "I don't think we realize the seriousness of this war. Jerry Banks down the street got his draft notice."

"At least we don't have to worry about Nicky here." His mother's brown eyes brimmed with confidence. "No one is going to pull such a bright boy out of medical school. Before long they'll be bringing the injured home, and we'll need trained physicians."

"And what about the battlefield?" his father commented. "Don't you think they'll need doctors there?"

"They'll have plenty of boys, Walter. Those eager to get medical training for free." His mother pushed out her high-backed lacquer chair and moved toward the kitchen before Nick's father could reply. "Does anyone need anything else? Drinks? Seconds?"

Nick took a deep breath and set down his fork. "Uh, Mom, Da—"

"She always does that." His father pointed his fork. "You'd think after thirty years, she'd let me finish one discussion!"

"She's right." Rita cut some small pieces from her pork chop and put them on her son Tony's plate. "Nick will make a fine doc for those returning."

Nick cleared his throat. "Dad, I—"

"Not the battlefield?" His father squared his shoulders. "Roger O'Reilly's son is training to be a medic. Just think, Luisa!" he yelled toward the kitchen. "Perhaps that's why our son fell in with that foreign girl. Perhaps the good Lord knew where his heart would be."

Nick folded his arms across his chest and leaned back as the conversation whipped around the room like a rag in an electric dryer. "Does anyone care what I think?"

The room stilled, and all eyes turned to Nick. Even little Linda paused and turned toward him. "It's already done," he said. "I received my draft notice this morning. I'm an army man now." He slipped the telegram out of his pocket.

"Nicky." His mother dropped back into her chair, her face drained of color.

"I would have joined up anyway, draft or no draft. Dad's right. I have no business staying here when I can help."

He tried to ignore the women's pained expressions. "Besides, I'll do anything to get Evie back. I have to do my part."

"Holy Moses." Nick's brother-in-law, Davis, let out a low whistle. "If love don't mess with everything."

✒   ✒   ✒

Evie fingered the miniature Statue of Liberty and thought of Nick as the Mercedes-Benz carried her and her parents through the predawn streets.

She'd imagined a different Vienna from what she saw through the car window. Christmas greenery still draped doorways and hung thick on awnings. Candles flickered in the windows of houses and storefronts. She'd heard rumors of rationing and hardship, yet theaters announced performances and new German films.

34

Evie caressed Liberty's torch and in her head composed a letter to Nick wishing him a Happy Birthday and telling him not to worry. Papa still insisted that no contact would be best for now, especially since all letters would be censored for "political material" and would draw attention to their family.

It was hard to believe that thousands of miles separated her from the man she loved. She'd gotten used to Nick dropping by the foreign language department between his classes. Since her mother refused to raise a "career woman," Evie wasn't allowed to attend classes. Instead, she worked as a volunteer, tutoring students her age who studied German. She'd always known when Nick was waiting by the door due to the flirtatious giggles of many of the coeds. She missed glancing up and seeing his small wave from the door. She missed the way his dark brown eyes concentrated on hers when she spoke. The way he tried to talk like a college-educated doctor, but too often allowed his words to slip back into New York slang.

The car turned a corner, and Evie noticed the spire of a small cathedral in the distance. *What was the name of that parish again?* Vienna was familiar, but in a detached sort of way—like something she remembered from a distant dream.

"Will Isak be home from work?" Evie leaned in close to her mother, feeling the brush of her fur collar against her cheek, taking in her familiar perfume. "Does he know we're arriving today?"

"Yes, Papa sent a telegram from the ship. He said

he'd be waiting. I imagine he's changed so much."

Evie tried to picture her brother's face all grown up. Even though she was a kid sister tagging along, Isak had always made her feel important and valued. When she'd tracked him through the nearby woods, he'd rewarded her with a survival lesson such as starting a campfire without matches or knowing how to tell direction by the moss on the trees. He taught her to shoot a rifle, bringing home rabbit for dinner—much to their mother's dismay and their housekeeper's delight.

"What about Ilse? I've missed her. Will she be there too?"

"She should be; it's her day to work. Although I'm not sure how she'll handle the influx of bodies after caring for Isak alone for so many years."

"Ilse? Are you kidding? She'll do fine. I bet she'll enjoy it even more. I even imagine she missed us."

The car turned down their street. The large homes stood proudly, protected by iron gates. Evie's mother took her hand. Her father glanced back from the front passenger's seat, and Evie spotted his concern. But before she had a chance to comment, her mother gave her a squeeze. "Here we are."

Evie peered over the driver's shoulder. "Mother, look at the maple trees in front, how tall they've grown! Oh, and what happened to my swing in the oak? Did Isak tear it—" Evie's voice failed as she saw something else different about their home. Two large flags fluttered from second-story windows—red flags with white disks and black swastikas.

Then a young man stepped out the front door, dressed in a dark suit. He waved and smiled.

"Stop the car. Tell me I'm seeing things."

The car slowed, and Evie jumped out. The frozen ground crunched under her feet. When she reached Isak, instead of stepping into his embrace, she put her hands forward to block it.

"Evie—" Her mother's voice was lost in her brother's welcoming hello.

"Isak? What is this?" She pointed to the flags and to the swastika pin on his lapel. "Do Mother and Father know?"

Isak took a step back and lowered his arms. "Of course they know. All Austrians are required to have two years of military service. Father's a party fellow also. Really now, Evie. Do you think you're still in America?"

Evie found it hard to catch her breath.

"Here now, little sis, things are not that bad. You are home now. *Wir sind zusammen, ja?* Yes, we are to-gether."

Evie stretched her arms toward her brother, not knowing what else to do. In spite of the warmth of his body, a chill traveled down her limbs. She clung to Isak and wondered what else she'd soon be forced to embrace.

❧   ❧   ❧

Dearest Evie,

I'm an army man now, doll. I have been for nearly one month. Hard to believe. It seems like time here has gone by so quickly. Then again, it seems like a lifetime since I held you.

As I wrote before, I only had three days to get my life in order and take the train to Pennsylvania. I discovered that because of my schooling, I'm an officer. Our group is directed by sergeants who are to be our instructors. Do I salute them, or do they salute me? I'm still not sure.

The day after we arrived, the marches began—in the rain, in the snow, in the slush. More than once I thought of how your mom always kept the furnace so high in your parents' apartment that we'd go out into the slushy snow to cool off. Those were the days!

When we aren't marching, we're listening to lectures. Because of the number of new medics being trained, the army's cramming a year's worth of field training and combat medicine into five months. And I thought medical school was hard!

Oh, I have to backtrack a little and tell you that I now have a "most embarrassing moment" that tops my world-class belly flop at the city pool. First, imagine a hundred nervous soldiers in boxers, lined up for their first round of inoculations. For some reason, the sight of those medics with their machinelike precision made me chuckle.

"I feel like I'm in a Ford Motor Company assembly line," I told the guy in front of me just as he stepped up. I guess he hadn't quite heard what I'd said, so he turned around. The medic's needle missed the guy's arm and plunged into his upper chest. Turns out he's okay, but I thought he would hate me for sure. And get this, the guy's assigned to my barracks. His name is Frank, but I call him Twitch, due to the fact that he shivers whenever someone mentions "needle."

Well, my wonderful gal, I gotta go. It's almost time for daily exercise. Today we get to march, as a unit, over rough terrain and then stand in the cold for two hours to hear a lecture. Oh, joy. But it will all be worth it if I can get to Europe, closer to you. Then I'll wrap these newly muscular arms (I guess army life is good for something!) around you and never let go.

Sending all my love,
Nick

P.S. I'm still waiting to hear from you, hoping your dad will find a way for us to communicate. I have probably twenty letters ready and waiting to send to you. Maybe today's mail will have a note from you. I can't imagine anything I long for more—except to be with you, of course.

Three

Otto strode into the banquet hall and surveyed the preparations in progress. Enormous swastikas draped the walls, and a large silver-plated eagle hovered over the musical instruments awaiting their players. Party leaders bustled around in full uniform, tending to last-minute details. In the center of the massive banquet hall, flowers and greenery adorned a six-foot-high bust of the Führer.

These types of events were genius, really. The suggested speeches, quotations, poems, and even the musical selections were chosen by event planners to create an emotional response from the attendees. Months before any government function found a spot on the official Reich calendar, supplemental information had already been distributed in the *Die Neue Gemeinschaft*.

"We have learned to see life's reality not as a problem but as a fighting mission," a Nazi Youth practiced onstage. "Our loyalty demands that we fulfill this mission, which binds us completely to the Führer as the agent of that law that we obey."

The speech ended, and Otto clapped. "Very well done," he called. "Your Führer would be proud."

The boy saluted, then stepped down from the stage. From the back of the room, the melody of "Germany, Holy Word" sounded from a piano. Otto's hands stilled as the song played, and he considered the battle cry to follow: "We greet our Führer, the first soldier of the Greater German Reich, with our battle cry: 'Adolf Hitler! Sieg Heil! Adolf Hitler!' "

Otto circled Hitler's copper-colored bust and plucked a bloodred carnation from the greenery. He breathed in the flower's sweet scent before securing it in the lapel of his black uniform jacket.

Otto knew that during the celebration to follow this very room would come alive with power, heat, and zeal. He'd witnessed it before. But after his experience in the bunker, Nazi fervor wasn't enough. Otto now longed for the *source*—the Presence behind the pageantry.

❧   ❧   ❧

If the radios and newspapers didn't constantly talk of the hardships of war, there were some circles in Vienna where no one would guess such a thing existed. Evie scanned the large ballroom of Hofburg, once the imperial palace of the Austro-Hungary dynasty. Men in uniform and women in fine gowns paraded through the room as they'd done for centuries. In the center of it all, Governor Baldur von Schirach, the self-proclaimed Nazi prince, mingled with his guests. Soon the doors would open, and they'd all be led into the chambers prepared for tonight's celebration of Hitler's birthday.

I can't believe I'm here, Evie thought. *I feel as if I've been sucked into some horrible nightmare.*

"We must keep up appearances," her father had urged her during the drive over. "If we do not attend, people will grow suspicious. If you ever hope to see Nick again, you need to play it safe. Play by the rules, Evie, for just a little while."

When the melody died away, Schirach left his clutch of admirers and strode to the small stage to the refrain of subdued applause. He raised his hands, and the clapping stopped.

"My dear friends, the celebrations will continue throughout the night. You have much that awaits you, but first, I must start the evening with a poem I penned for *der Führer.* I have already sent this poem ahead to his celebration in Berlin, and now I share it with you." The governor cleared his throat and read with reverence.

> *Many thousands of you are behind me,*
> *And you are I and I am you.*
> *I have no thoughts*
> *That do not dwell in your hearts.*

And when I form words, I know none
That are not at one with your will.
For I am you and you are I,
And we all believe, Germany, in you!

Evie rolled her eyes. Surely this was madness. She scoured the room for any sight of her father, hoping she could convince him to take her home. Her mother had regrettably gone to bed earlier with a headache, and Evie wished she had claimed a similar malady. She spotted her father seated at a large round table, surrounded by men in uniform.

Many of the older men, Evie knew, had been forced to support the new government. Some played their roles and wore the Nazi uniforms in order to survive. Then there were others—Nazi sympathizers and youth caught up in the fervor. These men embraced the new ideology.

She sighed as she lifted a glass from the tray of a passing waiter. The last thing she wanted was to be absorbed into *that* group. Instead, she strolled through the festive crowd, watching. She could tell by the way her father lifted his arms—as if holding an invisible gun— that he was retelling one of his old war stories. The young men laughed at the appropriate times, and from their movements it was evident when they started telling stories of their own.

"Evie, is that you?" A familiar voice interrupted her thoughts. She glanced over the rim of her glass, and her irritation vanished.

"Thomas!" She set her glass on a nearby table and

wrapped her arms around her childhood friend. She breathed in his wonderful scent of soap and a touch of expensive cologne. The smile and delight in his blue eyes caused her stomach to flip without her approval. "You're all grown up!" She pulled back for a second look and only then noticed the starched uniform and short military haircut.

"I was about to say the same to you." He placed his hand on her elbow and leaned close, raising his voice over the orchestra's harmonious strains. "I just arrived last night. Mother told me you were home. I was hoping to see you here."

Evie smiled, again ignoring the uniform, ignoring the warnings that sounded in her mind—it was Thomas, after all.

"It's been three months, and I admit that getting used to Vienna is harder than I thought." The orchestra paused between pieces, and she lowered her voice. "For example, I'm more used to American jazz, and I find myself spurting out English without thinking."

"Not a good thing," Thomas said. "Especially around here." He paused and studied her face. A small smile curled up the corners of his lips. "I'd love to say I have the same problem with spouting out French, but languages have never been my strong point. Of course, I don't need to tell you that. I would have failed an exam or two without your tutoring."

"One or two? You can't be serious. I remember a much higher number."

Thomas's eyes took on a dreamy gaze. "Sometimes I

long for the days before you left for New York. When my biggest concern was whether to ride my scooter or walk to school." He laughed. "Walking often won out, since Isak always ditched you, making you eager for companionship."

Thomas glanced at her jawline, and she knew he was eyeing her scar. "In fact, I remember . . ."

"Don't remind me." Evie fingered the place near her chin, then changed the subject. "You mentioned your mother. How is she?"

"Busier than ever—although doing what, I'll never know."

"So are you home for long?" Evie said, again amazed by how easy it was to recover their friendship after so many years.

"Yes, I'm here to stay. I've been transferred on special assignment. It seems the Führer feels the Jews are too numerous in Vienna." He laughed. "And I'm the lucky man who will help solve that problem. Schirach himself invited me to lunch next week to discuss transports. I'll be the military contact with Brunner and the civilian office. It pays pretty well, which means I'll have my own apartment soon. You'll have to come to dinner; I can treat you to some specialties I picked up in France."

Evie scanned his eyes for any evidence that Thomas was joking, but she saw no hint of embarrassment over his new position. *Deporting Jews from Vienna, as if they were trash that needed to be disposed of!* Since arriving home, she'd heard rumors that the Jews were being shipped out of town. Before moving to the States, her family had had many Jewish friends and colleagues, and she couldn't understand how seemingly overnight —because of one group's vehemence—they were suddenly targets of persecution.

Evie suddenly realized she had no interest in discovering exactly what Thomas's French specialties were, especially if he considered Jews a problem. She opened her mouth to give him a tongue-lashing, then remembered her father's request. This was the last place she should make a scene. *For Nick.*

Instead, she retrieved her fluted glass from the table. "A dinner date won't be possible. But thanks anyway." She took a long drink and glanced away. Still she could not swallow her anger. "Like your mother, I'm going to be quite busy over the next few months," she finally declared. "Doing what, I do not know."

Four

The train hissed to a stop, and Otto and another guard stepped down. The two trained SS men quickly scanned the area, then motioned that the coast was clear to the half-dozen men who followed.

The small white sign nailed to the equally tiny station read *Nelahozeves*—the same name as the imposing Renaissance château on the left bank of the Moldau River, just northwest of Prague. It had only taken an hour's train ride to reach this small Bohemian hamlet, but somehow Otto felt as though he had journeyed back fifty years.

Small cottages dotted the dirt lanes. Peasants' carts passed each other on the street, pulled by swayback horses. No wonder they'd taken the train. He couldn't imagine a car and cart having enough room to pass each other on the lane.

Otto's alert eyes observed the ill-dressed townspeople, who in turn viewed the group of SS men with suspicion. He spotted more than one curious glance as the uniformed assembly stepped from the train onto a set of muddy tracks, then hoisted themselves onto the station platform.

Mud splattered *Unterscharführer* Kametler's high-shined black boots, and a few spots of muck clung to his breeches. The *Unterscharführer* swore under his breath, cursing the barbarian location. Then the stream of harsh words ceased as the officer lifted his head and spotted their final destination.

In contrast to the humble dwellings of the townspeople, the great stone manor of Nelahozeves loomed over the village, guarded by a moat and thicket of trees.

"A Bohemian palace if I've ever seen one," Kametler commented as their group paraded across the dirt street and up the winding hillside. "I'm eager to discover the prizes awaiting inside."

Otto stayed twenty paces ahead of the others. His long legs kept up a quickened stride. His eyes darted from one side of the road to the other, probing for any sign of trouble.

He'd been to Czechoslovakia numerous times as a student musician, but never on a trip like this. In the past, his mission had been to see how many beautiful women he could woo with his handsome face, charm, and violin. But over the last few months his assignment had been to safeguard high-ranking officers, particularly SS *Unterscharführer* Kametler, on tour of the Protectorate.

The purpose was to travel the country, viewing the immense wealth at the disposal of the Nazi party. Their focus had not been the castles or cathedrals, nor bank accounts or treasuries, but rather artwork—both in museums and private collections. And with each discovery of art from the masters, Otto could see Kametler's eyes grow wide with greed. After all, the sale of only a few items could fund their army for a month, leaving thousands of additional pieces available for Reich museums.

But to Otto the art wasn't nearly as intriguing as Herr Kametler himself. Before transferring to Vienna, the officer had been a financial advisor to Hitler's inner circle. After viewing artwork during the day, Kametler often invited Otto to share deep, hearty Czech ales around the dinner table and into the wee hours. The officer loved weaving tales about their party's initial attempts to secure power. He spoke of former clandestine meetings and even hinted of an upcoming visit to *Berchtesgaden*, the Führer's retreat in the Bavarian Alps.

Otto knew this was his chance to break in. He was determined to make himself invaluable to Kametler. Longer hours, extra attentiveness to the officer's wishes —he'd do whatever it took to stand out.

They reached the top of the hill and came first to a substantial burgher's cottage.

"It's the childhood home of Antonín Dvořák, the Czech composer," Otto explained to Kametler. While his superior officer was very knowledgeable about artwork, he didn't know much about music and appreciated Otto's instruction. "His Symphony No. 9 was inspired by a Czech translation of the poem *Hiawatha* by Longfellow, the American poet. Hiawatha was an Indian, you know."

Otto's eyes moved to the outer walls of Nelahozeves. They were decorated with sgraffito art—colorful murals that seemed out of place in this simple setting. Some of the murals related to mythology; others depicted Roman history. Each had been scratched in lifelike proportions into gray stucco walls.

Otto smirked. *I'm sure Kametler considers such art a waste—since it cannot be moved or sold.*

The group reached the first doors, and an SS guard stationed at Nelahozeves greeted them. "Come inside. I've been told to lead you to Knights' Hall, then upstairs to the music room."

The uniformed group moved from the gallery toward Knights' Hall. Booted footsteps echoed off ancient walls.

Otto and the other Reich officials crisply followed the SS guard down the L-shaped passage. Just when he feared they'd never find the end to the manor, Knights' Hall opened before them. Knowing the building had already been secured, he turned his attention to the immense details of the room, feeling as if he'd walked into a long forgotten space left intact from the magical days of kings and queens, dragons, and sorcerers. He imagined being the master of this place, living in a world where magic and mystery did not dwell in fairy tales alone.

With a nod of appreciation, he took in the large stone fireplace and wall and ceiling paintings, perfectly preserved. He also couldn't help but grin at the Mannerist frescoes of rather tipsy-looking warriors. *My type of men . . .*

"Amazing." Kametler's hand glided over the surface of a side table. "Exquisite detail." He turned to an assistant and lowered his voice. "Have this delivered to my private residence. Use utmost care."

"Yes, sir."

"And see that it's there by Monday." Kametler stroked his chin. "My wife's birthday, you know."

"Wait until you see some of the treasures in the other rooms." The assistant's words spilled out. "Everything from medieval reliquaries and ceramics to costly musical instruments and original scores by Beethoven and Mozart."

Kametler nodded. "Please, lead the way."

After traversing through a maze of halls, the group was led to a large music room on an upper story. Unlike many of the other quarters, the doors of the room were closed. The assistant rapped sharply.

A small man with dark eyes magnified by large glasses opened the door. He gave a quick salute, then swung wide the door. They entered, and Otto recognized an overpowering odor of musty old papers—in this case, sheets of music. His eyes brightened when he spotted the violins on the table. One caught his eye immediately. *It can't be. . . .*

The men in the room greeted each other with the customary handshakes.

"Herr Doktor Michitsch—or may I call you Viktor? It appears you've been busy. What do we have here?" Kametler clasped his hands behind his back and walked the length of the table.

The little man, Viktor, swept his hand through his wild hair, then motioned toward the display of violins. "I'm still checking for authenticity, but many appear quite valuable." He hoisted a finely polished instrument high for Kametler to see. "Take this one, for example. The craftsmanship is exquisite—"

"It's an Amati." Otto risked interrupting. "Most likely crafted by Nicolo Amati around 1650. The gold-amber varnish appears to be original. Worth a large sum, but not the most valuable in the collection."

Kametler raised a single eyebrow and smiled.

Encouraged, Otto reached for the instrument he'd spotted the moment he entered the room. He lifted it gently, blowing a layer of dust from its surface. He turned to Viktor. "Where did you find this?"

Viktor's voice was shaky. "In the maid's chamber downstairs. It has a label, but the date has been scraped away. I'm in the process—"

Otto interrupted. "Did you note that the label reads *Antonius Stradivarius Cremonensis Faciebat*?"

Viktor looked at Otto with disdain. "You think me a fool? Thousands of violins have been made as tribute to Stradivari. They copy his model and bear similar labels. We have to study the instrument to know for—"

Otto cut off his words by lifting the instrument to his shoulder. He took the bow from the case and slid it across the strings. A note so clear, so perfect, rose from the violin that the hairs on the back of Otto's neck pricked. Without a moment's hesitation, he launched into Tchaikovsky's violin concerto, displaying the violin's range and versatility.

The eyes of the officer pierced him, and he knew he would either be exalted or reprimanded after this display. If he'd learned one thing from SS training, it was to obey without question—and plucking a violin from the hands of a Reich expert to prove a point was far from obedience.

When the last strain faded, Otto met Kametler's gaze. "It's a Stradivarius. I guarantee it."

Kametler crossed his arms against his chest. "Herr Akeman, it appears you've been holding back on us. You play quite well."

"Well, but not good enough. Five years ago I auditioned for the symphony orchestras in both Vienna and Prague, with no success."

Kametler clasped a strong hand on Otto's shoulder. "Good enough for me, soldier. It appears I've underestimated you."

Otto smiled. His heart pounded.

Kametler turned to Viktor. "Do you have some use for this boy?"

Viktor's eyes widened. "Today?"

"Today, tomorrow, the next day. It appears we are not using Herr Akeman to the best of his ability."

"Uh, I suppose I can think of something. In fact, today the Sonderstab Musik team will visit a repair shop in Prague. A very valuable violin, a Guarneri, from this collection is missing. One of the drivers remembers it being dropped off in Old Town at a repair shop owned by a man named Hanauer, a Jew. We have hopes there will be other pieces there too."

"Very good. Take this young man with you." Kametler turned to Otto. "Herr Akeman, I will see that your paperwork is put in order. As of this moment, you are relieved from my command and will join the Sonderstab Musik Aktion team. You are too valuable a man to waste."

What have I done? Otto attempted a pleasant smile, yet a sharp pain cramped his stomach. "Thank you, *Unterscharführer* Kametler. I will serve my Führer well!"

With a final salute and a "Heil Hitler," Kametler and the others marched from the room, demolishing Otto's dream with each parting step.

♪   ♪   ♪

Not two hours after arriving in Nelahozeves, Otto found himself back in Prague. He reclined in the backseat next to Viktor as the government car wound through the one-way cobblestone streets of the Mala Strana district.

"I appreciate your fine musical talents." Viktor removed his glasses and cleaned them with a handkerchief from his pocket. "You will be an asset to our team."

Otto cleared his throat. "I'm sorry about the scene with the vio—"

Viktor's hand shot up. "Stop. Each of us must look after his own interests in this war, correct? I have my motives. You have yours. In the end I've found myself with a skilled musician. I will use this to my advantage." He raised his voice and pointed. "There's the shop. Driver, please park here so as to not alert the Jew."

The driver did as instructed, and Otto eyed the humble shop connected to a narrow two-story house. A faded blue placard hung in front of the shop with a raised image of a violin.

"I believe I've been here before, years ago."

"All decent Czech musicians have." Viktor slid his hands into a pair of black leather gloves. "The shopkeeper is highly respected. So much so that the former owner of Nelahozeves willed the man a valuable violin."

Otto cocked an eyebrow. "Willed? I assumed it had only been dropped off for repairs." He spotted a group of six SS men marching toward the shop and reached for the door handle. Viktor grasped his arm.

"Wait. You grow hasty. Listen to me." Viktor's voice was stern. "To work with me you must realize two things. First, we always leave the dirty work for others and wait for the perfect opportunity. This means waiting until the shopkeeper is arrested. It's easier that way, not so messy.

"Second," he growled, "the Jews own nothing. All belongs to the German State. Our job is to take what is rightfully ours."

Otto watched as the SS men burst through the front door of the shop. A minute later two of the guards reappeared, dragging a bloodied man between them.

"Let's go."

Otto followed with long strides as they crossed the road. Citizens scattered at their presence.

Viktor paused before the Jew. "Where is the violin?"

"I—I don't know which one you speak of. I have many . . ."

The guard cranked back the man's head.

Viktor drew back his hand and slapped the Jew's face. "You know the one I speak of."

The Jew dropped his gaze. "The Guarneri?"

Chills raced up Otto's arms at the sound of that name. *Could it be? A man such as this owning the famed piece?*

"Of course," Viktor spat. "Where is it?"

"I—I gave it to a man who promised passports for my sons. I delivered the instrument, but the man was arrested before I received the papers. I can show you where he lived." Tears filled the man's eyes. "It was my only hope. . . ."

Viktor studied the man's gaze. "Take him away. Search both buildings!"

"And the man's family?" a third SS man asked. "A small boy was with him in the workshop—he ran upstairs."

"Leave them," Viktor snapped. "What good are Jewish vermin to me? Soon they'll be wiped from the Reich. But the violin—it has to be in this city somewhere. And if it is, we will find it."

※   ※   ※

Daniel will never find me here.

Jakub held back his chuckle and pressed his cheek onto the cool floor. It was dark under the bed . . . and dirty. His nose twitched as he inhaled a hint of dust from a ridge where the shiny wood floor met the plaster wall. To Mother, dirt was the devil itself. In fact, he was sure that even now as his mother visited Mrs. Lanik, her eyes had already found something in their neighbor's home that didn't meet her satisfaction.

Jakub held his breath as the floorboards vibrated under him. Daniel was coming, he knew. His brother's footsteps pounded faster up the stairs. Jakub scowled. Surely he had not counted to one hundred already. What was the rush?

Daniel's voice echoed down the hallway leading to the bedrooms. "Jakub! Jakub, come quick."

Jakub recognized the squeak of the door to the washroom. Next, Daniel flung open the door to their mother and father's room across the hall.

"Jakub!" he shouted again.

With his free hand, Jakub pulled the collar of his shirt to his mouth and muffled a snicker. Yet even there, under the shadow of the bed, something caught his eye.

He placed his hand over the patch on his shirt. He hated that yellow star. He closed his eyes and instead focused his thoughts on Daniel. His little brother had used this trick before to pry him into giving himself away. This time Jakub would not be fooled.

Every day it was the same. After music lessons, Daniel begged him to play hide-and-seek the way most children begged for candy. Jakub adored his younger brother and couldn't help but give in—though privately he thought that at twelve Daniel ought to be getting too old for such childish games.

The door to their room opened. There was a pause as if Daniel were scanning it, then he inhaled a deep breath. "Jakub! It's Father! He's been taken!" Daniel's voice trembled as he ran back down the hall, then descended the stairs.

A few seconds later the front door opened, then slammed. Had Daniel left? Hastily Jakub uncurled his long legs and pressed his feet against the wall. This was no game.

Using all his strength, he propelled himself into the light and jumped to his feet. His tall, lanky body was suddenly cold all over. What was going on? He thought he heard Daniel's voice still calling his name, only this time the voice intermingled with other noises from the street outside. Jakub ran to the window, jerked it open, and leaned out. A rush of wind and noise, plus the scent of rotting garbage, assaulted him.

"Daniel?" Jakub forced his voice into the street. He cranked his neck left toward the river, then right toward the city center. Then he spotted him. Spotted *them*. Daniel was desperately chasing two men, SS soldiers, who hauled their father between them. *Father!*

Jakub watched, eyes wide, as Daniel ran toward the men. "No! Come back!" Jakub shouted. "Daniel, stop!" The horn of a motorcar blared, drowning out his desperate plea.

Jakub watched as Daniel reached the men. As if in slow motion, he saw his younger brother stretching a hand for Father's coat. One SS soldier spun and hit Daniel in the shoulder with the butt of his rifle. Daniel crumpled to the ground, but his hands still clung to the coat. The second soldier joined in, hitting Daniel's hands again, again, again.

"No!" Jakub screamed. *Not his hands. Anything but his hands.*

He shoved away from the window, raced out of the room and down the stairs, and hurried onto the busy sidewalk. Just as the SS men disappeared around the corner with his father, more guards swarmed into Father's shop, like maggots on a carcass. Jakub wove in and out of the crowd gathered around the small fallen figure.

"Daniel." Jakub collapsed onto his knees and hovered over his brother.

Daniel's cheek was pressed to the cobblestone sidewalk, just as Jakub's had been pressed to the wooden floor only minutes before. Light brown curls fell over his forehead. His eyes were open, but his face was contorted with pain.

Jakub glanced at his hands. The broken, bloody hands. "No!" Jakub caressed his brother's cheek. "Brother. No." Jakub pictured how those hands had looked only minutes ago—fingertips lined with fine creases from hours of playing the violin.

"They took him, Jakub," Daniel sobbed. "They took Father. And look, now they're in his shop, stealing the instruments."

Jakub nodded, yet refused to look back over his shoulder. He could hear them. Hear the sounds of breaking glass and splintering wood.

Father. What will we do without Father?

But Jakub could not think of what would happen next. He was still trying to comprehend Daniel's broken, bleeding, priceless hands.

Five

The stuffy air of Jakub's house bore down on his shoulders, like the heavy quilt from his grandmother's bed. He had hidden under it once, pressing his body into the feathers until his form blended with the other lumps. But the quilt, pieced together from thick wool and corduroy, had covered him too heavily and pushed the air from his lungs. After what seemed like an hour, Jakub threw back the quilt, gulping and sucking in the coolness of the room.

He wished he could throw back this thick oppression of mourning as easily. Open the windows, open the doors, and suck in a breath of life. Everything within the boarded-up two-story house reeked of death. Yet no one had died. They'd received word that their father had joined a transport to the East. Daniel's fingers were badly injured, but he was far from dead. Or at least that's what the doctor said after sneaking in to examine him under cover of darkness. Medical services were no longer allowed for the Jews, yet their dear friend had risked his life to come.

Jakub stirred from his place on the living room floor. The sun dared to filter around the edges of the blackout curtain, casting a long ribbon of sunlight over his brother's sleeping form on the sofa. The curtains, made to hold in the artificial light glow, now served to intensify the darkness, blocking out all signs of life beyond the canvas shades. Yet it could not block out the threat of the enemy lurking at every corner. Jakub no longer felt safe. Not even in his home.

It had been over two years since the Nazis had invaded Caechoslovakia, and one suffering had been added upon another for the Jews. They were forced to wear the yellow star, forbidden to ride public transportation, and restricted in entering public places. But this was the first time Jakub understood that things would not get better. He'd thought for a time that if they followed the rules and obeyed their new leaders, they'd be left alone. Left to live together as a family— however humble an existence that may be. Obviously, this was not the case.

Daniel's ashen face drew Jakub's attention. He looked to the hands resting atop the blanket. Dried blood caked the bandages around his fingers.

Jakub slowly sat up and glanced at his mother, who slept on a feather mattress across the room. Blonde hair spilled over her tear-stained pillow. Just beyond her in the kitchen, dishes encrusted with dried food were piled in the sink. Her limp hand rested on the floor near some scattered potato peelings. Seeing this, Jakub was sure she'd gone mad overnight, first firing their housekeeper and nanny, then refusing visitors and frantically demanding that the two boys never leave her sight. So they had all bedded down on the first floor as she wept and mourned the loss of their father . . . and the loss of Daniel's hands.

Those fingers won't be much use to him anymore . . . bones broken . . . crippled . . . violin shouldn't be considered . . . with adequate medical supplies and a team of skilled surgeons, maybe some hope . . . not under these conditions . . . nothing for the Jews . . . no one to turn to.

The doctor's words echoed in his mind, and he ran his fingers through his overgrown hair. He examined Daniel for a moment, unable to imagine life without his brother's music. As if sensing Jakub's closeness, Daniel opened his eyes, and his lips curled into a weak smile.

Jakub inched closer, feeling Daniel's breath against his cheek. "How are you doing today?" he whispered.

Daniel's eyebrows made a V, and his mouth pushed out the words softly. "O-okay, I guess. Will the doctor be back soon?"

"He said if he couldn't make it before sunrise, not to count on him for a couple days." Jakub shook his head solemnly. "He has to come from the Jewish district, and I heard the SS in the street last night." There was no need to continue. They'd all heard it. The cries of families being separated, the breaking glass, the pounding on doors.

"You'll have to do it, then."

Jakub nodded. "He showed me how, remember?" He stood again and followed the instructions that played through his mind.

Light the fire. Heat the water. Jakub sensed Daniel's eyes upon him as he moved.

Tear clean towels into strips. He tugged, but the cloth fibers held tight. With one hard jerk they finally submitted with a loud rip. And still their mother slept.

When steam trickled from the kettle spout, Jakub poured water into a basin and scrubbed his hands. The water stung, and his hands turned pink, then red.

He soaked one piece of the rag, leaving the others for wrapping. Daniel lowered his gaze as Jakub neared, then stretched out his arm.

Jakub spread out a clean towel under the right hand, then began the tedious work of removing the bandages. Dried blood slowed the progress.

"Oh—ouch." Daniel clenched his teeth.

"Sorry." Jakub saw the pain in Daniel's brown eyes.

"No, keep going. I'll be okay—"

Jakub wet the bandages with the warm cloth until they loosened. As he slowly unwrapped them, pieces of torn flesh also tore away. Fragments of bone poked through blackened chunks of flesh. Head bent over, shoulders slouched, Jakub squinted in the dim light. He applied the sensitivity and care he'd seen his father exhibit over priceless violins in his shop. He continued. *Dab, peel back, gently, slowly—*

In spite of his efforts, the torn, broken fingers not only stuck to the cloth but also to each other. He squeezed hot water over the flesh.

"Aaugh!" Daniel thrashed his head against the pillow.

Before Jakub could offer an apology, their mother jumped up from her mattress. In four long strides she was upon them.

"No! What are you doing?" Her eyes were wild. "Leave him alone. Leave—"

Jakub winced as fists fell on him in blows.

"No, Mama!" Daniel cried. "He's helping. It is not his fault. He is doing well . . ."

Jakub dropped his rag. His back stung where she had struck, one, two, three times. But his heart pained worse. He had never felt his mother's hands upon him in anything but a caress.

A loud pounding at the door made his mother freeze midswing. Jakub, with his arms curled tight to his body, looked into her tear-streaked face.

"Don't hurt Daniel," Mama muttered, almost apologetically. She let her arms drop.

Jakub led her to the kitchen. "Mama, get ahold of yourself, please. Wait here while I see who it is." He ran to the door. Daniel's quiet cries followed.

As he pushed the cabinet away from the door and unlatched the numerous locks, he wondered why his mother didn't stop him. He also questioned if he should be opening it. *Perhaps it's the doctor.* He had to find out.

Jakub pushed the door open a crack. A breeze hit his face like a slap as he exhaled and wiped his eyes, for the first time realizing that he too had been crying.

The door swung open fully, and the man who waited was like someone from a distant dream. He stood tall. And despite the filthy cloak that fell from thin shoulders, the presence of greatness could not be denied.

Jakub stepped back, welcoming the visitor with a sweep of his hand. "Come in. Come in, sir." He bowed low.

The man glanced left, then right, and hurried inside. His cape made a loud whoosh as Jakub slammed the door shut behind him.

♪   ♪   ♪

Alexi Hořký stood like a tall, dark shadow in the dim entryway. He reminded Jakub of the Czech knights of old who fought so gallantly for King Charles IV. Only instead of brandishing a sword, Sir Alexi presented a dented violin case.

"I cannot stay long." Alexi's voice was low. "Here's some food, and I need to speak with your mother."

He thrust the case into Jakub's hands, and its heaviness took Jakub by surprise. Then he realized that it was the case that held the food. He pulled it tight to his chest and hurried to the kitchen.

In the short minutes it had taken Jakub to answer the door, his mother had somehow slipped on a clean apron—borrowed from the maid's closet—and straightened her blonde hair into a tight bun at the base of her neck. Her sunken, moist eyes were the only evidence of her outburst.

Jakub followed her into the living room. Suddenly he remembered Daniel's hands, unwrapped and un-attended. He hurried to the sofa where he found Alexi, al-ready kneeling, attempting to comfort the sniffling Daniel.

Alexi's eyes were filled with compassion as he cocked his shaded face and looked from Daniel to Mother to Jakub.

"Jakub, boy." Alexi rose. "Please continue here while I speak with your mother."

"*Ano,* yes, of course."

Alexi stretched his hand toward the door leading to Father's workshop. Mother nodded and led the way. Jakub settled next to Daniel and watched as his mother unlocked the workshop door with the key she wore around her neck. The two entered the room silently, closing the door most of the way behind them. Jakub strained but could not distinguish the muffled words.

He turned to Daniel, who also watched the door. His brother's tears had stopped, but his breaths still sucked in with little gasps, releasing with a sigh.

"G-go and lis-ten." Daniel sucked in, then sighed again.

"*Ne.*" Jakub shook his head. "That would be wrong."

"Wrong?" Daniel's voice was tense. "And you think how she acts is right? Mama's surely lost her mind. Are you hurt?"

Jakub shook his head.

Daniel continued. "We have to know what they're saying." He exhaled again, his voice growing stronger. "We have to."

Jakub rose and padded across the room. He stepped gingerly over the groaning plank by the piano and glanced back to Daniel, who nodded vigorously. Though younger, his brother had always been the confident one.

Jakub leaned close.

"Yes, Mr. Hořký," his mother was saying, "I trust you completely. But the violins, they've all been taken. The Germans came—it was horrible."

"But did you see it? The instrument with the light amber finish? Surely they couldn't have taken that one too."

Mother's voice was strained. "I don't know. I remember my husband saying he must hide a special piece, but I have no idea where. I know every square inch of this house. Perhaps he took it to a friend?"

Mr. Hořký's voice hinted of urgency. "Please try to remember. I'll come back, and maybe you'll think of something by then."

"I will try."

Jakub turned to hurry back across the room, but then the conversation continued.

"There's another matter. About the boys."

His mother was silent.

"I can find a secure place for them . . . possibly. The red streaks on Daniel's arms are a sure sign of infection. And Jakub—he's a big lad, large enough to be put to work in the camps. They might try to send him away."

"I know." Mother's voice was muffled, as if her hands covered her face.

The man lowered his voice. "I wish I could offer you a place—"

"No, I understand. The boys first."

"I'll be back. Two days, maybe three. The transports, you know. I only hope . . ." His voice was no more than a whisper. "I only hope we have enough time."

Footsteps vibrated the floorboards, and Jakub quickly shuffled across the floor toward Daniel.

Daniel's eyes were questioning. "Well?"

Jakub didn't answer. Alexi's words had kindled a memory. *The amber violin.* His father had coddled it and praised its beauty. The memory brought a smile—Father's approval was not an easy thing to obtain.

The door opened, and his mother and Mr. Hořký entered the living room. His mother locked the door behind her. Jakub glanced at their solemn faces. *Should I tell? If I do, they'll know I was eavesdropping.* The bodies moved toward him, and Jakub thought back to that day.

He had been hiding from Daniel underneath his father's workbench. Father had shooed him out of the workshop, reminding him it was not a play place. Jakub moved into the living room toward a spot between the piano and the wall that seemed too tight to fit into. Still, he had squeezed in. Then his father opened the door between the living quarters and the shop, propping it open with a stick of wood.

Jakub's father had looked around, not seeing him in his hiding spot. He picked up the large cushioned chair by the fireplace, then wrestled it into the workshop. An inner urge prompted Jakub to assist him, but a stronger impulse forced him to stay hidden. Father shut the door behind him, and then there was the sound of fabric tearing.

Jakub couldn't hold it in any longer. Surely they'd be thankful for his help, even if he *had* been listening to their conversation. "I know where it is!"

His mother looked at him, puzzled.

"Know where what is?" Mr. Hořký placed a large hand on Jakub's shoulder.

"The amber violin." He lunged from the sofa and ran into the kitchen, then returned with a large knife and moved to the cushioned, wing-backed chair. Before his mother could protest, he gingerly slid the knife down the fabric where the front and the back pieces joined.

Mr. Hořký rushed toward him. "In the chair back?"

Jakub nodded. "Remember, Mother, how Father insisted it be recovered? I remember him taking it into the workshop—"

Alexi ripped away the fabric, and Jakub saw a wooden crate wedged inside. Alexi smiled. Then he wiggled the crate from its prison and pried it open. Inside, wrapped in cloth, was the amber violin.

"My boy, you did it!"

Jakub looked to his mother for approval. She quickly turned her head, but not before he saw the rage that flared in her eyes.

Six

So how does it feel to be twenty-two, my darling?" Anja Kreig took Evie's hand in her gloved one as they strode down *Stephansplatz,* leaving the shadow of St. Stephan's cathedral behind.

"I really don't know yet." Evie glanced away from her mother's gaze as she kicked a rock on the sidewalk. "I've had better birthdays." She watched as the rock bounced across the cobblestones.

As a child, Evie loved coming to this downtown shopping district. She would imagine that a mysterious stranger, a handsome prince perhaps, waited around the medieval layout of lanes, alleys, and spacious court-yards. But her favorite part was having a delicious treat at the Sacher Hotel or the Konditorei Demel. Isak always chose the hotel for its famous Sacher torte. Today,

Evie picked Demel's. First, because she'd decided her next piece of Sacher torte would be with Nick. Second, because Isak wasn't there to protest.

After indulging her mother by choosing a few new outfits from their favorite shops, Evie and her mother entered through the elegant doors into the bakery. Perhaps she'd choose a crumbly fruit pastry or a piece of rich, creamy cake. Whatever she picked, Evie'd enjoy it with a mug of hot chocolate. As a child she'd once been invited behind the counter to watch as, with utmost care, the server at Demel's had boiled the milk slowly, adding pieces of chocolate and stirring until it looked like dark, sweet silk.

Evie's mouth began to water, and she thought that perhaps Mother was right: maybe chocolate *was* the key to getting her thoughts off Nick. Evie touched the French cameo that hung around her neck.

What Mother didn't know was that only half of her mind was on Nick. The other half was on Thomas. It sickened her each time she pondered her friend's position and his plans to rip innocent people from their homes and loved ones. How could her old friend be so cold and unfeeling?

A glass display case stretched from the door to the back wall. Small café tables were clustered under antique chandeliers. The Konditorei overflowed with Viennese citizens. Men with newspapers and pipes. Women wearing the latest fashions in hats, delicately nibbling their pastries.

"Have a seat." Her mother pointed to an open table

by the front window. "Would you like an éclair and hot chocolate?"

"Perfect." Evie offered her mother a smile and slid her bags under the window table.

Perfect, just as you like it. She watched her mother stride to the counter and greet the waiter with a smile. She pointed to the pastries with her gloved finger, then gave a soft chuckle—most likely in response to the waiter's flirting. Even now Mother's refined features sparkled in this city of culture. Always a lady, she never spoke out of line and always knew the right response. Anja Kreig had grown up during a time when Viennese society influenced much of Europe. She had married a cultured, ambitious man and was his perfect helpmate, supporting him as he fulfilled his dreams.

Unfortunately, Evie was nothing like her. She would rather scoot than sashay, laugh aloud than titter, and run through the woods than waltz. She didn't fit her mother's cultural mold. But in New York it hadn't mattered. Evie had not only reveled in the freedom of America but embraced the independence city life required. She cycled through lower-class neighborhoods, bought hot dogs from street vendors, tutored students not of her social status . . . and loved every minute of it.

The only thing her mother had approved of in New York was Nick. Handsome, charming, and a student of medicine. What more could a mother want for her daughter?

Gazing out the window, Evie observed again how slowly life moved in Vienna, in contrast to the bustle of the Big Apple. Delivery trucks rolled past, seemingly unconcerned with timetables. Pedestrians sauntered down sidewalks under the shifting shadows of Nazi flags fluttering in the breeze.

The flags reminded Evie of a holiday pageant she'd participated in as a child. She must have been about six when her class had created patriotic banners for their beloved Austria. In front of proud parents, the boys and girls had waved those flags and sung *"Heil Dir im Siegerkranz"*—which Evie later learned had the same tune as the American anthem "My Country 'Tis of Thee."

Mother returned from the counter, sat down, and removed her stole. "I love the smell of this place. The pastries weren't the same in New York. Don't you think?"

Evie attempted to smile.

"So what should we do after our treat? I hear the Vienna Boys' Choir has a performance tonight. Or perhaps your father can join us for dinner at *Griechenbeisl*. I told some friends about that place when we were in New York; they couldn't imagine eating at a restaurant that's been in business for five hundred years."

Evie placed her hand over her mother's. Mother always chattered when she was anxious. And her twittering had only gotten worse since arriving home.

"The choir or the dinner—either would be great," Evie answered.

Their waiter arrived and placed the hot chocolates before them. With a flourish he then presented their éclairs on Demel's fine china. Her mother clapped her hands lightly, like a child.

"Danke schön," they said in unison.

Evie lifted the mug, breathing in the luscious scent. But before she could take a sip, a commotion outside the window caught her attention. Evie plunked her cup on the saucer and stood. Her feet knocked a shopping bag to the floor, spilling its contents. Her chair clattered against the window.

"Evie, what is it?"

Half a dozen men in gestapo uniforms were circling a teenaged girl.

"What are they doing?"

One agent grasped the girl's arms, causing her leaflets to flutter through the air. Two more hoisted her legs. She struggled as they hauled her toward a waiting car and was rewarded with a club to the head. Blood flowed over her porcelain-like cheek and into her tight brown ringlets, but her clenched mouth refused to cry out.

"What has she done? Someone needs to stop them!" Evie moved toward the door, but strong arms caught her and held her back.

"Don't do it, miss." It was the waiter. His whisper was firm in her ear. "You run out there, and they'll take you too. In fact, leave immediately—don't look back. There are plainclothes agents in this very room. Nothing can be done for that girl now."

Evie's mother took her hand with a disapproving glance. "Let's go."

Hot chocolate and éclair forgotten, Evie allowed herself to be led down the winding streets and alleys to where their car and driver waited. She numbly slumped into the leather seat, hoping she'd wake from this nightmare.

They rode in silence for a few minutes, then her mother spoke. "The girl was handing out anti-Nazi propaganda. She should know better."

Evie said nothing.

"Your brother has to arrest such people all the time. You'd think they'd just obey the rules. No one would have to suffer if they just obeyed."

An image of Isak's freckled, twelve-year-old face popped into her mind. Did her brother, now grown up, behave like those brutes? Beating innocents, dragging them away. She couldn't picture Isak that way—didn't want to believe it.

It wasn't until she marched into the house and hid herself in the sanctuary of her bedroom that Evie thought about the chocolate treats they had left untouched on the table and the shopping bags they'd left underneath.

In exchange, Evie's heart had carried home something heavier.

🌿   🌿   🌿

Nick jumped up from the cement floor of the classroom, notebook in hand. There were plenty of wooden benches to sit on, but since they offered no back support, he often found himself hunkered against the wall as one army medical doctor after another lectured on medical techniques and patient care.

The teacher of the current course had been especially helpful. Having attended the injured in Pearl Harbor, the seasoned medic described in graphic detail the kinds of wounds one could expect to see in combat—and how to treat them. This was exactly the information Nick needed most.

Twitch strode up to Nick and patted his back. "Thanks for helpin' me study. You saved me from getting booted back to veterinary school."

"Anytime." Nick gave a thumbs-up as he strode through the front doors, hurrying to his next class. He grimaced to himself. If he didn't get things under control, he might be the one booted. He glanced at his notes on the page.

> *Amputee Care:*
> *Apply a tourniquet*
> *Cover the stump*
> *Inject morphine to prevent shock*
> *Get the patient in the shock position*
> *Keep him warm*

Funny thing. He didn't remember writing the list. His mind had been on Evie.

He looked to the notebook again. Under the notes for Amputee Care, he'd written:

She always tilted her head backward and closed her eyes when she laughed.

Any time she was deep in thought, she'd take a strand of her long, dark hair and twist it around her finger.

I bet she's lonely. . . . Maybe she feels like a part of her has been amputated. That's how I feel. I only wish I could be there to care for Evie's wound and to help prevent shock by keeping her warm.

🐚   🐚   🐚

Alexi Hořký hadn't been gone for more than a couple hours when their neighbor Mrs. Lanik pounded on the door. "There's been an assassination attempt on Reinhard Heydrich, the *Reichsprotektor*. It's on German radio right now."

The news blared across the airwaves. The highest-ranking SS officer had been on his way to work when members of the Czech resistance launched a small bomb into his green Mercedes. He was injured but still alive. The men responsible escaped, and the SS proclaimed that the whole city of Prague would be turned on its side until they were found.

Mother clicked off the radio. "I think we've heard enough."

Jakub and Daniel waited in the dim living room while the two women conferred in whispers. *What will this mean to us?* Jakub wondered.

Mrs. Lanik left, and Mother shut the door with a

slam. "How much more can I bear in one day?" She walked to the couch and slumped between the two boys, pressing her face into her hands.

"They are searching every Jewish home," she said, frantically repeating what they'd just heard on the radio. "Men and women are being rounded up and killed. Those without proper paperwork will be arrested. There is nothing we can do except wait."

The hours ticked slowly by as the three huddled behind closed doors. Reports continued to filter in from neighbors, and Jakub didn't know what to believe. It was said that twenty thousand police, gestapo, and SS troops had joined the search. And the tales of senseless murders seemed to be true. The sister of their neighbor Mrs. Pagler was shot when she couldn't account for herself during the time of the murders. It didn't seem to matter that she was a mother of small children.

Jakub glanced at his mother, who was again asleep on her mattress. After Alexi had left, Jakub had questioned her about the violin. He had also apologized for letting Alexi take it. She refused to speak to him about the instrument, but her eyes said enough—he'd made a big mistake.

His stomach rumbled. They had not eaten since breakfast, and it was now past dinnertime. Yet neither boy wanted to wake their mother. Jakub ignored the growling by thinking instead of the fairy tale that was a favorite of Jewish children living in Prague.

"Daniel, do you remember the story of Golem?"

"Yes," Daniel whispered, a pained look in his eyes. "But tell it to me again."

Jakub spoke softly, just as he did when they shared whispered stories in bed.

"It was a dark time in history. The Jews in Prague were under attack. They hid themselves behind the walls of a ghetto, but the Gentiles who roamed Prague were not satisfied. They wanted blood. Jewish blood." Jakub could hear echoes of his father in the rhythm and cadence of his own voice.

"How long ago was this?" Daniel asked, settling his head on his pillow.

"Hundreds of years ago."

"Things haven't changed much, have they?"

Jakub shook his head, then continued. "The great Rabbi Loew knew his people needed a protector. So he went into the streets and found clay to mold into the body of a giant. When he was finished, Rabbi Loew blew air into the large nostrils. Then he whispered in Golem's ear."

"Reminds me of when God created Adam," Daniel said.

"That's what I was thinking too."

A roar of jeeps outside caused Jakub's aching stomach to lurch.

He continued. "Golem strode out of the ghetto. The rabbi returned to the house of study to prepare for the Sabbath. But he knew Golem was slaying their enemies, putting an end to their troubles. Golem began his work on Wednesday and continued into Thursday and Friday, the beginning of the Sabbath.

"Soon the people of the ghetto were concerned, for Prague was filled with the bodies of Gentiles. 'Rabbi, if you don't stop Golem, there will be no Gentiles left for us to hire to light our Sabbath ovens or take down our Sabbath lamps.' So the rabbi began to recite a psalm for the Sabbath. Hearing the words, Golem returned to Rabbi Loew. Again the rabbi whispered something in the giant's ear. Only this time life was taken away, and Golem returned to clay."

Jakub paused. The noise outside increased, but still their mother slept. He was certain from the clamor that the scouring of their neighborhood had begun.

"Where is Golem now?" Daniel asked. His brother had hardly complained through the day, but Jakub could tell from his pale face that the pain in his hands had increased.

"He hides in the uppermost part of the synagogue, under a layer of cobwebs. He sleeps, waiting to be called into service once more."

"I wish someone would call him up now."

Booted feet stomped outside their door. The shouts grew closer.

Their mother's eyes opened, wild with fear.

Jakub wrapped his arms around his brother, not caring that they hadn't embraced in such a way since they were small boys. "Me too," he said, but his words were lost in the pounding at their door.

Seven

"It was the crown jewels, you know. They are what led to his downfall."

Otto eyed the security guard with suspicion as the stocky man led him through Prague University's large warehouse. Though nearly bulging with Jewish goods, the building did not emit the old, musty scent one might expect. Rather, as Otto strolled through the orderly aisles, he caught whiffs of cigar smoke and furniture polish from the newly cataloged items.

Sofas, cabinets, massive banquet tables—recently sorted, stacked, and draped with white linens—spread before Otto like a graveyard of fine furniture. He knew they would not rest here for long. Some would be transferred to the homes of fine German families. Others might be sold to support Hitler's regime. Some would just disappear.

"The crown jewels are the prize of our country, you

know," the guard said, glancing back at Otto with a lift of his eyebrows.

Otto didn't speak as they continued at a quickened pace. He clenched his fists, feeling his nails bite into his flesh. He'd made a fatal mistake. Now, instead of accompanying his superior to Hitler's Eagle's Nest, he found himself in a country he hated, amongst a people he despised, working with violins he'd sworn never to touch again.

Ornate claw feet peeked out from under white sheets as they passed one grand piano and then another. Otto scanned the aisles and noticed a dozen more pianos of varied models lining one aisle. Beyond them, music stands were clustered like a metallic floral arrangement. They continued on, passing a candelabra that stood at least six feet tall—its golden chains hanging in defeat. Otto could still make out red wax hardened on the metal frame.

The guard scurried ahead, glancing back over his shoulder. "I forgot, SS guards, or *esmen,* as we like to say, are of few words. Secrecy and all. But aren't you a bit curious? Don't you want to hear about the mystic legend?"

Otto raised one eyebrow. *Mystic legend?*

The man was old enough to be Otto's father. Still, one could not be too careful. Sometimes those who appeared most innocent were the deadliest enemies of the Reich.

Otto studied the man, smirking at the way his thin, gray hair spiraled in an awkward cowlick on the back of his head. Didn't the fool know he could be arrested for spreading rumors about the Reich? Many had been hanged for less, and especially since yesterday's assassination attempt on Reinhard Heydrich.

Yet something about the guard intrigued him. He watched as the fellow paused in front of an elaborately crafted grandfather clock and readjusted the protective cloth like a mother primping her child. The old man was harmless.

Otto cleared his throat. "And what *do* the crown jewels have to do with the attempt on Heydrich's life?"

The guard glanced back and smiled. He slowed until he matched Otto's stride. "Haven't been in Prague long, have you, *esman?* I can tell by that Viennese accent, still fresh."

"I've been here a month, this time anyway."

The man considered this, then lowered his voice. "So you know that the *Reichsprotektor* had moved into Prague Castle. Well, not long after, Heydrich hosted a ceremony for himself at St. Vitas Cathedral, home of the Bohemian crown jewels." The guard stopped, and Otto did the same. In slow motion the guard moved his hands, mimicking the actions of a key turning in a lock. He repeated his charade before continuing.

"Heydrich claimed for himself the seven keys that open the vault to the crown jewels. Then he had the jewels displayed—St. Wenceslas's crown and sword, the royal orb and sceptre, the vestments, and the gold reliquary cross.

"After that"—the guard leaned close as if relaying a

ghost story to a child—"in a secret ceremony, Heydrich crowned himself king of Bohemia and Moravia. But he didn't heed the warnings of the curse."

"What curse?"

"Hundreds of years ago, when Charles IV dedicated the royal crown to St. Wenceslas, he proclaimed that the kings of Bohemia were only to wear the crown during special celebrations, and only in Prague. King Charles also decreed that whoever wore the crown without authority would die."

Otto crossed his arms. But a tilt of his chin urged the man to continue.

"Heydrich laughed at the superstition, and he placed the Czech crown upon his head himself." The guard turned and continued walking. "That was less than a year ago. No one in Prague speaks a word of the curse. No one dares risk his life." He tapped an age-spotted finger on his graying head. "But everyone waits, knowing the curse will have its revenge. And then your people will know and will perhaps take more caution in dealing with things sacred. You'll tell them. You'll let your superiors know about the curse before anyone else is killed, won't you?"

Otto gave the man a look of disgust. "Your 'curse' isn't very effective. Heydrich was only injured. He still lives."

"Not for long." The guard pointed a finger into the air. "Mark my words."

The two turned one last corner and stopped before a dozen tables stacked with violin cases.

"Here they are, sir." He spoke with authority and confidence, the superstitious man of a few minutes ago replaced with a dutiful soldier. "The instruments of the Jewish musicians of Prague. I'll be back in an hour. Heil Hitler." He winked, saluted, and marched back through the labyrinth of confiscated treasures.

Otto scanned the room before turning to the instruments. The enormity of the amassed items was mind-boggling. *And this is only what was brought to storage.* He considered again his superior's request to deliver the side table from the castle directly to his home. How many officers did the same? With "guards" like this old man, how easy it would be for Otto to take his own share. For a moment, he contemplated what it would be like to possess such wealth.

No, this position wasn't what he'd planned. But perhaps it wasn't a total loss. He rubbed his hands together and began his examination by separating the instruments by kind. The violins outnumbered the others five to one.

His first assignment for the Musik Aktion team had been to search for the instrument missing from the repair shop. Viktor, the head of the Musik Team, had accepted Otto's addition to his staff warily. Yet, though Viktor was a man of few words, he'd treated Otto with a respect he'd not previously experienced in his military career.

Otto pushed away his anger of only moments before and instead decided to revel in the fact that Viktor thought him a genius. He also smirked, considering the odds of finding *that* Stradivarius. He could have picked it out amongst a thousand pieces. After all, during the months he'd prepared for auditions for the orchestra, it had been his. His hand had grown accustomed to the supreme instrument's rich surface. The pegs once turned by the great violin maker had tantalized his own fingers. He had been allowed to borrow the instrument for a time, but after he was denied a seat in Vienna, he had dreaded the thought of returning the priceless violin.

Yet the Stradivarius remained his for a while longer. His father's "good connections" landed him a tryout with the Prague Philharmonic. But when the philharmonic's conductor also rejected him, the expensive instrument was snatched away. His father's connections only went so far.

Otto shoved thoughts of the prideful orchestra conductor, Alexi Hořký, out of his mind before red-hot anger overshadowed all else. Besides, Hořký was a Jew. Most likely he was getting what he—and all the rest of that filth—deserved.

Otto turned his attention back to the violins. For good luck, he fingered a swastika into the dusty case resting before him. Then he examined the instrument as he'd seen his grandfather do thousands of times.

He turned over the piece in his hands, noting it had been well cared for. He didn't need a measuring tape to know it was a twenty-three-inch violin. He tilted the instrument toward the light and read the label pasted inside. *Giovanni Paolo Maggini, Brescia 16.* Handwritten underneath the stamp was the number *42*. Inside the case, Otto noted two bows with mother-of-pearl inserts. He returned the instrument to its cradle and snapped the cover closed.

Otto continued looking through the piles. Many of the violins bore the names of other masters: Amati, da Salo, Stainer. Yet all were facsimiles, created by dedicated followers in honor of a master's work, and he understood why anyone without prior training could question the value of such pieces. He opened a second case and withdrew a beautiful piece from the crimson lining. The deep burgundy varnish glowed on the instrument's soft curves.

Yet anyone who understood musical instruments also knew authenticity could only be determined through a comparative study of design, model, wood characteristics, and varnish texture—expertise gained through the examination of hundreds or possibly thousands of instruments. There was no substitute for an experienced eye, such as Otto had developed in his grandfather's workshop. Such a task should honor him. But Otto knew that working with the Musik Aktion team would take him further from the true prize he sought, which was entrance into the mystic world guarded by the Nazi elite.

Just be patient, a voice in his head told him. *Do your time, and you will achieve what you desire.*

The old guard returned too soon; Otto had barely gone through a quarter of the violins.

"Find anything?"

Otto offered the violin he'd been holding, and the old man took it gingerly.

"This piece is labeled *Antonius Stradivarius, Cremonenfis Faciebat Anno, 1742.*"

The guard's eyes widened.

"See that circular embellishment on the label?"

"Yes, a cross above the initials." The guard's voice rose an octave. "An A and S. I see it. And the last two digits of the date have been inked in by hand."

"Do you know what you're holding?" Otto asked.

"A Stradivarius," the guard whispered. He handed back the instrument, uncertain about holding such a gem. "Is it really—"

"No." Otto returned the violin to its case and shuffled it back into the pile. "A mere replica. One of thousands in circulation—though a good one, I'll admit."

The guard stepped back, put off by Otto's trickery. "If you're lucky, I'll be back to get you later." He limped away, shaking his finger. "Then again, I might just lock you in for the night."

Four hours later Otto followed the guard back outside. With a gloved hand he rubbed his stiff neck. His feet ached from standing. The amber violin hadn't been at the repair shop, and it wasn't in the warehouse either.

Where could it be? Nazi security forces had scoured the Jewish homes and businesses over the past two days. They guarded every border. Where would one hide such an instrument? Perhaps the Jewish repairman had an Aryan friend—a traitor was just as bad as a Jew —who had concealed it in an attic or basement.

Still, Otto knew, Jews talked. *And when they do,*
there is always someone willing to sell the information
for special privileges . . . or to save one's life.

🍂   🍂   🍂

"If you think Vienna's mad, you should hear the reports from Prague. Yesterday's attack on Heydrich will
bring a thousand times more destruction than any good
they could have accomplished."

It was Isak's voice. Evie quietly shut the kitchen cupboard and moved toward the closed dining room door,
hoping to hear more. Smells of dinner and warm pastry
had drawn her to the kitchen, despite her principled re-
fusal to dine with the family for the second day in a
row. Reinhard Heydrich, Evie knew, was the leading SS
officer and overseer of the Protectorate of Bohemia,
revered for his military brilliance and efficient plots to
extinguish enemies of the Nazi State.

Father lowered his voice. "The newspapers have
been vague about his injuries. What have you heard?"

Forks and knives scraping plates accented the conversation. From the sound of it, only Isak and their father dined together. If her mother were present, the
conversation wouldn't follow such a serious subject.
Anja Kreig didn't like talk of war.

"The bomb exploded just outside the car and blew
fragments into his body. His diaphragm, spleen, and
lungs were damaged. He also has broken ribs," Isak
said. "I hear Hitler's as angry with Heydrich as he is

with the Czech people. The man drove around Prague as if he were indestructible—in an open car without reinforced steel."

"Will he die?"

"Only time will tell."

A platter clattered on the table.

"And what about the attempted assassins?"

"The gestapo are purging the city of Prague. It gives them a good excuse to round up the hundreds of stubborn Czechs who won't bend to *der Führer*. I'll bet someone will talk. And when the rebels are captured, their punishment will ripple through the Czech countryside. It—"

Evie's eavesdropping was interrupted by the tinkle of china behind her. She turned quickly and spotted Ilse standing in the middle of the kitchen with a silver tray.

She moved away from the doorway, heat rising to her cheeks. "I didn't know you were there."

"I think *they* can say the same about you." Ilse smiled, and Evie was suddenly put at ease. Ilse wouldn't get her into trouble any more than she'd let her go hungry.

The German woman had been a part of their household since Evie was a baby. She was tall and thin, with soft curls around her face when her hair wasn't pinned up for work. And in the spring, Ilse always wore a wildflower in her hair, whether it was up or down. The curls used to be a golden blonde, which Evie had envied. But over the years, gray had overpowered the blonde, making Ilse's tresses appear as dull silver.

"I'm just taking dinner up to your mother. I was

going to check on you next." Ilse placed the silver tray on the countertop, with slower movements than Evie remembered. "Some birthday, I guess. I'm sorry. The last few days haven't been a great way to start a year. My poor little Evie."

Evie didn't ask Ilse how much she knew about their experience downtown. Ilse always knew. With no husband or children, Ilse's life had always been entwined in hers. They had exchanged letters nearly every week while Evie was in New York . . . so Ilse, more than anyone, knew how much she was missing Nick.

Evie spied the food on the tray. "Did you make my favorites again?"

"*Gefüllte Paprika* with *Apfelstrudel* for dessert. Sit. I will get some for you."

Evie settled at the small table where the paid staff took their meals. In less than ten minutes, a large green pepper was placed before her. It was stuffed with ground beef and rice and had been cooked in a spicy tomato sauce. Evie, suddenly realizing how famished she was, shoveled the food into her mouth.

"You always do that, you know," Ilse said with a tip of her head.

"What's that?" Evie slowed her pace, reminding herself that she was no longer a small child—even though she still felt like one in Ilse's kitchen.

"You eat when you're upset. I think that's why you returned from America so thin. You were very happy there."

Evie set down her fork and rested her chin on her

hand. "I was. That's what makes returning so miserable. If I'd stayed in Vienna all along—I don't know—I may have gotten used to the changes. I'm sure they didn't seem like a big deal, one step at a time. Who knows, I might have followed the same path as my brother." She sighed. "But I know things don't have to be like this. There's another world out there—and it's continuing without me."

Ilse pulled up a white wooden chair and sat across from Evie. "I missed having you around." She took Evie's hand in her own and gave it a gentle squeeze. "It's no fun taking care of just your brother. He's a bore. I miss the earful you'd give in exchange for your afternoon snack. Tell me, Evie, what do you think about most now?"

For the first time since she'd been home, Evie felt she could talk. "Sometimes when I go to bed at night, I think about my other home. I consider the New Yorkers getting off work. I remember the crazy, loud families sipping root beer, enthralled by *The Shadow* or *Little Orphan Annie* on the radio. The grimy street vendors packing up their wooden carts for the day."

She sectioned off a strand of hair and began to twirl it in her fingers. "Oh, Ilse, I think of Nick arriving home from classes and greeting his mother with a bear hug and smooch on the cheek, then joining the others around the dinner table. And there's an empty chair where I used to sit. I imagine his parents arguing over politics, and I wonder if they miss me being there."

"And what did they think about the war over here?"

"Oh, they don't like what Hitler's up to. They don't understand how such craziness can exist and why the people over here are allowing it. Surely, if ordinary citizens stood up for what was right, none of this would be happening."

Ilse's eyes narrowed, and she cocked her head. "Do you agree?"

"Of course. I mean, look what's happened to our country. I've heard the Jewish district is being cleared out, and the long trains in constant motion away from the city are filled with human cargo. How can we, as civilized people, allow such things to take place?"

Ilse looked away, and suddenly Evie's chest constricted. She let go of Ilse's hand, pulled her handkerchief from her pocket, and blew her nose. "Forgive my jabbering. May I have my *apfelstrudel* now?"

Ilse laughed nervously and rose from the table. "Yes, I know you well. You're like me in too many ways—feeling so much inside, yet not knowing how to get it out." She lowered her voice and glanced toward the dining room. "I need to talk to you—"

Ilse paused and sliced into the strudel. Steam rose as she slid a portion onto a plate and handed it to Evie.

"I'm listening." Evie sliced her fork into the pastry with a trembling hand, then paused. She noted a hint of desperation in Ilse's eyes. But it quickly vanished, and the familiar smile returned.

"See, just like you, there are no words. It's just that so much has changed since you've been gone." Ilse turned and wrapped a clean white dish towel over the remaining strudel. Then she turned toward Evie with a piercing gaze. "You will know when it's time. I must talk with a friend first."

Before Evie had a chance to prod further, Ilse opened the pantry door and retrieved a newspaper, which she placed before Evie.

"Anyway, you don't need to eavesdrop. It's all right here."

On the front page, Evie saw a photo of Heydrich's mangled car. A puddle of blood had pooled on the road. Next to the article, a photo of Heydrich's stoic profile graced the page.

"I must check on your mother." Ilse hurried toward the door. "I only hope the man survives, for the sake of the Czech people," she called back over her shoulder.

Evie glanced at the picture once more but didn't have enough compassion for the man to wish the same.

"I hope he dies," she muttered under her breath.

Eight

Otto trekked up the hillside toward Prague Castle behind Viktor, who carried a wreath of red and white flowers. The wind blew scents of early summer blossoms from the courtyard gardens as if protesting the morbid reason they gathered.

Ever since Otto heard the news of Heydrich's death three days before, the words of the warehouse guard had stirred through his mind. *Heydrich is cursed. He will not live. Tell your superiors to take more caution of things sacred.*

Now the streets bulged with citizens honoring their lost hero. For an occupied country, the number of people who turned out to pay their last respects to the *Reichsprotektor* surprised Otto. Thousands had already journeyed up Prague's cobblestone streets to lay flowers and wreaths at the base of the coffin. More still came.

Otto only wished he could step into eternity in such a manner—with women and children weeping uncontrollably and men lifting their arms in dedicated salutes.

These citizens, mainly Germans living in the protectorate, honored Heydrich for what he'd done for the common man. He'd provided jobs and goods—along with a sense of solidarity with the great German nation. Otto scanned the lamenting crowds and wondered if the curse dominated their thoughts as it did his.

Otto and Viktor mounted the top of the hill and made their way through streets lined by government offices. These "offices" were former royal homes, painted in pale hues of blue and pink, with ornate carvings trimming the windows and doors.

At the end of the street a wrought-iron gateway, flanked by eighteenth-century Battling Titans, led into the first courtyard of Prague Castle. They walked through the courtyard and under an arch that opened into a second courtyard. They strode past the Chapel of the True Cross and the old stables, which now housed the castle gallery. Then they proceeded to the third courtyard, where St. Vitas cathedral rose higher than everything around it, stretching its black spires into the clouds.

The cathedral itself inspired Otto, despite the fact that religion was a foolish hobby for the weak-minded. He paused and lifted his head in appreciation of the way the architects over the centuries had harmoniously combined Gothic, baroque, and Art Nouveau styles. Viktor paused too.

Otto spoke. "I lived near here when I was trying out for the Prague Philharmonic. Did you know the building of the cathedral began in 1344 and wasn't completed until thirteen years ago?"

"That is interesting," Viktor commented. "And what happened with the philharmonic?"

Otto turned his head and rubbed his nose with his finger. "I was denied a chair. But I'm not bothered by it."

"You lie. You should be angry with a man like Alexi Hořký."

"You know him?"

"Music is my world, Herr Akeman. Yes, I know the man, but I'm sure not as well as you. I assume he still haunts you."

Viktor switched the wreath to the other hand and turned his attention back to the cathedral. "You may appreciate such a building now, Herr Akeman, but in the end our Thousand-Year Reich will produce far greater exhibits of beauty. If we can create such a spectacle for a funeral, consider what permanent displays we'll erect in honor of final victories."

Otto followed Viktor's gaze and widened his eyes in appreciation. Nazi flags shrouded every window of the castle. Two large white banners hung, as from the sky, displaying the distinctive SS lightning-bolt runes. A lone casket rested at their base, ringed by a sea of flowers and greenery.

Otto and Viktor solemnly approached the coffin, guarded by Wehrmacht and SS officers. Otto's shoulders straightened as he watched Viktor lay a wreath over the salmon-colored funeral sash—a gift from the Führer as a sign of his personal friendship with Heydrich. Otto knew that after the state funeral in Berlin, the fine silk sash with gold-bullion fringe would be literally cut in pieces to be shared by the closest surviving relatives, a treasured memento of Hitler's high regard.

After a moment of silent respect, the two men stepped to the side, joining a group of Reich officials who prepared to embark on a solemn parade from the castle, over the Charles Bridge, to the main railroad station. From there SS *Obergruppenführer* Kurt Daluege would rest the flag-draped casket on a train to Berlin for Heydrich's last ride home.

Waiting for the procession to begin, Otto turned to Viktor. "What are the plans for the official state funeral? If there's this much pageantry in Prague, I can't imagine what Berlin will exhibit."

Viktor pushed his glasses up the bridge of his nose. "The funeral will be held at the Mosaic Hall of the new *Reichschancellery*. The Führer himself will speak. You're correct; this is nothing compared to what will take place there."

Otto stroked his chin. "Will we attend? I hear Heydrich was quite an accomplished musician."

"*Ja, freilich.* Heydrich's father founded the Halle Conservatory of Music and was a Wagnerian opera singer, while his mother was an accomplished pianist.

The night before the assassination attempt, I was invited to a concert celebrating his father's work."

"Did you attend?"

"No, I had work to do."

As they waited, Otto studied the small man, considering that perhaps he'd underestimated his new position. It was clear, despite his appearance of a timid intellectual, the Aktion Team supervisor had connections.

Otto readjusted his cap over his blond hair. "Any chance you could get us into that funeral? Didn't you say there's a violin that needs to be delivered to Berlin? Besides, it seems only right that someone from our team should be present—Heydrich loving all that we represent."

Viktor glanced at Otto with a wary gaze. "I'm not interested, but if you're that determined, I'll see what I can do."

♪   ♪   ♪

The next evening Otto found himself boarding the night train with dozens of other soldiers and a few citizens. In one hand was the Stradivarius he'd discovered at Nelahozeves, the one he'd once used as his own. In the other were a small suitcase and a ticket for Berlin. His mission was to meet Kametler, deliver the instrument, and join the officer at Heydrich's state funeral.

Otto quickened his pace and moved down the smoke-filled corridor, hoping to find a near-empty compartment.

He spotted a small six-person cabin with a sole occupant and slid the door open to join him. The man looked up from his newspaper, and his face drained of color at the sight of Otto's uniform. Otto grinned smugly at the reaction. He slid his suitcase into an overhead compartment. "Hello, sir. I'd say it's a lovely night for travel."

The man waved his hand as if agreeing and continued reading.

Otto slid the violin onto the plush seat next to him and unfastened his uniform jacket. The man's own coat appeared threadbare in contrast to Otto's. This too made Otto smile.

"Going to Berlin?" Otto asked. "Herr—?"

"Herr Breirather. Yes, I'm moving there. I'm traveling from Austria, actually."

Otto noted the man's Viennese accent. "Breirather, eh? Herr Brew Master." Otto smiled as he settled into his seat, crossing an ankle over one knee. "With that name, I imagine, sir, you'll miss the Weizengold. In my opinion, Germany doesn't make an equal wheat beer."

This was enough to break down the traveler's defenses. As the train pulled from the station and journeyed into the night, the men shared tales of the best of Viennese beer, dates, meals, and musicians. His fellow rider even broke out a bottle of cheap wine. When that was gone, Otto ordered another from the porter, and they reveled like old friends.

Otto's head weighed heavy, but it felt good to laugh. What had Breirather said, a Viennese dog's waste was better than Czech wine? Otto had almost fallen off his seat with that one. In good measure, Otto threw in a few cigarettes, which caused the man's tobacco-stained teeth to flash in a wide grin.

Hours later, the train rolled to a stop. Otto took a final swig of the cheap wine. "We are there already?"

"No, I've made this trip a thousand times, and we're not even close to Berlin yet." Breirather's words were slightly slurred. He lifted the blackout curtain and peered out the window. "I see a town in the distance. Looks like Dresden. I wonder what the problem could be."

The porter soon arrived at their compartment. "Sorry, friends, everyone out. There's been vandalism—the tracks ahead have been blown up. The underground resistance, no doubt. We'll have to walk to Dresden from here."

"What about Berlin?" Otto stood and ran a hand through his disheveled hair. "I have to get there by morning."

"Good luck," the porter said, moving on to spread the news to the other passengers. "There will be no trains continuing tonight, or tomorrow for that matter. If you're lucky, you might get there in a couple of days."

Otto's mind flashed to the image of the sanctioned funeral—the masses of people, and he himself standing amongst the Nazi leadership. He punched the seat next to him.

"Easy now." Breirather held up his hands, swaying slightly despite the fact the train now stood still. "I knew this was going to happen. And for this very reason I wrote down the address of a friend in Dresden." He patted his shirt pocket. "Come with me. I'm sure he'll put us up for the night."

Otto turned to the man. He wrapped his fist in the man's collar and jerked him nose to nose. "What do you mean, you knew this was going to happen? Are you part of the anti-Nazi movement? Did you know about the sabotage? I knew it as soon as I opened the door." Otto cocked back his fist.

"No, no! I'm not part of the underground. I am a seer, an occultist. At least I was, until the government shut me down. I can't explain. I just knew. . . ."

Otto released the man. Breirather staggered backward.

"If you are lying—" Otto couldn't stop his hands from trembling.

"Ask my friend Herr Weber. He will tell you. And if it weren't against the law, I would read your future myself."

Otto swiped his mouth and turned back to his seat. With quick movements, he slid on his jacket and grabbed the violin. "I will go with you and stay with your friend. But know this, you *will* tell me of your trade. I used to think such things were foolish, but now . . ." Otto pointed a finger at Breirather. "If you are lying—if you hold anything back—know that today will be your last day as a free man. Get my suitcase, will you? If we hurry, perhaps we can catch a ride to Berlin in the morning."

Otto hadn't slept all night. He was dressed and waiting in the kitchen when Breirather's friend Weber awoke. Weber eyed Otto warily. The man had to be at least seventy, yet there was quickness about his movements Otto admired.

Last night, after arriving at the small cottage on the outskirts of Dresden, Otto had heard the two self-claimed fortune-tellers arguing.

"Why have you brought him here? How could you have told him our profession?" Weber had moaned. "Do you want to get us killed?"

Now, tired of gazing out the window at the old, sturdy houses that loomed against the morning skyline, Otto watched the man as he filled his stove with wood and prepared to cook a meager meal.

Finally Otto folded his hands on the table and leaned forward. "What do you know about Hitler's involvement in the occult?"

A stick of wood tumbled from Weber's hands and bounced across the floor. He glanced over his shoulder, his eyes darting from Otto's face to his uniform and back to the stove. "Do you think I would allow myself to get arrested so easily? I'm not a fool."

"I'm not sure I even believe in your trade. Or at least I didn't used to. I'm just a seeker, like you. I promise." Otto lifted the violin case he'd stashed next to the table leg and placed it on the table. "It's a nice violin, worth a lot. A Stradivarius, in fact. I promise that if I cause you any harm, you can take this instrument and smash it into a thousand pieces."

Otto snapped open the case, and the man peered inside.

Weber's eyes flickered. He moved back to the stove and pulled an iron skillet off a hook on the wall. His words began slowly, then built with momentum. "I know elements in Hitler's horoscope promise prophetic ability. I know that from 1933 until September 1939, when the German troops invaded Poland, Hitler did not make a single international miscalculation. I know some doubted *der Führer* when, that September, France and Britain declared war, and the Germans faced the French on the border. Still, not a shot was fired. Hitler met their bluff again." Weber took a deep breath. "Very risky, unless one sees the future. I guess that alone should be enough to make one believe."

The front door opened, and Breirather entered with a small basket of eggs and a loaf of brown bread. The man nodded to Otto and Weber.

Otto ignored him. "Are you saying that Hitler can see the future?"

"It's not quite like that." Weber cracked the eggs into the skillet, the features on his wrinkled face relaxing. "No precog gets a clear view of the future. It's more like glimpses here and there."

"Like last night." Breirather poured three cups of ersatz coffee and passed one to Otto. "For some reason, I knew we'd not make it to Berlin. As I packed, an impression of my old friend Herr Weber filled my mind.

So I sought out his address and put it in my pocket. Don't ask me how it works; it just does. Besides, *esman,* what makes you so interested?"

Otto cleared his throat. "I was guarding some officials in a Viennese bunker when they—" Otto hesitated, unsure if he should continue, but something about these men made him feel as if they could be trusted. Or perhaps it was the lure of their power that pushed him on. "I was guarding some kind of ceremony. The chants, the symbols. It drew a power greater than any I've known. As I stood in that bunker, watching Nazi leaders evoke a force greater than themselves, I knew I wanted to tap into it.

"But that wasn't the first time. My interest has been growing for a while," Otto continued, rubbing the stubble on his chin. "There've been smaller incidents. Once during training, our instructor was so frustrated with our inadequate performance he had us close our eyes and visualize the spirits of the Ancients empowering us. Not long after, our group placed first in all the drills. No one discussed it, but I ache to feel that force again."

Weber set a plate of eggs before him, yet food was not what Otto hungered for.

"You know it's illegal to even speak of these things," Weber commented. "I've been out of work since 1934, when there was a ban on fortune-telling. Within months, my books were confiscated. But at the same time, I noticed the pagan symbols Hitler chose to display. The swastika, for instance, is a symbol of the sun and life. But Hitler had no interest in the Powers of Light. He reversed the original version and faced the rays backward as a symbol of death. And what about your black uniform and the necromantic death's head you wear on your cap? That cross and bones symbol is hard to miss, don't you think?"

"Yes, we learned all this at school," Otto said between bites, suddenly sensing a hunger in the pit of his stomach. "Or at least the part about the runes. But if this is all true, then I don't understand. Why would Hitler ban the occult? You'd think he'd embrace it."

Weber leaned forward, bringing his face within inches of Otto's. "There's just one word, my boy—competition. Hitler is not willing to share."

"And then there's the magic Hitler can't control," Breirather butted in. "Take Hess, for instance."

"You mean Rudolf Hess, and his recent flight to Scotland?"

"That is what the world knows of the story. But there's more." Weber leaned close. "This isn't public knowledge, but Hess embarked on that journey with the urging from his Secret Master, the magician Professor Karl Haushofer. It seems the whole thing began with a mystic vision. In a dream, Haushofer witnessed Hess striding through the aristocratic halls of an English castle on a mission of peace."

Breirather butted in. "Hess's betrayal of Hitler and his capture by the English shocked the world. But did you ever wonder why Hess sought out the Duke of Hamilton—a man who had no obvious political clout?

It seems Haushofer, the mystic, and the Duke of Hamilton were acquaintances."

Otto leaned back in his chair and trailed his fingers over the violin case. Everything was finally beginning to make sense.

Weber rose from the table, gathering up the empty plates. "Hitler, of course, was furious when Hess, one of his elite, betrayed him and sought a peace agreement behind his back. Hitler believed he'd been too easy on those in our trade. He was worried that more mystic visions would disrupt his plans. So last year, the gestapo swung into action and arrested occultists throughout Germany."

Breirather tilted his chin toward his friend. "Weber here even spent some time in jail. It was a who's who of the mystical world, that's for sure. Followers of Haushofer and other transcendentalists. Clairvoyants, faith healers, astrologers—anyone who could have been in touch with Hess. In fact . . ." Breirather turned to Weber and cocked one eyebrow. "It was exactly a year ago today when the arrests were made."

Weber resumed his seat with a thud, as if overcome by Breirather's words. His blue-gray eyes met Otto's, and Otto sensed the man could read something deep inside him. He longed to look away but couldn't.

"One year from the day I was arrested, another SS man crosses my doorstep. The last Nazis sought to end my visions. This Nazi seeks to know them." Weber's voice was slow and sweet, his honey-tongued words causing Otto's chest to fill with warmth.

"It can only mean one thing." Weber took Otto's warm fingers into his icy clutches. "It can only mean that I have a prophecy you are meant to hear."

Nine

CAMP CARLISLE, PENNSYLVANIA
JUNE 9, 1942

Nick rubbed his fingers over his crew-cut hair and stretched out on the hard bunk.

"That's not good enough, soldier!" the voice of the newly appointed "brown bar" shouted from outside. "Try that salute again! Again!"

Nick could hear the slapping of the officer's riding quirt striking the ground with impatience, and he felt sorry for the poor sap unfortunate enough to have thrown up a mediocre salute.

Nick's legs and back ached from last night's seven-mile hike. *You'd think we'd be used to it after nearly three months.* But lack of sleep had left his head throbbing—lights out at 12:45 with wake-up at 4:30 wasn't his idea of a good night's rest.

Throughout the barracks, the other medical officers spent their little leisure time discussing everything from Roosevelt to Benny Goodman to the fact that the price of a car had skyrocketed to $1,100.

In the background, a radio announcer discussed a recent air battle in the Pacific. "It was a hound-and-rabbit affair," the announcer claimed, with the American pilots being the rabbits.

Nick had hoped for a more positive report. *That's okay; we'll get 'em next time.*

He closed his eyes and hummed a Glenn Miller ditty, forcing his body to relax. *I got a gal in Kalamazoo.* But even Glenn couldn't help. In fifteen minutes, they'd leave for the "K" range, and there was nothing relaxing about the ear-piercing thunder of dozens of Enfield bolt-action thirty-caliber rifles being fired simultaneously. Despite the fact that they wouldn't be allowed to carry weapons into battle, the medics still needed to know how to use them. Today was their final day of shooting at the full-sized paper-and-wood tanks. Of course, Nick was no match for the country boys, who'd been shooting possum since before they could walk. Still, his score wasn't too shabby.

He rubbed his temples, hoping to ease the pounding. *And the guys back at medical school complain about lack of sleep.*

"Mail call! Whew-whee, look who's got himself a letter." Twitch's voice carried through the barracks as if he were yelling through a megaphone.

"It better be me." Nick opened his eyes. "I need a

pick-me-up here, or they'll be waving Maggie's Drawers at me tonight."

"Maggie's Drawers" was the name of the red flags attached to long poles that were waved downrange when someone missed a target. Nick had seen them waved his direction more than once as he fired five shots from each position—prone, kneeling, sitting, and standing.

A few guys snickered as Twitch plopped down on Nick's bunk, pushing Nick's legs to the side.

"Don't you ever wonder about ol' Maggie?" Twitch rubbed his chin. "I mean, who was she? And did she really wear big, red drawers? Or maybe that's what they looked like on the clothesline, blowing in the breeze—"

Nick nudged Twitch with his leg and hoisted himself onto one elbow. "C'mon, Twitch, stop stalling. Just give me the letter."

Twitch handed it over, and from the moment Nick glanced at the envelope, he knew a message about Evie waited inside. His mother's handwriting wasn't normal. It appeared hurried, maybe even excited.

"Look at his eyes, boys. I think I smell perfume on that letter," Jones called from across the room. "Is that lipstick on the flap?"

Nick ignored them and opened the envelope, pulling out a single sheet.

Dear Nicky,

Good news! A carrier arrived today from the embassy. Evie's father says they have arrived safely.

Evie is having a hard time adjusting, but you are on her heart. He was sorry he couldn't send more details but wants you to know you're missed.

I'll write more later. I just wanted to get this out before the postman comes.

Love,
Mother

Nick's heart soared. After months he finally knew. She was home. Safe. And she missed him.

Nick couldn't hide the grin on his face. He sank back on his bunk. *Funny. No more headache.*

"Is it news about your girl?" Twitch asked.

"Ya."

"You going to read it to me?"

"Nah, it's just a few lines."

"I read my letters to you sometimes."

Nick tapped Twitch with his booted foot, trying to reclaim his space on the bed. "Don't you think I know that?"

"Fine then, keep news of your girl secret. But when I get a girl, I won't tell you anything about her."

Nick smirked. He knew that if Twitch ever got a girl, the whole East Coast would hear about it.

"And you'll be getting yourself a girl soon?" Nick teased. "I'm thinking the pickings are pretty slim around here."

Twitch lowered his voice. "I have a plan."

Nick glanced at his watch. They had five minutes left—he hoped Twitch's plan wasn't a long one. "Well?"

"I want to go to church with you on Sunday. Fisk said he and a few of the guys went, and they were invited to the pastor's house for dinner. I hear he's got a good-looking daughter."

"Oh, I get ya. I've been taking the wrong tactic. Instead of talking about the comfort and consolation of religion, I should've mentioned all the single ladies at church."

"So you've seen her?"

Nick furrowed his brow and scratched his head, pretending to stir a memory. "Seein' how I go there every week, I guess I have."

"She a looker?"

Nick waved his letter in the air and rose from his bunk. "Not as pretty as my girl, but I guess she's not bad."

"Heck, far as you're concerned, no one's as pretty as your gal."

Nick closed his eyes again. He could see Evie now, walking toward him with her small wave. It was more like a flexing of her fingers, really, and a toss of her long hair.

He opened his eyes and shrugged. "Sorry, you're right. No one even comes close."

≈   ≈   ≈

PRAGUE, CZECHOSLOVAKIA

A knock sounded at the door. Before Jakub could open it, a pink slip slid underneath and rested at his feet. He lifted it with trembling fingers and read the brief notation:

Martha Hanauer. Jakub Hanauer. Daniel Hanauer. Summoned for June 10, 1942, at 8:00 A.M. to the secondary school on Merhaut Street for the purpose of deportation.

For the next hour, Jakub read the words over and over as he waited for the sunlight to brighten the edges of the dark drapes. When he couldn't carry the knowledge alone any longer, he tiptoed to his mother's bed.

"Mama." He touched her shoulder and brushed her golden hair from her cheek. His mother's brown eyes fluttered open.

"Jakub," she whispered. "What's wrong?"

Jakub's chest flooded with warmth as he gazed into his mother's eyes. It was as if the past few months had only been a bad memory, and his sweet, loving mother had returned.

She sat up and rubbed her eyes. "What's in your hand?"

Jakub longed to make the moment last longer, but there wasn't time. He stretched out his hand, and his mother grabbed the pink paper.

"No," she moaned after reading it. "Dear Abraham, Isaac, and Jacob, haven't we endured enough?" She pounded her pillow. "Why this? Why now?"

Daniel stirred from his place on the couch.

"I can go to the community center for you," Jakub

said, eager to bring his loving mother back. "Maybe something can be done. Perhaps because of Daniel's condition?"

His mother's determined look swept away the sweet embrace of only a few moments before.

"Good idea, Jakub." She stood, pressing her hand on her wrinkled gown. "But I must go. You're right; Daniel is not fit to travel. I will tell them that. In the meantime, clean his wounds, so the infection won't get worse." She grabbed her brush from the counter and ran it through her hair. "You do it so well."

Jakub nodded, then walked to his brother. Daniel lay on the couch with a look of disbelief in his sleepy gaze.

"It's our turn?" He pressed the bandaged hands to his chest, as if protecting his heart from the news.

"Tomorrow morning, 8:00 A.M. You can help. Tell me what we need, and I'll pack it."

Daniel attempted to smile, but Jakub was not fooled. It was the smile Daniel always flashed when trying to hide his fear.

❧   ❧   ❧

VIENNA, AUSTRIA

The sound of footsteps outside her room stirred Evie from a deep sleep. She glanced at the clock, shocked to see that it was past ten o'clock. She'd been up late writing a letter to Nick. She now had a stack of at least

119

two dozen ready to be mailed as soon as her father found a suitable way. Her letter written, she had tried to pray, but there were no words. God felt far off—as if she'd also left Him in New York.

When she still couldn't sleep, she had stayed up reading *West with the Night* by Beryl Markham. She'd picked up the book in New York, and in the dark hours she'd been entranced by the prose.

> *There are all kinds of silences and each of them means a different thing. There is the silence that comes with morning in a forest, and this is different from the silence of a sleeping city. There is silence after a rainstorm, and before a rainstorm, and these are not the same. There is the silence of emptiness, the silence of fear, the silence of doubt.*

She had read that last sentence more than once, her soul resonating with its truth. It described her—empty, fearful, full of doubt.

Someone knocked gently. Evie knew she couldn't ignore it, despite the fact it was most likely her mother, coming to offer more well-meaning advice.

"Evie, it's me." It was Ilse's voice.

Evie combed her fingers through her hair and sat up against her pillows. "Come in."

The housekeeper stepped into the room, closing the door behind her. Her face was pale, and her lower lip trembled.

"What's the matter?" Evie kicked the covers off her feet and patted the bed.

Ilse sank down beside her. "I don't want to do this to you, but I have no other choice. I—"

Evie placed her hand on the woman's arm. "Ilse, please. What are you trying to say?"

"I need your help. I wouldn't ask. It's just that—" Her eyes met Evie's. "I've been watching you, and I know you feel the same. You feel helpless and angry. I heard about your reaction at the bakery. And your comments to your father. The way you treated your own Thomas."

"Wait, Ilse. How do you know these things?"

"It's a different place, Evie. In our new country, both sides watch each other. Like players in a game of chess, each must know where to move and when . . . or you lose."

"Please, this isn't making sense. Just tell me what you need." Evie took a sip from the crystal water glass at her beside.

Ilse moved across the room to Evie's silver-edged desk. Her fingers trailed over *Songs of Praise*.

"I know I can trust you. I've sworn to the others that they can too." She met Evie's eyes once again. "I'm part of the Resistance. For a year—"

Evie choked on her water. "Ilse! You can't be serious."

Ilse brushed back a strand of hair from her neck. "Oh, please tell me I can trust you."

"Of course you can trust me. I'm just surprised. I

mean, I've heard of the Resistance—read about them in the paper. But to know someone involved . . . please tell me more."

Ilse's shoulders relaxed, and she took on an almost business-like air. "Our efforts are scattered. It's been difficult to form the many small groups into an effective fighting unit. We finally found a leader and have come up with a four-part plan. I won't go into details, but we need help to carry it out."

The older woman's courage surprised her. Evie crossed her arms across her chest. She'd wanted to do something, but now that the moment had arrived, she didn't feel as brave. She thought of her father's warnings. She remembered the girl on the street, knowing the young woman's life was mostly likely cut short because of her protests. She thought about Nick and her hopes of seeing him again—that was most important. And how would her mother face the humiliation of going to prison for her daughter's actions?

"Ilse, I'm just not sure."

Ilse's gaze dropped. "I understand. You won't tell anyone?" She turned to go. "Breakfast will be ready in half an hour."

"Wait . . . you will be able to find someone else to help, won't you?"

"No, I really don't trust anyone else. I had hoped . . ." She let her words trail off.

Evie's chest tightened. How could she turn her back on efforts to fight against what she despised most? The thought of actually doing something suddenly sent strength to her limbs.

Ilse walked back toward the bed. "We always have trouble coming up with enough ration cards for those in hiding. We need money for them and to buy weapons."

A sense of relief coursed through Evie. This she could do. "I don't know what I was thinking, Ilse. Of course I will help."

A knock sounded. "Evie? It's Isak. May I come in?"

Ilse's eyes widened.

Evie grabbed her robe and slipped it over her nightgown. She lowered her voice. "I'll have the money by tomorrow. We'll talk then."

Evie hurried to the door. When she opened it, she discovered her brother in his military police uniform with a gold swastika pin on his lapel. "Isak, come in. Ilse was just asking about breakfast. She always takes such good care of me."

"Look, we need to talk. But if this isn't a good time—"

"No, I'm just leaving. Pancakes and eggs American style, right away." Ilse squeezed through the doorway, her eyes on the floor.

But it wasn't Ilse's eyes that concerned Evie. It was the piercing gaze Isak gave her as she scurried down the hall.

Ten

It was noon, and Jakub's mother returned from the Central Office for Jewish Emigration with a look of resignation heavy on her features.

"They don't know where the transport is headed," she said in defeat. "Some say thousands are being sent to the East as a punishment for the death of Heydrich. Others believe all transports go to Terezín first—a sort of 'waiting spot' before getting to the horrible camps."

Terezín. Jakub had heard the name whispered by his parents and their friends more than once. He remembered learning about the fortress town in school. Built as a military fort in the late eighteenth century, Terezín had been designed to protect Prague from northern invaders. Joseph II, king of the Hapsburg dynasty, had named this village after his mother, Maria Teresia.

But why would they be sent to a place like that? Why couldn't they just stay in their home? Before Jakub had a chance to ask, a knock sounded at the door, and he turned to his mother.

"You answer it, Jakub," she called from the kitchen area. Their meager food was spread out before her on the counter, and she hurriedly wrapped it for the journey ahead.

If only Father were here. He'd know what to do. Jakub opened the door to his neighbors' somber faces.

"Let them in," his mother called. "They have come to help us pack."

A flurry of activity consumed the remainder of the day as they worked to pare down their items to fifty kilos each.

Mrs. Lanik helped by stitching their thickest blankets into sleeping bags. Another neighbor provided rucksacks that were filled with toiletries and basic necessities.

In the midst of it all, an Aryan neighbor, Mrs. Novy —whom Jakub hardly knew—offered to keep their valuables and photographs in safe hiding.

"The SS have already taken all the instruments," his mother told the woman, with a note of sadness in her voice. "But we do have the silver, linens, and a few pieces of art. Jakub, would you carry them to Mrs. Novy's, please?"

As night descended over the city, Mrs. Lanik placed their items on the scale and wiped her brow. "Looks like you're still five kilos over the limit for the three of you. You have to cut back."

Wearily, Mother grabbed Jakub's satchel and took out one set of his clothes. Next, she sifted through Daniel's things.

"What is this? Music hidden with your bandages?" Jakub had never heard his mother speak so harshly to Daniel. "Can you eat music? Can you wear it?" She threw the pages onto the floor.

Daniel's shoulders trembled as the sheets scattered, sliding under the velveteen sofa and Father's chair.

His mother began to repack the rucksack. Quietly Jakub retrieved the sheets from under the furniture and carefully stacked them into a pile. He slipped Daniel's favorite piece into his rucksack and was rewarded by a weak smile from his little brother.

Jakub's stomach felt pinched. How would Daniel fare on this journey? Jakub only wished they'd heard from Mr. Hořký. Hadn't he said he'd try to find a safe place for them to go? Maybe Mother knew something about the man that Jakub didn't. Maybe their father's friend couldn't be trusted after all.

When the clock neared the 9:00 P.M. curfew, the women left with hugs and prayers.

"What about the carpets and furniture?" Mother wondered aloud, when the last visitor was gone.

Jakub knew there was no need to answer. The gestapo would take care of that.

When both Daniel and Mother had drifted off to sleep, Jakub peered through the darkened room, knowing he would never see this place again. Earlier, he and Daniel had said good-bye to their bedroom and their childish things, closing the door behind them.

Now, as he lay in the darkness, a rumble of Nazi jeeps patrolling the streets filled his ears. The sound joined that of the grandfather clock's familiar rhythm. Jakub blinked back tears as he stared at the chandelier hovering over his head, for the first time noticing how beautiful it was.

With a sigh, he turned his attention to the solid wood door that led to his father's workshop, wishing he could see the warm glow of his father's work lamp. He had once overheard Father telling Daniel that music inspired him, and he worked better after attending a concert at the opera house. Jakub was proud of Father's work, redeeming broken instruments, bringing music to the world. It was important, significant.

But his father wasn't waiting on the other side of the door. And he never would be. Those times were only sweet memories. In the morning, his fears would break from his nightmares and become reality.

Suddenly a new thought made Jakub's heart pound. What if their father was released and returned home? Would he be able to find them? Would the neighbors tell him where they'd gone?

Jakub spotted the photo album his mother had gone through earlier. She had sent the best pictures with Mrs. Novy, but still a few remained. Jakub rose from his mattress on the floor and tiptoed to the album. He flipped through the nearly empty pages until he found what he was looking for. It was a photo of the four of them in mountain snow. He and Daniel were younger, smaller. The photo was four years old—it was that many years since they'd been free to travel like everyone else.

The picture was slightly out of focus, as if the photographer had been laughing when the picture was snapped, but that didn't matter. It was good enough to help Jakub remember when the world was still a decent place. He slipped the photo from the corner tabs and pressed it to his chest.

Jakub flipped through the other pages and paused at another photo left behind. This one was of Jakub and Daniel together. It wasn't blurry or out of focus. No, it was a professional shot taken when Jakub was seven, nearly eight. Daniel had just turned six. The brothers stood side by side on the stage of the National Opera House.

Jakub's throat tightened, remembering. He and Daniel had practiced for months on a violin concerto by Beethoven. One of his father's friends had heard the brothers and had insisted they perform together.

Daniel was a natural. He loved to perform. But Jakub, though he'd been playing longer, knew he didn't have such a gift. *Why should I play too?* he wondered. *I'm not nearly as good as Daniel.* But one thing had urged him on.

Jakub closed his eyes and remembered his father's smile and excitement. "Father can hardly sleep," Mother had confessed to Jakub. "He's proud to have one son as a professional musician, but to have two—he's beside himself!"

When the night of the concert arrived, Father proudly led his sons through the front doors of the opera house. The foyer overflowed with men in fine suits and women in exquisite dresses. They smelled of cigars and perfume. Mother had purchased new suits for both of the boys.

The musicians backstage cheered when the brothers' turn came to perform. Excitement stirred as Jakub followed Daniel into the lights. And then it happened. Someone in the audience coughed. Jakub strained to see into the dim auditorium, and then he saw one face, then another. Suddenly he couldn't remember the music. Not one note.

Daniel lifted his violin and began. Jakub did not join in. Daniel started again and eyed his older brother. Jakub stood frozen like a statue.

Jakub looked at the photo in the album again. The photograph had captured the horror in his gaze. It also captured Daniel's clear annoyance. Seconds later Jakub ran off the stage in tears. Daniel continued the performance alone.

Despite his father's urging, Jakub did not go back onstage that night. Or a hundred nights that followed. But for Daniel it was only the beginning.

Jakub wiped a tear and closed the book. Then he quietly crossed the room and slipped the photo of the ski trip into his satchel, next to the bandages and food.

Jakub glanced back over his shoulder at their home. Aside from the boarded-up windows in Father's shop, the house looked just as it had any other day when, for so many years, he'd hidden in its recesses feeling secure and safe.

His mother locked the door and handed the key to the Nazi *blockwart*. Then they marched. Like a wearied group of soldiers who'd recently lost a battle, they shuffled in single file. Jakub's shoulders sagged under the weight of their possessions. His heart felt equally heavy.

They walked through the main shopping district, where loudspeakers attached to street lamps broadcasted news of brave German troops, boats sinking, and executions, as well as raucous patriotic songs.

Years ago, Jakub had not understood why his father and mother had cursed the Germans. Yes, they were citizens of the Czech Republic, but their family seemed equally German. They spoke the language, celebrated its customs, and even ate the same food as their neighbors. But walking into the frightening unknown with friends and strangers, he understood. It was not the culture his parents had cursed but the darkened hearts of its people. Whispered rumors spread amongst the yellow-starred citizens as they walked. Words like "death camps," "heading east," and "no return" sent icy-cold fear piercing through him.

The secondary school stood silent as heavy-laden Jews from around the city converged on its gate. SS

131

men barked commands. With quick jabs from his walking stick, a guard prodded those entering.

"Quickly, quickly now!" he shouted, poking the shoulders, heads, and backs of anyone within reach.

"He reminds me of the cowboy in that Western book we've got—we had." Daniel shoved his hands deeper into his jacket pockets for protection. "I feel like a cow being rounded up."

Jakub looked around at the frantic eyes and tear-streaked faces of those pushing against him. His mother had heard that there would be a thousand deportees in all. It seemed like more.

Sentinels guarding the doors pointed toward the gymnasium, where cohorts assembled small family groups into long lines.

Additional SS men stalked the rows, scrutinizing the victims who would pay the price for the death of their great leader, Reinhard Heydrich. Without a moment's peace, their voices bellowed above the din of the crowd. "If anyone is caught hiding money, jewelry, or other valuables and doesn't hand them over immediately—he will be shot!"

Jakub's mother did not hesitate. Within minutes of finding their place in line, she ripped out the hidden pocket she'd carefully stitched into her skirt and waved the last of her jewels and money toward the guard closest to her. He snatched it from her hand. But instead of depositing it with the piles of confiscated booty, the soldier slipped the treasure into his pants pocket and resumed shouting.

Their paperwork was in order. Jakub, his mother, and his brother were taken to the *Messepalast*—a large wooden hall divided into many sections. Mother gasped when the stench of body odor and decaying food assaulted them. Filthy mattresses covered the entire floor of the hall. Upon these mattresses, destitute families huddled together and awaited their fate. The high windows in the room were shut tight, making the air thick and warm.

They soon found an empty mattress, and now they too waited. Their hearts pounded with the fear of the unknown. Jakub glanced at Daniel, curled in his mother's lap in spite of being nearly as large as she was. His brother's face was white from pain, and he could hardly support his head.

Along with the stench, the noise assailed Jakub. Younger children screamed as they chased each other, as if they were attending one large sleepover. Adults huddled in groups, feeding each other rumors. Rabbis and other Orthodox Jews slept, huddled next to those who—like Jakub's family—considered themselves Jewish by nationality only. Jakub felt especially sorry for the half-Jewish children here alone, their Aryan family members unable to stop their fate.

Their mother made conversation with a young woman named Esther, who shared their mattress. She was newly married and, instead of staying for a later transport, had voluntarily signed up to be with her husband. Yet

Esther came alone. The gestapo had arrested her husband the previous night, taking him in for questioning.

That night, Jakub watched Daniel's fitful slumber, unable to submit to his own weariness. Instead, he studied the people who moved around the room. He recognized the butcher whom his mother often went to for kosher meat. The large man and his family huddled together on a mattress, the mother holding the hands of her two nearly grown daughters even as she slept.

There was the librarian from the school he'd attended his first year. Her two small sons raced from one wall to the next, refusing to comply with their mother's desperate pleas. As he watched them, covering his ears to block out the pounding of their small feet, Jakub wondered where their father was, and if he too had already been taken away. Jakub again thought of Father and wondered where he was now.

On the second morning, just before dawn, Jakub recognized a man who used to play in the orchestra with Daniel. The man came over and sat next to Jakub, whispering so as not to wake the others.

"I heard about your father and your brother." He leaned close, his breath warm on Jakub's cheek.

Jakub sat up straighter. "You heard about Father? Do you know where he's been taken?"

"No, only that he'd been arrested."

Jakub lowered his head.

"What about Daniel? Will he be able to play again?"

"We can always hope. But if you could see his hands . . ." Jakub lowered his gaze. "I guess not."

"I suppose it will be up to you now." The man, whose name Jakub could not remember, rocked back and forth on his haunches as he spoke. "It's up to us to play together again in the great concert halls of Prague. And Daniel can be our conductor, yes?"

"Yes. When we get home, we will do that."

The man winked and patted Jakub's knee. "I better go back and check on my family." He rose and walked away with a small wave. "Until we meet again," he said, barely above a whisper.

"Until we meet again," Jakub echoed, wondering if it would be in this lifetime.

♪   ♪   ♪

As evening of the second day drew near, Jakub knew he couldn't wait any longer to clean his brother's wounds. He worried about the infection already setting in. But where could he change the bandages, and how?

The "bathroom" for this mass of people was simply a large bucket in a back corner that was emptied periodically. Jakub had scanned the large room a hundred times. There was no running water, let alone a stovetop to sterilize bandages. Perhaps if he asked one of the guards.

Jakub hunched on his knees, preparing to stand, when his mother grabbed his arm. "No movement; sit still." Her eyes were wild.

"But—Daniel. His wounds need to be cleaned."

135

His mother gripped tighter, and just as Jakub opened his mouth to plead with her, the dim room was immersed in light. SS men with flashlights filled the doorways, barking commands.

"*Raus, raus!* Line up outside by groups!"

The quiet room burst into noise and movement.

Daniel awoke, his eyes red and full of confusion.

"Grab our rucksacks and canteen," their mother cried, pulling Daniel to his feet.

Bodies pressed around Jakub, pushing him forward. A man holding a small child pressed into Jakub's back. The child let out a piercing scream, right in Jakub's ears. Oh, to be able to cover them, to shield them from the screams! But this was not possible, for Jakub's arms were burdened with the last of their possessions.

Despite the large number of people, the crowd flexed and moved through the warm evening at a quickened pace. Outside the room, shadows flickered on the walls like obscure paintings that changed with the movement of bodies.

They moved down the stairs and then outside to line up in rows of four. Jakub took a large gulp of fresh air. His mother and brother followed him into a row with a lone man. The man stared into the darkened summer sky as if already dead, but Jakub refused to allow his captors to see him in such a defeated state. He squared his shoulders despite the heavy load and marched with the command to move forward.

Fearful of treading out of order, the mass of people stepped together. They moved through the school's oval driveway, which was circled with torches rising from the ground. SS men stood between the torches like fierce statues—their white faces the only spot of color on their black frames.

The mass of people struggled forward, caged in by men and lights, and Jakub knew that escape was impossible.

🙖   🙖   🙖

"Forgive me, God, for what I'm about to do," Evie muttered as she reached for her father's office door. It was unlocked, of course. She quickly entered the room, which smelled of cigar smoke and leather. She then hurried to the paneled wall next to the tall bookcase.

Evie had first discovered her father's safe by accident. When she was eleven, Isak had gone next door to visit the Bauer family. Since their son Anton was even younger than she was, Evie knew Isak was wanting to visit the older sister Maria. It was the first time Isak had shown interest in a girl.

So using the spying tactics her brother had taught her, Evie had made a beeline path to their father's office —the best place to watch the Bauers' backyard.

She had not been disappointed. Years later she'd confessed to Isak that she witnessed his first kiss under the Bauers' oak tree. But what she didn't tell him was that she'd also spied on someone else that day.

Evie had been peering out the window when she heard footsteps nearing. Darting behind the heavy velvet drapes, she peeked out as her father entered and strode to the fireplace. From a vase on the mantel, he removed what appeared to be a key. Then he moved to the paneling next to his bookcase. Sliding his fingers along one groove, he gave it a quick jerk, and the panel swung open. As Evie watched, her father unlocked the safe, withdrew some papers, then locked it again and returned the key to its hiding place.

That had been over ten years ago, but Evie hadn't attempted to open the safe until now. As she walked through the room, her shoes echoed on the glossy wooden floor. Her hands trembled.

"You're doing the right thing," she whispered to herself. "There are people who need your help." She approached the vase, wondering if the key was still hidden inside after all the years. She flipped it over, and a single silver key slid out. She cautiously moved to the paneling and slid her fingers along the crevice, just as her father had done. She grasped the small latch and gave it a quick tug. The door swung open with ease.

Evie blew out a breath, then cocked her ear toward the door. She was the only one in the house, but that didn't stop the fear from tightening a knot in her throat. She moved the key to the lock, then lifted her fingers to the safe handle. Holding her breath, she pulled on the door and then gasped.

Growing up, Evie had known their family had money. They'd lived amongst the nicest houses in town and never lacked for anything. Still, it was surprising to see the stacks of German marks in her father's safe. Big bills.

Evie reached for a small stack, then thought better of it. Her father most likely knew exactly how many stacks there were. Instead, she slid one bill from each of the dozen piles. It was more German marks than she'd ever held at one time, and she again prayed God would forgive her dishonest actions. Evie stepped back from the safe and closed the door with a click. She then pushed back the paneling. The money burnt in her hands.

I'm doing the right thing, aren't I? She thought of the girl arrested for handing out pamphlets, and she longed to help. *Is there anything else I could give them of value? Anything that's mine to give?* A few of the bills slipped from her grasp and dropped to the floor. Evie bent to retrieve them. As she did, her French cameo slipped from her blouse and hung before her face.

Lord, are You trying to tell me something? She fingered the cameo with her free hand, then reopened the safe, returning the money to each of the stacks. *It's all I have from Nick,* she wanted to argue. But she knew it wasn't true. She still had the little things he'd offered during their last good-bye. She still had the memories. She clung to the cameo and wiped back the tears, then hurried out of the room.

Stepping softly, Evie moved through the house toward the kitchen door. She glanced over her shoulder once, then moved down the rock walkway that wound through the backyard.

Earlier that morning, Ilse had pleaded her case again. The underground was desperate for funds. With a quick hug before heading to the grocery, Ilse had told

Evie to hide money, or anything of value that she could spare in the base of the angel statue.

Evie smiled. As a small child, she had discovered the hollow angel in the backyard during one of her adventures. It had been a perfect spot to hide her treasures. The secret of the angel had been hers alone for many years, until one day her mother spotted her sneaking items into the angel's base. After that, Evie would often open it to discover small treasures—candy wrapped in waxed paper and small notes in her mother's handwriting. She had even spotted Ilse bent over the angel once, making a delivery for her mother.

Evie had never let on that she knew they were the ones leaving her treats. The angel had been their little secret—and it still was. Only she was quite sure Mother wouldn't approve of the treasure she was now planning to hide in the angel.

Evie unlatched the necklace, then balled it in her hand. She reached the small cherub. It was smaller than she remembered. As a child, she'd struggled to lift it, but now she picked it up with ease. She slid the necklace into its base, whispering a prayer for those it might help to protect.

૪   ૪   ૪

PRAGUE, CZECHOSLOVAKIA

They hurried through town to the station, marching down the same streets through which the Nazis had carried the body of their leader a few days before.

Jakub had always considered the train station a happy place. Within these walls, his family had waited in preparation for vacations or greeted Father when he arrived home from his business trips.

Tonight the station had a haunted feeling. Darkness, due to blackout conditions, encompassed the building. Other than the moon, the only lights were the beams from the SS flashlights. Like beacons of death, the beams directed the crowds to waiting freight cars.

"Stay in the middle," he urged his mother and brother as cries rose from the weak and unfortunate who straggled along the outer edges. Jakub winced at the sound of boots kicking the downed bodies of old people and young children. His heart ached at the moans of family members now separated.

"Forty-and-eight," said an older man pressed next to Jakub. "I rode in those during the first war. Forty men or eight horses. Cattle cars used for transport. Last time I rode in one, I was a war hero. Guess they forgot."

"Shhh," the man's wife urged. "They'll hear you."

Jakub knew the man's words would be impossible to distinguish amongst the cries of those being shoved into the cars. Ahead, the fearful pleas mixed with the sounds of dogs barking—an additional deterrent for anyone who contemplated escape. As they drew near the boxcar, his own mother's cries rose with the rest.

"Mama, please. Quiet. It will be all right." It was Daniel now who offered comfort.

She listened and attempted to muffle her sobs, but they rose again as the doors on the car in front of them slammed shut, and they were herded forward to the next car.

"Locked like animals," she moaned under her breath. "We are not animals. We are wealthy citizens of Prague."

"Shh." Jakub hoisted Daniel into the car and helped his mother in also. "We know who we are, and that's what matters." It was something his father had said when they were forced to wear the yellow star, forced to walk instead of ride the trolley. But climbing into a cattle car that reeked of human waste, Jakub wondered if he believed his own words.

Pressed in the train car with dozens of others, Jakub struggled to breathe. His hand was still curled around the handle to their rucksack. Their bedroll stood as a barrier between him and his mother. And with each struggling breath, Jakub worried about their small satchel. He'd dropped it while getting into the train. Did it get kicked under the train? Had someone behind him tossed it inside? Jakub doubted it was in the car, for with the barking of savage dogs filling their ears, no one would have slowed to retrieve a mere satchel.

Voices and moans radiated throughout the car as the SS men counted and recounted. Finally, the large doors slammed shut with a loud metal clanging, and Jakub heard the large bolt being fastened on the outside.

Locked in.

"Daniel," Jakub whispered. There was no answer

from the darkness, only cries from the people packed around him.

"Daniel," he said louder.

"Jakub, what is it?" Daniel's voice sounded pained, and Jakub ached at the thought of those wounded hands being pressed by bodies.

"I have lost the satchel with your bandages and medicine." Jakub strained to see his brother through the darkness, longing to see his face—to see how bad off he really was.

"We'll get more. At the camp. We'll visit the nurse, and she will help."

Jakub didn't respond. He knew it was a lie, and most likely Daniel did too. But hope never hurt, did it? Even temporary hope? It was fear that acted like a fist to the stomach.

From outside their pen, they heard shouted orders and a single train whistle. The train jerked forward and back again. Then forward with increasing speed.

For the first few hours, Jakub's senses peaked at full alert. The smells of human body odor and waste filled his nostrils. The heat of the bodies packed together like mice in a box was overwhelming, and beads of sweat trickled down his brow.

His only solace was the view through the slits between the boards. Diligently, Jakub observed the shapes of darkened city buildings whooshing by. Soon they hurled past a sleeping countryside. He spotted farm animals snuggled down in summer pastures. Candlelight brightened cottage windows.

Do those villagers know of the cargo this train car-ries? Jakub wondered. *Do they know what passes their windows as they sleep?*

The voices around him quieted as the hours passed, but the weeping did not. As soon as one person ceased crying, another began.

"May I use your shoulder for a pillow?" Daniel asked. Light was beginning to filter in, and Jakub spotted Daniel's bandaged hands pressed to his chest. His face was pale.

"Of course, try to rest," Jakub said, although he knew it was impossible. How could one rest in such conditions?

Through the slits in the boards, Jakub watched the dawn's light brighten into morning. And just as the first full rays peeked over the distant horizon, the train slowed, then came to a stop with a jerk. The doors opened, flooding the packed compartment with light.

"*Raus, raus,* everyone out!" SS guards shouted.

Jakub pushed forward, ensuring his mother and brother stayed with him. As they climbed down from the train, he noticed a small sign at the two-track station. *Bohusovice-Bauschowitz* the sign read.

"I need air; I need to sit." His mother pushed her way through the crowd, her blonde hair plastered in a filthy tuft around her face.

Behind her, Daniel followed. Jakub trudged farther back, too weary to protest. He longed to tell her to stay in the middle, where it was safe, yet he knew that in the end it would make no difference. His head ached, and his heart weighed in his chest like a lead ball.

The SS men allowed them to sit, congregated in families. Hard bread was passed out—one-sixth of a loaf for each person. Jakub's hunger was powerful, but when he bit into the green-tinged bread, he had to force himself not to spit it out.

Around them, other families unwrapped the food they'd packed. Neither Daniel nor Mother said a word as they gnawed the bread—their food supply had been in the same satchel as the bandages, forever lost.

As they sat, the SS men counted and counted again. A thousand occupants from a dozen cars rested on the lush grass of an untended field. A few of the guards argued. Jakub attempted to make out their words, but they were too far away. Besides, the clamor from the crowd made focusing on a single voice impossible.

An hour later, the SS guards herded them back into their cars. Jakub reached for Daniel as he struggled to his feet.

"Let's stay in the back, please," Daniel begged. "I need the air, and my hands hurt. I don't want to be pressed in again."

Memories of shoving guards and barking dogs haunted Jakub, but he didn't argue. *The clear air does feel good,* he thought as he took another deep breath.

As they neared the train cars, the last of the crowd was stopped. "Too many, too many," one SS guard shouted to another. "Our orders are 1,000 to the East. These make 1,050. They must stay. We cannot take them farther!"

An argument erupted again, and shouts from the two SS soldiers filled the air—their black uniforms and tall frames standing in contrast to the bedraggled group of prisoners who silently waited.

The younger man finally submitted with a wave of his hand. "Fine, we'll march to Theresienstadt. Go on with your cargo. Go now."

PART TWO

Therefore is judgment far from us,
neither doth justice overtake us:
we wait for light, but behold obscurity;
for brightness, but we walk in darkness.
Isaiah 59:9

Eleven

The trains pulled away, and Jakub watched as the bloated cars moved past. Inside were men, women, boys, and girls whom he'd lived next to his entire life—packed together, destined for the unknown. Were those on the train better off, or did a more promising fate await the fifty who remained?

"We will be shot and buried, right here in this spot," his mother moaned, her shoulders slumping forward.

"I don't think so," Daniel said. "Look."

Jakub followed Daniel's gaze. On the other side of the tracks, they could now see what the train had hidden. Before them, a road stretched toward a small town approximately three kilometers away. *Terezín.*

"It's the old fortress town," Jakub told Daniel. "I saw a picture of it in school. It was built to secure the bridge over the Eger. The Germans call it *Theresien-stadt* and—"

Jakub was interrupted by a guard forcing them to line up and march down the road. "Move on, move on. Let's go!"

Another soldier led them at a quickened pace. "Come along! Hurry now!"

Jakub jogged to keep up. He noticed the discarded luggage and torn rucksacks that littered the sides of the road. As he hustled past, he noted one suitcase ripped in two, as if pounced on and clawed by people eager to see what valuables were hidden inside. Except for a few scattered contents, a hollow void was all that remained where someone's cherished heirlooms and basic necessities had been so carefully packed.

As they trudged forward in midmorning heat, sweat trickled down Jakub's face. His arms and legs ached, and the heavy load he carried shot a throbbing pain through his shoulders. *If only Father were here.*

On his back he lugged the remnants of three people's worldly possessions. No, he wouldn't give in to the aches, wouldn't leave their things along this road to be sifted through and scattered like the items of those who'd gone before him. For Mother, for Daniel, for Father . . . he'd plod on.

They moved toward the city gates. Little could he have guessed, when he had studied this garrison town years ago, that it would one day be turned into a ghetto for Jews—and that he would be locked inside.

After passing through the gates, their group crossed

a drawbridge over a trench. The former moats had been emptied of water and now were cultivated into a well-tended vegetable garden. Steep, grassy hills rose from the trench, meeting the tall brick walls.

The gates closed behind them, and the armed guards slammed the locks into place. Jakub's burden grew heavier, and his legs faltered. Daniel looked as if he could not move another step. Under his breath, Jakub prayed for strength.

From beyond the wall, they entered a miniature town with a central square facing a park. Large trees shaded a sandy parade ground. As their group straggled into the center, the side streets seemed to come alive with bodies. Fellow Jews poured from large houses and storefronts, which appeared to have been remodeled for housing. Old men and women, even small children, trod toward them like the walking dead. Thin and gaunt, their white faces wild with hunger.

Jakub's gaze met Daniel's, and he knew they wondered the same thing. *Would this soon be them?*

Like shadows falling over their group, the prisoners eyed the newcomers. Jakub understood. They hunted for familiar faces of family members and friends. Their mother walked numbly, whispering Father's name.

A cry of joy sounded from behind Jakub, and he turned. A woman from their group dropped her satchel and ran toward a man in tattered clothing who was moving her direction. Before she'd taken two steps, blows fell upon her.

"Stay in line!" a guard cried, clubbing her head. She

crumpled to the ground and didn't move. Two of the prisoner-children ran up, and Jakub thought that perhaps they knew her. Instead, they snatched the satchel and darted away before the guards had a chance to stop them.

"Watches, money, valuables. Turn them in!" German shouts filled the air.

Daniel, who was not nearly as schooled in German, turned to Jakub for an explanation. Jakub shook his head, too terrified to speak.

One of the prisoners walked past the guard and took Jakub's rucksack. Jakub straightened with the weight lifted from his shoulders, then reached for the rucksack, wondering if he should put up a fight.

"Come with me." The man gave a toothless grin. "You too, boy." He pointed to Daniel.

The gaunt man walked with an air of importance, and Jakub noted the yellow band around his black cap. "The infirmary first in the Ustí barracks." Other men in similar attire led others in their group, including Mother, the same direction.

Had the man said "infirmary"? Jakub clutched Daniel's shoulder. "My brother. Will he find help for his hands?"

"No," the man called back over his shoulder. "Sorry, son. First they check you for lice, then you'll get a serum for typhoid. You'll spend the first two nights in quarantine. Later, maybe later, a nurse will examine those hands."

Their small group entered the building, and the band of *Bademeisters* led them to a delousing station.

"What's new in Prague?" A dark-haired man with bulging eyes sought information as he sprinkled delousing powder all over Jakub and Daniel's naked bodies. "I heard our statue of St. Wenceslas has been demolished, and the Nazis have the Czech crown jewels. What about the coffeehouses? Do they still have real coffee, or ersatz, or are they closed too?"

Jakub attempted to answer the man's questions as best he could. He turned, looking to his mother for support, and for the first time realized she was not with them.

"My mother," Jakub asked the man. "Where have they taken her?"

"Don't worry, boy. You'll be with her soon—for a little while anyway. After the days in quarantine, you'll be separated. That's how things work here. Men with men. Children with children. Women stay with women." He made quick work of his task, handing their clothes back to them. "How old are you?" he asked Jakub.

"Nearly fourteen. And my brother's twelve."

"Good. You'll most likely be moved into one of the boys' homes. They get better food, better housing. But I don't know about your brother. With that injury I'm afraid he'll be taken from quarantine to the hospital."

Jakub pulled his brother to him. "Please, can I stay with Daniel? We can't be separated."

The man's smile disappeared, and he gave Jakub a piercing look. "That's how things work, so you can either fight it or you can live. I suggest the latter."

When they put their clothes back on, they were led

to Hohnenelbe, a military hospital barracks under the shade of giant chestnuts.

Daniel paused on the steps before entering the building. Jakub turned back. Noticing his brother's upward gaze, he glanced up to see what Daniel was looking at. Only trees and sky loomed above.

"Daniel, what's wrong?"

"If you look up, Jakub, it looks like any other park. Let's do that, okay? Every time we go out, let's look up and pretend we're at Kampa Park on the banks of the Moldau."

"Good idea." Jakub patted his brother's shoulder. "I promise to try."

Inside, shouts of welcome greeted them. Some of the others from their train came with hugs and pats. Their mother rushed to them, arms open wide.

Together, the three were led to a small room with running water and a nice heater. Wood shavings covered the floor. Five others waited—two women with three young sons between them. As soon as they entered, the women began asking questions about their trip and their dates of transport.

Jakub's mother was soon drawn in as she shared news of the train ride and their march to the camp. Jakub looked at her with brow furrowed. His mother blathered about their travels as if she were discussing a trip to the spa at Marianske Lazne, not a nightmare journey to a deportation camp.

"Well, now, this isn't as bad as we imagined, is it? It's just like a little town that we're all tucked inside."

154

She brushed back the hair from her face. "The citizens seem relatively free to move about. The guards seem friendly enough. I think I can handle this ghetto."

The women smiled at Mother, yet it was not an ordinary smile. Something in their eyes worried Jakub.

Twelve

Night darkened the sky . . . their third away from home. His mother and Daniel were still with him—and for that Jakub was thankful.

He stared down at his small bowl of lentil soup. This second meal at Terezín was just as tasteless and unappealing as the first. At noon they had been given disgusting white turnip soup, called *wrucken*. Jakub had gagged it down, picking out bits of turnip leaves. He even noticed sand in the bottom of his bowl, as if the turnips hadn't been cleaned before being thrown into the pot. For lunch they'd each received one plain boiled potato.

As he ate, Jakub remembered how picky he used to be. He'd complained about the meals their housekeeper had prepared. Now he'd give anything for her goulash or stew and dumplings.

The three small boys who shared their corner room

had been whining all day. They complained of hunger and wanted to go home. After gobbling down their meal, they settled into a fitful sleep, whimpering and curling against each other like helpless puppies. Their mothers, who were sisters, sat back-to-back sharing a cigarette.

Jakub's mother had paced the room throughout the day. Not able to watch her active worry, Jakub and Daniel had lounged beneath the shady trees outside their barracks. Mother refused to leave their room to get her dinner, saying she wouldn't take a step outside until she had her things and was given a chance to freshen up. The boys attempted to bring her meal to her, only to be told that it wasn't allowed.

As Jakub slurped the last of his soup, his mother stopped her pacing and sank onto the floor. "Jakub, when you went out today, did they say when they'd bring our things?"

One of the women—the one with unnaturally bright red hair—laughed. "You really think you'll see your things again?" She took an extra-long drag of the cigarette, then continued, the smoke escaping with her words. "Your suitcases and rucksacks have been taken to the *schleuse*—the channel. The same thing happened to us a few days ago. Our suitcases, pillows, and feather beds are all gone. I guarantee your precious things have already been cleaned out, sorted, and are headed for Germany."

Jakub's mother sat up straighter. "Don't tease me like that. They told us to pack fifty kilos of what we'd need most. They said—"

The other woman cut in. "Yeah, well, they say a lot of things. Did you think this was a spa for Prague socialites? I talked to one of the guards yesterday. The SS steals the best stuff, and the next best is sent to 'poor' people in Germany. Then they pick out some things to use here in the ghetto, and whatever's left over is put in the camp 'store' they promise to open soon. That's where we're allowed to purchase items with the ghetto money they pay us for working."

"We have to buy back our own things?" Mother's face turned pale. "I have nothing?"

"You have your sons and your life," the redhead answered curtly. "Consider yourself lucky, sister. Most Jews don't have either anymore."

ᖮ   ᖮ   ᖮ

BERLIN, GERMANY
JUNE 13, 1942

An SS chauffeur awaited Otto's arrival at the Savoy Hotel in Berlin. Days earlier Otto had sent a message to Kametler and received a reply, in which the SS officer stated the importance of his receiving the violin by the thirteenth. Though Otto wouldn't have minded a few more hours of Breirather and Weber's compelling conversation, instead he hired a car to drive him to the capital.

The waiting chauffeur clicked his heels and swiftly opened the door to Kametler's Mercedes. Otto slid wearily into the backseat.

"The cottage is not far out of town. It will be but a twenty-minute trip," the driver informed him.

Otto nodded, then turned his attention out the window. The streets of Berlin were full of excitement and tension—a very busy metropolis littered with Brownshirts and gestapo uniforms. Trolleys clattered and jangled, and the only evidence of the massive funeral ceremony for Reinhard Heydrich was a photo he'd discovered on the front page of yesterday's newspaper. In the center of the photo Hitler stood tall, giving an address. In the background, amongst the mass of Nazi leadership, Otto clearly made out Kametler's profile.

Gritting his teeth, Otto ripped the paper in two. *He* should have been rubbing shoulders with Hitler's key men, not Kametler. Instead, he had listened to Heydrich's state funeral broadcast while sitting between two out-of-work fortune-tellers. With fervor stirred by the moving ceremony, the announcer had breathlessly described each member of the Nazi leadership in attendance and raved over the thousands of black-uniformed SS guards who protected the procession.

Over the radio, the three men had listened to the Berlin Philharmonic Orchestra play Wagner's funeral march, followed by Himmler's praises of a man "feared by lower racial types and subhumans, hated and defamed by Jews and criminals." Clearly choked up, Hitler ended the event with a short but stirring eulogy.

But that had been only a small part of Otto's experience at Weber's table. When the radio was finally clicked off, Weber took Otto's hands in his own, squeezing them tightly as he spoke.

"What you assume to be a dead end, Herr Otto Akeman, will lead to your heart's desire. Along this path you will discover a treasure even more valuable than the one you now carry. It will be yours until the day you breathe your last."

As the car cruised around a sharp turn, Otto glanced at the violin sitting on the leather seat next to him. This was the treasure he carried. *What could be worth more than a vintage Stradivarius?* His thoughts flashed to the still-missing Guarneri, but he quickly pushed it out of his mind. *Too valuable, too sought after, too impossible.*

The Mercedes turned down a short driveway lined with thick pines. The driveway opened to a three-story house graced with white marble pillars.

"If this is a cottage, I'd like to see what his main house looks like," Otto said with a smirk, making eye contact with the driver in the rearview mirror. He recalled the side table Kametler had appropriated. "I'm sure Frau Kametler enjoys her husband's position."

The driver eyed the newcomer to town. "Oh no, sir. This is not the home of Frau Kametler. This is where Herr Kametler keeps his mistress—a music student from the conservatory. They are expecting their first child soon, and today is her birthday."

Otto didn't know why he hadn't figured it out sooner. Many German officers had "Gretchens" in Berlin,

Munich, and Nuremberg and provided for them by the fine shoes, clothes, and other merchandise they'd confiscated. It was simply one of the perks of the job.

He didn't respond as the car pulled to a stop. He pressed his sweaty palms down his shirtfront and attempted to fix a smile upon his lips. "A music student from the conservatory. I see." His assumption that Kametler would turn the violin over to the Berlin Music Museum, he now realized, was gravely incorrect.

🎵   🎵   🎵

"You should have seen it. The funeral was something else." Kametler's voice ricocheted through the marble foyer as he led Otto to the front sitting area. A bulbous chandelier hung two stories up. A large mural painting of an English foxhunt hung over a river-rock fireplace. Otto was sure they'd discovered the piece in the large manor house near Brno.

He slipped his cap from his head, taking in the room with a full turn.

"Heydrich's coffin, draped in the swastika, was drawn by four jet-black horses in procession to the Veterans' Cemetery. The city was decorated in military decorum," Kametler continued. "And while the Führer put on a calm front for the masses, behind the scenes he was beside himself with rage. He vows revenge. Hundreds of Czechs with doubtful political allegiance have already been rounded up and shot. And just a few days ago an entire village was leveled for sheltering the assassins.

Those murderers might as well give themselves up; they'll only bring down more justice on their people."

Kametler sank into the sofa and reached his hands toward Otto. "Oh yes, the violin."

Otto handed over the case, and Kametler flipped open the top.

"Rikka, darling, look what I have for you!" Kametler's voice echoed through the halls. He motioned for Otto to sit. "I see you didn't have any trouble getting the violin here on time. It's a gift for my dear friend. Her birthday, you know."

Otto's eyes widened as a strikingly beautiful blonde woman entered the room, trailing the scent of French perfume. Clearly young and definitely pregnant, she cast Otto a demure smile before gliding to Kametler's side.

"For me?" She covered her mouth with one hand, blinking back tears. Otto hadn't seen such dramatic acting since Hedy Lamarr's last film.

Rikka lifted the violin from the case and placed it on her shoulder. She gingerly fingered the bow and began to play a Beethoven romance.

Otto grimaced inwardly, thinking of hundreds of musicians more worthy of such an instrument. Kametler placed his hand over the woman's stomach and closed his eyes while he swayed to the music. Nausea overwhelmed Otto.

When the impromptu recital was mercifully over, Otto stood and moved toward the door, his boots echoing on the marble floor.

Kametler's eyes popped opened. "Herr Akeman, are you leaving already? But you just arrived. At least stay for dinner."

"Really, I must be going. I told Viktor I'd only be gone a few days. The train catastrophe has already put me behind schedule."

Kametler rose, flashing a wide grin. He slid an arm around Rikka's thick waist. "That's the way, always putting the Reich above all else."

Donning his cap in a final farewell, Otto headed out the door and toward the waiting car.

One thing's for sure. He slid into the leather seat for the return ride to his hotel. *I will ensure Weber's prophecy does come true. Never again will I mindlessly give my all to the Reich. The next great treasure I discover will be my own.*

🦋   🦋   🦋

From the back of the black Mercedes, Otto Akeman pondered the possibility of possessing a violin such as the one he'd just handed to Kametler's little "friend." What would it take to work alone, to smuggle, for his own possession, valuable items as he came upon them? He knew it would be necessary to gain Viktor's trust. But even more, he'd have to bewitch the lower sops, such as the Czech security guard, who held keys for important warehouses.

From this point on, Otto needed to consider not a man's status but his possible worth concerning Otto's future needs. A few favors, a little charm, and mock authority were sure to do the trick.

"So do you know much about the Wannsee district?" the driver asked, interrupting his thoughts.

Otto sighed, preparing to get short with the man. He quickly changed his mind and instead shot the driver a broad, beguiling smile. "I know about the Wannsee Conference held earlier this year. If I remember correctly, all the top Nazis attended it. But I'm afraid my knowledge is lacking—this being my first time in Berlin and all. I'm sure a notable public servant like yourself could fill me in."

"Berlin is only truly known by Berliners." The driver smiled. He straightened in his seat. "Right now, we are on the outskirts of the finest residential district of the city. Do you have to get back to your hotel any time soon? If you have an extra hour, I'll gladly give you a tour."

Otto shrugged, appearing nonchalant. "I don't have anywhere I need to be. My train leaves in the morning."

"Would you like to see some of the most elegant villas on the Kleiner Wannsee? It's a beautiful lake, the larger of twins."

"Yes, I would like that." Otto crossed his right ankle over his left knee and settled in for the ride, his body sinking deeper into the leather.

The driver slowed the car and took the next right. His voice lowered an octave as he took on the air of a travel guide. "The road we just turned onto is known as *Am Großen Wannsee*. It runs along the western bank of the larger lake of Wannsee. I'll drive you by the Wannsee

Villa, which was the scene of the famous conference. It is said that the fate of all enemies of the Reich was decided there."

As they drove past opulent homes, Otto's senses peaked. The park landscapes and stylized gardens caused his eyes to widen; yet even more startling was the inward stirring he felt. He thought back to the lessons he'd learned during his year of SS tutelage. The faithful who sought the way of the Ancients would be led on the correct path, he had been told.

The discovery of the violin, the promotion to his new and privileged position, the meeting on the train with Breirather, the prophecy from Weber, and this unexpected detour to Wannsee—surely these were not mere coincidences. Otto knew deep inside he was called for a greater purpose, and in time the purpose would let itself be known.

The car turned the next corner, and the driver slammed on his brakes. Otto braced himself as his body smashed into the back of the front seat. A curse rose on his lips, but he swallowed it. On the side of the road, a black Mercedes with a blown tire dangerously protruded into the roadway.

Otto's driver pulled to the side of the road and parked. Otto glanced back at the disabled car. The passenger wore a finely cut suit with shiny black loafers—most likely a home owner in this exclusive district.

The driver turned in the seat and faced Otto. "Sorry about the quick stop. Do you mind if I offer my assistance?"

"No, by all means."

Otto resisted the urge to watch. *Act like one of great importance. Like one who is not awed by wealth and stature.*

Within a few minutes, the driver returned with a man by his side.

"If you don't mind, Herr Akeman, I have offered a ride to the stranded man. It seems this fellow, who happens to be the manager of the Wannsee Villa, will be late for dinner otherwise." The driver's eyes sparkled, and Otto understood.

"The Wannsee Villa, how interesting," Otto said to the man standing before him. "I was just asking my driver about the place. By all means. I'd be happy to share my seat." Otto patted the leather.

The white-haired gentleman placed a hand over his heart. "I am grateful. Thank you ever so much." He climbed into the car beside Otto for the short drive to the villa. "My name is Fane."

A few minutes later, he motioned to the house as they turned into the driveway. "Please, sir, come in and join my wife and me for dinner. Due to your generosity, I'm sure I've kept you from your own arrangements. Won't you join us?"

Otto stepped from the car and placed his cap with the death's head emblem on his head with a flourish. "I'd be delighted."

Thirteen

Following the manager through the front door, Otto matched his stride to the man's short, snappy steps. From the front entrance he had a clear view to the back patio and the lake beyond.

"On the left is the library. On the right, the conservatory. Beyond this, the hallway is connected to salons and a large dining room."

Herr Fanc removed his jacket and hat and hung them inside a mirrored armoire. "My wife will be seeking me out for dinner soon. We'll be partaking in the dining room where the conference was held."

Otto hung his jacket and hat. "That will be delightful, thank you."

Herr Fane led Otto back toward the dining room, which they entered through wide double doors. The first thing Otto noticed were the arched windows that gave a stunning view of the lake. The second thing was the table, where just a few months earlier the Nazi elite had gathered.

"Fifteen top officials were in attendance," Herr Fane began. "It was here they devised their plans concerning the Final Solution of our Jewish enemies. Would you like to sit in the seat of Heydrich, Himmler, or Hitler himself?"

Otto smiled at his host. "Any seat would be an honor."

"While I find my wife, please make yourself comfortable. Look around." He moved back toward the doors. "We are in the middle of renovating, but before long this villa will be open to visiting SS officials. The hotels in Berlin are mostly overfilled and exceptionally expensive. Soon this house will provide them an affordable, respectable place to stay, along with the opportunity to enjoy the companionship of their fellow officers."

Otto stepped toward the huge tapestry depicting a Roman guard and citizens, tilting his head to scan its length from floor to ceiling. He felt an urge to stroke the detailed needlework but contained himself. *Wondrous.*

૨   ૨   ૨

Twenty minutes later, Otto found himself seated at the dining room table with the manager and his wife. He hadn't asked in whose chair he now sat, but he was sure he felt the touch of power still resonating through the cushions.

He lifted his crystal wineglass by the stem and clinked it first with Herr Fane and then his wife.

"Prosit," Otto said, taking a sip of Franz Keller *rot wein,* bottled in 1937. He looked into the eyes of the manager and lifted the glass just slightly.

"Guten Appetit," Herr Fane responded. "Enjoy your meal."

"For a young man, Herr Akeman," Frau Fane began, passing a platter of roasted lamb, "you have quite a position with the Musik Aktion team. What are your other interests?"

"I enjoy women, appreciate fine food, and hunger for power." Satisfied with himself, Otto gave a half smile.

The couple laughed.

"Sounds like a good Nazi to me." Herr Fane leaned back in his chair, lacing his fingers together on his lap. "So tell me, where does your hunger for power lead you?"

"It leads me many places, but currently it has led me to your table."

"That's interesting." The manager picked up his fork and knife and continued with his meal. "After dinner, I planned on showing you the artwork throughout the house, but I feel you would be more intrigued by the secret art of the Reich."

"Secret art? I have traveled around the *Reichsprotektorates* for many months, but I haven't heard of such a thing."

Herr Fane finished swallowing a bite of *rosti,* pan-fried potatoes. "This is a class of art that one finds all through the Reich, yet many do not know how to interpret the pieces. You are aware, I assume, of our spiritual heritage?"

"I learned in SS training that we are of a superior race, the elite, descendents of the Ancients, and destined to rule the world once again."

"I see you learn well. Ancients encapsulated the art of which I speak in runes. Today, all those serving the Reich bear its image. Yet the world has no idea of the power of this secret language of the spirit."

Herr Fane raised his glass and took a sip before locking his eyes on Otto's own. "It's meant to be understood only by those who have developed the sensitivity to its truths."

"I know what you speak of: the swastika, the symbol of death's head, the lightning runes. They are ancient symbols that I agree are imbedded with power. The swastika, for instance, has been used by many nations, such as Tibet, as a symbol of infinity and good luck."

Herr Fane paused and tilted his head. "I see you are one of the chosen. In fact, I knew that the moment you sat in the chair of Himmler—the true follower of the Ancients. Remember this, Searcher: symbols are the keyholes that can open the door to eternity. They are figures pregnant with power. You will continue your journey from here, but you can be assured that what you seek you will find."

℘   ℘   ℘

The tired and dirty occupants of the quarantine room ate their portion of black bread and sipped their ersatz coffee to the sound of a large cart being pushed down the street.

"It's the funeral cart," the redheaded roommate commented, not even bothering to glance out the window. "They're picking up those who died in the night. The old people drop like flies around here." She ran her fingers through her tangled hair. "And if you're wondering, it's the same cart they just used to deliver your bread."

"How do you know all this?" Jakub's mother's face turned pale, and she pushed her stale bread to the side.

"If you left this building for one hour, you'd know all about this place," the sister commented. Her diatribe was cut short by the entrance of a Jewish ghetto guard wearing a funny peaked cap bordered in yellow. Trailing him were the three small boys who'd been running through the halls playing "war" since dawn, raising the noise level in the barracks with each native holler.

"Sisters, please come. Your time in quarantine is over. You'll be taken to your barracks now. We'll go to the children's home first and get these boys settled in." He arched one bushy eyebrow.

They hustled out of the room, and Jakub and Daniel looked at each other with a sigh of relief. Then they laughed and resumed eating. Jakub took a small bite of bread and broke off a chunk to feed his brother.

"I don't know why you're laughing." Mother stood and paced the room.

Sleeping or pacing, that's all she does. Jakub knew better than to glance away. *Or yelling . . .* he thought as she raised her voice.

"Your father should have been there. He would have known what to do. Jakub, you shouldn't have done it. You shouldn't have told that man where the violin was. We could have used it. Could have escaped."

Daniel cocked his chin toward her. "You mean you knew where it was hidden?" He glanced at Jakub with a look of disbelief.

She paused and crossed her arms, and Jakub noticed for the first time how thin she had become.

"That's not the point," she muttered. "Our lives were at stake. *Are* at stake. It was your father's most prized possession. Who knows where it is now?" She leaned against the wall for support, sinking to the ground. "It's your father's fault. If he would have listened, we could have left long ago. I told him to sell it. I told him months and months ago. What use is it now?"

Silence filled the small room. The minutes ticked by with the sound of workers and voices conversing outside the window. Jakub knew if he tried hard enough, he could convince himself that Terezín was just like any other town, with men and women heading off to work. If he tried, he could also convince himself that his mother loved him and didn't blame him for their fate.

Unsure of what to do next, the boys leaned on each other for support and finished eating until a tall form filled the doorway.

"Excuse me, are you the Hanauer family?" An older man stood quietly, hat in hand. A well-worn leather belt cinched his filthy pants as tight as they could go, and still his trousers hung awkwardly.

Jakub heard his mother gasp, and then noticed the reason. He held a rucksack in his hand—their rucksack.

"Yes, we are." His mother rose to her feet and gave the man a quick embrace.

His face reddened, and he glanced at the floor. "Sorry to interrupt, but I recognized your name and address on some bags that came through yesterday. I knew your husband, ma'am. He was a good man. A few months ago he purchased an old cello from me. He gave me more than it was worth, and that money fed me and my children until we were called for transport. I am forever grateful."

The man stretched out his offering. "I wasn't able to save it all. Only this. I also went through the other bags and grabbed a few things—another change of clothes for you, ma'am, and your son's music."

He pulled the folded sheets from his pants pocket and handed them to Jakub. "I figured you could play with the orchestra here."

"Oh, these are for my brother." Jakub unfolded them and placed them on Daniel's lap. "He'll love to play as soon as he is well!" Jakub continued on before

Daniel could protest. "I had no idea they had such a thing here. An orchestra, really?"

Jakub's mother took the sack from the man's arms. She opened it and burst into tears. "Soap, a thread and needle, a can opener. Look at all this!"

The man's eyes glistened as he leaned down and patted Jakub's shoulder. "We don't have much, son, as you can see. But one thing we do have is music—concerts nearly every night. Simply follow the strains of the melodies. You will stumble upon some of the finest musicians of Czechoslovakia and Austria. They feed our souls with song."

Fourteen

Nick stood and lifted the old red hymnal, raising his voice with the others for the final song of the morning. Twitch stood by his side and joined in on the stanza of "A Mighty Fortress Is Our God":

And though this world, with devils filled,
Should threaten to undo us;
We will not fear, for God hath willed
His truth to triumph through us.

As he sang, Nick's mind wandered to his friend. For though they'd sat side by side as Pastor Green talked about the young David's faith in God overcoming the giant in his life, Nick was certain Twitch hadn't heard a word. Instead, his friend—as expected—had been focused on the pastor's daughter.

As she did every Sunday, Barbara Green nestled in the front row between her mother and younger siblings. Barbara couldn't be older than twenty, with long, sunkissed blonde hair that spread over her shoulders like a golden shawl. Most attractive was her coy smile, which seemed almost sinful to display amongst a chapel full of lonely soldiers.

Twitch hadn't been the only one staring. More than once Nick had caught Barbara casually flipping her hair over her shoulder in a sly effort to eye his eager friend seated four rows behind her.

When the beat-up old organ's music faded, the congregation placed their hymnals into the racks and gathered their things. Though barely after noon, the sun had already heated the small sanctuary like an oven. Nick stepped into the middle aisle and wiped his brow. He felt Twitch's hand on his shoulder.

"Since you didn't pay attention to the sermon, I hope you enjoyed the view," Nick whispered.

"I was listening." It was a female voice. He spun and found Barbara's face only inches from his. He took a step back as Twitch's laughter echoed through the room.

"Excuse me, ma'am." Nick twisted his cap in his hand.

She cast him a coquettish smile and pointed to her father. "My daddy asked me to invite you and your friend for lunch. He likes to get to know the boys of the congregation, and you've been a familiar face for some time."

Nick didn't have to confer with Twitch before responding. "Of course, we'd be honored. We haven't had a home-cooked meal in months."

"Great! I'll get my things and walk with you. It's only a few blocks. Meet you outside?" She turned and made her way toward the front of the sanctuary, her pleated skirt swishing with each step.

Twitch sidled up to him, and together they moved amongst the family clusters toward the door.

Nick glanced over as they stepped into the warm summer air and made their way to the shade of the nearest oak tree. Spring had developed into summer, darkening the hills around Carlisle with lush green foliage. Extending from the town was a patchwork quilt of pastures, farmhouses, and small towns. Many of the city boys, Nick included, had been appreciative of Cumberland County's plethora of creeks for quick dips during weekend leave. They also marveled at the country lads who made even better use of the streams, returning to base with trout, large- and small-mouth bass, pickerel, and walleyes—much to the cooks' delight.

"So do you think she likes me?" Twitch asked.

Nick socked his friend's shoulder. "You caught her glancing back, didn't you?"

"Yeah, but I couldn't tell if she was eyeing me or you."

"Oh, it was you, all right. You're here one time, and we get an invitation to lunch. Think that's a coincidence?"

Twitch stood a little straighter and ran his hand through his white-blond hair. His grin widened.

"Besides, I've got a girl, remember?" Nick whispered.

Twitch didn't respond. His eyes were glued on to Barbara as she sauntered over with a wave and a smile.

🍂   🍂   🍂

Thirty minutes later, Frank and Nick graced Barbara like bookends at the Greens' dining room table. The scent of pot roast and biscuits caused Nick's stomach to rumble. He thought he also recognized the aroma of homemade strawberry pie.

"Let's pray," said the pastor.

Without hesitation, Barbara's small hand slid into Nick's left one. With his other, he took Mrs. Green's hand. She gave it a slight, motherly squeeze.

The pastor raised his voice. "Dear Lord, we thank Thee for this meal we are about to receive."

Nick attempted to concentrate on the pastor's prayer, but he couldn't ignore the feeling of Barbara's hand in his. It had been over six months since he'd enjoyed a feminine touch. Her hand was so warm and soft—

"Amen," erupted around him.

"Amen," Nick echoed, chiding his wayward thoughts. *She reminds me of Evie, that's all.*

"Here, Nick, have some potatoes." Mrs. Green passed them his direction. "Barbara made them herself."

"They look fantastic." Nick scooped a large serving onto his plate, then turned to Barbara. Their fingers grazed during the pass off.

"Thank you," she said.

Their eyes met for the briefest moment, but it was enough for Nick to notice how full of life and joy they were. He quickly glanced away. This girl was nothing like Evie. Evie was small and dark, spunky and full of laughter. The girl sitting beside him was like an actress from Hollywood, tall and blonde with a quiet, almost mysterious, demeanor.

Nick attempted to focus across the table, where Barbara's three younger brothers and one sister sat bunched together on a long bench. Yet Barbara was full of questions about their training and schooling.

"So what did you do before you joined?" Barbara turned to Nick, as she raised her fork to her mouth.

"I was in medical school. Residency, actually."

Her eyebrows rose in approval.

Pastor Green leaned forward in his seat. "Really? Tell me about that. Do you have a specialty?"

"I was torn between general practice and pediatrics." Nick took a sip of lemonade.

"So you like children?" Mrs. Green smiled.

"How could I not? I have a half-dozen nieces and nephews at home . . . but did you know that Frank, here, was also studying medicine?"

"Really?" Mrs. Green seemed doubly pleased.

"Veterinary medicine." Twitch seemed thrilled to take over the conversation where Nick left off. "Back on the farm, I've been helping to birth cows for as long as I can remember. I was almost done with my schooling and was looking into starting my own practice when they drafted me into the medical corps. I laughed and told them I had experience tending to sick animals, not sick people—and I don't expect to be assisting in any calf births on the battlefield."

"Yuck!" one of the younger kids called out. The room exploded with laughter.

When they all had their fill of lunch, Nick rose and lifted his plate from the table.

"Please, you're our guest." Mrs. Green placed her hand on his arm. "Why don't you boys have a visit with Barbara on the porch? I'll bring out some pie in a few minutes."

Nick didn't protest, and the three moved toward the front porch. Barbara sat on the small bench and patted the seat beside her. "I think we can all fit if we squeeze."

"That's okay; the steps will work fine." Nick settled on the top step. Twitch joined Barbara on the bench.

Nick eyed the neighborhood filled with family homes. Large trees shaded the streets. Well-tended lawns with a rainbow of colorful flowers lined the cement walkways. Nick noticed that on the Greens' sidewalk, a handprint had been pressed into the cement at the bottom of the steps. It was a small hand with the word "Barbie" printed underneath it in childish scrawl.

"May I ask you boys something personal?" Barbara's voice interrupted Nick's thoughts.

"Sure," Twitch answered for both of them.

"Aren't you scared traveling across the sea to fight? Will you be going to the South Pacific or Europe?"

"Who knows exactly?" Twitch said. "With the army, you never know until you're there."

"I've heard rumors of Europe lately," Nick added.

"That's so far from home, fighting against those nasty Germans."

"We won't be on the front lines," Twitch corrected. "We'll be assigned to the surgical stations behind the lines, which means there's a good chance we won't see fighting at all. It's not like the aid men, who are on the field with the guys."

"That's good," Barbara commented. "I'd hate to worry."

The front screen door opened, and Mrs. Green poked her head out. "Frank, could you help for a minute? It seems the boys got a rubber ball stuck in a tree out back. I'm afraid I'm not tall enough to reach."

Twitch jumped to his feet. "Sure thing, ma'am." He glanced over his shoulder at Barbara. "Be right back."

She smiled and nodded.

Across the street an old woman worked in her garden—her wide-brimmed hat barely visible next to the sunflowers nodding in the slight breeze.

Nick felt the vibration of Barbara's footsteps on the wooden planks. With a soft sigh, she settled next to him. She twirled the end of a blonde curl between her fingers and followed Nick's gaze.

"That's Mrs. Demmers. She lost her husband in the

183

Great War. She's not very old; she just acts like it."
Barbara's voice was solemn.

"Well, as Frank said, we most likely won't see fighting. So we're pretty sure we're coming back."

"That's good. I'd hate for anything to happen. . . ."
Her voice trailed off. "Nick?"

He could feel her eyes on him, but he continued to focus on Mrs. Demmers's hat.

"Do you like it here?"

"It's different from New York City, that's for sure. But it's very nice." He fingered a fragrant lilac growing on the bush beside the steps.

"Do you like our church? I've seen you every week."

"It's a great church. I'm so glad I can feel God's closeness when I'm away from home."

"I've been watching you. Lots of guys come and go. Sometimes there are more uniforms in the pews than regular folk. But there's something different about you." Barbara paused. "You seem to know what you want in life. You seem to really care. You'll make a really good medic."

Nick chuckled. "You got all that from seeing me sing a few hymns and listen to your daddy's sermons?"

"I'm a good judge of character." She tilted her head toward Nick. Her gaze softened and she smiled. "I can see goodness in your eyes."

Nick traced his finger along a lavender cluster.

"Nick?"

"Hmmm?"

"I want to ask you something."

"Okay."

"Do you mind if I pray for you? And maybe write you a letter now and then? I'm sure it can get lonely being so far from home."

Nick plucked a leaf off the bush and studied its intricate pattern of fine veins. A chill traveled down his spine. "Sure, I'd like that."

Nick turned and peered into Barbara's eyes, for the first time realizing they were not true blue but hazel, with tiny specks of yellow that made them glimmer.

"Do you have anything specific I can pray for?"

He noticed how smooth and soft her skin was. She had a slight golden tan that caused her face to glow beneath her halo of curls.

Nick thought for a minute. "Yeah, pray I'll make a difference—that I'll be at the right place at the right time. This is a big war, and—well, I'd just like to know that my contribution matters."

Barbara grinned. "Sure, why don't we pray right now?" She took Nick's hand and closed her eyes. "Dear God, be with my friend Nick. Give him the knowledge and ability to help those who are hurting. Put him in the right place at the right time. And mostly, give him an opportunity to help at least one person in a way that only he can. In Jesus' name. Amen."

Nick squeezed Barbara's hand but didn't let go. "Thank you." He looked into her face and felt his chest fill with a gentle peace. "That means so much—"

The sound of the screen door startled them. They

both pulled back. Nick released Barbara's hand, and his eyes darted to the door. Twitch stood there, balancing three pieces of pie on his right arm.

Twitch cleared his throat. "We got the ball . . . and here's your pie."

Nick took the plate and fork from Twitch's hand. He scooted even closer to the edge of the steps.

"Thank you."

"Yes, thank you, Frank." Barbara glanced at Nick from the corner of her eye. She rose and made her way back to the bench, accepting the plate.

Instead of joining her, Twitch sat down next to Nick on the steps, digging into his pie with fervor. As Nick watched Twitch plunge his fork through the crust, jabbing a strawberry, he could guess whose face Twitch was picturing with each jab.

℀   ℀   ℀

"I didn't initiate it, if that's what you're thinking," Nick said as they walked toward their barracks a few hours later.

"I didn't say you did." Twitch cocked his head and appeared to be studying the night sky.

"I told Barbara when I left that nothing will come of it. I told her I had a girl—" Nick shoved his hands deeper into his pockets, feeling like a traitor twice over.

"Of course you did."

Nick paused and reached a hand toward Twitch's shoulder. Twitch refused to face him.

"Look, I know it's only been a few months, and we're from places as different as they come, but you're the best buddy a guy can have." Nick squeezed his shoulder tighter. "I don't want any dumb girl to come between us, got it?"

Twitch turned, and Nick could tell he was far from forgiven.

His friend sighed. "I'm not going to let this blonde dame get between us. I know it's pretty stupid. I only saw her for the first time today. I was just, y'know . . . hoping."

Nick lifted his face and realized they'd been walking under a canopy of bright stars. "I know. Let's forget the girl. But I would like you to continue to come to church with me. I'd love—"

Twitch held up his hands in defense. "Hey, I'm not ready for that, okay? I attended church with you once; that doesn't mean I'm ready to join the choir." He looked away, and they continued their walk toward the barracks.

The tumult of men's voices floated from the doors and windows, which were open to let in the cool evening breeze.

Nick bit his lip. "I understand, man. I won't push. Friends?" He stretched out his hand.

Twitch paused and took the hand with a firm grip. "You got it. On one condition."

Nick grinned, feeling a heaviness lift from his chest. "You name it."

Twitch scratched his head. "As far as the guys are

concerned, the pastor's daughter was no Betty Grable. And she gave us both the cold shoulder, agreed?"

Nick laughed. "You've got nothing to worry about. Neither does Evie, for that matter."

Fifteen

Jakub plucked a blade of grass and twirled it between two fingers as he sat on the grass and waited for his bunk leader to arrive.

A young man jogged up the walkway with a wave. "Hi there."

Jakub looked back over his shoulder to make sure the man was talking to him.

He stopped at Jakub's feet. "You must be Jakub. I'm Adler Meyers. Come with me."

Jakub jumped to his feet.

Adler, a thin man about Jakub's height, looked not a day over twenty-five. Jakub cast another look at Adler as they walked down the street. His clothes were patched and dingy, like everyone else's in Terezín. His hair stuck out in all directions, and he smelled like spoiled milk. But by far his most dominating feature was the smile that lit his face.

"You just may like where we're going." Adler ruffled Jakub's hair. "Our home is in the former school building of Terezín. It's not too bad, really." They walked through the wide streets, past the parade grounds to the large, yellow building, and moved up the brick steps. "It's called L417 in ghetto terms." He pointed to his right. "We have those first two windows on the ground floor."

Adler held the door open for Jakub. "Forty-one boys reside in Home No. 1. All of them are thirteen and fourteen years old. You make forty-two."

Jakub sensed emptiness, and looking back over his shoulder, he wished that Daniel or Mother were there for support. Mother had been taken to the Dresdner barracks and Daniel to the infirmary, where nurses would tend his wounds.

Jakub followed Adler into the crowded room. Boys sprawled about and lounged upon the bunks. Two boys kicked around a balled sock, chasing it through the jumble of bodies. The room's smell reminded Jakub of sweaty soccer games he'd once played with friends.

As Adler and Jakub entered, the noise and commotion ceased. All eyes turned toward the newcomer.

"Boys, I'd like you to meet Jakub." Adler patted Jakub's shoulder.

Calls of "Hi, Jakub," "Welcome," and "Greetings" filled the room.

One of the smaller boys stepped closer. The top of

his curly hair barely reached Jakub's shoulders. "Follow me." He set out with long strides.

Adler nodded his approval.

The curly-headed boy led Jakub to a three-tiered bunk by the window. "You can put your stuff in the middle bunk."

Jakub glanced at the tight spot, noticing that there wasn't enough room for him to sit up straight. Getting in and out would be a squeeze.

A blond-headed boy sat cross-legged on the bottom bunk. He looked up at Jakub and smiled.

Jakub's tour guide held out his hand. "I'm Yuri. And you're going to love Addie—as we call our bunk leader. He used to work at vacation camps, and sometimes we pretend we're at camp too."

"He seems very nice." Jakub scanned the room. Directly across from their bunk, in the center of all the beds, sat a big table.

Yuri followed Jakub's gaze. "That's where we hold school—although if we are caught, we'll deny it. School's illegal, you know."

"No, I didn't know." Jakub placed his few meager items on the bunk.

"Things work on a steady schedule around here. We do our best to get along. The thing we dread most, of course, is transports. Boys leave, and new ones take their place."

Jakub patted his thin mattress. More than anything, he wanted to ask about the boy who had previously slept in this bed. *Whom had he replaced?*

Yuri shrugged his shoulders. "That's life around here, and nothing we can do about it. At least the new kids are all right. We're family just the same. I'm your brother now, and you're mine."

The word "brother" burnt like a red coal in Jakub's chest. He turned away before Yuri could see the moisture building in his eyes.

"Thank you," Jakub muttered.

"It's almost time for dinner, so I'll be back to get you. We can walk together."

"Anything else I need to know?"

"Just one more thing." Yuri puffed out his chest, proud to be of service. "You'll be getting a job tomorrow." He crossed his arms and leaned against the bunk. "The best jobs are in the gardens. Even though it's hard work, sometimes the gardeners let you have a radish or some lettuce to bring home. Some of us work in maintenance or in different workshops. For now, I work in the fields. But when I first got here last winter, I had to clean toilets for the old people. That was horrible." Yuri scrunched his face so tight Jakub expected his ears to touch his nose.

A laugh escaped Jakub's lips, catching him by surprise. "If we have to work, when do we have time for school?"

"Oh, there's always time for that. We make time. There are many poets, artists, and musicians here in the ghetto. They visit when they can, usually in the evenings, and give us great lectures. We share books and read a lot too. But I better go. I have to finish my chores. We

192

all trade chores once a week. I'll tell you more about that when we walk to dinner. See you."

He hustled away, and Jakub couldn't help but smile again at the flow of words that had gushed from Yuri's mouth.

"Do you like the middle?" The blond boy from the bottom bunk peered up at Jakub with large blue eyes. With that hair and those eyes, he looked more Aryan than Jewish.

Jakub met the boy's gaze. "Sure, the middle's fine."

"You can sit by me if you like. I have a little more room. I was ready for a break anyway."

Pens and pencils, brushes and paints surrounded the boy. Paper had been scattered over the mattress like a colorful blanket. Jakub's eyes widened at the treasure, and he wondered how the boy had managed to smuggle it in.

Slowly, meticulously, the boy stacked his papers, then patted a place for Jakub to sit.

"Henri used to sleep up there." The blond boy pointed up. "He was quite the daredevil. Broke his nose three times. He snored terribly. Do you snore?"

Jakub folded his hands in his lap. "I don't know. I don't think so. Surely Daniel would have told me." The boy didn't ask about Daniel as Jakub suspected he might. And Jakub didn't ask about Henri.

"I'm Michael, by the way." He stretched out his ink-stained hand.

Jakub took it with a firm grip. "I'm Jakub. Nice to meet you."

"Well, Jakub, welcome to Home No. 1. It's not so bad here, considering." Placing the papers on the bed, Michael stood quickly, ducking so he wouldn't hit his head. "Time for dinner. We'd better hurry."

With amazing agility, he scaled the three-tiered bunk like a circus monkey. His head stopped just inches from the ceiling. Then, with both hands and the top of his head, he pushed against a small panel in the ceiling. The panel opened, revealing a crawl space. "Hand me those things, will ya?"

Jakub did as asked. He picked up the paper and pens and stretched his long arms toward Michael.

"Fantastic. You're the perfect height!" Michael took the items from Jakub's hands and slid them into a cloth sack. Within a minute, the drawings were safely tucked away. Michael closed the panel and scaled down the bed to the floor.

"Come on now; let's hurry. We'll find Yuri and sit together."

Before Jakub could answer, Michael turned and hustled toward the door—past the dozens of other bunks, past the large table in the middle of the room.

Jakub followed, his long strides taking one step for every two of the smaller boy's.

"Long arms for reaching, long steps for keeping up. Fantastic, just what I needed!" Michael called as they scurried down the front steps into the cool evening.

It was just a short walk down the paved street packed with destitute pedestrians, to the courtyard of L318. Soon the boys entered the warm building that smelled of baking bread and gathered around a large table at the *Kinderkuche,* the children's kitchen. Lentil soup was served again, but this time a piece of fat floated in his bowl. Each boy also received a biscuit.

"They call Home No. 1 the 'boys home.'" Yuri took a large bite of his biscuit. "But no one here much feels like a boy. Some guys have been on their own for years —living on the streets, camping out in hiding places, or seeking out relatives before finally being sent here. Still, we call ourselves boys, because children get special privileges, even though we don't get a lot. We're more protected. We get better food too."

Jakub slurped a spoonful of the tasteless, watery soup and nearly gagged. *If this food is better, what are Mother and Daniel eating?* Still, the warm gruel was better than nothing.

"So, who else do you have around here?" Michael lifted his bowl to his lips and slurped down the remainder of his soup.

"My mother was taken to Dresdner today, and my younger brother to the infirmary. His hands were injured pretty bad by the SS, and they're going to look after him there."

"Do you want to go visit him after dinner?" Michael asked.

"Can we?" Jakub plopped the spoon on the table. "Today?"

"Sure, we just need to let Addie know," Yuri butted in. "After five-thirty, the place swarms like a beehive, with everyone checking on their loved ones. I have an uncle in the infirmary too. He has stomach problems, and my father says he won't be around long."

Jakub studied Yuri's face. How could he speak of death so matter-of-factly? He pushed his soup to the side.

An hour later, the three boys ventured across the garrison town to the infirmary. Jakub's eyes scanned the mass of people, the buildings with a constant flow of traffic in and out, and the storefronts that reminded him of the small businesses in Prague—only these buildings were in the process of being renovated to hold the collection of people transported into the town.

When they arrived, Jakub noticed that the large, airy infirmary looked more suitable for housing a museum than a hospital. He scanned the tall, arched ceilings and floor-to-ceiling windows. Then their worn shoes shuffled along the hardwood floors as they searched the metal beds for Daniel. Finally Jakub found him and rushed to his side. He lay like a white statue.

"Daniel?"

His brother stirred and opened his heavy eyes. Then he yawned. "Jakub!" Instant tears gathered around his lids. "You've come to see me. How did you do it?"

Jakub took a step back. "These are my friends, Michael and Yuri. They brought me and told me I can come every evening."

"Really?" Daniel attempted to hoist himself up on his elbows but fell back, weary from the effort. He sighed. "I'm not doing so well. They say my hands are infected. You should see them. My fingers are all swollen and red, and some are black. They hurt like crazy. And the nurses say they have nothing to give me for the pain."

"But you'll be all right soon. I'm sure they'll see to that."

Daniel's eyes fluttered, then closed completely. "Of course. You sneaked in my music for me, remember? I'll be playing with the orchestra soon. I'll play a special song for you. Now, tell me about the boys' home, because when I get out of here, that's where I'll be too."

For the next thirty minutes, Yuri and Michael dominated the conversation, telling Daniel about their daily schedules and competitions in Home 1.

"They give us points for fixing our beds, for studies —which we do even though we're not supposed to. You name it," Yuri said, his hands moving with his words.

"You get points for drawing too." Michael held up his stained fingers. "I get lots of points for that."

"Do you win anything?" Daniel asked in a groggy voice.

"Yes, you win your name on the blackboard. But Michael's name is always on the top." Yuri crossed his arms, feigning anger.

As the end of visiting hours neared, the children's nurse ambled over, her dark hair pulled back tightly, displaying her motherly features. "Shoosh now. Daniel needs his sleep." She waved her hands toward the boys.

Jakub patted Daniel's shoulder. "I'll be back tomorrow. See you then." He gulped down the emotions that threatened to break through, then turned to leave.

"Jakub, wait."

Jakub glanced at the nurse for approval.

She nodded with a compassionate gaze. "Two minutes. I'll leave you two alone." She placed her hands on Yuri's and Michael's shoulders. "Come on, boys, why don't you wait outside?"

Jakub sank onto the bed and leaned close to Daniel's pale face.

"I want you to know that my music is under this mattress. My extra set of clothes too, in case you need them."

Jakub furrowed his brow. "Why in the world would I need them?"

Daniel shrugged. "Oh, I was just thinking. In case you meet a musician—someone with a violin—and you want to play the Ravel for me, then that's where the music is."

"Never. I can't play 'Tzigane.' You're the prodigy, remember?"

"You underestimate yourself. You always have." Daniel yawned. "Papa says that you have what it takes too. You just need confidence—"

"And practice."

"Yeah, but just because it doesn't come as easily, doesn't mean you don't have talent. Some people just have to work harder, that's all."

Jakub tucked the blankets around his brother. He was reminded of the time when Daniel was six and had to go to the hospital with pneumonia. Jakub was powerless to help then too.

"Okay, I'll see what I can do. I doubt I can find someone to just lend me a violin. But I'll try. For you, I will try."

"Thank you." Daniel's voice was no more than a whisper. "See you tomorrow."

"See you tomorrow." Jakub rose and walked slowly out of the building.

Outside, in the fading sunlight, Yuri and Michael were waiting patiently on the front steps. They jumped to their feet when they saw Jakub.

"Hurry now," Yuri called. "Professor Emers has promised to come read to us tonight. The story's about the Republic of Shkid, the name of the school for homeless orphans in St. Petersburg. You're going to love it."

Jakub broke into a jog alongside the other boys, weaving in and out of the citizens who hurried home before curfew. Yet while his legs propelled him forward, he felt tethered to what he'd left behind. If only he could stay by Daniel's side, to tell him stories of Golem or whisper promises of what they'd do when they regained their freedom.

But he couldn't. And he also couldn't shake the nagging worry that clung to his chest. *What if the infection got worse? What if Daniel—*

He pushed that thought from his mind.

When he, Yuri, and Michael entered Home 1, the lecture had already started. They silently took seats at the table. Jakub's stomach still ached from hunger. He felt awkward and out of place. And as he listened to the literary readings of the eloquent university professor, he wondered what type of strange world he'd been dropped into.

🙠   🙠   🙠

VIENNA, AUSTRIA
JUNE 16, 1942

Evie poured cold milk from the tall jar into a glass, then sliced off another piece of Ilse's coffee cake. She was sure she'd gained ten pounds since leaving New York. The most work she'd done all week had been to help roll bandages at the Red Cross office. The rest of the time she'd lounged around, looked over old photos of her time in New York with Nick, and ate sweets— this was her second piece of cake today.

The sound of footsteps neared, and Evie prayed it wasn't her mother. She had come home from more than one outing with complaints that Evie was giving their family a bad name.

"I don't understand why you won't return Thomas's phone calls," she had fussed. "He even sent flowers this afternoon. Everyone's saying you think you're too good for them, and you've changed while in the States. I understand your devotion to Nick, but at least let Thomas take you to dinner once, won't you?"

She was trying to steer clear of her mother, lest she be roped into giving a proper public appearance. She was also fearful that her mother would notice she no longer wore the necklace from Nick. But as the door to

200

the kitchen opened, Evie saw that it was Ilse. She let out a slow breath and pointed to the cake with a thumbs-up signal.

Now Ilse smiled as she crossed the room. She opened a drawer and slid a stack of freshly ironed linens inside. "I'm glad you're enjoying that cake," she said in a singsong voice. "No one else seems to be touching it."

Evie studied the housekeeper as she moved to the sink and began running hot water for dishes. She wouldn't meet Evie's gaze.

"Is something wrong?" Evie placed her glass on the kitchen table and walked to Ilse's side. "Something seems to be bothering you."

Ilse let out a slow breath. "I'm just tired, that's all." She rolled up her sleeves and plunged her hands into the water.

"Oh, my goodness, look at you." Evie lifted Ilse's sudsy hand into the air. "You're skin and bones." She dropped the hand and poked Ilse's shoulder with her finger. "And that's not an exaggeration. Don't you eat?"

Ilse lowered her voice. "I do, but there are just so many mouths to feed in—in our group. We have so little, and it must go a long way." She made quick work of the dishes, scrubbing them with fervor. "And I'm not going to bother you about it. The necklace will help. You've done enough."

"Are you kidding?" The sweetness of the cake in her mouth suddenly made Evie's stomach turn.

"Kidding?" Ilse asked. "I'm not sure what that American term means."

"It means 'are you joking?' Because here I am eating more than my fill, and there are others not getting enough. I can't just sit around while that happens. I want to help. I have to help."

She moved to the pantry, swinging open the door. "Look at this. We have plenty. It's foolish that some people live on rations, when others have more than they need.

"Dry your hands," Evie continued. "I have a quick job for you before you get started on dinner." She lifted a ten-pound sack of flour and handed it to Ilse. "Take this and some eggs. Oh, and that extra milk too. Run them to your house, or wherever you need to take them. Don't be long. I'll get started on the meal, if you need me to."

Ilse did as Evie said.

"You are too kind." She hoisted the flour to her shoulder. "You were a great child, but I'm amazed by what a wonderful young woman you've turned out to be." She took a step toward the icebox. "Now, if I wrap everything, I think I can carry—"

Ilse's words were cut short by the kitchen door swinging open. Isak strode into the kitchen with a puzzled look on his face. "Carry what? Where on earth do you need to carry that to?"

Ilse's jaw dropped, and Evie took a step toward Isak.

"Really now, where else would she be taking those

things except home? I found out it's her mother's birthday tomorrow, and she doesn't have the ingredients for a cake—the rations are just dreadful, you know."

Isak peered down at Evie with one eyebrow raised. "Ten pounds of flour for a cake?"

She took his hand and gave it a quick squeeze. "Of course not, but we should consider it a gift." Evie moved back to the icebox and wrapped up the eggs in a bundle, handing them to Ilse. "After all, we have so much."

Ilse stood silent, her arms full.

"Well, good thing I got off early." Isak lifted the glass jar of milk. "Here, Ilse. Let me help you home with that. I'll give you a ride in my car." He took the flour from her hands and moved to the door with quick steps. "I know you have to get dinner on soon, so we'd better hurry. Come now. Won't your mother be pleased?"

Ilse glanced back at Evie and shrugged as she followed Isak out the back door. As soon as the door shut, Evie slumped onto a kitchen chair and rested her forehead on her hands.

Almost a thief. Now a liar. What's next?

Sixteen

Evie hurried down the large staircase short of breath. She'd covered every inch of the massive house, including guest bedrooms she hadn't set foot in for years. Ilse was nowhere to be found. Evie opened the side door, preparing to search the yard again, when she heard the kitchen cupboards open and shut. Immediately, her pounding heart began to slow.

"There you are! I've been looking all over for you," she called into the kitchen as she neared. "It's not like you to be gone for so long."

She pushed the swinging kitchen doors open, then stopped short. It was her mother who stood in the kitchen, hands on hips.

"Goodness, Evie. Haven't I told you not to yell across the house like an Indian?" Her mother moved toward the pantry, her fine tailored suit looking out of place. Evie heard her rustling around inside the pantry. In a moment she reemerged.

"Do you have any idea where the aspirin powder is kept? I have a terrible headache." Mother pressed the tips of her fingers to her temples, emphasizing her point.

Evie shook her head. "No, I have no idea. Where's Ilse? She knows. I've been looking for her all day. Is she sick?"

Mother moved to the kitchen table and sat down, crossing her legs demurely. In voice, vocabulary, and manner, her mother did not slouch. "No, I fired her. But I should have asked before she left where she kept a few things."

"Fired her?" Evie was sure she'd misunderstood. "Ilse's been with us since before I was born."

Her mother looked up, and for the first time Evie noticed her puffy eyes.

"Tell me, Evie, why were you giving Ilse food? And why did you lie? I know when her mother's birthday is, and every year I offer supplies from our kitchen for Ilse to make Gerta a cake."

Evie glanced away. "I—I gave Ilse food because she needed it. Didn't you see how thin she was? The rations aren't nearly enough." She crossed her arms over her chest, attempting to keep her tone even. "You . . . you had no right to fire her for something I did. You should have come to me. I was just trying to help."

"You would lie to me!" Her mother rose and spun

Evie toward her. "She was getting you involved in foolish, illegal activities. Isak warned me. He's only thinking of your best interest. He doesn't want you hurt." She squeezed her forehead. "Besides, if you were caught, our whole family would be imprisoned—sent to who knows where. Do you think your father can handle such a thing at his age? Do you think I could ever show my face in public again?"

"I don't know what you're talking about." Evie turned away.

"You can't deceive me. I'm your mother, remember? Ilse did not give birth to you—no matter how much you wish she had."

Evie's cheeks flushed. It was true. How many times as a girl had she longed for Ilse to be her mother?

"Besides, you're only looking at the negative," her mother continued, unaware of the accuracy of her blow. "What about the good the Germans have brought? Hundreds of thousands of Austrians have work, and our country exudes a pride we haven't felt since the reign of the Hapsburgs."

"Mother, you can't possibly be that blind! You only say that because you and father are just as weak and cowardly as everyone else—"

Evie's face felt the sting of her mother's hand before she thought to block it. She touched her cheek, her eyes wide.

Her mother looked at her hand, as if surprised herself. She closed her eyes, then opened them, her gaze unwavering. She lowered her voice. "If you get involved in *anything,* it will be the end of us. Think about that, will you? If you care nothing for yourself, at least think about what your actions could do to your family."

🍃   🍃   🍃

Evie entered the door next to the tailor's shop. It had been years since she'd been to Ilse's home, but the sound of whirring sewing machines brought it all back. She climbed the tall flight of steps permeated with dinnertime scents of sausage and sauerkraut.

She glanced at the peeling paint and sagging steps and wondered what it would be like to grow up within these paper-thin walls, with neighbors able to hear your dinner conversations or even your whispered secrets in bed at night.

At the first landing, Evie made her way to the farthest door and knocked. The door opened a crack, and half of a wrinkled face peered out at her.

"Yes, what do you want?" an old woman's voice croaked.

"I'm looking for Ilse. Is she home?"

The door cracked open a bit more. "Who's asking?"

"Evie Kreig. Ilse works—worked for our family."

The door opened wider, and a strong grip tugged on her arm. With a strength that surprised Evie, the elderly woman jerked her inside and quickly shut the door. It was Gerta, Ilse's mother.

"Evie, you're so grown up . . . but what in the world are you doing here? Do you have news of Ilse?"

"News?" Evie scanned the apartment, which appeared even smaller than she remembered. The worn furniture smelled of mildew and looked as if it had occupied the same spots for the last fifty years. An ornate silver crucifix, the only object of value, hung on the whitewashed wall.

Evie cleared her throat. "I was hoping you could tell me where she is."

The woman settled into a roughly upholstered chair that perfectly fit her shape. "Ilse came home last night, crying. She left not thirty minutes ago, saying she needed to meet some friends." The woman's chin trembled. "I swear, if anything happens to that girl, I don't know what I will do. She's all I have left." She leaned forward, a delicate, blue-veined hand covering her cracked lips.

Evie kneeled before Gerta, placing her hands on the woman's thin shoulders.

"I'll help you find her. Do you have any idea where she went?"

The old woman smiled and patted Evie's cheek. "Ilse always said you were a nice girl. So helpful . . ." She studied Evie's eyes for a moment. "I think I can trust you."

She pointed a gnarled finger toward the window. "That way. Ilse said she was to meet someone near the bridge in the park." The woman shrugged her shoulders. "I'm sorry; that's all I know."

There had to be hundreds of parks in Vienna, with dozens of bridges—but only one that could be seen from Gerta's window.

"The Prater? Did she go there?"

The woman nodded.

"Thank you. If I find anything—"

"Watch out for curfew. It's in an hour."

"Don't worry. I'll make it home before dark." Evie kissed the woman's hand. "Thank you for your help." Evie strode to the door. She glanced back over her shoulder and noticed that Gerta had pulled prayer beads from her pocket and was already at work rubbing them between her fingers. The old woman lifted Evie's and Ilse's names in mumbled prayers.

⁊   ⁊   ⁊

The skies darkened, and Evie realized that the park was farther away than she thought. Her footsteps echoed on the quiet street. The city hid under a shroud of gray and black. Her only marker was the tall steeple of St. Stephan's, slicing the white moon in half with its projection.

She felt a stirring inside her. *Go home.*

Evie ignored the voice. *I just have to talk to Ilse. . . .* She slowed as she turned the corner to the park, fully expecting her anxiety to be stilled by Ilse's smiling presence. Yet the street was empty.

She entered the woodsy park and moved to the main bridge. In the distance, the amusement rides at the Prater stood silent—there would be no nighttime carnivals or brightly lit Ferris wheel rides with Allied bombing raids coming ever closer. Evie looked up at the tall

210

ride. She had never ridden on it before and could barely glance up at it without a wave of nausea flooding over her.

Beyond the dormant rides, the trickle of the Danube reached her ears. A rustling caused Evie to spin, but it was only tree branches scraping in the wind.

You're not a child, scared of the dark. The river nymph in the Danube is only a child's story, remember?

More rustling to her right. Not a tree branch this time. She paused, the sound of her own breathing filling her ears.

Moonlight slanting between maples revealed the top of a blonde head as it ducked under a limb and darted behind a patch of bushes.

Evie stumbled ahead in full pursuit. It had to be Ilse. She ducked, barely missing a projecting tree limb. Her foot twisted on the soft ground, but she refused to give up. Her handbag struck against her side with each stride.

Without warning, a thin arm reached out and halted her. Evie screamed.

The hand, which smelled of cleaning solution and mud, clamped over her mouth. Seconds later a face appeared inches from hers. It was Ilse, her eyes filled with a fury Evie had never seen.

"What are you doing here?" she hissed. "Do you know what kind of danger you could put us in if you were followed?"

Evie stared at Ilse. Overnight her friend's face had transformed into a network of wrinkles. Strands of dirty hair veiled Ilse's eyes, and mud caked the side of her face.

"Mother told me you were fired. It's all my fault. I'm so sorry."

Ilse pushed Evie behind a wide oak and shoved her to the ground. A root protruded into Evie's ribs.

She sucked in a breath. "I had to find you. I can't sit around there any longer. I'm ready—"

"Shhh!" Ilse pushed Evie's head down, smashing her cheek into the moist dirt. "We don't need naive do-gooders. This is no time to play hero, Evie. I told you what we need. Valuable items. Money."

Evie froze, shocked by her friend's harshness. "I—I just want to . . ."

Ilse's eyes narrowed. "Go home, now. Do you hear?"

"But—"

The sound of footsteps surprised them both. Ilse glanced over her shoulder, eyes wide. "Get out of here, Evie. Go now!"

Evie let out a moan and retraced her steps, regretting her foolishness. She pushed through the brush, ignoring the spiked limbs scratching her face and arms. She dashed toward the clearing, toward the street—away from whoever belonged to those footsteps. Visions of holding cells, her mother in hand irons, her father sleeping on a lice-infected mattress inundated her mind.

A pain cramped her side. Out of breath, Evie slowed.

"No." Evie planted her fists on her hips. "I won't let them frighten me."

Ilse's words replayed in her mind. *This is no time to play hero, Evie. Go home.*

Yes, she'd go home. But she was far from giving up.

A streetlight hung above her unlit, due to blackout conditions, and she attempted to straighten her hair, preparing for the long walk home. There were no trolleys out at this hour. She'd be lucky to make it there by morning.

Warm liquid trickled down her cheek, and she wiped it with her sleeve. First her mother's slap and now this. *How am I going to explain these scratches? And being out after curfew?*

Suddenly Evie stopped, sensing that she was being watched. Ahead, a lone car was parked on the otherwise empty boulevard. Then she saw him. Beside the car, a man stood in the shadows, watching her. Gestapo.

Evie turned to run, but hesitated. Something about the man . . .

"Thomas? Is that you . . . ?" She hurried toward him.

"Well, hello, Miss Kreig." He crossed his arms over his chest. "May I ask what you're doing out at such a late hour?"

"Miss Kreig? Thomas, please." She neared, her heart pounding at the sight of him.

"I asked what you are doing, Evie." He didn't give her a chance to respond. Thomas grasped her upper arm, at the same moment pulling a pistol from his jacket pocket.

"Thomas, you can't be serious! What are you doing?"

"I want to know what you're doing lurking around an area that harbors members of the anti-Nazi movement. You haven't gotten yourself involved with them, have you? Did your housekeeper rope you in?"

He moved his face inches from hers.

"*Ja,* we've been watching your maid, Ilse, for quite a while, my darling. Watching you too—your display at the bakery. Your aloofness at Hitler's birthday party. Your complete disregard for old friends. Why would you shun the very person who has always cared for you most?" Thomas lowered his voice, sliding her closer. "You've saddened me, my love. You've refused to let me care for you."

Thomas pulled Evie tight to his chest. He forced his lips onto hers, and the gun pressed even harder into her side.

Evie jerked her head back and gasped. "Thomas, wait. I can explain. I—"

He pushed her from his arms with a smirk. "Come with me. I'm sure my commander downtown would also appreciate your story." He shoved her toward a green police car waiting by the curb.

"Thomas, you can't do this—"

"Quiet." He grabbed her arm again. "Let's see what good your freedom-fighting pals are to you now." He thrust Evie into the back of the car, slamming the door shut, then climbed into the driver's seat.

Evie tried both door handles, but it was no use.

Thomas reached for the ignition. The sound of a gunshot pierced Evie's ears. Glass from the driver's side door exploded, and Thomas slumped forward.

Evie dived to the car's floor, expecting to be next.

But her own Ilse stood next to the car, shoving a pistol into the waistband of her work skirt.

Evie's door opened. Hands jerked her onto the street. Her legs gave out, and she stumbled.

Thomas—

"Let's go!" Ilse yanked her back toward the park. "They'll be here soon."

"But, Thomas—" Evie craned her neck to see him.

Thomas's shoulder was bright with blood. He lifted his head.

"Thomas!"

His arm shifted across his lap.

"No!" Evie lunged toward Ilse as a second gunshot blasted.

The force of a bullet sent Ilse crumpling to the pavement.

Seventeen

"Ilse, please!" Evie cradled Ilse's head in her lap, taking a fleeting glance toward the car. Thomas was slumped over the steering wheel, apparently unconscious.

Evie brushed the loose dirt from her friend's face and smoothed back the straggly locks of hair. Blood seeped from a chest wound—Ilse's black blouse made darker by the oozing wound near her heart.

"Please, God," Evie pleaded. "I know I've been far off lately. But I need You. Now more than ever. Save Ilse, please."

Evie searched Ilse's wide-open eyes, but even in the dim light she knew no life remained. "No, please, no."

More gunshots exploded around her. The plunk of bullets ricocheted off the car. Then figures emerged— two sprinted toward her from out of the park. She felt heat against her back and turned to find the night sky ablaze with flames. The car was on fire, and a man was feeding it with something out of a large can. Flames licked around Thomas's body. *Thomas.*

Evie closed Ilse's empty eyes with shaky hands and rested her head on the road. "Good-bye, my friend." She choked back sobs and rushed toward the car. Flames from the front seat popped and burst as the heat melted the leather interior. Sparks hit the sleeve of Thomas's uniform jacket, igniting it.

Evie yanked on the door handle, burning her hand. It was stuck. "Thomas!" She yanked harder, but it wouldn't budge. She reached through the shattered glass of the window, coughing back smoke. "Thomas, wake up! You have to get out!"

Voices broke through her screams. "We only have a few seconds. We have no choice!"

Evie turned and spotted two men in black carting Ilse's body toward the blazing car. "No!" she shrieked. *Were they mad?*

A woman rushed up and grabbed Evie's purse from her shoulder, tossing it to the sidewalk. "Come with me now!"

But Evie's feet remained planted by the car. She covered her mouth from the smoke and watched in horror as the woman emptied a can of gasoline over Ilse's body. The men then slid Ilse into the backseat.

Dear God, no.

Hands pulled against Evie, drawing her away from the flames. She struggled, and the strong hands attempted to cover her eyes.

"Stop, no!"

A second set of male arms joined the first and lifted Evie's feet from the ground. She kicked and flailed. Her mind flashed to the image of the young girl she'd seen arrested on the street.

Evie struggled harder and twisted her head until the hand no longer covered her eyes. A young, bearded man carried her torso. Another man gripped her legs.

Evie shook her head until her mouth was freed. "Stop. Let me go!"

"Quiet. We are trying to help!"

"No, stop. Please!"

"Somebody shut her up." It was the woman's voice.

Sirens screamed in the distance. Evie thought again of the girl on the street and wasn't surprised as the blur of a club came into view, bearing down on her.

An explosion sounded in the distance. Followed by darkness.

🍂　　🍂　　🍂

Evie awoke to the strong odor of onions. She felt beneath her and found she was lying on a dirt floor. Pulsating pain hammered her head.

She struggled to open her eyes. Her hands searched around her. Cool walls and a sack of rotting onions an arm's length away. *Where am I?*

It all came back in a rush. Gunshots ringing in her ears, a fire's heat on her back. And . . . Ilse, Thomas— disappearing forever in exploding flames. She hugged her knees and let the tears flow. She longed to pray, but no words came.

Finally she forced her eyes open. She spotted a ladder leading up to a trapdoor. Light filtered down around the edges of the opening.

Evie crawled to the ladder. She attempted to pull herself up the first few rungs but collapsed.

"Dear God, help me." She clung to the rung. "I don't know where I am, but I need You now."

She slumped to the dirt floor again. If she was in prison, this was unlike any she'd ever heard of.

And those people at the scene. They had to be part of Ilse's underground group. But why had they torched Ilse's body?

It hurt too much to think. She tilted her chin to the light. "Someone, please help me. God, please, help!"

Footsteps from the floor above echoed around her. Evie's jaw clenched as the trapdoor scraped open. She shielded her eyes from the light now streaming from above.

From the brilliant beams pouring into the hole, she guessed it had to be past noon. *Father. Mother.* Surely, they were sick with worry.

"Cut the crying, will you?" a woman's voice snapped. "Promise me you'll stop, and I'll get you out."

Evie wiped her cheeks. "Yes. I . . . I'll stop. Please just help me."

"Move out of the way."

The woman trudged down the ladder and, with thick, callused hands, helped Evie to her feet.

"Grab the rungs and pull yourself up. I'll push from behind. You're pretty weak, but that's to be expected after being unconscious for two days."

Two days? Evie grabbed the next rung, for the first time taking in her surroundings. A blanket had been spread on the floor near where she'd been lying. A bottle of water had been left for her too.

"Where am I? Who are you?" Evie asked as she struggled upward.

"Hush now. You just get yourself to the top of this ladder, and we'll answer your questions." The woman gave a hard push from beneath. "And you can be sure you'll have a few questions to answer too."

⁊   ⁊   ⁊

The dark-haired woman, about Evie's height, led her into a small kitchen and seated her at a table. Curtains blocked Evie's attempt to catch a glimpse of the outside, but it was clear she was no longer in Vienna. Instead of city sounds, she heard only silence. Then male voices from an adjoining room punctuated the tranquility.

The woman left and returned with two men, one middle-aged and one younger, with a beard and a muscular frame. Evie sat up straighter and brushed stray hair from her face. Her fingers contacted a cotton bandage, then detected dried blood on her forehead. Her stomach churned.

The younger man moved and spoke with authority.

"I'm sure she has quite a headache. Make her something to eat, but not too much."

He's the one who held me from the flames, Evie realized.

The woman didn't budge. "We have so little—and where will we keep her? This place isn't safe. Even the cellar isn't a long-term option."

The man lifted a coffeepot from the stovetop and poured a hot, dark liquid into a ceramic mug. He placed the steaming cup before her, then turned back to his friends.

Evie lifted the cup to her mouth. It smelled like coffee. She took a sip but had to force herself not to spit out the foul liquid.

"What about the farm? I'm sure they could use another pair of hands there," the man said.

"Humph, like she's worked a day in her life—"

Evie slammed the cup on the table. The coffee sloshed over the side and burnt her hand. She quickly wiped it on her torn skirt. "May I say something?"

The three faces turned.

"I am not brain damaged—despite the blow you gave me. I do have ears." She attempted to rise, then slumped back into the chair.

The bearded man hurried to her side. "Don't try to get up."

The woman rolled her eyes and poured herself a cup.

Evie pressed her fingers to her temples. "I think I deserve some answers. Who are you? Have I really been out for two days, and what—why did you do that to my friends?" Evie looked down and noticed her hands trembling. "What—what are you going to do to me?"

The man tapped his knuckles on the table. "One question at a time, please."

"We saved you. Why do you think we'd harm you?" The woman's voice was harsh. "Felix, tell her we saved her."

The bearded man, Felix, leaned close and spoke softly. "We saved you." He patted her back.

"Oh, you've got to be kidding." The woman's voice rose an octave. "Don't treat her like a child. Look what she's done. She almost got us all killed."

"Stop, would you?" The jaggedness of Evie's tone surprised even herself. "You don't have to worry about helping me or keeping me. I just want to go home. I want this whole nightmare to be over. I want to see my parents and sleep in my own bed."

Felix opened his mouth and then closed it again, as if unsure of his words.

"What?" She glared at Felix, then at the woman. "Someone please tell me what's going on."

The woman settled in the chair next to Evie. "You can't go back, because your family thinks you're dead."

Evie sucked in a breath.

"Korina, please!" Felix rose from the chair and ran his fingers through his brown hair.

"Well, it's true."

"Yes, but sometimes the truth is difficult to hear."

Korina slid a newspaper across the table, pushing it closer to Evie. "Look for yourself."

Evie read the headline. " 'Young Viennese socialite found dead after murder-suicide plot.' " Her eyes moved to the first paragraph.

The body of Evie Kreig, a young Viennese woman from a notable family, was found burnt beyond recognition in what appears to be a murder by a jilted lover. The body of her boyfriend, Thomas Wolff, was also found burnt with a self-inflicted gun wound. Investigators suspect that after Miss Kreig broke off their relationship, the gestapo agent kidnapped and murdered Miss Kreig, then caught the car on fire before turning the gun on himself. . . .

Evie couldn't read any more. She rose from the table and struggled toward the back door. "No, this can't be. I have to tell my parents. They must be beside themselves!"

"Evie, sit." Felix's voice was strong. "We planned it like this. It's the only way."

She paused and looked at Felix. Even in her anger, Evie noted compassion in his gaze. "What do you mean you planned it like this? You *planned* my death?"

"Evie, sit down, and I'll explain."

"I don't want to sit. I want to know what's going on."

Felix took her by the arm and led her to the chair.

"We had no choice. Ilse was dead, and if we allowed

the gestapo agent to live, many more lives would be at risk, including yours. He'd been following you for some time. And he most likely knew about Ilse's connection to the underground."

Evie thought back to Thomas's words of accusation. It seemed like years, not days, ago.

Felix stood and crossed his arms.

"If we had let him live, you would have been arrested, your parents, and Isak too. Then they would have hunted us down."

"Wait." Evie cocked her head. "You know Isak?"

Felix quickly glanced away. "I think we've determined that the less you know, the better."

Korina cut in. "We saved your life, just as I said. Protected your family too."

"But the police think I'm dead . . . why did they think that was me instead of Ilse in the car?"

"Your purse on the sidewalk helped," Felix said. "Our friends on the inside assisted too. Don't worry; your death has been confirmed. The certificate's been issued. The . . . funeral will be held tomorrow."

Funeral. My funeral?

"But what about Ilse? What will they think happened to her? I visited her mother. Gerta knows I was looking for her."

The second man stepped forward from the corner of the room. He was tall and thin, middle-aged, with horn-rimmed glasses. Evie had almost forgotten he was there.

"I'm Sascha. Il-Ilse and I were cl-close," he stammered. Gray circles sagged beneath his eyes. "I visited her mother. Gerta believes Ilse is staying with friends in Linz. I didn't have the heart to tell her otherwise."

"It's too much. I can't think. Where will I go? What will I do?"

Finally the thought she'd been pushing aside forced itself to the surface. Her heart clenched, and new sobs threatened to emerge.

Nick.

"What about Nick?" she whispered.

Eighteen

An unexpected visitor had forced them to leave Sascha's cottage sooner than expected. Felix walked at Evie's side, holding her hand as they played the part of lovers out for an afternoon stroll. It was less than a mile's walk from the small farm to her new home.

Her mind refused to focus, yet she knew she must try. Her bandaged head was hidden under a large sun hat. A light cotton peasant dress, at least a size too large, hung from her frame. Sunglasses shielded her face.

Felix had mumbled to himself what she was sure were curse words in Romansh, or was it Italian, as he threw some women's clothes, a blanket, and a pillow into a satchel. He didn't have any identification papers for Evie—nothing to keep her from being arrested if stopped. Now she shuffled next to Felix, attempting to appear casual, yet the memories of Ilse and Thomas haunted her. *They're dead because of me.*

"Lift your head. Don't be afraid to glance at the automobiles as they pass," Felix warned. "If you lower your chin like that, they'll think you are hiding something."

But I am hiding something. My whole life.

She lifted her eyes and scanned the countryside. Though Grinzing was on the outskirts of Vienna, she'd never been in this area before.

As they walked along the country road, houses appeared more frequently. Soon they entered what appeared to be a residential area. The small cottages reminded Evie of something out of a child's picture book. Though pressed together as a single unit facing the road, the individual residences sported varying rooflines and colors of paint.

An old woman swept her front steps with a straw broom while a half-dozen clucking chickens circled her feet. Evie smiled at the woman, but she granted Evie no more than a sideways glance.

Felix spoke low and close to her ear. "We are going to the *Altes Presshaus* restaurant. There is a tunnel that runs from the field through the wine cellar to the basement of a nearby church. Hundreds of years ago, winegrowers used it to escape from marauding tribesmen. We use it for much the same purposes today."

"I'll be living in a restaurant?"

"We feed a lot of people there who assist with our efforts. You'll help with the cooking. There's a small room in the basement for you to sleep."

"But I've never cooked before—"

Felix chuckled. "Guess it's time to learn."

They wandered down a side street, then entered through the back door of the restaurant.

Korina sat at a small table, reading the newspaper. She glanced at Evie, then turned her attention to Felix.

"Look at this." She slid the paper across the table for Felix to get a better look. "Tonight's the night."

Felix hurried over and glanced at the print. "You're right. You better go get Sascha."

Korina rose, plucked a slice of bread from the cutting board, and hurried out the door, letting it slam behind her. Her pounding head allowed Evie to understand what her mother had always complained about. *It only takes two seconds to shut it properly.*

Felix pulled out a scuffed wooden chair and took a seat at the large rectangular table. He motioned for Evie to join him. She placed her hat and glasses in the seat next to her as she sat, relieved to be done with the deception.

Felix moved his finger over a small ad. Then he closed his eyes, pressing his hands to his forehead. His lips moved slightly as if he were making a list in his mind.

Evie peered over and attempted to read the newsprint.

Darling Riita,
*   Our precious passion makes my life complete.*
*   Happy 5th Anniversary, darling.*
*   Forever, Hammond*

"A love note?" Evie asked.

Felix lifted his head and gazed at her, stroking his beard.

Evie crossed her arms over her chest, pulling them tight to her. "Felix, I know I've caused you a lot of work and frustration, but I have nowhere to go. If I leave, I'm dead. I'm completely dependent on you. I want to help. I want to gain your trust. I understand if you can't tell me everything—"

Felix chuckled. "Do you always rattle on like that?"

Heat crept up Evie's cheeks.

He studied her eyes for a moment, then sighed. "Perhaps you were only trying to help, but it will take time before we can completely trust you as Ilse did."

He rose from the chair, walked to the back window, and looked out. "I will tell you this much. It will be your first lesson. Hidden meanings are the language of the Resistance." He returned to his chair, scraping the planks as he scooted in. "We've become the masters of hiding information between ordinary phrases. It completely eludes the Nazis. All the radio stations and newspapers are closely monitored, but patriotic messages are broadcast and printed almost every day. They seem obvious to the careful listener, but the Nazis don't understand."

"This letter is a secret message?"

"Yes. The editor of the newspaper is a friend. Any time he has a message, he puts an ad in the left corner of the second page. See, right here."

Felix pointed to the words. "Read the first letter of each word."

"D-R-O-P . . . P-M . . . L-M-C? There's some type of drop tonight? Yes, that must be it. But the rest of these letters don't make sense."

"They stand for possible locations. There will be a drop tonight, yes. I can't tell you where. And I don't know if it's men or weapons."

"They drop men? From planes?"

"Patriots from Czechoslovakia, Austria, and France, who've escaped. They get Resistance training in England and sometimes parachute in. It's very dangerous, but the assistance they give is invaluable."

"Is that what the five in '5th Anniversary' stands for? Five parachutists, perhaps?"

Felix shook his head. "No, the five stands for five campfires. We light them near the safest prearranged location. The plane travels the route given in this code. Five fires means it's okay to drop. If there is another number of campfires or no flames, he continues on."

The door swung open, and Korina reentered. Sascha was at her side, dressed in a farmer's bib overalls. His blond hair framed his wrinkled face.

"He was already on his way over," Korina explained. "He saw the message too."

Sascha settled next to Felix and pushed his black-rimmed glasses up from the brim of his nose. "Tonight's the night."

"You know what to do?"

"I sure do. I'll meet you at the end of the tunnel before dawn with—whatever I find."

Felix placed a hand on Sascha's shoulder. "Good luck."

"Thanks." Sascha grinned. "I'll take all the luck I can get."

Evie rose from her spot next to Felix. "Thank you for trusting me. I have so much to learn." She smoothed her dress, thinking how her mother would faint if she saw her in such a rag. The thought of home caused Evie's chest to ache. She swallowed the mounting emotions. "What do you want me to do first? Anything to get my mind off—"

Korina laughed derisively and pushed a strand of hair behind her ear. "You think you can just dive right in? Have you forgotten that people think you're dead? What if someone gets a glimpse into the kitchen and recognizes you?" She took Evie's arm and led her to a doorway. "We have much to do. A haircut, new clothes, a new ration card. It will most likely take a few days."

Evie stroked her hair, which fell over her shoulders and down her back. "A haircut?"

Korina glanced at Felix and Sascha. "She's a scrawny thing, isn't she? Perhaps we should transform her into a boy."

Evie yanked her arm out of the woman's grasp.

"Come now, Korina," Felix chided. "A haircut, change of color. Maybe some glasses. We want to protect the lady, not humiliate her."

Korina opened a side door. Steps led downward into what Evie assumed was the wine cellar.

"Come on, girlie. I'll show you to your new room, and then we'll do something about that hair."

ᔆ   ᔆ   ᔆ

TEREZÍN, CZECHOSLOVAKIA
JUNE 20, 1942

Michael walked alongside Jakub, hands in pockets. "When they first brought me here a few months ago, I felt like I was visiting a foreign country. Really. The customs are different. Even the language is unique to the ghetto. I couldn't believe they just let us walk around. Everyone has duties, of course, but once those are complete, we're free to explore this odd new world."

"My brother would say we were Magellan seeking out new territories," Jakub chuckled, feigning cheerfulness.

Michael grinned. "Hey, I like that."

They turned down a side street, where a large black-painted administrative building loomed ahead. The three-story structure resembled the other barracks with the sparse courtyards. Walking toward the white stone gate, Michael pointed out the keystone with its two horses crossing their heads. "Those can be our exploring horses." Michael tilted his head up and gave Jakub a wink.

"Good idea."

A Jewish ghetto guard with bright yellow lapels on his jacket guarded the gate. A Czech gendarme in green uniform stood on the other side.

"That place is Magdeburger, the main office building of the ghetto. The Jewish Council of Elders works there. They're the ones who make the laws for the Jews here—with Nazi approval, of course. They keep track of the transports too—the number of people coming in, the number going out, their ages and transport numbers. Of course, the real power belongs to the German High Command Headquarters. That's the building in Town Square."

"So how far is it to my mother's barracks?" Jakub quickened his steps past the guards.

"We're almost there. You won't be able to see her, since it's not visiting hours yet. But I'll show you where to go."

A few minutes later, a sprawling, three-story building with a steeply pitched roof came into view. The sign near the door read *Dresdner.*

"My mother lives in there? It looks dark and dirty."

Michael glanced up and shielded his eyes against the sun. "It used to be an infantry barracks for soldiers. No one's here now. They're at work at the mica or the box plants. You should see this place at five-thirty. The women perch in the outdoor arcades on little stools or on the banisters gossiping. There's not enough room for all of them. The only thing there is room for is lice and fleas."

Jakub wrinkled his nose.

"I can come back with you tonight if you'd like, to find your mother."

"Don't you have someone to visit?"

"Oh, uh . . ." Michael kicked a dirt clod. "They were already transported out. . . ."

They resumed walking back the direction they'd come.

"So I can come with you, if you want," Michael said again.

"Thanks, but I'm going to visit my brother tonight. He didn't look so good yesterday."

"Oh!" Michael stopped suddenly. "Did you hear? A choral group is singing in the Dresdner barracks tonight. Want to go? After you visit your brother?"

They walked by a group of elderly men huddled on a bench. The men eyed Jakub as he passed, their faces waxy and gray. Open sores and scabs covered their heads, and their threadbare clothes hung like blankets draped over gaunt bodies. Jakub thought of his own grandfather, so round and happy until his last moments. A sickening feeling traveled through his limbs.

"Uh, what did you say about singing? I missed it."

"A choral group is singing tonight. The performances are always fantastic. I could go early and save us seats."

"Nah, I think I'll stay with Daniel as long as possible. He has no one to talk to all day."

Michael shrugged. "Suit yourself."

Nineteen

Jakub found Daniel awake when he entered the hospital. With the high arched ceilings and tall windows, the room was filled with sunshine, spilling over the beds and patients.

Daniel's pale face broke into a wide smile when he spotted his older brother. "Jakub, do you know . . . what I dreamed about . . . last night?" His speech was slow, as if he struggled with each word. His breathing was raspy as well.

"What?" Jakub moved closer to his brother and stroked his arm. It was burning to the touch. Daniel looked so frail and white. . . . *Maybe I should get a nurse.*

"Remember when we were small . . . and Grandma and Grandpa were still alive . . . and we visited Vrbatky on May Day?" Daniel's eyes lit up. "The village band played . . . folk waltzes and polkas. They had trumpets and drums and fiddles." His voice rose, then was interrupted by a wheezing spell.

Jakub stroked Daniel's back until he quieted. "Maybe you should get some rest." He brushed his brother's overgrown hair back into place.

Daniel ignored him. "Remember how they would play in front of each house for five or ten minutes, and then the master of the house would come out to give them money? They stopped at Grandpa's house, and Father took Mother in his arms. They danced." Daniel sighed.

"Yes, I remember."

Daniel's voice began to fade. "And the maypole in the square. The little tree on top with red, white, and blue ribbons dancing in the breeze." Daniel's eyes blinked slowly, and he smiled. "I've waited all day so I could tell you."

"Thank you, Daniel. I'd forgotten about that—"

"Do you still have the music?" Mother's voice came from behind Jakub, interrupting them.

Jakub turned and wrapped his arms around his mother's neck. She squeezed with one arm, placing a kiss on his forehead.

"The music," Mother repeated. "You didn't lose it, did you, Daniel?" Mother leaned over the bed to place a kiss on his cheek.

"No, of course not. It's under my mattress."

"Well, perhaps Jakub can play it."

Jakub eyed his mother with curiosity. Gone were the elegant blouse and skirt she'd arrived in. Instead she wore a dingy gray frock, stained and faded as if it had spent too many days in the fields—the red flowers in the print had completely worn off in several places.

"Play? On what?" Daniel asked.

Mother pulled a violin from behind her back. "It's not much. Nothing like what you had at home, but Jakub can make music with it."

"How did you get it? I mean, who would give up a violin?" Daniel's chest rose and fell with raspy breaths.

"The violin belonged to my roommate's husband, who died a few weeks ago. She had no use of it, so I struck a bargain."

"A trade?" Jakub asked. Then suddenly he knew. He glanced at the frock, and his heart warmed. He stood and placed another kiss upon his mother's cheek.

Mother waved her hand in the air as if it were no concern. "Jakub, here. Play for your brother."

Jakub stepped backward, nearly tripping over Daniel's bed. "No. I—I can't."

"Yes, you can. We didn't get you all those lessons for nothing."

Daniel attempted to sit up on his elbows, then slumped back onto the straw mattress.

Jakub reluctantly took the violin. "But it's such a hard piece, Daniel. I could never play it as well as you."

Mother slid her hand between the straw mattress and the planks. She pulled out the music and unfolded it, spreading it like a blanket over Daniel's thin legs. "Try it, Jakub. . . ."

Jakub took a deep breath and lifted the violin to his

left shoulder. He leaned over to study the notes, then he connected the bow to the strings. A note rang out, and all clamor in the room faded. Jakub's heart pounded as his fingers fumbled over the strings. He tried his best, but the bow seemed to move with a mind of its own, and the result was a jumble of discordant notes not at all pleasing to the ear.

Jakub's shoulders sank. When he looked to his mother, he was surprised to see that she wore a smile. And Daniel's face glowed as if illuminated by an inner light source.

"It wasn't very good," Jakub muttered.

"It was perfect." Daniel wearily shut his heavy eyes. "Play again, Jakub, one more time. Please."

🍃   🍃   🍃

The next evening, as soon as visiting hours began, Jakub hurried to Daniel's bedside with the violin. If anything could make Daniel get better, it was music. He'd play every night until they kicked him out—and Daniel's eyes would brighten as they had the night before.

Jakub drew near Daniel's bed, but his brother didn't wake. His breathing was shallow and uneven. Jakub sank to the ground beside the bed and closed his eyes. He imagined they were back at home in Prague, and Daniel was peacefully sleeping on the feather bed they once shared.

"Daniel," he whispered, "if you wake up and get

better, I'll play your song for you again. Or we could play hide-and-seek. There are all kinds of places to hide around here—coal bins, up in the tall trees, behind the gazebo in the park."

Daniel did not respond.

Jakub lifted his fingers and combed them through his brother's grimy hair. Daniel had always been with him. A pest at times, but mostly a playmate, a treasured friend. He couldn't imagine life without his brother's silly grin, his squealing laugh, his kind heart. He looked at Daniel through a blur of tears. *I wish Mother were here.*

Lately work had increased in the mica plant, and the women were forced to labor late into the night. Last night when he saw her, her fingers were raw from peeling apart the mica. Still he wished her arms were around him now. He couldn't deal with this alone.

Or Father.

The thought of seeing him again seemed so unlikely. It had been so long without word. . . .

Why did the Nazis have to do this—tear apart our family?

"Please wake up, Daniel. Please. I need you. I can't face this place alone." Jakub's shoulders shook, and he pressed his face to his brother's soft cheek, breathing in his scent. "Please, Daniel."

Around him other patients stirred, their coughs and moans creating a heaviness in the morbid ward. The nurses were mechanically making their rounds for the night. One glanced in their direction, then looked

241

quickly away, shaking her head. He could see it in her eyes. Daniel was dying.

Jakub pulled the folded music from his pocket and spread it over Daniel's legs. He lifted the violin from where he had rested it on the floor, then wiped his tears with the back of his hand. "I'll play. Would you like that? I'll play your song over and over."

Jakub lifted the violin and played. He didn't consider the bow or his fingers on the fingerboard. He thought only of Daniel. His earliest memory was of sitting with his brother in the old bathtub. He couldn't remember a day in their home when he hadn't fallen asleep with Daniel's breathing in his ear. He'd felt proud to watch his younger brother onstage. Yet like all brothers, there were days when he'd wished that Daniel weren't around. Wished *he* were the special one.

Why did I wish that? I need my little brother. I don't know life without him.

Jakub's shoulders shook.

When the song was finished, he began again. After the third time through, racking sobs overwhelmed him and he could play no more. He wiped his face with his sleeve and looked at his brother.

Daniel lay motionless, the smallest hint of a smile on his face.

No. Jakub sank to his knees beside the bed. The thin shirt covering Daniel's chest neither rose nor fell. His brother, his closest friend, was gone.

242

Twenty

Fire in the middle of the parade grounds illuminated the dark night. Twenty young men had lined up in a long row, waiting to face the fire—proving to themselves and the crowd they were indeed worthy to wear the uniform of Nazi Youth. Swastika flags fluttered in the breeze as if to the tempo of the crowd's clapping.

Otto joined the group of fifty or sixty Nazi loyalists and soldiers who cheered the young boys on.

"Here they go!" one soldier shouted.

The first in the line, a lean, handsome blond boy, dashed full speed and stretched out his body, leaping over the bonfire. He cleared it only by inches, causing the crowd of soldiers and citizens to roar with excitement. The next youth followed.

Otto laughed with the rest and applauded the boys' agility and strength.

He hadn't been back in Vienna long. After days and nights of restless anxiety—and thoughts of Berlin that swirled around in his head—he was grateful for a chance to enjoy himself.

The midsummer celebration was the perfect way to do it—the day when the sun's power was at its height. This new holiday was promoted to bring Austria back to Germanic ways. Otto took in a deep breath, reveling in the scent of burning wood and evergreens.

He scanned the crowd and noted the wreaths held by chosen soldiers. The circles of greenery were dedicated to party martyrs and war heroes. As soon as the youth were finished, and before the fire speech, the wreaths would be thrown into the flames. It was a representation of complete sacrifice given to the Nazi party—and their beloved Führer.

Otto watched one boy who stood out amongst the rest. He was tall, strong, the perfect Nazi Youth, yet his eyes never rose from the ground for more than a few seconds. Otto watched closer as the boy leaped and landed with a stumble. The crowd gasped as he nearly fell back into the fire. *If only he realized that strength begins in the mind,* Otto thought.

Your search is for such a boy.

Otto didn't know where the voice came from. At first he tried to ignore it, yet as he continued to look into the fire, a new surge of strength forced him to straighten his weary shoulders. Somehow Otto knew he ought to listen.

When the crowd moved closer to the flames in preparation for the tossing of the wreaths, Otto searched for the tall boy. He found him standing off to the side, watching his group of friends tussle and play in the darkness.

Otto marched over with a salute. "Hello there, young man."

The boy straightened and saluted in return. "Heil Hitler!"

"Heil Hitler," Otto echoed.

Now that he had the boy's attention, Otto didn't know what to say. The voice spoke in his mind again. *Your search is for such a boy.*

Such a boy? he wondered. *Not this boy?* Otto frowned. It made no sense. Why did he need a boy at all?

Otto cleared his throat. "Tell me, son, have you been in the Nazi Youth long?"

"For as long as I can remember, sir."

"Do you enjoy it?"

"Yes, sir!"

Otto could see in his firelit gaze that this was not the truth. "Thank you, that is all." He turned to walk away. Then he paused and looked back into the boy's face. "What is your name?"

"Jacob. Jacob Sterner. Heil Hitler!"

"Jacob, indeed," Otto muttered striding from the group. *Your search is for such a boy,* Otto reminded himself.

245

Jakub heard the sheep before he saw them. He turned and watched them ramble down the same road he'd traveled what seemed like a lifetime ago.

He had been working as a shepherd for over a week, and he didn't mind at all. His duty was to keep track of a small flock—which meant lying in the pastures under a bright summer sun.

During these days, Jakub had studied the landscape a hundred times. Barbed wire twisted through the meadows and blue hills, and animal sheds now contained people, due to an overflow in the ghetto. At least counting the curls of barbed wire kept his mind busy. When he wasn't counting, though, Jakub thought about life—how it was and how it would be.

The day after Daniel died, he and his mother had stood by the small pine coffin in the courtyard of the Dresdner barracks. His mother had wailed uncontrollably, but he only stood silent. That bothered him now as he thought of it. Why hadn't he cried?

Former neighbors who heard of Daniel's passing came from all corners of the ghetto to pay their respects. Many of them shared stories of hearing Daniel onstage —the youngest musician ever accepted to the Prague Philharmonic. A genius. A prodigy. What a waste!

Jakub thought of his father. Was he even alive? If he

was, hearing of Daniel's death would perhaps be more than his father could handle. Jakub again thought of the look on his father's face when he'd watch Daniel play onstage. He thought of his father's wide grin to hear the applause for the youngest son.

But to Jakub, Daniel was so much more than a gifted violinist. He was a warm body to cuddle back-to-back with on a cold night, a best friend to whisper stories with and share jokes. Losing Daniel was like losing half of himself.

Even though Jakub's new friends had only met Daniel once, Michael and Yuri attended the funeral as well. Michael drew a picture of Daniel, and Jakub was amazed by the likeness, especially coming from someone who barely knew his brother. Afterward, Yuri fastened the picture to the underside of the top bunk for Jakub to look at any time he wished.

The bleating grew louder as a larger flock of sheep moved down the small lane. Jakub's charges added to the noise.

Emaus, a boy older and far thinner than Jakub, hunkered down at Jakub's side.

"Know where those sheep came from?"

Jakub shook his head. He hadn't a clue, nor did he care.

"Lidice. Word is that the Nazis wiped it out. Could be the town is only rubble now. Or just the people were killed. Wouldn't put it past the SS to do either."

"But why would the Nazis do that—wipe out a whole village?"

"I heard some stupid freedom fighter from the town helped the guys who killed Heydrich. But who knows? They don't need an excuse for half the stuff they do."

Emaus stood and sauntered back toward his own flock. One small lamb trailed the others, a scrawny thing with a singed rump. It bleated with more strength than it appeared to possess.

Jakub's heart went out to the little guy, most likely torn from his family. He wondered if the lamb would someday be made into a nice meal for a bad German. Jakub sighed and stretched back in the grass once more. At least for today, the lamb lived. The Nazis believed the lamb was of value, so it would be taken care of.

If only that could have been said about the poor people in Lidice. About all of us.

ρ   ρ   ρ

CAMP CARLISLE, PENNSYLVANIA
JULY 29, 1942

Nick strode across the parade grounds, thankful for the cool summer evening. He stood in the grassy center and thought of the many soldiers who'd marched this circular route before they were shipped out. In less than a week it would be his turn.

Around him in all directions, Camp Carlisle shimmered with lights and voices carrying through the darkness. But Nick's favorite spot was here, alone under the stars, where he could think about Evie. She was somewhere out there. . . .

He dug both hands into his trouser pockets and rubbed his fingers on the smooth metal covers of two small Bibles—one in each hand. The kid at the supply store had claimed the metal on the cover was strong enough to deflect a bullet, but Nick didn't care about that. He knew the words inside were his true salvation.

Nick had seen less and less of Twitch lately. After the first few weeks of training, Twitch had been selected to become a frontline medic, while Nick continued to study for surgical medicine. But tonight he'd make an effort to give him this gift.

"Gee whiz, they're putting me out there with all the action," Twitch had said with a laugh, fastening the metal helmet on his head and the Red Cross band on his left arm. "Just what I want—to be bandaging up wounds while bullets are flying, and with a perfect white target on my arm!"

Twitch's words troubled Nick for days. That's when he discovered the Bibles. He caressed the cover again. He'd even marked some of his favorite verses for Twitch. One replayed in his mind. *Wait on the Lord; be of good courage, and he shall strengthen thine heart; wait, I say, on the Lord.* It was a truth Twitch needed to hear.

Well, it's now or never. Nick headed back to the barracks where he waited for his friend to arrive.

Twitch walked in thirty minutes later, laughter spilling from deep in his gut. "Oh, man, you missed it!

Cary Grant was at his peak tonight. You should have seen him; he played this—" Twitch looked at Nick and paused. "Hey, what's going on?"

Nick cocked one eyebrow. "Nothing. Why do you ask?"

"Because you look so serious." Twitch unbuttoned his uniform shirt and slid it off. He rubbed a hand over his white T-shirt.

"Do I? Uh, actually, I just wanted to give you a small gift. I picked something up for you at the supply store." Nick slid the Bible from his pocket and handed it to Twitch.

"A metal cover. Neat." He flipped through the pages. "Looks like it's been used."

"No, I did that." Nick sighed. "I underlined some of my favorite passages."

"Thanks. I'll take a look at that." Twitch tossed the Bible onto his bunk, then plopped down to untie his shoes. "Oh, by the way . . ."

He stood again and pulled a couple letters from his pocket. "I forgot to give you these yesterday." He tossed them to Nick. "One from home. And one from a pretty blonde we know so well. I don't know why she bothers to write. She just lives across town, and you see her, or should I say ignore her, every Sunday."

Nick glanced at the return addresses. Barbara Green was written neatly in the corner of one envelope. "Nah, she's not here. I think I heard she's visiting her grandparents for the summer." He opened his footlocker and slid it inside, unopened, next to three others from

Barbara—and next to the dozen or so he'd written to Evie.

Looks like I need to send another batch of letters for Evie to my mom for safekeeping.

The second letter was from his mother.

"I thought we weren't allowed to pick up each other's mail anymore." Nick slid his finger under the flap.

Twitch shrugged. "What can I say? They like me."

Nick pulled out the folded piece of his mother's stationery. As he did, a yellowed newspaper clipping fluttered to the floor.

Dear Nick,

An old friend—who used to work for Mr. Kreig at the embassy—brought this clipping to us. It took so long getting to New York because it had to be routed through friends in Switzerland. The former embassy official translated it for us. I tried to call. Said it was an emergency, but since it wasn't information about an immediate family member, they wouldn't allow me through. Nick, sweetheart, Evie is dead. It seems a gestapo agent murdered her.

Needless to say, there are no words to describe our sorrow. We had a small ceremony at church to pay our last respects—many of us knew Evie and loved her so. It was a beautiful service. And while we don't understand what happened . . .

Nick tossed the stationery to the bed, his heart pounding. He grabbed the newspaper clipping, picking out Evie's name in the first line of German text. But he couldn't read the rest. And he didn't know if he wanted to.

"No." Nick placed a hand to his chest, wanting to make the pain stop.

"Hey, man, what's going on? You're all white."

Nick handed the letter to Twitch.

Twitch's eyes widened as he read. "This can't be—"

Nick snatched the letter back. "Can you leave me alone for a while? I—"

Twitch moved to the door, his eyes searching Nick's face. "Anything, man. I understand."

When the door shut behind Twitch, Nick reread his mother's letter. *Killed by a gestapo agent?*

His breath came in small gasps. *This has to be some type of mistake.*

Nick grasped the newsprint and folded it until it was only a small square in his hands. Then he sank to his knees.

℞   ℞   ℞

USS WAKEFIELD,
SOMEWHERE IN THE ATLANTIC
AUGUST 2, 1942

Dear Evie,

I don't know if I can't believe it, or don't want to believe it, but I find myself still writing to you. This can't be happening. I've lost you once; my heart can't take losing you forever.

I'm writing from the bow of the USS Wakefield taking me across the Atlantic. Nine months ago we were together. We were happy, and now you're gone and I'm heading into battle. What did I do to deserve this?

All those months without you I'd often think, "Train hard, do your best, and the army will send you closer to her." I just can't comprehend that you're not there.

My parents, my sisters, all the kids met me at the harbor. We were allowed a couple of hours together before loading up. You should see how little Linda has grown—remember

Sorry. I had to leave this letter for a while and come back to it. I feel ill, and I don't think it's simple seasickness. Our bunks are stacked four high, and I've found one near the top. Away from curious eyes, muffled by the engine sounds from those bunked near me. People say that men shouldn't cry. I guess they've never lost someone like you.

Forever in love with you,
Nick

☙   ☙   ☙

GRINZING, AUSTRIA
SEPTEMBER 17, 1942

Evie panted as she followed Sascha up the tall hill. It was her first time out of the restaurant. Though her arms were strong from the peeling of what seemed like a million potatoes, her legs felt ready to give out. But she had begged Felix to let her journey with Sascha during his delivery.

"Just a few more meters," Sascha called over his shoulder. His foot slipped on a rock, then he righted himself. "We're almost there."

Evie committed the rest of her energy to carrying herself over the final rise. Then she collapsed onto a layer of red and golden leaves—the first of the season to carpet the ground with bright hues of color.

She lay back and stared into the treetops. The sky was overcast, and a slight mist hovered above the rolling meadows. She took in a deep breath of the Vienna woods, inhaling the earthy, fresh scents.

She placed one hand in her overall pocket, and with the other she pushed a strand of blonde shoulder-length hair from her cheek. "For someone who's been dead for three months, my legs sure ache."

Evie could see that Sascha didn't consider her joke funny.

"We were engaged, you know." He plucked a leaf from the ground and crushed it in his fist, then let the breeze sweep away the powdery pieces.

"Engaged?" Evie sat up and leaned against a moss-covered rock.

"Ilse and I. We found each other late in life, but last Christmas I proposed, and she accepted."

Evie felt the deep, familiar ache surface in her chest. Soft raindrops erupted from the sky. Evie wiped the wetness from her face, unsure which were tears and which were raindrops.

"Sascha, I'm so sorry. I had no idea. It is painful losing a great love." Nick's face flashed into her mind as it did a hundred times a day.

Sascha removed his rain-splattered glasses and wiped them on his damp shirt. "She talked about you often. She'd joke and say she raised you well—taught you to think of others, to care."

Evie opened her mouth to speak, but words failed her.

Sascha stood. "We'd better hurry, before it gets too dark. We still have to make it back tonight."

Evie followed. She stumbled, overwhelmed by bittersweet memories. Memories of Ilse. Thoughts of Thomas and Isak playing with her in woods similar to these.

Just when Evie was sure she couldn't take another step, Sascha motioned for her to stop, then blew through his fingers, mimicking a bird's whistle. A similar whistle was returned. Sascha smiled and moved forward.

"Now that we're almost there, can you tell me what this whole thing is about?"

"You'll see soon enough." Sascha trudged toward a cluster of boulders.

"Sascha!" A boy no older than four or five scurried from behind the nearest boulder and wrapped his small arms around Sascha's legs.

"Abram!" Sascha hoisted the boy into his arms. A man and woman climbed out from behind the boulders. Dirt caked their too-large clothes. The woman's short hair jaggedly framed her face, as if she'd grown tired of it and cut it off without the assistance of a mirror.

"Ishar and Rebecca, meet Theresa."

Even after all these months, Evie was not used to her new name. Though she answered to it at the restaurant, it usually took the others two or three attempts to get her attention. Evie stretched out her hand to the couple, who offered their filthy hands in return.

"Is your home near here?" Evie's eyes scanned the trees, looking for some type of shelter.

Abram laughed. "No, Theresa. Our home *is* here." The small boy grabbed Evie's hand and led her around the boulders. The rocks formed a natural outcropping where a small cave had been burrowed.

Evie forced her brightest voice. "What a great adventure." She smiled at the child.

Rebecca's voice attempted to be cheerful. "Sascha hopes to get us a home soon. Perhaps a barn or a basement for the winter. I tell myself it won't be too long."

Evie thought of her own warm spot back at the restaurant. She had cried herself to sleep a dozen times as she remembered her soft bed at her parents' home. Now she felt ashamed.

She held out her hand to the boy. "Come, Abram. I helped Sascha pack some food. I'm sure you're hungry."

Twenty-One

Twitch read his letter aloud as he and Nick crossed their large encampment, mud sucking down their boots with each step.

Dear Dad and Mom,

No doubt you'd like to know what I've been up to and where I've been, but, sorry, can't tell you. You probably guessed we crossed the Atlantic Ocean in September. I'd love to describe the ship (we didn't swim), my first time sailing on the ocean, the insane schedule we kept—again, can't. What I can tell you is I didn't get seasick, we only ate two meals a day, and those sleeping quarters were really crowded—imagine how nasty a roomful of sweaty soldiers smells, whew! Guess I shouldn't complain, as I was pretty ripe myself.

Our camp is a typical small army camp in England. Mom, you'd love the countryside. Reminds me of something from those old books you're always reading. There's cattle grazing in the pastures, and the gentle rolling hills are scattered with trees, stone houses, and fences. The only thing really wrong with this place is that it lives up to its damp reputation. It rains for a while so you throw on your poncho, then it stops and the sun shines for a few minutes so you take it off, then it starts all over again. And it's cold here even on the few clear days. So far I've only seen one castle, but the old Roman bridges and rock work are neat. Guess we're not here for sightseeing. It's a shame, though.

So far we've got plenty of cigarettes, but candy is scarce and my sweet tooth is aching! If you wouldn't mind sending a scarf and candy in the first order, that'd be great. Later on, I may want lined leather driving gloves and handkerchiefs.

That's all for now, cheerio, pip-pip, and God save the King.

Love,
Frank

Nick pulled his collar tight around his neck. "That's good, Twitch. Only one thing you forgot—tell them how the kids follow us around, saying, 'Got any goom, choom?' until we finally hand over a stick of Wrigley's."

"Oh, that's good. I'll add it as a P.S. And maybe I'll let them know about the thatched roofs, fish and chips, and mild and bitters too." Twitch leaned in closer as they trudged along. "I think I forgot to tell you, but I wrote Mom and Dad and told them about Evie. They said they were very sorry. After all my letters they feel like you're one of theirs too."

"Tell them thanks." Nick kept his eyes focused ahead. "Tell them that means a lot."

They moved past their quarters, which were nothing more than half a corrugated tin cylinder laid on the ground with a door at each end and rough planks laid down for the floor. Finally they entered the camp "church"—a tent set up at the far end. Soldiers sat packed together on long benches. Nick scanned the faces of his friends, spotting many more than had ever attended church in the States. The reason was clear: they were sailing for North Africa in the morning.

After three months of waiting in England, their division would be involved in the first invasion in the East. Nick was now part of the 48th Surgical Hospital, and his detachment consisted of six officers, six nurses, and twenty enlisted medics. They'd be joining the 26th Regimental Combat Team, 1st Division, which was set to hit the beaches east of Oran, in North Africa. Nick had wanted to travel the opposite direction, toward Austria, but at least they were doing *something*.

They soon were to be invading the French in Morocco. Word was that the U.S. and British hoped no shots would be fired. After all, the Allies were attempting to protect the area from German invasion. But not many soldiers, or medical staff, had their hopes up. This morning's gathering was proof. And it didn't help that they'd be crossing German-infested waters where approximately two hundred Allied vessels were being sunk each month.

Nick scanned the faces of the stoic soldiers. Scores of fearful, barely of-age men stared intently as the young, squinty-eyed chaplain read from Psalm 91.

"He that dwelleth in the secret place of the most High shall abide under the shadow of the Almighty. I will say of the Lord, He is my refuge and my fortress: my God; in him will I trust."

Nick couldn't help but smile to himself as Twitch pulled out the metal-covered Bible and read along.

The chaplain preached a simple sermon and finished by encouraging the young men. "You may not know what will happen tomorrow, my friends, or the next day after that. But you can know what awaits you in the hereafter. Trust Jesus, men. He will never leave your side."

The chaplain led them in a time of prayer, during which Nick prayed diligently for his comrades—especially Twitch. *Please, Lord, don't let Twitch die without knowing You. Keep him safe.*

After the amen, the chaplain scanned the crowd until his eyes met Nick's. "Which song, Fletcher?"

"God Be with You 'Til We Meet Again." Nick looked at each of the faces once more, wondering who in this tent he'd not meet on this earth again. Their voices rose in unison.

God be with you 'til we meet again,
Keep love's banner floating o'er you,
Smite death's threat'ning wave before you:
God be with you 'til we meet again.

℔   ℔   ℔

48TH SURGICAL HOSPITAL
NOVEMBER 10, 1942

Dear Evie,

Blood. Death. The cries of the injured. Too many voices calling for me, needing my help. I've heard it said that you can't understand war until you've lived it. And though I now understand it, it's too hard to explain.

I wish I knew that you'd someday get these letters. Maybe I'm crazy still writing to you like this. I guess I'm just not ready to let go. Can't I still pretend you're out there somewhere, thinking of me?

Your ol' Nick is now part of history. Our medical unit was on hand during America's first offensive in Europe. I wish I could say that it was an invasion of France or Belgium—or someplace closer to Austria.

Since this letter will never be mailed, I suppose it's okay to write that we've invaded North Africa during "Operation Torch." It all started with the code "Play Ball." After that, millions of leaflets were dropped over Casablanca, which is occupied by the French, and the other landing sites. "The immediate purpose of the invasion," explained the leaflet, "is to protect French North Africa against the menace of an Italo-German invasion."

It wasn't a typical invasion. Under the cover of darkness, the huge fleet crept close enough to let out the landing craft. We were hoping that the French defenders in Morocco and Algeria would welcome us as friends. It was not to be. Since Hitler now controls France, we discovered later that he'd given a ultimatum to the commander of the French in North Africa: resist or he would attack Vichy.

For me the war began when I climbed over the side of a ship off the coast and down an iron ladder into small assault boats. Each boat carried five nurses, three medical officers, and twenty enlisted men. We carried full packs, mussette bags, and gas masks as we waded ashore near the coastal town of Arzew. Tens of thousands of troops huddled behind sand dunes as sporadic French Resistance took potshots at anything that moved.

One of the worst things was that medics were as much targets as the soldiers. Even though we were unarmed and wore a Red Cross brassard, we were shot at. Later when the French POWs were interrogated, they swore that the single brassard worn on the left arm wasn't always visible. I plan to put one on my right arm too. Maybe I'll even paint a red cross on my helmet.

We first took shelter in some abandoned beach houses. Late into the night we moved to an abandoned civilian hospital. Casualties poured in. There was no electricity or running water. The only medical supplies were those we packed in.

I've watched operations performed hundreds of times. I always thought my first encounter would be in a sterile, well-lit hospital with an experienced surgeon by my side. Instead I performed my first operations that night with inadequate supplies and lit by flashlights held by the nurses—or anyone else I could grab. Blood pooled around those lying on the floor—since there weren't enough beds. If this wasn't bad enough, the sniper fire continued, and we had to steer clear of doors and windows.

Despite the lack of supplies and the continuous fighting, most of the injured survived. I can honestly say that I felt God's hand upon me as I worked. I can't count the number of operations I performed in those two days. The nurses were amazing. Now, two days later, the supplies have come. But it's too late for some.

The wounded are still coming in. And the guns are still firing. Who knows how many lives will be lost over this piece of soil? I'm sure it will be thousands.

I haven't heard from Twitch yet, and I hope he made it. He's up the coast, nearer to Algiers. The *goal of this operation was to get a foothold into French Morocco on the Atlantic, in order to secure bases for continued and intensified air, ground, and sea operations. I would say, my darling, that our foot is in the door. I only wish it meant I were one step closer to you.*

Love forever,
Nick

༄   ༄   ༄

TEREZÍN, CZECHOSLOVAKIA
NOVEMBER 23, 1942

Jakub held his ticket, towel, and soap sliver in his hand. He had worked exceedingly hard all week long on his studies and was rewarded by Addie with a trip to *Vrchlabí*—the main bathhouse. He entered and handed his ticket to the man by the door.

The man checked Jakub's head and body for lice before letting him pass. "No lice, no sores. All clear, get in."

Jakub turned the knob and lifted his face to the clean water flowing over him. It was barely warm, yet it felt good to scrub the dirt from his hair and skin. He rubbed the sliver of soap over his body and smiled. Mama would be delighted to see him clean.

He thought of home and how she used to inspect him and Daniel after their baths to ensure they hadn't missed a spot. *Daniel.* He hardly had a childhood memory that didn't involve his brother, and he struggled between trying to remember those innocent times and trying to forget in order to ease the pain.

Mostly in the past few months, Jakub worked to become accustomed to the ebb and flow of Terezín. He visited his mother nearly every evening, and he found it odd. The worse things became, the better his mother seemed to act. The madness she'd shown in Prague was only a memory.

One night he joined her, and they listened to a lecture on art, another time they joined in a sing-along of Czech songs. Sometimes they visited the small *Ghettozentralbücherei*—the Ghetto Central Library, which had recently opened. Michael and Yuri often tagged along too, Yuri because he was tired of visiting sick relatives, and Michael because he had no relatives to visit.

"Time's up," the ticket man called.

Jakub shut off the knob and quickly toweled himself off with a handkerchief-sized rag, then pulled on his same dirty clothes. His pants, at least three inches too short, exposed his bony ankles, and his shirt collar sported a dark brown ring of dirt and body oil he couldn't wash out.

As he journeyed back to Home 1, Jakub hurried past the blockhouses filled with German Jews. His mother had told him about the people inside, suffering from dysentery, lying on top of one another on urine-soaked mattresses. They couldn't remove the dead fast enough, so the half alive squeezed together with corpses.

The cold air nipped at Jakub's cheeks and filtered through his thin shirt. He increased his pace to a jog and noticed two boys ahead from Home 5, the other home for boys his age. Home 1, Jakub's group, focused on education. But Home 5 was better known for their patriotic songs and practice of Boy Scout theology.

He waved at the two boys in the plaza. Between them swung a stretcher carrying a dead body. Jakub slowed, yet still hopped from foot to foot to keep the warmth moving through his limbs.

"I'm sorry; is it a family member?" Jakub asked the boys, blowing in his hands.

The boy with curly hair shrugged his shoulders. "Nah. We saw two old men struggling with this poor chap, so we offered to help."

Jakub nodded. "Your good deed for the day?"

"Yup." The other boy laughed as they hurried on. "More points to add to our badge!"

Jakub continued on. "Good for you!" he called, trying to ignore the fixed-eyed gaze of the body on the stretcher. He had gotten use to some things here, but not everything. No matter how many times he witnessed it, death caused a deep ache in his gut, a sweating on his brow, every time.

☙   ☙   ☙

The next morning, Addie's voice called out through their room. "Rise and shine, gentlemen. Rise and shine!"

"Not yet," Pavel called out.

"Please, just ten more minutes?" Jan added in. "Can't we sleep until 6:10?"

"Boys, no arguments, please. I haven't put up the day's latrine detail yet, and surely you'd rather not have your name on *that* list."

Boys staggered from their bunks. Jakub glanced at the drawing of Daniel posted above his head, then joined them. He headed to the washroom to clean up under a dribble of cold water.

Every weekday stuck to the same morning schedule: clean up the beds, corridors, lavatories, and the court-yard, followed by breakfast, roll call, and work detail. The evenings were spent studying lessons around the long table in the Home—illegally, of course. As some worked, others watched out for ghetto guards who randomly in-spected the barracks and children's homes in search of banned items such as books, cigarettes, or hot plates.

For work duty, each had a job in the ghetto. Now that snow had fallen, Jakub no longer ventured into the fields with his sheep. Instead, he'd been given the envi-able job of working in the kitchen, where he was able to sneak bits of food throughout the day.

After making his bed—smoothing and tucking in his one thin blanket—Jakub read the work detail posted on the chalkboard. It was his day to clean the courtyard, which meant hazarding out into the cold.

Securing his thin shirt to the top button, he scurried outside. Across the courtyard, a piece of torn newspa-per fluttered in the cold breeze. Jakub ran to fetch it. He reached for the paper as it rustled at his feet, but it scooted ahead of him into the street. Jakub ran after it and nearly bumped into an old man walking past, whistling a tune.

Jakub paused and tilted his head. "Beethoven's Razumovsky Quartet!" he called to the man.

The man stopped and looked Jakub over from top to bottom. "Boy, how do you know such a thing?"

Jakub felt heat rising to his cheeks. "My father, sir, loved Beethoven. I've been to many concerts." He felt his throat thicken. "And my—my brother used to play at the National Theater in Prague."

"Really now?" The old gentleman stepped forward, adjusting his glasses. "So tell me, what is your brother's name?"

"Daniel. Daniel Hanauer, sir." A cold wind struck Jakub's face, and he pulled his arms tight against him, newspaper in hand.

"Ah." The old man nodded. "I've heard of him. A young master." The old man puffed out his chest. "I am a former member of the Berlin Philharmonic myself." He wore a heavy coat and seemed unaffected by the cold wind. "Tell me, son. Do you also play the violin?"

Jakub didn't know how to answer. He shrugged. "A little."

"Do you have an instrument?"

"It is old and beat-up."

"It will do. We need a violin for our simple orchestra. Our last violinist was shipped off. Do you know where the Hannover barracks are?"

Jakub nodded.

"Meet us tonight in the attic. Seven o'clock sharp. We are practicing for Smetana's opera, *The Bartered Bride*." The man turned and continued his whistling before Jakub had a chance to say no.

Jakub turned and hurried up the steps to Home 1, regretting that he ever struck up a conversation with the elderly gentleman.

♪   ♪   ♪

That evening Jakub was headed out the door, violin in hand, when Michael rushed into the room. The small boy's ears and nose were bright red from the cold.

"There is a large transport leaving to the East. I've heard maybe as soon as tomorrow."

Jakub's knees grew weak. He retraced his steps, sitting down at the long table next to his friends. Every week two transports arrived from Prague, but they departed only every few weeks. When word came that a transport was leaving, everyone wondered if his turn had come.

"What does that mean?" he asked Michael. "I mean, where is 'the East'?"

"I'm sure it's just rumors," Pavel called, refusing to move from his place on the bunk.

"No, it's not." Michael shook his fist in the air. "I heard it with my own ears. Some say it's going to Birkenau. Others say Třinec. But either way they're leaving."

At just that moment, Addie walked into the room, hat in hand. His face was pinched, and though their leader was young, he stooped and hobbled like a sixty-year-old man.

"Boys, I'm just back from Leitung. I've read the transport list, and it's sad news. There are quite a few boys from Home 5 going. There are also a few from our room."

Jakub looked around. They all gazed at each other, wondering whose names would be read.

In his hand Addie held four pink slips listing the boys' names and transport numbers with time of departure. "Jan, Zdeněk, Erik, Yuri," Addie read solemnly. "I'm sorry. You leave tomorrow."

Jakub looked to Yuri, everyone's favorite.

The young boy shrugged his shoulders and attempted to smile. "We'll be okay. We'll be fine. You'll see."

Michael stood up, breaking the silence. "Come on. Let's not just sit here. We all know what to do. We must pack for them before lights out."

Suddenly, a strong sense of solidarity emerged amongst the group. The four boys rose, and the others gathered around them as if they were honored guests. For the next few minutes, the boys from Home 1 worked feverishly to help their friends in any way possible. Being caught up in the spirit, Jakub rushed to his bunk and took out some of his most prized possessions. Taking them into his hands, he moved to Yuri's bunk.

"Here are some extra socks. I was saving them, but I have a feeling you'll need them more. They were knitted by my grandmother and used to belong to my father."

Yuri paused from rolling up his bedroll. His arms

stretched around Jakub, and the roll unraveled itself.

"Thanks. I'll use them every day!" Yuri grinned and held his treasure high. "Guys, look what Jakub gave me!"

Heads bobbed up and down in acknowledgment.

Addie slumped onto the bed and combed his fingers through his thinning hair. "Looks like we're done. What about one more story?" He tried to sound cheerful. "What do you say? In honor of our friends here. Who will begin?"

Jan told of a time he fell beneath the ice while skating. Even though the room was now warm from the heat of dozens of boys, Jakub shivered under his thin blanket. Michael went next, then more boys followed. Each one told of a time before Terezín. They shared boyish tales that did not involve transports, lists, or lines for daily soup.

As the night wore on, Jakub couldn't keep his eyes open. He fell asleep to the sound of Yuri's voice in his ears as his friend wove a fantastic tale about St. George and the dragon coming back to life in Prague and joining their forces to conquer the Nazis.

☙   ☙   ☙

Jakub struggled to distinguish shapes in the darkness, wondering what had awakened him. He listened closely. A rat scratched in the corner of the room. No, that wasn't it. There was a new, different sound.

He heard it again—like the bleating of a young

271

lamb. Jakub realized it came from a bunk across the room. It was not a lamb, of course, but a boy.

In the empty darkness, Jakub knew the sobs came from Yuri. His friend would soon be taken from all he knew and loved—again. *What awaits him? Will he be okay?*

Some said the boys were going to work camps. Jakub doubted that; there also were hundreds of old people and small children leaving in this group.

Others whispered "death camps" when those destined for transport were out of earshot. Tomorrow, as soon as morning dawned, one thousand souls would travel to an unknown fate. Jakub wondered how soon it would be his fate too.

He pressed his face into the pillow, letting it muffle his sobs and soak up his tears. He cried for Yuri. And he cried knowing that one day his turn might come.

Twenty-Two

Otto hurried through his flat toward the small black trunk in the corner of his bedroom. For the past few weeks he'd been working in the music conservatory with Viktor, studying and categorizing the musical instruments that flooded in from all areas of the German stronghold. The tedious work bothered him. Years ago Grandfather Akeman had coddled each instrument, praising its uniqueness, like a schoolteacher rejoicing over the variety and differences of his students.

Otto, on the other hand, saw the violin as a means to an end. He would find a special piece, choosing her as carefully as he would someday choose a wife. And she would be his passport to rising out of this world of normality. She would usher him into the notoriety and power that courted him in his dreams.

A bloodred sunset filtered through the window as Otto sank to the floor in front of the trunk. Last night's dream refused to rest, even during the day. As he'd outwardly studied the new crop of instruments harvested from the Budapest Jews, images and phrases of his SS training had flashed through his mind.

In Otto's dream, he'd been transported back as a student in the academy at Dachau. But instead of participating in the typical physical tests and feats, he had been locked inside the classroom and asked to read through stacks of SS books, pamphlets, and teaching texts.

In his sleep he'd read about the seven levels of human evolution, the mystery of the blood, and the soul of the Aryan race. And he'd felt strengthened, realizing anew his part of a holy, secret, and powerful force. Awake, he longed for more.

He lifted the lid of the trunk and sifted through its contents. He pulled out Nazi banners, party lapel pins, and other memorabilia he'd collected since his training. Then, at the bottom of the trunk, he found what he was looking for—a book by Hoerbiger, pamphlets, and copies of the magazine *The Key to World Events*.

Otto lifted one of the pamphlets from the stack, "Why the Aryan Law?" and thumbed through it. Then he spotted a book that each graduate had received as a gift for his children, present or future—*The Poisonous Mushroom*. Otto read the first page. "Just as it is often hard to tell a toadstool from an edible mushroom, so too it is often very hard to recognize the Jew as a swindler and criminal."

A spurt of laughter escaped Otto's lips. Yes, he would enjoy going through these things. Like a peasant discovering nuggets of gold while preparing to claim bankruptcy, Otto knew these sacred teachings had been protected for the moment he needed them most.

⁊   ⁊   ⁊

TEREZÍN, CZECHOSLOVAKIA
DECEMBER 8, 1942

"Things look hopeful," Jakub's mother told him as she parted his hair and brushed it back from his face with a broken comb. "The transports to Poland have stopped. And did you see? There's a new café open in the main square." She sighed. "There is no food to purchase, of course, but it's a great place to socialize and listen to music. Daniel would have loved hanging out there with other musicians. Your father, too, for that matter."

Jakub nodded and hunched down for her, so she could finish combing his hair. He had grown in the six months since they had come to Terezín, and he now stretched taller than his mother. Still, she fussed over him as if he were a child.

"I talked to Herr Kappel and explained to him why you didn't show up at their practice a few weeks ago." She stepped back and eyed her work. "They've already given out the parts for *The Bartered Bride*, but he said they will be practicing for a new opera soon." She pinched his cheek. "Go and do your best."

275

Jakub held his violin case to his chest. Slowly he trudged across their garrison town and entered the men's barracks. He looked into one of the rooms as he passed and noticed it had the same type of bunks as in Home 1, only here more beds were packed into the room, with twice as many bodies spread over them and across the floor. Thin men, pale and weather-beaten from a hard day's work, ate from their tins, slept, or talked. One laughed and told how he'd found himself chewing on his shirt collar in his sleep, dreaming about eating a tough steak.

Jakub continued on, climbing up three flights of stairs. The nearer he got to the top of the building, the louder the music grew. When he reached the top story, he discovered a mass of bodies stretched across the floor, listening to the music. They parted like a miniature Red Sea, and Jakub walked through, pausing before the door. He recognized the upbeat tune but couldn't remember the composer. Taking a deep breath, he pushed the door open.

The music faded away, and the conductor left his orchestra standing in their places—they had no chairs. He hurried to Jakub's side, stroking his weedy mustache. He patted Jakub's back and grinned. "So it's true, a famous young musician is in our presence. Good to have you. Please come with me. I'm Oldrich."

"No, no, you don't understand. The famous one, that was my brother. I'm *Jakub* Hanauer, not Daniel."

The conductor turned back. "So do you play then? Hmm?"

"A little."

Oldrich threw his hands into the air. "Oh, so you are modest, are you? Come, come, let us play!" Pulling Jakub by the arm, he led him to a music stand made of bent wire attached to a broken chair. "Here will be your spot. Our violinist was taken on the last transport. We are in desperate need. Since we do not have a complete orchestra, everyone fills in where they can. Before he left, our violinist revised the score to fit our needs."

Jakub glanced toward the music stand and saw that a staff had been drawn around the edges of a Nazi propaganda flyer. A picture of Hitler smiling was printed in the center of the "sheet music."

"This is your music. Begin when ready." Oldrich moved to his spot. "The others will join in on my cue."

Jakub pulled the violin from its case. He lifted the instrument to his shoulder and took his time tuning it. Then, holding the bow with shaky fingers, he attempted to focus on the notes before him. The shapes blurred before him. He blew out a deep breath.

The man beside him coughed, and then the room was silent once more. Jakub's heart pounded, and he couldn't catch his breath. He played the first note. Then the page before him faded to shades of gray, and before Jakub could catch himself, his legs sank beneath him.

♪   ♪   ♪

It was a horrible day. Evie had dreaded its coming for weeks. Just one year before, she'd had the perfect life—an apartment with her parents in New York, a wonderful church, and a boyfriend who loved her. *Why, God? What did I do to cause this to happen?*

As she worked in the restaurant kitchen, helping dish up the food, Evie replayed the day Nick had proposed. They'd seen a show and later walked to The Danube restaurant where—

"Theresa, you're getting behind." Korina's voice cut through Evie's thoughts. "Can you hand me those plates? The restaurant's hopping tonight."

Theresa! My name is not Theresa, Evie wanted to shout. Instead she took two plates from the chef, added a dollop of potatoes to each one, and handed them to Korina. The other woman turned and hurried back into the restaurant—the noise of the dinner crowd waxed and waned as the door opened and shut. The disturbed thoughts in Evie's mind also grew louder, then quieter, as she worked.

While wine had run out in many parts of Austria, it still flowed here in the Grinzing area, a ten-minute drive from Vienna—especially after this year's yield. Because of that, the cooks and waitresses had hardly been able to keep up.

At least she was useful in her new position. When Korina returned a few minutes later, Evie met her gaze.

"Would you like me to clear some tables? I imagine you could use some help out there."

Korina bit her lip, resting her hands on her hips. "Well, there are two in the back that desperately need to be done." She pointed at Evie. "Hurry in, hurry out, and keep your head down the whole time. Felix would kill me if he knew I was letting you do this."

Evie nodded and replaced her soiled apron with a fresh one. She brushed her short blonde hair closer to her face, then hustled into the busy restaurant.

A soft haze of cigarette smoke hung in the air. Men's and women's laughter circled around her, and the closeness of the crowd was nearly intoxicating. In her old life, Evie had sat through a hundred dinners in restaurants such as these, but now she wished to have just one more—to be able to sit and laugh and dine.

Working quickly to clear the two tables, she lowered her head and moved toward the kitchen door. Suddenly a loud crash sounded behind her, followed by a screech. Evie looked back to see Korina's hand lifted in the air, blood dripping down her arm. Without thinking, Evie grabbed a cloth napkin and rushed to Korina's side. She wrapped her hand, then squatted down to scoop up the broken glass.

"Careful, you don't want to cut yourself," a woman whispered to her.

Evie knew that voice.

She lifted her head automatically, and stared directly into the face of her mother. Mother tilted her head and gave Evie a knowing smile, then quickly looked away.

Evie lowered her gaze and continued picking up pieces of glass. Why didn't her mother say anything, do anything?

Mother leaned toward Evie's father, blocking his view of Evie. Her voice rose above the volume in the room. "Did I tell you I asked the gardener to clean up the backyard and prepare everything for winter? I just hate this time of year, don't you, when the last leaves fall and we have to wait until spring to see new life bloom again? I'm worried about Isak. Since he has his new place, we never see him. It's too quiet around the house, don't you agree?"

"Anja, please," her father's voice cut in. "You're babbling like a madwoman. Is something wrong?"

"No, nothing. It must be the wine. Everything is great. Perfect."

Evie picked up the last of the broken glass and hurried back to the kitchen. She dumped the pieces into the trash, then placed her hand over her pounding heart.

"Theresa, did you cut yourself too? Your face is pale."

"No, I, um, I'm fine. Actually, I do need some fresh air. I'll be outside." Evie hurried out the back door. She planted her feet and willed herself not to go back in there. More than anything she longed to throw herself into her parents' arms. Or hoped that they would follow her out. Her mother had seen her. *Why wasn't she surprised? Why doesn't she come to me now?*

God, why is this happening? What I want most of all will bring harm to those I love. I don't know what to do. . . .

Twenty-Three

Evie waited a full week before bringing up the subject of her mother with Felix. He'd been angry with her—and angrier with Korina for letting it happen. Without a moment's notice, he whisked Evie away, taking her deeper into the countryside. She was now staying with an elderly farmer and his wife near Baden bei Wien, a small town on the edge of the *Wienerwald*—the Vienna Woods. Evie shared a secret room under their barn with an old printing press.

But before being moved, Evie had again taken on a new look. Her new cherry-red hair barely brushed her jawline. Though short, the color was so outrageous she usually tucked it under a scarf like the one she'd seen on American posters of Rosie the Riveter.

"Are you sure your mother recognized you?" Felix asked.

Evie stopped turning the hand crank on the printing press and rolled her eyes. "Please, it was my mother. Anyone else, maybe not, but her, yes."

"And she didn't look shocked?" Though he attempted anger, Felix's dark eyes hinted more of concern.

Evie resumed pumping, moving the handle round and round. Her voice rose above the din. "That was the strange part. Even though she seemed surprised to see me, she didn't appear surprised that I was alive. How could she have known?"

Felix took a stack of sheets from the table and began to fold them. "There are people in Vienna who know, of course. Trusted sources. But they would never tell. Too much would be risked. Perhaps your mother's heart told her you were not really dead. Maybe since she never viewed your body, she secretly hoped you lived."

Felix brushed a strand of hair from his eyes, leaving an ink streak just over his fuzzy eyebrows. He too had taken a new look, shaving his beard and allowing his brown hair to grow longer in the front like a schoolboy's. Evie had been surprised to discover that he was quite handsome under the beard. In fact, he reminded her of a young Clark Gable, only with a Viennese accent.

Evie diverted her eyes back to her work. *Fellow Fighters in the Resistance!* she read over and over as the pages were fed through the press.

Felix broke the silence. "It's a strange reaction, that's for sure."

"And then Mother started babbling about the garden, and about Isak no longer being at home. My father could tell something was wrong. We all know my mother too well."

"Maybe she was trying to send a secret message."

"My mother? I don't think so."

"Well, I'm pretty sure that I understand what her comment of Isak being gone meant. She wants you to visit her. She was letting you know that it's safe."

The printing press stopped. Evie sought out Felix's eyes. "Would it be possible?"

He was silent for a moment, then he cleared his throat. "If there were something that would be of redeeming value to our cause, it could be considered."

"Like more money for weapons or ration cards?" Evie bit her lip, hopeful.

Felix stood and grabbed a flour sack. He placed a small stack of flyers in the bag, then covered them with flour. He repeated the process until the bag was full, then leaned it against the wall. It was Evie's job to use her new sewing skills to stitch the sacks closed.

Felix turned to her, brushing his hair from his face. "I'm still not sure of the risk. The house is probably being watched. If someone did go, it wouldn't be you."

He sat back in his chair. "Forget what I said. Just because she didn't give you away at the restaurant doesn't mean she can be trusted. People like to believe they're brave, believe they'd do anything to protect their family members. But there are only a rare few who can hold their tongues when they are put to the test."

He shook his head. "No, we'd better not. Not unless you can decipher a possible hidden meaning behind her words—and we feel what she can offer is worth the risk."

Evie turned her mother's words over in her mind as her arm spun the crank. If the comment about Isak was meant to let her know it was safe to visit, what did the garden have to do with anything? *Garden . . . flowers . . . benches . . . angel.*

"I've got it!" Evie stopped the press. "I know what Mother was talking about!"

❧   ❧   ❧

TEREZÍN, CZECHOSLOVAKIA
DECEMBER 18, 1942

Jakub didn't like his new job in the ghetto nearly as much as he'd liked scrubbing pots in the kitchen. Since winter had fully hit their garrison town, more and more people died each day from dysentery, exposure, and starvation. His new job was pushing the funeral cart, stopping at each of the barracks and waiting for the leaders to bring out their dead.

There was only one good thing about this job—the heat from the crematorium. Four ovens worked day and night to incinerate the bodies. Anyone within fifty meters had the warmest spot in the frozen city.

Jakub pushed the loaded funeral cart through the snow to the door, leaving it for the crematorium workers to worry about. He glanced at the clock in the church's baroque tower, checking how much time he had before reporting back for duty. Ten minutes to get warm.

With quick steps, he hurried past the ghetto cop who waited outside the door. *I don't know what he's guarding,* Jakub thought. *He doesn't have to worry about people escaping.* The *Ordnerwache* looked intimidating with his heavy winter coat, wide belt, dark breeches, and heavy boots. Especially frightening were his truncheon and the badge that swung from his chest. He said nothing as Jakub opened the door and stepped into the warmth of the building.

Jakub never went into the room where the ovens worked but remained in the small foyer. He moved to the corner and pressed his chilled body against the brick wall, his skin awakening with the warmth.

The roar of oven fires seeped through the walls. More than once Jakub found himself nodding off. After his body was fully warmed, he rose to make another round. He could imagine Michael's complaints when he finally hurried to afternoon lessons.

"You've been sleeping with the ashes, haven't you?" his friend would always say. Though Jakub went away from this building warm, he also carried with him the lingering scent of burnt flesh.

ᴿ   ᴿ   ᴿ

That night Michael said nothing of the foul odor that permeated Jakub's clothes and hair. He ran to Jakub, his blue eyes wide with excitement.

"Tonight's the night! I talked to Addie. Come help me get everything ready."

A few hours later, every boy was gathered around the long table.

Michael rose. "We've been discussing starting our own secret government. And since our favorite teacher, Professor Emers, has endeared to us the book *The Republic of Shkid*, we have agreed to call our organization by the same name. If you don't mind, I'd like to read an address for this occasion."

Cheers of "Hear, hear" rose from the group.

"Home 1's own flag has been raised, the symbol of our future and our communal life," Michael began.

Jakub was enthralled, as were the other boys. Michael went on to speak about their unwillingness to remain an accidental group of boys without a purpose. Their new *raison d'être*, Michael explained, would be to create a well-ordered society, together with voluntary discipline and mutual trust.

Michael put down his prepared sheet and spoke the last sentence from his heart. "Torn from our people by this terrible evil, we shall not allow our hearts to be hardened by hatred and anger, but today and forever, our highest aim shall be love of our fellow men, and contempt for racial, religious, and national strife!"

Cheers erupted from the group, and Jakub felt his

heart fill with hope. While what they envisioned could never replace what was lost, it was a start.

"Now, who has contributions for this week's edition of *Vedem*?" Michael asked.

The magazine of Home 1, *Vedem,* wasn't actually printed and distributed. Rather it was a collection of stories and poems they wrote and read out loud each week. When they were finished with their readings, Michael collected the pages. He had even designed a cover for their "magazine," which consisted of a Jules Verne spaceship and a star that represented their future.

This was only the third week they'd gathered to read their contributions. It was also the first time Jakub had lifted his hand to read his work out loud.

"The title of this piece is 'Secrets.' The author is Anonymous." Jakub looked to his story with a smile. The other boys quietly waited. Jakub felt his heart pound but began:

> *Many people think I'm quiet. What they don't realize is I'm just careful. Too often I'm afraid to open my mouth because I don't want to reveal a secret I've been sworn to keep. What horror to say something to the wrong person at the wrong time!*
>
> *For example, Addie's coal-stealing expeditions after dark. Do all the boys know about this? Or do they believe the coal simply appears when it's needed most? And if they don't know, what is the reason? What else is Addie, our fearless adult leader, trying to hide? Doesn't anyone else have a secret*

about our beloved bunk commander they'd like to share? Anonymous is open to receiving equally anonymous letters.

Laughter erupted from the group.

Or what about Aaron's interest in the older girls he meets at the park? There are too many lovely ladies to name. Am I the only one with the observation that he's begun shaving on a regular basis, despite the fact he must do so with a dull blade?

A moan tore from Aaron's mouth, followed by more laughter from the group.

Also, do we truly believe that lights-out at 10:00 P.M. means we go to sleep? Who are we trying to keep our late-night story times a secret from?

And finally, there is one secret that I've promised to myself never to divulge—no matter who tries to pry it from me. But since this is only an article, written by an anonymous writer, I guess I'll share it now.

The secret is this . . . although I miss my old life terribly . . . although I cannot get the thought of delicious meals around a family table off my mind, and although I'd give anything to have my father back . . . and my brother . . . I'm secretly glad I've been put here with this group of boys. There are many worse places I could be—a concentration camp, for example. We have a secret strength that lifts me when I am weak. Who else but these new brothers could make me laugh when all I want to do is cry?

So if you see me sitting quietly, this is why. I have secrets I'm trying to keep. Secrets I may just whisper in my sleep if anyone happens to be listening past curfew!

Laughter flowed from the group again, along with applause and pats on the back from those closest to Jakub. A few more boys read contributions that ranged from childhood memories to patriotic poems, jokes, and silly rhymes. They concluded by singing their own anthem, which Jakub had helped Michael write. They sang to the tune of the workers' song "Like a Tempest 'Round the World."

> *What joy is ours after the strife,*
> *In Number One we've made our bid.*
> *Self-government has come to life,*
> *Long live the Republic of Shkid.*
>
> *Every person is our brother,*
> *Whether a Christian or a Jew,*
> *Proudly we are marching forward.*
> *The Republic of Shkid is me and you.*

꙰   ꙰   ꙰

Dear Mom and Dad,

    After two months, I've finally received the package you sent. The candy and extra socks were very much appreciated. I also received a letter from my friend Twitch, who is a few hundred miles away doing the same work as me. I can't really say much about where I'm at, except that I'm somewhere in North Africa. I hope you've received the letter I've previously sent and know that I'm doing fairly well. I won't lie and tell you that my heart isn't still broken into a million pieces because of Evie.

    I've struck up some friendships with a few nurses. They're real troupers, and since we've been working in our field hospital, they've really come through for our country. Someone said that this is the closest women have worked to the front lines in any American war, and I believe it. Our hospital is bivouacked on a damp hillside, and we're the first help for those injured on the front lines. The ground rumbles beneath us most of the day as we stabilize the patients and move them back to the clearing station. From there, the troops receive additional care, and the ones needing serious attention are shipped even farther back.

    If the earth-jarring explosions aren't bad enough, the terrific outbursts of antiaircraft fire put my pounding heart at full alert. It means that Jerry planes are overhead, and as I work I quietly pray they don't mistake our hospital for an ammunition dump.

Yet things have quieted the last few days. Christmas Eve wasn't very spiritual, but it was festive. I'm in a small town now for a few days' rest. It's fairly warm, and palm trees bend and flex in the breeze. The hills around us are white, not from snow but from the small, whitewashed houses that cover the hillsides.

We will be having a Christmas dinner tonight, and everyone's trying to spiffy up for it. We washed our uniforms the best we could and gave each other haircuts. One of the signalmen picked up a BBC broadcast of Bing Crosby singing "White Christmas," and that really brightened our day. It helps to know that all of you were gathered together, and we were celebrating the birth of Christ together in our hearts despite the miles.

Continue to lift me in prayer until the good Lord grants me the opportunity to celebrate a happy return.

Sending all my love,
Nick

Twenty-Four

TUNIS, NORTH AFRICA
MAY 20, 1943

The past six months had been a blur. The injured, the sick, the thousands of land mines left by the Germans that cost lives daily, the desolate waste that war brought to North Africa. And now he was leaving it all behind.

Just last week, the French who'd fought the Allied arrival now cheered the victory over the Italians and Germans on May 13. Just this morning thousands of citizens had celebrated during the official victory parade through Tunis. The 34th Infantry Division had marched down a wide road lined with swaying palms. Nick and the other medics had been happy to follow in a jeep, listening to the crowds shriek, *"Vieve l'Amerique! Vieve l'Amerique!"*

Now, with a slivered moon hanging in the sky, Nick

sighed, reached over, and flipped on the light, illuminating the hotel room. It was a tiny rectangle, hardly large enough for the bed. Though nearly midnight, the heat from the day still made the room unbearable despite the open window.

On a whim, Nick had grabbed up the letters from Barbara and flipped through them. Numbering over a dozen, they sat on the nightstand unopened. Every time he had thought about reading them, a nagging feeling wouldn't leave—no matter how often he reminded himself he wasn't betraying Evie. How could he? She was gone.

He studied the fancy script on the first envelope, then slid his finger under the flap. The letter was written on pink stationery.

> *Dear Nick,*
> *One day a waitress brings her patron a cup of coffee.*
> *Waitress: "Looks like rain."*
> *Patron: "Tastes like it too. Bring me some tea."*
> *See! I told you getting a letter from me would bring a smile to your face! Isn't coffee rationing the worst? So how are you?*

Nick laughed out loud and read the rest of the letter. Barbara shared news about her summer in Nebraska, home, church, and funny antics that her brothers and sister attempted to pull off. She ended the note with a prayer for his safety.

When he finished with that letter, he put it aside and reached for the next in the pile.

Dear Nick,

I haven't heard from you but hope you're doing fine. Here's something to make you smile:

A rookie passing the mess hall asked the head cook, "Say, what's on the menu tonight?"

"Oh, we have thousands of things to eat tonight," replied the cook.

"What are they?"

"Beans!"

Nick laughed again, then abruptly stopped, hoping he hadn't awakened his neighbors. He closed his eyes and leaned back on the bed, trying to remember the feel of Barbara's hand in his when she prayed for him. *She has a pretty face and a kind heart.*

Nick reached for another letter and scolded himself for not reading them sooner. He looked around the room, spying the hotel stationery and pen on a small desk in the corner. Who knew? Maybe he would even write one in return. Tell her he would be back in a few weeks—back to take the role as the veteran of the front lines, teaching the new recruits just what they could expect in this bloody war. Perhaps Barbara would be the key to getting over his pained heart.

℞   ℞   ℞

Evie skirted the predawn streets of the quaint resort town, wondering if today she would hear from Sascha. He had left over a week ago to visit the garden behind her parents' home. It had taken nearly six months for Evie to talk someone into checking to see if her hunch was correct.

"When I was little—before I began to rebel about wearing dresses and attending social teas—my mother and I had a secret game of hiding messages for each other in an angel statue in the garden," she had hurriedly explained to Felix. "Perhaps that was what my mother meant. Maybe I, or someone else, could check?"

"The gestapo controls every movement in and out of Vienna," Felix complained. "Would it be worth risking a person's life for the remote possibility that something is there?"

When Evie refused to give up, Sascha agreed to go. Felix visited Evie in Baden with the news.

"Perhaps he believes you, Theresa. Or perhaps he just wants to quiet you," Felix had said with a smirk.

That was a week ago. *Is he okay? Did he run into danger?* Evie knew that worrying wouldn't help. She glanced up at the stars and was thankful that the God who created that great expanse also watched over Sascha. She pushed thoughts of Sascha out of her mind and enjoyed this moment when night and morning tussled for position.

Over the last six months, these crisp morning hours had become her friend. While Felix refused to allow Evie to venture into Baden, home to many wealthy Austrians, she'd convinced him to let her take these walks by first light—before even the gestapo took to the streets. In Baden, it seemed, the gestapo enjoyed a good night's sleep.

Baden had always been known for its healing waters. That was one of the reasons Emperor Francis I had chosen this idyllic town for his summer residence during his reign in the 1800s. Evie found a sanctuary in the waters too.

The small roadway soon narrowed to a hiking trail. She traipsed through the familiar landmarks with only the first rays of dawn as her guide. She pushed back the low hanging branches and stepped over the muddy rocks, venturing down a footpath known only to locals. She breathed in the smell of fresh pine and damp earth and smiled. Then a new scent mingled in the air—a faint sulfur aroma that reminded her of eggs. She soon found herself at the edge of a thermal pool.

Evie slipped off her clothes, shivering in the morning chill. She let them fall to the stony ground, then stepped off a rock jutting into the heated waters. "Healing waters" is what Frau Stahl, the farmer's wife, called them. And Evie had come to believe it.

She pushed off the rock with her feet and floated through the natural, heated pool before turning to her back and lifting her face to the brightening sky. The warmth wrapped around her and reminded her of the heated towels Ilse used to prepare. Ilse would always lay the fluffy bath towels over the furnace so they would be toasty warm when Evie climbed from the tub. *Oh, Ilse.*

Evie's throat tightened at the thought of her friend. She turned and reached for the rock edge and found her favorite spot—a natural slope of the rock that made a perfect seat, like a large hand to hold her. Like God's hand. *Oh, God, why did things have to turn out this way?*

Evie trailed her fingers over the surface of the water. *Lord, I thank You for safety. For caring friends. But I miss my parents, miss Nick so much.*

She pushed her hands deeper into the warmth, then let them float back to the surface. *I know I'm always forcing my way into things. Thanks for showing me how wrong that is.* She attempted a smile. *Guess it's good to be humbled. Please help me to wait on You.*

God's voice had been hard to hear at first. The first few months underground, pretending to be someone else, were the hardest. And though she struggled with losing herself to Theresa, Evie discovered that God still spoke when she took the time to listen. God spoke through Herr Stahl, as he read from God's Word every evening. God's tenderness sang through the birds' melodies that accompanied her walks in the dark mornings and in the delicate new life that bloomed with the arrival of spring. God had also given her a gift of friendship with Sascha, Felix, and even Korina. She knew they cared for her and worked hard to keep her safe.

Evie dived under the water one last time and resurfaced at the water's edge. She reached for a rock, preparing to climb out, when the silhouette of a man startled her. She sucked in a breath, gulping down water with it.

Choking and coughing, she saw the man move toward her, as if to offer help. She motioned him to stay away. Then her eyes widened as she realized who it was.

She caught her breath and called out. "Felix, what are you doing? Trying to make me drown?" She wrapped her arms around her body, though she knew it was impossible for Felix to see her form in the darkness of the heated waters.

"I—I, uh, just came to tell you that Sascha has returned." Felix turned away. "I'm sorry. Frau Stahl told me you'd be here. I had no idea you'd be bathing. I'll wait for you on the road." He took a step forward.

"Wait!" Evie called. She stretched her hand toward him. "Sascha is back? Is he okay? Did he find anything?"

Felix turned his head slightly in her direction. "There is always trouble making it in and out of Vienna. But he's back, safe. And, yes, you were right, Theresa. There were items hidden in the angel statue. We just don't know what they mean."

          *   *   *

Evie's damp red hair hung around her face as she stared at the small package resting on the big farmhouse breakfast table.

"Did you already look inside?" She glanced at Sascha.

"Yes, but . . . well, you'll see."

Evie unwrapped the brown paper. The parcel was smaller than she'd imagined.

Moisture filled her eyes when she unwrapped three items. First, the tears came because she knew these things were meaningless to her friends. Sascha had risked his life for nothing. Second, she cried because she could not have asked for a more precious gift for herself. A gift to help her remember who she was on the inside.

"There was no note. Nothing," Sascha explained.

Evie's fingers grabbed the photo—a picture of her and Nick at their last Thanksgiving together. She was sitting on his lap as they smiled into the camera. Her fingers caressed the image of his handsome face. Her heart ached at the sight of him. Even her daily memories hadn't done him justice.

Embarrassed, she quickly wiped her eyes with the back of her hand. "This is my fian—boyfriend." She took in a breath. "He lives in America. I haven't heard from him in nearly two years."

Felix cleared his throat as he faced the back window.

Next Evie lifted the miniature Statue of Liberty and stroked it with her fingers. Finally, she unfolded a single thin sheet of paper that had been carefully torn out of her hymnal—the gift from Nick. Her eyes immediately moved to the first verse.

Gracious Spirit, dwell with me;
I myself would gracious be;
And with words that help and heal
Would Thy life in mine reveal;
And with actions bold and meek
Would for Christ my Savior speak.

Evie wiped her face again and rose from the chair. "I'm sorry. I know this is not what you were hoping for. Perhaps if we want to risk it, we can leave a note asking for money or whatever we need. . . . But I have to admit this is just what I needed most."

Evie offered Sascha a hug. "Thank you so much for doing this for me."

"You're welcome," he whispered.

She turned to Felix. "I want to thank you too. I—" She placed a hand on his arm, but when he turned, a knot formed in her throat. She wasn't the only one struggling to hold back tears. Felix lifted her hand to his lips. "If only," he whispered.

〰   〰   〰

TEREZÍN, CZECHOSLOVAKIA
OCTOBER 15, 1943

Chanukkah, New Year's, Passover, and even Rosh Hashanah had passed with their meager attempts at celebration. Yet celebrating the Jewish High Holy Days

301

with his friends had been a comfort to Jakub during the fifteen months he'd called Terezín his home.

Having been Jewish by race only, his family had taken little notice of the Holy Days. So when they gathered to celebrate First Night, Jakub's friends had patiently explained the purpose of the celebration. Rosh Hashanah, the Jewish New Year, was a time of spiritual renewal through prayer and deep personal reflection. It was a time for families and friends to make amends, ask forgiveness, and strive to make the next year better.

Since there were no women in their house, Addie, the "head of their household," lit the candles eighteen minutes before sunset, and together they said the blessings. Jakub couldn't remember all of it, but one phrase had stuck in his head. *Blessed are You, Lord our God, King of the universe, who has granted us life, sustained us, and enabled us to reach this occasion.* As he looked around, he wondered just which of them would be sustained in the year to come. . . .

Jakub's mother made no comment when he told her about the First Night ceremony. After the incident in the attic with the orchestra, they'd spent less and less time together. Even when they were together, she mostly complained of his not joining the orchestra.

After moping around for days, Jakub had told Addie about his blacking out in the attic. Other times his nervousness hadn't been so bad, simply shaking knees and a tense throat that caused him to freeze.

"It's called stage fright." Addie had looked at him

302

with compassion. "I've heard there are things you can do to get over that."

"No, thank you," Jakub had responded. "I think I'd just rather keep away from stages altogether."

"Sure, I understand," Addie had said with a pat on Jakub's shoulder.

Jakub's mother hadn't been quite as sympathetic. "You are a fine musician. You and Daniel were equal once. Don't let your fears hold you back." Then her tone grew serious. "Perhaps if they saw your value as a musician . . . things could be better for you, like extra protection."

Instead, Jakub kept the violin in the hiding place above their bunk with Michael's art supplies. He'd only brought it out when the warmer days arrived, and he'd been given the job of shepherd again. While he watched the sheep milling through the grassy fields beyond town, he played the songs he remembered from home. Addie had told them stories about a shepherd named David who had praised God with a harp. Perhaps his violin was an adequate substitute.

Jakub's pets—as he liked to refer to the lambs—didn't seem to mind when he lost his place while playing the melodies in his head. They also didn't care when he closed his eyes and pictured himself playing for Daniel.

Today Jakub left the autumn fields early and hurried to Home 1. Michael had asked him to help prepare for their weekly reading of *Vedem*. It was his favorite part of the week. At home, his parents had always tried to shelter the boys from "world events." But in Home 1, the boys speculated about whether the Americans and British would liberate France. Or if the Russians were really pushing back the Nazis.

Jakub had also learned through *Vedem* about Terezín's new Council of Elders. From the time the ghetto opened, the elders were forced to decide who would stay and who would go. Often their choices seemed completely random, as if they just pointed to names on the page. Other times they were asked by the Germans to group together young men for a work camp. After a while, the power over life and death became too much to bear, especially when the Germans' requests for one thousand souls to ship out became more frequent. So one wintry day, when the transport was short by three people, the elders, who oversaw the daily activities of Terezín, simply rose from their desks and climbed onto the train themselves. The Germans, unfazed, simply found three others to replace them.

Jakub also learned about the German surrender in Stalingrad and America's advance in Tripoli. Though sometimes the news didn't arrive until months after the event, reports like this strengthened the hearts of those who longed for an end to the war, an end to their suffering.

Jakub stamped his feet outside the door, shaking off the dirt and leaves from the fields, then entered their home. The heat from the furnace brought a smile, but he knew he wouldn't have time to warm himself. Michael ran up with his shirttails flapping and his socks bunched at his ankles like accordions.

"I have good news!" he exclaimed. "Professor Emers

is coming to hear our readings tonight. He promises to award a lump of sugar to the boys with the best contributions."

"Real sugar?" Jakub's mouth watered.

❧   ❧   ❧

That night they all eyed the small pile of sugar cubes as they sat around the table. The professor took a spot at the head of the table as their privileged guest.

Jakub looked around, appreciating the faces and personalities of his friends. Each one unique, and each with a story written on whatever paper he'd managed to find.

Michael went first, reading an investigative report he'd written about the mica plant just outside the gates of Terezín. "They call it the Glimmer Factory. The women I interviewed say they have two jobs. The first is to strip the mica core of its worthless surface layer. Second is to split the mica into thin slices. Mica is an insulating material needed for airplane production and—"

Suddenly the boy closest to the front window stood. "Visitors!" he yelled. They all moved with precision, in the manner they'd practiced dozens of times. Michael quickly darted toward his bunk and scaled to the top. Jakub grabbed the magazine articles from the other boys. He ran them to Michael, handing them up with his long arms.

With a flip of his wrist, Michael tossed the sheets into the dusty crawl space, then returned the paneling to its rightful place. By the time the guards entered, the boys were either chasing each other around the room in a game of impromptu tag or busily making the beds they had just messed up.

"Attention. All eyes up here!" At the guard's command, the commotion of the room stopped.

Addie stepped forward, feigning surprise at the guards' appearance. "May I help you, gentlemen?"

"We have a new list for transport!" The guard handed over the pink sheet, turned, and stalked out of the room. Everyone waited.

In a low voice Addie began to read. "Aaron, Artur, Samuel, Michael . . ."

Jakub couldn't focus on what Addie was saying about preparations and times of departure. The words swirled past him as he looked at his friend, still perched on the top bunk. All he saw were Michael's wide eyes.

꿈   꿈   꿈

The next day Addie took over Jakub's work so he could walk Michael to the *Schleuse*. A crowd of women, children, and old men milled round the barracks, hoping to get a last look at their sons, husbands, fathers, brothers.

Transports made no sense in Terezín. One time it would be all old people. Another time only women and children. This time it was some of the men sixteen and over—Michael's birthday had been the week before.

306

Jakub dug his hands into his pockets as he faced his friend, not knowing what to say.

Michael took on a serious tone. "You know where all the copies of the magazine are hidden. You have to keep them safe. Make the other boys keep writing."

"Are you sure you don't want to take them?"

Michael tipped his chin up. "Nah, just extra stuff to carry. I trust you, Jakub; you can do it. You're going to make it through this war."

"As are you." Jakub gave his friend's shoulder a squeeze.

"Of course I will. And after the war we'll get a house together. We'll call it Home 1 in honor of this place. I'll write books, and you'll play your violin. Our wives will make us big dinners of chicken and dumplings."

Jakub laughed. "And our kids will play hide-and-seek and never have to do chores."

Michael's eyes zeroed in on Jakub's. He put out his hand, but Jakub pulled him into a hug.

"I wouldn't have survived here without you."

"I'll miss you." Tears welled in Michael's eyes as they pulled apart. "I have to go. See you . . . soon."

For the rest of the day, Jakub hung around the *schleuse*. Men waiting to leave leaned out the windows of the large building, pushing each other aside to snag a final glance at their loved ones. Gendarmes in leather coats and green hats with tufts guarded the exits with automatic weapons.

Finally, as evening neared, the train pulled into the

station. The long group of defeated men marched out in groups of fifty, shivering and huddled together with transport numbers swinging around their necks.

They waved and said good-bye with their eyes. Some stared straight ahead, trying to be brave. Most sobbed.

Jakub returned home, his head hung low. He entered the room silently and climbed onto his bed. A lump formed in his throat as he glanced at the bunk above. Next to the pinned picture of Daniel, Michael had drawn one of himself.

To remember me, he had written in the corner.

Twenty-Five

VIENNA, AUSTRIA
NOVEMBER 18, 1943

Die Fahne ist wichtiger als der Tod.
"The banner is more important than death." Otto read the slogan aloud as he walked through the bustling streets of downtown Vienna. He studied the postcard in his hand. *Meet me. Alt Wien, November 18, 20:00 Uhr* was written under the motto in neat script.

Whoever had mailed the note to Otto's private address had known when he was due to return home from his most recent trip with the Musik Aktion team. The sender also knew his taste. *Alt Wien*, the pub on *Bächerstrasse*, happened to be one of Otto's favorites. The illustration of the buxom blonde on the postcard also appealed to his male sensibilities.

He checked his watch as he quickly strode past a dozen sidewalk cafés. Their neon signs reflected off the damp cobblestones. Evening paperboys stood on each corner calling out the latest headlines. One boy beckoned louder than the others. "Royal Air Force Drops Bombs on Berlin. Light Damage to City, Nine English Planes Lost!"

On a whim, Otto bought a paper and tucked it under his arm. He entered the small pub—eyes darting to see who watched him. SS soldiers and Brownshirts mingled with local girls. He strolled by the bar and ducked into a small side room with two booths against each wall. The room held few customers, and only one of the table's candles was lit.

Otto settled into a chair and lit a cigarette. He waited, sensing that he was being watched. He scanned the room, finally stopping on a pair of green eyes peering out of the shadowed corner booth. He needn't have worried about finding his contact.

The blonde woman in the corner took a long drag from her cigarette, then sauntered to his side, sliding onto a chair next to his. She calmly crushed her cigarette into the ashtray and turned to Otto with a sly grin. "Hello there, Herr Akeman."

Otto pressed the postcard onto the table, tracing the drawing of the blonde. "The pen-and-ink likeness doesn't do you justice."

The lady laughed as she stretched her hand toward him. Otto kissed it tenderly.

"My friend said you were a charmer." The corners of her wet lips curved upward. "He didn't let on how good-looking you were."

"Is your friend the one who arranged this meeting?" Otto asked. "Who is this friend?"

"All I can say is that he's someone you've met in the past year."

Otto's brow furrowed. "Many people fit that description."

"Yes, but I doubt any of them will offer such a proposition as I."

Otto leaned closer, breathing in her musky scent. "I'm listening."

"My friend is in the market for a violin. He's willing to make it worth your while. It must be an extraordinary piece, of course. A Stradivarius, Amati, or especially a Guarneri."

Otto straightened. "If I were ever to find such an instrument, what makes you think I'd hand it over to you? I'm an officer of the Reich, after all."

"Of course you are. But everyone can be bought for a price. Besides, I have no doubt that you've seen how the system works. Those at the top funnel what they want first. Tell me, have all your supervisors been completely loyal to the Reich?"

Otto raised an eyebrow, thinking of the violin and other items skimmed by Kametler.

The lady smiled. "I'm right, aren't I?"

"Perhaps. But how do I know you're not a plant— someone sent to try to bring me down?"

"For one thing, if I were trying to bring someone down, it would be a bigger someone than you." She clicked her fingernails against the table. "My contact needed someone with access. And someone who enjoys the finer things in life."

Otto straightened his shoulders. "Well, if I did find a violin, I'd—"

"What?" the lady interrupted. "You'd keep it for yourself? I doubt that, Herr Akeman. I think you'd try to sell it." She grazed a manicured figure along his chin. "I know your kind. You desire money and power. Plenty of both." She laughed as she let her hand drop on his. "The only problem, my dear, is you need my help."

"Really?" Otto brushed her hand away. "And just what can you offer?"

The woman leaned in close. "First, buy me a drink and kiss me. Someone might be watching. We should make this look like a meeting of pleasure rather than business, don't you think?"

Otto first indulged the kiss, then lifted a finger to summon a waiter. "Herr Ober," he called.

A waiter in a crisp white shirt and black vest hurried over.

"A bottle of your finest red for myself and the lady, please."

The lady grinned and tossed her hair over her shoulder, exposing the creamy white smoothness of her neck. "Good. I think we can begin."

🙞　　　🙞　　　🙞

Once the wine began flowing, the lady eagerly disclosed her plan. "A few years ago, I felt like an actor in a play, with Hitler the only one knowing the script," she said with a pout. "But after my journey to Tibet, things have become clearer. In a way, I feel I've discovered the path to the Scriptwriter."

"Tibet?" Otto echoed, taking a sip of his Cabernet.

She leaned closer. "'The banner is more important than death' is a common phrase in the Reich. But in my travels, I stumbled upon the powers behind the banner. My friend tells me you're interested in the Ancient powers behind the Reich too. I'm sure you've studied some of the Nazi symbols that originated in Tibet?"

"I've found numerous references in my reading." His chest began to fill with the warmth he'd come to know so well. "Tell me more about your discoveries."

"It began on the 19th of January 1939, when five members of the Waffen SS passed through the ancient arched gateway leading into the sacred city of Lhasa. They'd been commissioned by Himmler to learn more about the Tibetan ancient practices. When we arrived, we had no idea what to expect."

"We?"

"Yes, I traveled with the group as a—how shall I say it—companion to one of the men. There is just too much to explain about the Ancient customs there. Instead, I'd like to offer you access to the mystical land, a chance to discover these things for yourself. In fact, my friend is offering to fund such a trip."

"And in exchange, what does your friend ask of me?"

"He desires an exquisite violin. He will pay a high

price for the right piece. Enough to book two passages to Tibet and—"

"Two passages?"

"I'll go with you, of course."

"Go with me? I don't even know your name."

"If you will let me continue . . ." She took a sip of her wine and lit another cigarette. "Once we get to Tibet, we can live as royalty in the land where the Ancient power stems—"

Otto rose and spoke in a loud whisper. "Okay. I don't know what type of joke this is, but you're creating a fancy tale. Do you honestly believe that I would leave my post and travel to Tibet in the middle of a war?"

He slowly buttoned his jacket, lowering his voice. "How would we get there? We're talking a two-month journey through war-torn Burma and China. I'm sure I can find enough Ancient powers around here to keep me busy. In fact, I've recently read about a special sanctuary high in the German Alps, near *Garmisch-Partenkirch*. Someplace I can get to on a weekend pass. . . ."

The woman's eyes grew frantic. "Please, Herr Akeman. Give me a chance to explain." She reached up and pulled on his collar until he submitted, again sliding to her side.

"I'm not talking about now." She flicked ashes into a tray on the table. "After the war is over, when we have control of our land and that of the Ancients." She patted Otto's newspaper, her fingers tapping over the headline of the bombing on Berlin. "It also doesn't hurt to be prepared if the war turns against us. Someday it just may be necessary for us to escape."

"Or I could find such a violin and make my own plans."

The blonde took a long drag, blowing it out slowly between soft lips. "But you forget . . . I have a buyer. I also have the connections in the mystical land. Not just anyone is allowed into Lhasa. Not just anyone has access to the power of the Ancients. Think about it." She rose from the table. "I'll meet you here tomorrow. Same time, same table."

"There's only one problem." Otto stood, towering over her. "As of yet, I have only come across one such violin. How will I ever find another?"

The woman also rose, leaned forward, and pressed her lips against his. When she withdrew, she looked directly into his eyes. "I think you are a man who always gets what he wants." She stepped past him, then turned back. "By the way, you may call me Maddalena."

"Tell your friend thanks for the offer, and . . ." Otto grasped her arm forcefully. "There will be no need to wait until tomorrow. I can give you my answer now."

℞   ℞   ℞

VIENNA, AUSTRIA
DECEMBER 24, 1943

Evie's heart pounded as their car sputtered down the street. She stared at the darkened city—the first time

315

she'd laid eyes on it since being taken into hiding.

"I need your help in Vienna," Felix had said a few days earlier on a visit to Baden. "We have a cache of weapons we are unable to get to. They are hidden away. We need someone your size to get them for us."

"My size?" Evie questioned.

"Yes, one of our operatives has been killed. She was petite like you. She hid the weapons in a narrow spot. We're all too big to fit."

At first Evie had not wanted to go. The reality of patriots dying made her nervous. She'd grown comfortable living at the farmhouse with the Stahls. She lived a quiet life with early morning swims, offering meager help in Frau Stahl's kitchen. Dare she say it: she even enjoyed running the antiquated printing press, though her ink-stained fingers often ached from the work.

But finally she had given in, praying the phrase from her hymn—that her actions, *bold and meek, would for Christ her Savior speak.*

Now there was no turning back. The city streets lay quiet, as most of the Viennese citizens celebrated Christmas Eve at home with family and friends. Felix parked next to a small parish church alongside three dozen other cars.

As soon as the engine clicked off, Korina hurried from the car and moved into the sanctuary, where a Christmas Mass was being held.

"She's our lookout," Felix muttered as he and Sascha opened the trunk and pulled out empty clothes sacks and a few lengths of rope.

"You hid weapons in a church, and now you want me to break in during Mass to retrieve them?" Evie readjusted her black tunic and pulled her dark knitted cap tighter around her head. "Am I missing something?"

"Mass has just started. We have at least an hour," Felix whispered as they moved to the back of the church. "The caroling will cover our movements, and our car is perfectly camouflaged amongst the others. No one will be the wiser."

Uneasiness roiled in Evie's stomach, but she knew Felix was right. Wasn't this the kind of thing she'd been wanting to help with? Still, her hands grew clammy.

"Give us ten minutes, and we'll be on our way home." Sascha looked up at the highest point of the church—an old bell tower. "I'm following right behind you. We'll be up there and back before you know it."

Evie looked up, and through the trees she noticed a miniature window. "Up there? You've got to be kidding."

Felix tied a length of rope around her waist. Evie clawed his hand. "You're *joking,* right?"

"Listen to Sascha. We'll be done in a few minutes. We just need you to scale the tree limbs to the window. He'll be right behind you, and the end of this rope will be wrapped around my waist for safety. We just need you to climb in through the window, pass the bags of weapons to Sascha, and then climb down. It's that simple."

Evie tried to control the trembling in her knees. "You have no idea what you're asking me." She ran a finger across the scar on her jaw. "I fell out of a tree

317

once. I was with Thomas—my friend, and we were playing around. I wanted to prove I could climb higher than the boys. I succeeded but I fell."

She glanced at Felix and Sascha. Felix ran a hand down his face, attempting to keep his composure. *They've done so much; I can't let them down.* She placed her hands on her hips. "All right, I'll give it a try."

Evie reached for the lowest limb, then her head began to spin. She was sure she'd faint any moment. She felt a push from behind. She reached for the next, ignored the sinking feeling in her stomach, and . . .

Evie's head jerked, and she found herself hanging by the rope tied around her waist. She hadn't even made it to the second level of tree branches before the dizziness had overtaken her. She scurried to get back on her feet. "I'm sorry. I'll try that again. I'm sure I can do it this time."

Felix cursed, then raked his fingers through his hair. "Theresa, you blacked out barely fifteen feet off the ground."

"Really, I'll try again."

"And what, get your head split open?" Felix clenched his fist. "No, let's get out of here before we are seen."

Sascha stepped forward. "But what about the weapons?"

"Enough! Go get Korina," Felix said in a loud whisper. From inside the church, the melody of the choir could be heard lifting their voices in a heavenly refrain. "We'll figure something else out. Obviously Theresa will not be able to help us."

Twenty-Six

Jakub stood in the doorway and peered into the dusty attic that pulsated with screeching pandemonium and suffocating heat. Children of all ages spread throughout the cobwebbed room, their voices and laughter causing the floorboards to vibrate.

At his mother's urging, he had agreed to meet the director of the new children's opera. What she didn't know was that he'd left his violin back at Home 1, still tucked away in the ceiling panels over his bed.

"Children, little ones, come. Gather around Uncle Rudi, and I will tell you of Hans Krasa's opera *Brundibár,* which we will perform in Czech!" The young director with bright eyes waved them closer, bending low to pat a few heads. "Then . . . we will begin auditions!"

The obedient children settled onto the floor, a sea of black, brown, and blonde heads, peering up at Uncle Rudi.

Jakub towered over them like a giant in a room of dwarfs. He quickly crossed to the back, where adult supervisors waited.

"This is the tale of two children, Pepicek and Aninku, on a mission to buy milk for their sick mother." Uncle Rudi tousled the hair of the child closest to his feet. "As they sing to raise money for the milk, their earnings are stolen by the evil old organ-grinder, Brundibár, who is displeased by the competition."

Rudi stretched his fingers like claws and roared at the children, who laughed and screamed in delight. He righted himself and winked. "Thankfully, these children got help from a Sparrow, a Cat, and a Dog—who, of course, will be played by three of you."

Murmurs erupted as the children glanced around, wondering who would receive the coveted parts.

When the whispers settled, Rudi continued. "In the course of the opera, brother and sister are able to outwit Brundibár, reclaim their money, and finally bring the milk home to their mother. Now, children, can you tell me what this story represents?"

A dozen hands shot up. The director tapped his lips, and then pointed to a curly-headed girl in the front row.

She leaped to her feet. "That good people will win over the bad ones in the end!"

Uncle Rudi clapped his hands together. "Good, good. Now there are a lot of children here, but don't worry. Everyone will get a job. We'll need an orchestra and a children's choir—including ten soloists. Now, show me your hands. Who likes to sing?"

Hands sprang into the air.

"Great! Now who plays an instrument?"

A few hands went up. Jakub's hand remained tucked to his side.

Rudi frowned. "Hmm, it seems we may need some help from the adults."

Rudi scanned the grown-up faces in the back of the room. His eyes met Jakub's. "You, boy. Don't you play? I believe I've seen you walking through town with a violin case."

Jakub felt his throat grow tight. "Uh, no, sir. That was my brother's instrument—and he is no longer with us."

"Too bad, too bad. Having a violinist would really help us." Rudi squinted at Jakub and dropped his hands to his sides. "What about the instrument? Do you still have it? Maybe we can find someone else to play."

Jakub looked down at his feet, scuffing them on the ground. He didn't want to play, but he didn't want to get rid of his last connection with Daniel either.

"Never mind, boy." Rudi lowered his voice. "I understand. We'll figure something out, now, won't we, children?"

🎵   🎵   🎵

Jakub laughed at the volume radiating from the children, who were practicing a new song for the opera.

We won a victory
Over the tyrant mean,
Sound trumpets, beat your drums,
And show us your esteem!

We won a victory,
Since we were not fearful,
Since we were not tearful,
Because we marched along
Singing our happy song,
Bright, joyful, and cheerful.

The children's voices energized the air. They sang with heads tilted toward the sparse lights that beamed down on their makeshift stage.

On days when he wasn't tending sheep, Jakub came here to entertain the children with stories as they waited for their turn to practice. He didn't have an official role, but he supposed if he were to claim one, it would be that of encourager. More than one youngster had erupted into tears after trying out for a solo part, standing before Uncle Rudi, singing, "La, la, la," only to be disappointed.

"We *all* have our special jobs." Jakub squeezed the shoulder of a young boy who was passed over for the role of Dog. "Can you imagine what a flop it would be if the lead actors tried to perform alone—without back-up singers or a crew to help with the curtains and lights? This opera needs many players!" Jakub gave the boy a quick hug. "There, now, get back in the chorus and sing your heart out."

As he watched the boy scurry away, Jakub felt a tapping on his shoulder. He turned to find Pavel. The boy's face was red. He was arched over, hands on knees, attempting to catch a breath.

"What's wrong?" Jakub bent low to get a better look at his friend's face.

"Addie sent me. All Home 1 . . . work detail."

Jakub waited until Pavel caught his breath, then together they hurried to Home 1.

"I've heard over the Jewish *Bonkes* that a Red Cross council is coming to inspect our town," Pavel said. "Maybe that's the reason for all this fuss."

"But the rumor radio isn't always correct," Jakub said just to debate. He knew the report was most likely true. In the past few months, improvements had taken place all over the garrison town. Along the main streets, green turf, flowers, and benches had been installed. In the "café"—a favorite spot for musicians and poets—furniture, drapes, and even flower boxes had been added.

Addie was waiting on the front steps when Jakub and Pavel rounded the corner to Home 1. He jumped up. "Let's go. We have a list of jobs to get started on."

With quickened steps, Addie led them to Town

Square. "We're having visitors soon, and this place must be brought to order."

Jakub and Pavel's eyes met, and Pavel lifted his eyebrows as if to say, *I told you so*. By the time they reached Town Square, the other boys were already hard at work.

"It's about time you joined us!" Jan grabbed a wooden fence post and pried it from the ground. The three dozen other boys had spread around the perimeter of the large square and were doing the same.

"What happened to the box factory? How did they get it down so fast?" Jakub scratched his head. He usually didn't walk this way and was surprised to find bright blue sky where two huge circus tents holding a working box factory had previously stood.

"Where have you been for the last few days?" Pavel grabbed the next post. "They took it all down. They're making this a park again. I even heard they're building a music pavilion in the center."

"But what about all the workers from the factory?"

Pavel didn't answer. Instead he gave Jakub's shoulder a gentle push as he moved toward another fence post. "Are you going to work or talk all day?"

"Yeah," Jan butted in. "And I think we should make a new rule. Last one here gets digging duty!"

Jakub grabbed the next fence post in line. He pushed and pulled on it, trying to loosen the dirt around its base. "Digging duty?"

"Yup, the camp commander stopped by moments

ago. He's purchased rosebushes from Holland. Guess who gets to plant them?"

"Rosebushes?" Jakub rocked the fence post even harder. "That shouldn't be too bad."

Jan paused and placed a filthy hand on Jakub's shoulder. "Oh, did I forget to mention? There will be twelve hundred of them!"

Jakub released the post and wiped a trail of sweat that had already formed on his brow. "Twelve hundred? We don't have enough to eat, and we've been wearing the same clothes for two years." He glanced at his ragged shirt and trousers. "Ah, why am I complaining? At least we'll get to see some pretty flowers while they're in season—a bit of beauty in this drab place."

Yet Jakub knew that once the flowers were planted and the town fixed up, one obstacle remained. Buildings still packed with sickly, emaciated people would disrupt the facade. Ten thousand had already been sent away in three months' time. His guess was that more transports would be leaving soon.

Jakub didn't have to wait long to discover that his guess was right. When the boys trudged back from work that night, a visitor waited with a pile of pink slips in his hands.

The boys filed in quietly, eyes fixed on Addie as they waited for him to read the names.

Their leader cleared his throat. "Emaus, Pavel, Jakub . . ."

Jakub stood by the gate to the mica plant, waiting for his mother to arrive for work. He'd been up all night considering what to say to her. How would she handle his being shipped off? How would she handle being alone?

Thin and weary women trudged past. Jakub scanned huddled groups, but his mother wasn't with them. Had something happened? He hadn't heard from her in a few days. Was she sick?

Jakub hurried down the street, anxious to get to the Dresdner barracks. A voice called to him from down a side street and he turned. An old, sickly woman staggered toward him. *Mother?*

"Mama!" Jakub turned and ran toward her. He allowed himself to be pulled into her bony embrace. Men and women hurrying to work streamed around them.

Mother mumbled in his ear. "I was so worried. Your bunk leader said you'd left early to find me. Please don't tell me—"

Jakub stepped back and pulled his pink slip from his pocket.

A gurgled cry escaped his mother's lips. A man walking by gave them a questioning look, but Jakub ignored him.

"Don't worry, Mama. I'm probably being sent to a work camp. You'll be okay too. Things will be safer here for you."

His mother shook her head, her dingy hair swishing

around her face. "You don't understand. I was hoping you'd be the one to remain. It's bad here, but at least we know—"

Jakub touched a hand to her cheek. "Does this mean . . . you too?"

Mother looked up at him, then opened the palm of her hand to reveal a wadded-up pink slip.

Later that afternoon, as a last good-bye, Jakub visited the barracks where the children practiced. Rudi walked into the room rapidly and perched upon the stage with hands on knees. Then he jumped up again.

"My little Cat is gone," he blurted to no one in particular. "A dozen choir members are to be shipped off." He pressed his fingers to the bridge of his nose. "Now how do they expect us to perform for the delegation?"

Jakub offered a quick hug to the little ones who remained, then slipped out. There was nothing he could do to help now—even if he had enough courage to play.

Rudi's voice followed him down the stairs. "Ruth, you practiced with our Cat, no? Come, come . . ."

Later that night as Jakub climbed into bed, Rudi's words echoed through his mind. "My little Cat is gone."

He thought of the little girl with the sparkling eyes who would join their group tomorrow. The thought of her crammed into the packed boxcars with so little air hurt him even more than the thought of his own pain.

Later, after lights were out and everyone had said

their last good-byes, Jakub heard the shuffling of feet across the room. Someone was nearing his bunk. He squinted in the dark and was amazed to see that it was Addie.

Addie leaned in close. "Jakub, are you still awake?"

"Yes," Jakub whispered.

"Do you have everything you need? I know the boys gave everything they could."

"It will be fine. And I have my violin."

Addie's breath felt warm on Jakub's face. "Good, son. I'm glad you're taking it. I—I just wanted to let you know that we will miss you. You will not be forgotten." Addie patted his chest, then turned and shuffled toward the next boy on the transport list.

Jakub swallowed hard and pulled his thin blanket tighter against his chin.

How long, Jakub wondered, *will this madness continue?* The madness of numbers on a page representing thousands of individuals sent to their deaths. And the madness of those who remain—attempting to live a normal life while trying not to forget those sent ahead.

♪   ♪   ♪

BADEN BEI WIEN, AUSTRIA
MAY 12, 1944

Evie clicked off the shoe box–sized tube radio and sat amongst the piles of weapon parts stacked on the floor around the printing press.

Felix had only visited once since Christmas. He'd come the previous week to check on her and to bring her another job—separating boxes of stolen machine-gun parts into piles. The gun parts had been pilfered from armament dumps with the cooperation of Austrian soldiers who sympathized with the Resistance. Evie was the lucky one chosen to make sense of the mess.

Footsteps could be heard from the barn floor above, followed by the clucking of chickens. Frau Stahl hadn't sounded the dinner bell—their warning signal—so Evie knew it was a friend. She combed her fingers through her hair and looked up toward the hatch.

She was rewarded by dirt falling into her face.

The trapdoor scraped across the ground, and Sascha's face appeared. "Hello, there. How's my little mouse?"

"Waiting for her cheese." Evie balled her hands into fists and positioned them on her head like ears.

Sascha chuckled as he climbed down the ladder. He adjusted his glasses and scanned the room. "Looks like you've been busy."

She looked past Sascha, hoping to see Felix's face next.

"Sorry, Theresa." Sascha replaced the hatch. "He decided not to come this time. But he did ask me to bring you this."

Evie sighed, trying to hide her disappointment. Felix had been on her mind lately, his gentleness, his forgiveness for all she'd done to mess things up. He cared for her too, she knew. And sometimes when she felt especially lonely, she considered what would happen if she watered those small seeds of affection. Could they ever grow to be something beautiful, something as powerful as she had with Nick? It had been so long since she'd heard from him. Did she dare believe that he waited for her as she did for him?

Evie pushed those thoughts out of her mind and snatched a paper sack from Sascha's hand, her eyebrows twisted with curiosity. She pulled out a stack of drawings and tried to hide her disappointment.

"What are these for?" She turned the page and saw that they were sketches of guns that included step-by-step directions for assembly. A sinking feeling stirred her gut. "Don't say you expect me to put these together." She looked at the numerous piles and saw pieces ranging from wooden stocks to tiny firing mechanisms. "It's impossible—"

Sascha cut her short. "Theresa, you know things are getting desperate. If you've been listening to the German radio, I'm sure you've heard that just today the Nazis sentenced thirty-three Resistance fighters to death."

He sank down on the dirt floor. She joined him, tucking her legs under her check-printed frock.

"Well, Sascha." She looked at him through determined eyes. "Good news. When I was little, my brother let me hold his rifle, I think maybe two times. So you see, I have experience." She grinned. "But the not-so-good news is that I haven't touched one since. Still, I'll do my best. Show me what to do."

330

Sascha clasped his hands together. "That's my girl. Don't worry. I'll stay with you until you get the hang of it."

Evie reached over and lifted some type of trigger from the top of a pile. "You know, Sascha, I'm going to make some guy a good wife someday. I can mix up a batch of bread and while it's rising assemble a German-made, semiautomatic machine gun."

The fragrance of newly transplanted roses, which were just beginning to bloom, floated on a gentle spring breeze as Jakub waited in line to enter the next cattle car headed for Auschwitz. *Those stupid roses.* He knew they would be fully open, blossoming with color, when the Red Cross delegation arrived. Everything would be perfect by then—a resplendent hoax. The clean ghetto, flowers, well-fed Jews, happy children dancing and singing.

Jakub closed his eyes as he considered today's dress rehearsal—the noise, confusion, and disorder of dozens of children excited about their show. His mind skipped ahead and considered the upcoming performance before the delegation. Would little Marta, who played Mother, remember her lines? Who would they find to play Cat? Little Ruth?

A foul-smelling body shoved against Jakub, and he opened his eyes. The train whistle blew; the engines churned. A long trail of cars pulled away from the station. Jakub knew their turn was next.

Jakub's mother squeezed his hand. More gray than blonde streaked her hair. Hollow cheeks stretched in a smile. "At least we're together. You have your violin—"

"Yes, of course," Jakub said. "Perhaps they have an orchestra where we are going. Maybe it will be someplace just like this where the Nazis don't discourage the prisoners from playing."

A man shuffled by with the aid of a cane. He stumbled, and Jakub reached to steady him. The man mouthed "Thank you," but a louder voice burst through the clamor.

"Load up. Groups of fifty. Hustle, faster!" The guard jabbed the air and signaled them forward with his wooden baton.

Jakub shuffled. Bodies pressed. He hoisted himself up and reached for Mother, his fingers completely wrapping around her upper arm. Cries filled his ears from the mass of people around him. The air had already begun to thicken with the odor of unclean bodies.

"Let's try to reach a wall," he said, leading her. Jakub thought of his last trip, when he could look out through a crack and view the passing countryside. This time he'd not be so lucky. There wasn't room to move, let alone vie for position. Jakub released the violin case and the small bundle, which landed on the top of his feet—knowing they wouldn't move from that spot. When he heard the train whistle, he widened his stance in preparation for the car's jerk as it pulled away from the station.

His mother stood next to him in silence. There were

no tears, no words. Her eyes were fixed in front of her, and Jakub wondered if she too were thinking of Daniel and Father.

A lurching movement propelled the train forward, and Jakub knew that if he could see out, he'd observe a music pavilion built in just a few days with the labor of dozens of workers. He'd also see twelve hundred rose-bushes, and a playground in Stadt Park built for the remaining children.

He closed his eyes and heard the children's voices singing in his mind to the clackety-clack rhythm of the track. *We won a victory over the tyrant mean. Sound trumpets, beat your drums. And show us your esteem!*

PART THREE

For I have eaten ashes like bread,
and mingled my drink with weeping,

My days are like a shadow that declineth;
and I am withered like grass.
Psalm 102:9, 11

Twenty-Seven

Jakub's body shuddered. A bright light hit his face. He opened his eyes, expecting to see the pen-and-ink drawings of Daniel's and Michael's faces pinned on his bunk in Home 1. Instead, he realized he'd been asleep standing up when the train stopped. The doors were flung open, and whispers of "Auschwitz" filled his ears.

Though it was dark, spotlights hit them from every direction. Guards shouted through the doors. "Out! Faster. Come on. Faster!"

A surge of people thrust forward, jumping to the ground. Jakub reached for his mother's hand. She took it, clinging to him. Together they jumped onto the station platform and hurried to keep up with the others.

Jakub's throat felt dry and thick, and he'd lost all

track of time. How many days had they journeyed without food or drink? Two? Three?

His mother stopped midstep. "Your bundle and your violin!"

Jakub looked to his empty hand, then glanced back over his shoulder. Too late. His violin case had been kicked onto the pavement and trampled by dozens of feet.

Jakub's mother began to cry. He pulled her forward, speeding up, his weak legs protesting every step. Finally the movement of the crowd slowed, and they found themselves in a long line.

Prisoners in striped uniforms jerked forward toward the train, like walking dead. They began to clean out the left-behind contents and human waste in the cattle cars.

"Excuse me," a woman behind Jakub called out to one of the uniformed prisoners. "Will some of us be sent on to a different destination?"

The prisoner smiled, exhibiting broken teeth. "Sure." He pointed to the blackened sky. "Through the chimney. That's where the transports go." Then he spat disgustedly.

The man in front of Jakub turned around. "Don't worry. He's only trying to scare you. I received a post-card from my sister, and she said they have a small camp here for the families from Terezín. *Theresien-städter Familienlager,* they call it. The mothers, fathers, and children live in separate barracks, but they can spend their days together."

Jakub lifted his eyes toward the camp, but he couldn't make out anything beyond the spotlights and barbed wire. The familiar smell of burning bodies, however, sickened his stomach.

Mother squeezed Jakub's hand. "As long as we're together, it will be bearable."

Dogs barked from all directions. An SS guard in a spotless uniform glared down at them with a slanted smile. His whip slashed through the air impatiently. "Come on, you miserable Jews!"

At the head of the line, a young SS officer pointed his thumb to either the right or the left for each person who neared. Behind the officer's left side hovered mothers, old people, and children. Young men and some women waited on the right.

The man ahead of them turned around again. "See, the ones on the left are going to the family camp. The ones on the right must be going to work detail."

"Quiet, Jew!" The guard marched over and slammed his club on the man's head. "Turn around!"

Jakub winced, and Mother tried to quiet her sobs.

When it was their turn, a guard stepped between Jakub and his mother. "To the left," the SS guard shouted to Mother. He pushed Jakub to the right.

"No, wait." Jakub lunged toward his mother. "I want to stay with her."

The SS guard smiled. "Fine, go ahead." He stepped aside for Jakub to pass.

Despite the warm night air, they waited as a shivering mass. When the last group of prisoners drew near,

Jakub spotted Pavel and Emaus near the rear of the other line.

"Mother, there are my friends."

"Yes, I see them." She looked around—her eyes searching the faces of those huddled with them.

"Jakub," she whispered, "there are no other young men in our group."

Her eyes locked on his, and she reached up and caressed his face. "Please move back to the other side. You'll probably get better rations there. They always feed the workers better."

"But I can't leave—"

"Stop that." She yanked her hand away. "Will you disobey me?" She quickly wiped away a tear, then gave him a little shove. "Look, the guard isn't paying attention. Go now."

Something inside told Jakub to obey his mother's wishes, yet it tore at him to leave her. The guard turned his back. Jakub took five steps, crossing into line with his friends.

Pavel wrapped an arm around Jakub's neck.

Jakub glanced back over his shoulder and noticed his mother already shuffling ahead with her group, moving toward a half-dozen Red Cross ambulances. Yet he noticed the drivers were SS guards, in their foreboding dark uniforms.

"They are not real Red Cross," someone muttered. "The poor souls have no idea their ride ends at the ovens."

"Shut up!" another person shouted. "You lie."

Mother glanced back, gave him a small wave, then lowered her head and hurried to keep up.

≈   ≈   ≈

Jakub shivered in the chill of the morning. A week after arriving, he still couldn't get used to the horror. He'd been shaved, given a tattered, striped suit, and had a burgundy number etched on his arm.

As he walked back and forth to work, he scanned the fenced yards for any sign of his mother—without success. That didn't surprise him, since the camp was enormous. Hundreds of barracks, each covered with green tar paper, formed a long rectangular network of streets. Prisoners in striped burlap filled the barracks to overflowing. And above them all, elevated watchtowers jutted thirty feet into the air. No matter where he went, SS guards leaned against machine guns mounted on tripods—their eyes fixed on his every move. There were no secret schools, no cafés for artists to meet in this place. Only death, which stalked Jakub like a rabid wolf.

The second hour of roll call dragged on. Jakub's shoulders ached from holding the perfectly straight posture. From the corner of his eye, he glanced at Pavel's bruised cheek and puffy split lip. Pavel had dared to make eye contact with a guard. At least Jakub knew he lived. They'd not seen Emaus since he was taken away on a work detail the first day.

As they waited, a group of officers strode up and

down the aisles, looking the prisoners over as if they were heads of cattle.

"Has anyone ever assembled weapons before?"

Jakub dared not look around, but from what he could see no one raised his hand.

"Anyone?" the guard asked again.

Just then, Jakub heard a whisper in his ear.

"Raise your hand," the man behind him said.

Jakub's brow furrowed. Should he lie?

The man said it again, louder. "Raise your hand."

Jakub wondered who would dare risk his life in such a way. Maybe the man knew something he didn't. Jakub stretched his arm into the air.

Pavel turned and gawked.

An officer marched closer. "You, boy, tell me your previous experience."

Jakub paused before speaking, choosing his words carefully so as not to lie. "My father . . . he had a workshop attached to our house. He was very skilled, and I used to watch him work. I helped him sometimes too."

The guard studied Jakub's eyes, as if determining whether he told the truth. "Fine, you come with me."

"Load this boy up with the others," he called to the SS guard. "But first get him something to eat. He looks half starved."

Jakub stepped out of line and turned to thank the man. His jaw dropped. No one stood behind him.

℞   ℞   ℞

Jakub found himself in the back of another train car. Only this time it wasn't nearly as crowded. He sat and stretched his legs.

He thought about his mother. His last memory was of her climbing into the back of the Red Cross van. Had she really been taken to the family camp with the others from Terezín? Or had the other man, the one who spoke of the ovens, told the truth?

He chose to believe the former, even smiled slightly, picturing Mother reunited in the family camp with Michael and Yuri, his two best friends. He'd like to imagine them together, just like a small Terezín. *They will care for her. . . .*

And what about Father? Where was he? Did he also think of them? *God knows,* Jakub thought as the train hurled down the tracks. *He can see those I love even when I can't.* That thought brought Jakub comfort.

One man with a red, scarred cheek finished with the waste bucket, then settled next to Jakub.

"Do you really work with weapons?" The man's hands trembled as he talked. Sores covered his head.

Jakub glanced away. "No. I heard someone . . ." He paused. It would be too hard to explain something he didn't understand himself. "No, I told them only that my father had a shop that I worked in—but he actually fixed violins."

The man patted Jakub's leg and chuckled. "Well, stick with me. I used to work for a munitions factory in Brno." A cough racked the man's body. "I was the supervisor. My wife and I had a large villa on the hill."

Jakub turned back to the man, and seeing his oozing sores made his own skin crawl. "I don't understand. Why do they need people to assemble weapons? Are we being sent to a factory?"

"You don't know? We're going to Mauthausen, in Austria. It's a work camp. One of the most brutal."

Jakub moaned. "What have I got myself into?"

"There are factories in underground tunnels. After the defeat in Stalingrad, the Reich needs more arms." The man's breathing was labored. "I . . . need rest." He curled up on the filthy straw.

The train rocked. Jakub's mind wavered with worry. *What am I doing, leaving Mama, Pavel, possibly others in the family camp?* His chest began to ache.

Jakub looked at the man. "I'll take you up on your offer. I'll do what I can to learn."

The man's eyes opened slightly, but he didn't answer.

"Sir?" Jakub shook him slightly, but there was no response.

Twenty-Eight

Otto stretched out on the sofa, his head resting on Maddalena's lap. She had become a familiar presence, visiting him each night when he returned home from work.

"Anything interesting happen today?" She placed a kiss on his forehead.

"If you're asking whether I found a priceless violin, the answer is no. Don't you think I'd tell you if I did?"

Maddalena gave Otto a fake pout.

"But we still have instruments coming in from Hungary," he quickly added. "There were some nice pieces from Budapest, but nothing worth packing up our things and heading out of town for."

Otto stood, strode across the room, and poured whiskey into a small shot glass. "Of course, my boss,

Viktor, will be out of town for a while—this would be the perfect time to smuggle out a piece or two." Otto scoffed, "The fool has the insane idea of checking out the various 'orchestras' in the concentration camps."

He poured a second shot and carried it to Maddalena. Her red-tipped fingers took it from him.

"You can't be serious. I had no idea there were such things!"

Otto took a sip. "Many of the Jewish musicians have been allowed to take their instruments into the camps. Some were even allowed to write home and have their pieces sent in. Viktor believes valuable pieces may be inside. Can you imagine? Priceless instruments played by imprisoned vermin?"

Maddalena joined in his laughter. He settled down by her side, and she nestled her head on his shoulder. Otto breathed in her scent, but instead of peace settling over him, a question stirred in his mind. He stroked her long, blonde hair. "Darling, may I ask you something?"

She sat up and looked into his eyes. "Of course. What is it?"

"When will you tell me who your contact is?"

Frustration flashed in her eyes. "We've been over this. I think it would be better for both of us if I didn't say."

"For both of us?" Otto smirked. "I doubt that. Besides . . . what if we don't find an instrument? I mean— you've let your intentions be known from that first day."

Maddalena put down her glass and grasped his

hand. "Otto, do you really think, after all this time, that a violin is all I'm interested in?"

She kicked off her red leather pumps and slid her silken legs across his lap. "True, that's how it all began. I may have started as a messenger, but I've ended up falling for *you*." She ran a hand down his jawline. "I plan on sticking around, Otto. The violin will just be a bonus." She planted a kiss on his cheek, then caressed his temples with her fingertips.

"Mmm," Otto whispered. "You know exactly what I like."

"Yes. I also know that you love to hear stories about my journey to Tibet. Now close your eyes, and I'll tell you about our first night in the Buddhist temple."

Instead, Otto studied Maddalena's face. A pain shot through the pit of his stomach. He knew why she acted so tenderly, and it wasn't love. He could see it in her eyes.

He only wished he knew what it was she feared.

ꝛ　　　　ꝛ　　　　ꝛ

KZ MAUTHAUSEN, AUSTRIA
MAY 22, 1944

The train clanked to a stop, letting out a long hiss of steam. The wheels had barely stopped rolling when the bolts were unfastened and the doors flung open. Dozens of SS waited with huge, snarling dogs.

"*Raus! Raus!* Out!"

Jakub joined the others, running the gauntlet through the blows from the guards and bites of the German shepherds. He finally reached the station platform.

"*Angetreten!* Line up into groups of five!"

Jakub obeyed quickly. A dog snapped its sharp fangs at his heels with every step.

The other prisoners staggered from the train car and lined up behind him, crying out from under a flailing of bludgeons.

"Join arms; head out!"

Arms linked together, they marched from the station toward the village. Jakub dared to lift his eyes and scour the homes as he passed. The town of Mauthausen appeared as a larger-than-life garden terrace with quaint houses and storefronts sprouting from the mountain.

The marching stopped. "We will cross the village. Anyone who stops will be shot!"

They wearily traversed through the still town. A church steeple rose on the left, another on the right. Jakub scanned the small grocery and post office. No one walked on the streets. His eyes searched the windows for any sign of humanity.

Then he saw her—a young, blonde woman staring out as a mute witness. Jakub noticed tears on her cheeks, and he felt a lump in his throat at this sign of sympathy. The woman's eyes met Jakub's. She shook her head, then stepped out of view.

The road forked, and the guards picked up the pace. Jakub raised his eyes to the tall hill before him. He felt weak, and he prayed he'd be able to make it up the rough path to the camp.

"We have three kilometers to go," one guard called out. "Anyone who tries to escape will be eaten alive by the dogs!"

"*Jetzt komm mit uns!* Now you come with us! *Los! Schnell!*" A second SS guard yelled, pointing his whip up the mountain.

The bedraggled men in tattered uniforms surged up the path. The guards walked on higher ground on either side, raining blows on the unfortunate souls who struggled along the edges. Behind them, dogs continued to bay. They bounded at those who lingered, snapping and snarling.

Soon their frantic group had broken from fives into groups of twos, with weaker prisoners falling behind. They reached a turn, and then Jakub saw it—the granite walls of a massive fortress. He panted heavily, fear gripping his chest. At the top of the hill, the beasts of prey herded their frightened flock into the garage yard. A large granite staircase rose to the main camp—an ascent into the gates of hell.

"Undress! Undress!"

Jakub obeyed swiftly, his wide eyes darting from the high sentry walks to the machine guns trained upon him. When they at last stood, a naked, shivering mass, furious guards clubbed them up the steps through wood-and-iron gates.

"*Rechts gehen!* Go to the right. To the wall!"

Jakub ran and pressed himself against a wall lined with iron ring. His tears trailed down the stone.

ꝑ   ꝑ   ꝑ

Jakub was awakened with a shove, and his mind reeled as he attempted to remember why his body ached. *Mauthausen.* Terror of the work camp had preceded this place, but the rumors paled in comparison to reality.

After standing at the "Wall of Lamentations" for hours, his group had been shoved down more narrow steps into a small, sparse washroom where the *Friseur* shaved them with a notched scalpel.

They moved to the next room, and when he read *Duschen* on the door, Jakub knew the end had come. Yet, instead of deadly gas bubbling from the showerheads, water sprayed down, alternating from scalding to freezing.

One prisoner, a man about Addie's age, scorched by the hot water, jumped out of the way with a cry, only to be beaten over the skull with a guard's cudgel.

"This belonged to a fellow Jew," said an SS guard as he threw a filthy uniform at Jakub's wet body. "He committed suicide on the wire. We advise all Jews to do the same. Saves us the hassle of dealing with them!" He laughed.

And that had only been the first day. What would day two hold?

Before he received a second shove, Jakub struggled

to stand. There had been no bunks to sleep on, only pallets on the ground. Jakub's ankle twisted in his shoes, which consisted of nothing more than strips of canvas nailed to wooden soles. They weren't even the same size.

"You'll be in Block 18, the quarantine unit," the *gruppen* leader growled. "In a few days you will be taken to the quarry to carry stones. The average life span of a quarry worker is six weeks. Those are the lucky ones. Follow the rules, and you will live longer. Disobey, and you will be considered ripe for the crematorium."

Quarry? What about the weapons assembly? Jakub didn't dare question the leader. He hugged his arms tight around his shrunken stomach and realized he'd made a horrible mistake. Six weeks. That's all that remains? *If I last that long.*

His shoes clopped with the others as they followed their fearsome guide. Jakub's eyes focused on the back of the man's bald head and the large, red scar that stretched nearly from ear to ear. Survival of the fittest, the evolutionist Darwin had explained.

What about the rest of us? Jakub wondered.

The block leader looked back over his shoulder. His mouth curled into a gruesome smirk. "Do you hear the orchestra playing? That means it's time for work."

Jakub's slumped shoulders lifted. Orchestra?

Twenty-Nine

Jakub followed the two guards and the other workers as he lugged his bucket with dog waste from the main roll call square. The guard dogs—teeth bared —were a constant presence in the camp. And for newcomers, cleaning their waste from the *Appellplatz* was considered one of the "easy" tasks.

Jakub and the three others on this small work detail were led through the gates. At a quickened pace, they moved toward the hillside overlooking the quarry to dump the feces.

Since arriving, Jakub had heard the thunderous sounds of the rock work inside the camp, but now he gasped as he neared the edged of the hillside and got his first look into the pit: prisoners in striped suits, the explosions of rock, the guards with whips, and more dogs that snarled and barked at those who lagged under their burdens.

Jakub's gaze followed the parade of workers. The rhythmic beat of a thousand wooden clogs pounded up and down the flint steps and echoed off granite cliffs that shimmered in the summer sun. *So many men,* Jakub thought. Like striped worker ants, the sea of uniformed prisoners laboriously carried their loads up the rock staircase. They moved at a military pace, under the bludgeons of SS and kapos—the fierce prisoner-guards.

Jakub's eyes moved to the uppermost level where, not one hundred meters away, those who'd survived the trip to the top loaded their burden into V-shaped carts. Jakub thought of the ghetto. How he'd hated the jobs they'd given him. Now he longed for the long hours tending sheep or planting roses. Even the funeral cart seemed like a blessing.

The day before, as they huddled in groups near the quarantine hut, news of their upcoming assignment to the quarry had come as a shock.

"We're supposed to be in the tunnels, assembling weapons," one of the men from Auschwitz had complained. He looked about twenty years old and spoke with an unfamiliar accent. "Maybe someone should inform them."

The others, haggard and dejected, gave no response. Instead, they pooled around the large tureen filled with putrid "soup."

"Fine, I'll say something." The young man puffed

out his chest. "And when I save us from the hole of death, you'll all thank me!"

The cocky prisoner strode to the nearest SS guard. Jakub lowered his head and listened closely to the prisoner's complaint.

The SS man nodded and patted the man's back. "I see your dilemma. They tell you one job, then when you arrive they assign you to the quarry. Not to worry. I have the perfect solution."

Jakub dared to look up just in time to see the guard whip out his pistol. He slowly lifted it to the man's forehead and pulled the trigger.

Flinching, Jakub looked away, continuing to slurp soup from his bowl, begging his stomach not to heave it back up. Over his slurps, he heard the sound of a booted foot kicking the man's body.

"If that's the way you feel, no quarry for you." The guard's voice had been calm. Almost gentle. "No quarry for you."

Now Jakub forced himself to hum as he righted his smelly bucket and looked away from the quarry. He wished for the song in his head to block out the thumping of wooden clogs.

"Let's go! Pick up your pace!" the guard shouted, his machine gun pointed at Jakub.

The bucket swung in Jakub's hand and he moved even faster, humming a quicker tune. From the quarry the sound of exploding rock filled his ears. Metal-studded boots paced just behind him.

"Faster. Move it!"

Jakub's breath came in gasps. *How will I do it?* It was hard enough carrying himself without stumbling. *How will I ever be able to cart such a load up those steps?*

Jakub hustled in line with the others as they hurried toward the camp gates at a quickened pace. Behind him, someone stumbled. An SS guard's shout was followed by the sickening thud of a gun's wooden stock against bone, and a man's scream.

That night, as they lay crammed together like spoons in a tray, shivering in the darkness, one man had dared to whisper. "The quarry is called *Wiener Graben*. I learned about it from the man who delivered our soup. Prisoners work from six in the morning until noon, then receive a half-hour break. Then work continues until dark, depending on the daily quota."

Jakub let out the breath he didn't realize he'd been holding.

"Of course, those are summer hours. It's much less in the winter." The man's raspy voice quieted as if he shared a secret. "The guards are afraid of the dark. In the winter they won't leave the safety of their gates until after sunrise. They head back before the sun sets. Who would really believe that such weakened, unarmed prisoners could hurt them?"

"Soon our fight for survival begins," he continued. "We must quickly learn how to step and when to lower our eyes. Remember, never speak unless spoken to, and absolutely never draw attention to yourself." The man yawned. "And the most important rule: when you live with wolves, you have to behave nicely toward them."

And like a distant dream, Jakub thought of Addie's retelling of the biblical stories from the Pentateuch. The Hebrews had cried out under the burden of their slavery in Egypt. God had heard their cries and delivered them.

Dear God, how can I ever survive this? Where is my deliverance?

As the others slept, Jakub decided on a plan. He would end this hell himself. Before he took one step as a quarry slave, he would stride out of line.

The next morning as he stood in roll call, Jakub built up his resolve. By the time they moved ahead, their footsteps sounding as one, he was ready. He knew just a few wrong steps out of line was all it would take.

As he marched in unison with the others, he wondered when it should happen. Inside the gates, or outside? Perhaps he should wait to glimpse the Austrian hills one last time.

Then, as if breaking through the fog, a noise startled him. Music. Somewhere an orchestra played.

Jakub cocked his head and dared to peer around the man who marched in front of him. Yes, it was as he thought. A real orchestra played for the men marching to work. Winds, brass, percussion . . . strings.

A conductor stood before the haggard group, his back to the marching prisoners. Jakub noticed that even in his striped uniform the man stood tall. Jakub's heart pounded harder, faster to the tempo of the music. They were playing the overture to *The Kiss* by Smetana.

If I am to die, at least I die to the sound of music!

They marched closer, and Jakub closed his eyes. His body moved to the right, out of step, toward the music. Jakub was certain he could already hear the growling of dogs.

"Get back in line!" A truncheon struck his back. Once, then twice.

Jakub stumbled and cried out in pain. *Daniel, I am coming.* . . . Pain erupted in his head. He crumbled. His knees crashed onto the granite square. Music echoed in his ears.

Suddenly hands grabbed his shoulders. He flinched, anticipating more blows.

"Son, look at me!" A gentle voice called to him over the music.

Jakub opened his eyes and sucked in a breath. He peered into a familiar face. *Alexi.*

"Am I already dead?" Jakub asked.

The guard lifted his truncheon, and Alexi blocked Jakub with his body. "Stop! I know this boy!"

"What good does that do me?" The SS guard lifted his stick again. "He's as good as dead!"

"Move on. Keep going!" a second SS man shouted to the rest of the group. A third guard from farther back in line hurried toward Jakub with two dogs on leashes. The dogs' barking grew louder. Jakub braced for their attack, praying it would be over quickly.

Alexi stepped forward. The music faltered. "You would kill one of the greatest prodigies of all time?" His words were hurried. "You are getting married in two weeks, yes? What better gift can you give your wife than a violin solo by one of the greatest young musicians of the century?"

The guard hesitated. Questioning eyes stared down at Jakub. He waved his fellow guard and the dogs away.

"He does not look like a great musician." The guard spat.

Alexi yanked on his own uniform. "And I do not look like a great conductor! I have performed for you hundreds of times . . . do you think I would risk my life if it were not the truth?"

"If you are lying, this boy will be killed. You will be killed! All of you!"

Alexi bowed low. "Yes, plan on us being at the wedding. We will not disappoint you."

The guard straightened, then gave Jakub a swift kick. "Fine, take this piece of trash with you. A good excuse to send you all up the chimney!" Without a second glance, he stalked away.

After the last prisoner had marched by, and the orchestra's morning playing was complete, Alexi grabbed Jakub's arm and pulled him along.

"To live you must work. We are in the orchestra, and that allows for easier labor. But we must work for our keep like the rest."

They walked into a large room of latrines.

"You know how to clean?" He thrust rags and strong cleaner into Jakub's hands.

Jakub nodded, still uncertain about what had just happened. *He thinks I am Daniel . . . how does he not know? Doesn't he remember the injury to my brother's hands?*

"I will be back. Work fast; work hard." Then the conductor disappeared.

Alexi returned a while later, as promised. He eyed Jakub's work, then nodded with approval. With quickened steps, he led Jakub to his new barracks. All eyes turned Jakub's direction as they entered, many of their gazes narrowed in anger.

Alexi placed a hand on Jakub's shoulder. "This is a Hanauer boy. The older son. I've known him since he was a small child taking music lessons. What I told you about his music was no lie. Many of you may have known his father, Samuel."

Recognition flashed on one man's face, then another.

"Owner of a violin repair shop? In Prague?" The small man with large ears reminded Jakub of the dwarf in the book of Grimms' tales he once owned. "His son? You don't say?"

Alexi pushed Jakub forward and whispered in his ear. "Go ahead; tell them, Jakub. Spit out your name."

Jakub looked to the men. Four dozen pairs of eyes studied him. They were thin and tired, yet with the simple mention of his father's name, their faces had brightened. *Yes, Samuel Hanauer has one son who remains. Only one son to carry his name.*

Jakub closed his eyes and imagined the expression on his father's face when Daniel's small steps had carried him to center stage under the lights at the National Theater. All eyes had been on Daniel. All eyes except Jakub's. Instead, Jakub had studied his father's rapt attention and flushed cheeks. *If only one son should live on* . . .

Jakub opened his eyes and lifted his head. "I am Daniel Hanauer," he said finally. "I am the son who remains to carry on my father's name, my family's music."

Thirty

At the sound of Daniel's name, the men began talking at once.

"I heard you play in Prague once."

"Do you have an instrument?"

"Our lives rest in the hands of a boy?"

"You can practice on my violin."

Alexi eyed Jakub warily. He held up his hands, quieting the others.

"Gentleman, please. Let the boy breathe. I haven't even had the chance to speak with him myself. We still have our afternoon work assignments before this evening's march, remember? Get your lunch, finish your work, and we'll meet at our usual practice time."

The men scattered, grabbing their soup tins. Wooden bunks, three-tiered high and covered with straw, stretched across the length of the room. Various instruments rested on splintered benches.

Alexi retrieved a tin and handed it to Jakub. "Here is mine; use it until we retrieve yours. Lunch is served in the small courtyard between barracks."

"What about your lunch?"

Alexi waved a hand in the air. "My job takes me by the kitchen. I'll get something later." He placed an arm around Jakub's shoulder. "Now, *Daniel,* is it? They will be expecting you to play with us tonight. Are you up to it?"

Jakub imagined the men gathered in this dank room, eyes intent upon him. Seasoned musicians who could not be fooled. Alexi's face began to fade. Jakub reached for the nearest bunk post.

"Look at me." Alexi's voice was stern.

Jakub forced his eyes to focus.

"They expect you to play, yes? They are counting on you."

I didn't want this. I wanted to die! Jakub wanted to shout. Instead he nodded, sucking in a deep breath.

"Can you think of something you know well enough to play for the others tonight?"

"I do know my brother's—uh, my favorite. By Ravel. But I lost the music."

"Do you need the music? Surely you can play it without."

Jakub's mind flashed back to his solos at his brother's bedside. He had played the same melody in the fields— often with his eyes closed. Still, the printed page was like a security blanket. "I think I can play it . . . without the music."

Alexi smiled, then strode to the farthest length of the bench to retrieve a violin case. He opened it and presented it to Jakub. "This belongs to Janos. He won't mind. Practice this afternoon, and be ready for tonight."

"But . . . but what about my duties? Won't they find me out if I skip out? Will they send me back to the quarry?"

"Thank the Almighty, we in the orchestra have lighter duties. We're also given time in the evenings for practice. These extra favors make our load lighter. I will do your work for you, for today."

Alexi turned to leave.

"Wait . . . please. I need to know."

Alexi paused, looking back.

"Was he serious? The guard. Did he mean what he said about killing us all?"

Alexi sighed and placed his worn cap over his shaved head. "I've never heard Mueller back down on a threat yet."

𝓫   𝓫   𝓫

Jakub practiced the Tzigane all afternoon. His fingers were stiff, and he had trouble remembering one of the movements. And as the afternoon turned to evening, his stomach ached from lack of food. The small bits he had swallowed for breakfast and lunch did little to ease the constant hunger hounding him, ever growling, like the SS dogs.

Alexi entered the room. Sweat trickled down his face. "Well?" he raised his eyebrows. "How are you doing? The others will be here soon."

Jakub lifted the violin and began to play. Before he'd finished three measures, Alexi interrupted.

"Wait, wait." He strode up to Jakub's side. "You're rushing things. Slow down, breathe, take your time. Finish the note you've started before you launch on to the next one."

Jakub breathed in deeply and forced his fingers to match the melody in his head. Amazingly, the music sounded clearer. Jakub finished the song and felt a pride he'd never known.

"Very good!" Alexi clapped his hands. "That's a very difficult piece. You just need to trust yourself more. Trust the melody in your mind; trust your fingers as they move. If only you had a better instrument—this is such a second-rate fiddle. Oh, something else for me to stay up worrying about." He placed a hand on Jakub's shoulder. "You'll be fine, son."

Jakub's eyes widened. "No, wait, I can't." Jakub thought of his "performance" in the attic at Terezín. The feeling of the eyes upon him, and his failure. Things had not changed since his first days of attempting to perform. The instrument trembled in his fingers.

"I have a problem. I play okay by myself. I did fine playing for my brother too. It's just crowds. All those people looking at me. The faces grow blurry and my knees get weak." He crumpled onto the nearest bunk.

Alexi sat beside him. He patted Jakub's knee. "Close your eyes."

"What?"

"Forget that everyone is in the room. You don't have any music, remember? There's nothing to look at."

Jakub peered into Alexi's dark brown eyes, wanting more than anything not to disappoint him.

"Just close your eyes," Alexi said again. "Breathe and play. It's just you and the violin. Why don't we try it?"

"Are you serious?" Jakub could hear clomping footsteps outside the barracks.

"Yes. Up quick. The others will be in coming soon. We have to play for the workers marching in for the day. Hurry now. Up, up."

Jakub stood.

Alexi grabbed his shoulders and turned him to face the bunk. "Now, close your eyes and begin."

Jakub lifted the instrument to his shoulder and slid out the first note. He heard footsteps behind him and began to speed up. *Slow down. Breathe. Play.* He pictured Daniel in the hospital bed. How he loved this song. He trusted the music in his head, trusted his fingers to do their work. Before he knew it, the last refrain echoed through the room, followed by silence.

Jakub dropped the bow to his side and took a breath. Applause filled the room. He turned. The whole orchestra was there. Smiles lit their gaunt faces.

Alexi applauded the loudest. "That was good. See?

367

What did I tell you? You will stay with us. We'll find you an instrument."

"But what about the wedding?" One man limped forward—his pegged leg stiff and straight as he walked. "What will he play? Will two weeks be enough time to prepare?"

"One thing at a time. Janos, do not worry so." Alexi shook his finger in the air. "First, I'll see what I can do about a violin. Then we will put our heads together and come up with the perfect piece." Alexi placed a hand on Jakub's head. "With Eastern Europe's finest orchestra working with this brilliant boy . . . how could he not succeed?"

"Now, we mustn't be late for our duties." Alexi swept up his baton and hurried to the door. "Tonight, we will work together. We have become a team, have we not—masters from national symphonies and orchestras joined with Bohemian village minstrels? If together we create beautiful music, surely we can fashion an equally beautiful musician, no?"

♫   ♫   ♫

BADEN BEI WIEN, AUSTRIA

Evie lifted the Schmeisser MP 38/40 machine gun—as she had learned it was called—and finished stroking the metal with a soft cloth. Sascha would be pleased. From the pieces he'd given her, she'd managed to assemble twenty Schmeissers for use by the Resistance.

She heard someone walking above. *Finally.* She desperately needed someone besides the Stahls to talk to. The trapdoor slid back. Evie looked up to see Sascha's face, but he was not smiling.

"Evie, come. The others are in the farmhouse. It's safe . . . we just need to talk."

Evie climbed up the ladder and hurried alongside Sascha. "Others. Do you mean Korina?"

"And Felix," Sascha added. "Don't worry, he's over the incident at the church—at least mostly over it."

Felix. Evie tried to hide her smile.

They entered the kitchen, and the scent of stew simmering on the stove greeted them. Evie's stomach rumbled. She hurried past the food into the small living room area where Felix and Korina waited.

Korina looked to Felix as Evie entered. "I don't know. I don't think she's ready. I could just—"

Felix turned to the woman. "Korina, hush. Give this a chance, please. I've thought it over."

Evie settled into a rocking chair, leaning forward. "What's going on?"

"Felix wants to give you another chance to help, but after Vienna—"

"Korina, do I need to ask you to leave?"

Korina sank back against the faded cushion, her arms crossed over her chest.

"Theresa, we have a job for you," Felix said. "We need you to make a delivery for us. It's very important."

"A delivery? Where to?"

369

"Near Linz. We have something that needs to be hand delivered. It's very important."

"Is it the weapons? I just finished them. Will someone go with me?"

"You'll be going alone, traveling by train. You'll set out early tomorrow morning."

"In daylight? But what about my papers? I have some forged ones, but they're not very good."

"See, I told you she'd refuse."

Felix glared at Korina, then turned back to Evie. "I have those taken care of." He reached into his jacket and handed a small packet to Evie.

She opened the envelope, pulling out identity papers as perfect as her originals. *Theresa Bradl*. She glanced at the photo. "Wait, this is me."

It was a perfect shot of her looking into the camera. She looked closer, recognizing it. "Nick took this picture in New York. I don't think I even showed it to my parents. How did you get this photo?"

Felix simply shook his head.

"You have someone inside my house; I know it. Is it a new maid?" She studied Felix's face. "Or . . . is it one of my family members? Is that how they knew I was alive? Is that why my mother wasn't surprised? Could it be Isak?" Evie saw a flash of knowing on Felix's face before the protective mask returned.

She rose, then knelt before Felix, taking his hands in hers. "You have to tell me."

He pulled her hands to his broad chest. His features

softened. "You know I can't tell you. But, yes, someone on the inside knows."

Evie felt like kissing Felix straight on the lips. "Yes, what do you need me to do? Anything."

He released her, then reached to the side of the old sofa and pulled out a violin case. "We need you to deliver an instrument, a very expensive violin, to a small town called Mauthausen—"

"Wait, isn't there a concentration camp there?"

"Yes, but you will have no need to go near the camp. You'll meet a contact, pass off the item, and return home the next day."

"But why me?"

"Well, for starters, none of us can play the part of a beautiful, educated musician quite as well. We've heard you used to play the violin?"

"Did you hear it from your friend on the inside?" Evie smiled. "I had lessons when I was younger, but that was years ago."

Felix smiled. "You don't have to play *well*; just play. Also, these clothes won't fit any of us."

He handed her a bag, and she pulled out a navy blue dress, stockings, matching heeled shoes, gloves, and her favorite turban hat that was pretty, but not too elegant. The perfect traveling attire.

Evie covered her forehead with a hand. "*My clothes.* I had no idea—no idea these things would mean so much." She grabbed up her dress in her arms, then wiped her eyes with the sleeve of her plaid work shirt.

"We have a few more things packed in your valise."

Sascha held up the small pink suitcase. "All the things a lady needs when she travels."

"And this is the violin." Felix opened the case to reveal an instrument of light amber color.

Evie reached to touch it, then stopped herself. "It's beautiful. I can tell it's expensive, but I probably don't want to know how expensive."

Felix let his fingers glide over the bow. "The Resistance worked hard to smuggle this out of Prague. It was almost found once, when one of our leaders was arrested. Now this very man has asked for it to be brought to him inside Mauthausen. I'm not the one in charge, and it doesn't make sense to me, but it's our job to get it there."

He snapped the case closed and handed it to her. "And, no, you don't want to know how valuable it is."

Evie took the case. "When did you say I'm going?"

"Tomorrow."

"Which means we have to do something with that hair," Korina butted in.

Evie stood and hugged her dress to her chest. "Actually, Korina, I think I'll take care of that myself, if you don't mind."

Thirty-One

BADEN BEI WIEN, AUSTRIA
MAY 29, 1944

Felix met Evie at the train station, where a few other well-dressed passengers waited. Evie smiled at the sight of the new, ill-fitting suit hanging on his athletic frame.

Red touched Felix's cheeks. "You look nice. I like the sunglasses."

"Thanks for dressing up for the occasion." Evie adjusted the collar on his shirt. She thought of Nick and quickly dropped her hands. "I'm surprised you came, since we already said good-bye at the farmhouse."

Felix glanced at the other passengers with mock sternness. "Just had to make sure all was well. You never know." He eyed the plain brown case she held at her side. "I see you have the violin."

She patted it. "Right here."

"And you know what to do?"

"Of course. I won't mess up, just as long as there are no heights." She grinned.

"Okay, then. Remember, meet your uncle at the station, have a nice visit, and I'll see you in two days."

"I said I knew what I was doing. But . . ." She paused, wrinkling up her nose. "Will he be wearing a white daisy or a yellow carnation? And he's a young, handsome guy, right?"

Felix frowned.

"Just fooling," she whispered, leaning close. "I will go with him to a guesthouse, where I'll be given a room. Then my Uncle Katz will trade violins, and I'll take the train back home. It sounds simple, and I get to venture out and experience the world again."

"Simple, yes," Felix warned. "But beware, it's often the simple tasks that lead to the most trouble."

Evie set the valise on the ground and gave him a quick hug. "I have God watching out for me, remember?"

She said it as much to remind herself as Felix.

      🍂   🍂   🍂

At the station, the conductor checked her paperwork, then led her to the train with a smile.

You are a young, naive girl, visiting her uncle. You have not a care in the world, she reminded herself.

On board, a young, good-looking SS guard rechecked her papers, then handed them back with a wink. Evie managed a coy smile, took them from his hand, and slipped them back inside her small purse.

"So tell me, will you be riding this train all the way to St. Georgen?" She slipped her sunglasses off her face. "I haven't visited my uncle since I was a child, and I would love to have someone to sit with who could point out all the small towns as we pass."

"Oh, I'm sorry, miss. I have to watch the doors. You never know what criminals might try to sneak on or off—even in motion."

Evie laughed. "Of course. What was I thinking?"

Six hours later, the train rolled into the stop. Evie carried her violin case and the valise down the aisle, bumping the chair backs as she passed.

The same SS guard waited at the door. "I wish this were my stop. I'd buy you a drink."

Evie offered him a pout. "I would have liked that."

"The least I can do is help you down." He held her arm gently and led her down the steps.

"Thank you ever so much."

Evie turned and scanned the station. A sea of German uniforms swallowed up the platform and wrought-iron benches. Wooden batons rested on the laps of many. German shepherds lounged in the sun.

"Do you see him?" the guard asked next to Evie's ear, still holding her arm.

"My uncle? Not yet. Wait—" She spotted a gray-haired man with a slight limp. A white daisy was pinned to his lapel. "Yes, there he is! Thank you."

Without waiting for a response, Evie rushed forward.

She set the violin and the valise at her feet and accepted the stranger's embrace.

"Welcome, Theresa. It's been too long. You're all grown up. Here, let me take these." Uncle Katz lifted her cases.

Evie turned and waved at the guard from the train. He waved back with a smile.

They hurried off the platform. "I would say you're a natural, but I'm not sure that would be a compliment. Come, I live right down the street. It's the large yellow building on the corner."

"Just so you won't be alarmed," he added, "several SS officers are living in my guesthouse. I told them my young niece would be visiting. They will most likely expect you to play for them."

"Play?" Evie asked.

The old man paused. "You can play the violin, can't you?"

"Of course, I've—uh—practiced. Just be warned. I'm not very good. My greatest feat so far has been squeaking out a few lullabies."

Uncle Katz smiled. "Anything will be fine."

℔   ℔   ℔

Jakub plunged the shovel into the ground, dumped his load of dirt, and then started the same process again, remembering Alexi's advice. *It's very important to watch the guards at all times and to take a break when not being observed. It's the only way to survive here.*

"How many tents will go up?" Stein squinted, eyeing the rambling, rock-strewn field. They worked together digging a long, narrow trench for a latrine.

"A dozen, I believe." Janos hobbled by, his peg leg sinking into the soft dirt.

"You know what this means, don't you, Daniel?" Stein leaned close.

Jakub dropped his shovelful of dirt. "What?"

"It means more prisoners, coming down from the north. The Russians are moving in—it's just a matter of time."

"Matter of time?" Jakub struck a rock and bent to wiggle it from the ground.

"Before we're liberated. Free to go, you know? In March, nearly five thousand Russians were brought here. They were POWs from camps closer to the border. They'd been locked in gated barracks and practically left to die. The Nazis brought them here because it's the farthest camp from the front lines. I just wonder how far away the Russians are now. Maybe we'll be free by fall. No?"

Jakub continued to dig, humming as he plunged down his dull shovel. Stein joined in.

"Beethoven's Rondo in G Major." Janos smiled. "I heard you play it at the National Theater. You were much smaller then."

"Yes." Jakub wiped his brow. He eyed the guard, whose gaze was intent on them. He dug his shovel in deep, refusing to pause. He began to work even faster, moving farther down the line. "But I . . . I don't remember the things I played so long ago."

"Don't worry!" Stein called. "We have a great deal of music. Before things got too bad, the Nazis allowed us to send for music, and for our instruments too."

Janos cut in. "We have lots of Wagner—Hitler's favorite." He lowered his voice. "We also found Jewish folk songs and other banned music. We even found the music for the national anthem of the United States—although if we played it, it would be certain death to us all."

Stein caught up to them again. "But I have been thinking—for the wedding, it has to be Bach. I know we have the A Minor Sonata."

Janos bobbed his head in agreement. "Perfect. Nothing else will do."

Jakub moved faster, increasing the gap between himself and the other two men. His shovel worked in an even tempo, and he hoped they couldn't see the trembling in his shoulders. The Bach A Minor for unaccompanied violin? That was impossible.

Dead. We'll all be dead soon because of me. Why had Alexi given them hope?

      🎝   🎝   🎝

ST. GEORGEN, AUSTRIA
MAY 29, 1944

Evie tucked a strand of newly died auburn hair behind her ear, then patted her cheeks, warm from the male attention of the dozen SS guards circled around her.

"That's so nice of you to visit your uncle," said one officer who lounged in full uniform on the sofa. "I see you've brought a violin. Won't you play for us?"

"I'm very rusty," she protested, as she opened the case. She attempted to hide her shock when, instead of the beautiful amber instrument, a worn, dark brown violin rested in its place. She glanced at Uncle Katz, and he urged her on with a nod. *He's already made the switch. That was quick.*

She lifted the violin and put it into position, then squeaked out a tune.

The men applauded but did not ask for another song.

One guard with dark hair, a square face, and narrow-set eyes watched as she returned it to the case. He cleared his throat. "So how long have you played?"

"I started at five."

He raised an eyebrow.

She laughed. "Oh, but I only played for a couple years, and then I gave it up. I began again recently out of boredom. With all those hours I've spent in bomb shelters lately, I've needed something to occupy my time."

"And the others don't mind your playing?" he asked.

"I haven't asked. Maybe that's why they sent me to visit Uncle for a few days."

The men's laughter joined hers.

Sixty men were gathered in the crowded room. Jakub was sure there had never been such a ragtag group of musicians or instruments. But he felt more frightened than he had on the stage in Prague so many years before.

He stared at the sheet of music in front of him, an overture by Wagner.

"Play with us, son," Janos whispered. "I will help you."

Jakub looked to the music. His hands began to quiver as he lifted the borrowed violin to his shoulder. *Play like Daniel. Play like Daniel.* Jakub attempted the first series of notes, but he knew it wasn't right.

A violist at the next stand turned to Janos. "Did you give the boy the wrong piece?"

Jakub took a step forward. "No, it's not the music. It's me. I just have a hard time. . . ." He paused and looked around.

Alexi stood. "What the boy's saying is that he needs someone to play it for him first. To get him started. He's had a rough few years and needs help getting back into the swing of things."

Stein took the violin from Jakub and squinted at the music on the stand. The music flowed from the violin, and Jakub smiled. *Yes, I recognize this melody.*

Stein handed the violin back to the boy. Jakub closed his eyes, hearing the music in his head. His hands played the melody in his mind.

There was silence when he finished.

Jakub opened his eyes.

"You do not realize, do you?" Alexi's eyes seemed to smile.

"Realize what?"

"You were not even looking at your music."

Warmth climbed up Jakub's cheeks. He remembered his first teacher. Every time Jakub had attempted to close his eyes, the teacher had urged him to open his eyes and play to the notes on the page.

"I'm sorry," he said. "I'll try again."

"No, please don't. Don't you see? The music does not come from seeing the notes on a page. It comes from the heart, once you know it in your head of course. I think you learn better by ear." Alexi shuffled across the room. "Franz, pick out a tune, any tune, and play it on the fiddle."

Franz obeyed, choosing a snappy gypsy number.

"Okay, now your turn."

Jakub matched the song on his violin with quick strokes of the bow. A grin spread across his face.

"Now, Julius, on the cello." Julius, a small man with large ears, played a line of a slow ballad, filled with emotion.

"Now for you . . ."

Jakub followed note for note, excitement stirring his chest, like the tingling of angel kisses in his heart.

"That's it!" Alexi beamed. "When you trust yourself, trust the music in you, it is endless what you can play."

He turned to the orchestra. "Gentlemen, we can have this young master playing all our music in no time.

All we need to do is play his parts for him—hum them if need be."

Stein nodded. "Yes, but 'no time' is exactly how long we have. Can he have the Bach A Minor ready for the wedding in ten days?"

"Do we have a choice?" Janos limped across the room. He took Jakub by the arm. "Come, boy. It's almost light's out. You can sleep next to me. I'll hum you the Andante. That's the movement you'll play for the wedding."

"There is still one thing he needs," said Stein as Jakub was led toward the bunk, "one thing that would ensure our safety. A fine violin. Better than any we have. These castaways don't do the music justice."

Jakub turned and eyed Alexi, wanting to see the conductor's smiling face and approving gaze one more time.

"I agree," said Alexi with a twinkle in his eyes. "Perhaps one will be delivered . . . to deliver us."

℀   ℀   ℀

ST. GEORGEN, AUSTRIA
MAY 30, 1944

Evie awoke to the smell of coffee—or something similar. She dressed quickly, ran a brush through her auburn hair, and tiptoed to the kitchen. An excitement stirred through her at the thought of sharing her success with Felix.

"Good morning," she whispered to Uncle Katz, who was busily cleaning up the breakfast dishes.

"No need to whisper, dear. The early shift has already left, and the late one hasn't arrived yet. Would you like some eggs and ersatz coffee?"

"Yes, please."

Within a few minutes, he placed a plate and a cup before her. He took the opposite chair, running his hand over graying whiskers. "There's something I need to talk to you about."

Evie took a large bite of the fluffy fresh eggs and lifted her eyebrows. "Hmmm?"

"I've just heard the news. One of our friends has been arrested. He was the one who was to deliver the violin." Uncle Katz's words became hurried. "We have a connection inside the police department, so I'm sure we can get our friend out of prison soon. But until then, it's urgent that we get this violin to its owner."

Evie's pulse quickened. "So you need me to visit someone's house and make a delivery? I'm sure I can do that." She pushed the eggs to the side.

Uncle Katz cleared his throat. "The violin needs to be delivered *into* the concentration camp. And it's not that easy. We can't just march up the hill and say, 'Special Delivery for Prisoner X.'"

"Well, what *was* your plan?"

"We had a job at the bakery waiting for my friend. They deliver bread for the SS kitchen, and it was arranged that he would start making the deliveries. The violin, of course, would be hidden under the loaves, along with a 'gift' for the guard."

Evie folded her hands in her lap, knowing what she should do. Still, the thought of going near a camp . . .

"Do you think I could pull it off?" she finally said. "There is one problem. All the SS guards think I'm going back to Vienna tomorrow. Unless . . . can you tell me, did the city happen to be bombed last night?"

Uncle Katz peered at her over the top of his glasses. "I'm sure it was. Recently there has been some type of activity almost every night—but mostly on the outskirts, where the refineries are."

Evie leaned forward in her seat. "So . . . what if we say the bombing was closer in town, and my family's apartment was destroyed? We could then say my parents sent a wire asking me to stay here until it's safe. What do you think?"

Uncle Katz rose from the chair. "I see what you're getting at. So you take a job at the bakery to help out . . ."

". . . and I make the delivery myself. Do you think it will work?"

"We have no choice. Many lives are depending on this instrument." He pushed his chair back and slipped a worn jacket over his shoulders, then placed an equally frayed hat upon his head. "Let's go." He held the kitchen door for her. "You have a job to apply for."

"How will we get word to Felix? He's planning to meet me at the station."

Uncle Katz waved a hand toward her. "We'll worry about that later."

Thirty-Two

Evie slipped on her sensible, floral dress and flat-heeled shoes for work. She fastened her auburn hair in a bun on the top of her head. A few stray strands fell against her cheeks. She walked into the kitchen in the predawn hours and noticed a lone SS officer at the table, just finishing breakfast. He looked up, and she recognized him as the one who'd asked her to play the violin. Uncle Katz was busy frying ham for the other soldiers, who no doubt would be down soon.

Uncle Katz hurried to the table and pulled out a chair. "Theresa, Officer Seidler has been kind enough to offer to escort you to work. He works at Mauthausen and will be making the trip the same time as you every morning."

"Oh, Uncle, how kind." She pasted a smile on her

face, then turned to the officer. Trying to keep her eyes off of the skull and crossbones symbol on his cap, she said, "Shall we go?"

He wiped his mouth with the cloth napkin. "Yes, I'd be honored."

They walked side by side through the predawn darkness. The wind had shifted from the previous day, and a putrid smell wafted through St. Georgen.

Evie's eyes began to water, but the guard seemed unaffected. As they walked, he discussed his new position at the main camp and his hopes of finding living quarters closer to Mauthausen.

"There are barracks for the soldiers inside, but others—mainly officers with families—have homes in town. I've lived with your uncle for over a year. There have been, on occasion, problems with the train, and I hate showing up late for duty. Of course, I'd need a family to qualify for housing in Mauthausen." He grinned and shouldered close to Evie.

She listened, commenting at the right moments, but her attention had turned to the white flakes that fell from the sky. From the smell, she knew immediately that it was ash from the large crematorium chimneys she could see from the guesthouse. *Oh, God, how can this really be happening?*

As she walked, the horror stories she'd heard from Felix and the others became real. This is what their underground efforts were fighting against. These camps, these guards, were reality to thousands of people—reality to the person who'd just made the trip up the chimney. If they didn't stop this madness, it would be the end of them all.

She clutched her stomach.

"Theresa, are you all right?"

She offered a weak smile. "Oh, I always get this way when starting a new job. Especially a job that matters so much. I—I mean, people need to eat."

Officer Seidler patted her arm. "Don't worry, my dear. It's not a life-or-death situation, is it now? You'll do fine."

"No, no, no!" Alexi stopped the group in the middle of a phrase and stamped his wooden clog on the ground. "Did you hear that? Someone was off. One of the violins. Stein, was it you? Janos? Whoever, please get it right."

Jakub sank back against the wall, surprised by Alexi's anger. Since Jakub didn't have a violin of his own, his practicing had been put on hold in order to prepare for an SS concert to take place the following evening.

His stomach cramped from dinner's ill-tasting food. His eyelids were heavy from being up too many nights.

"*Buh, bum, pah, pah*," Janos had whispered in his ear in the darkness. "Did you hear that last fading note? *Buh, bum, pah, pah-h-h.*"

Janos, with the peg leg, was Jakub's favorite—and not simply because the wooden leg allowed more room for Jakub to stretch out. Janos was also the most patient, humming the melodies again and again until Jakub recorded them in his mind.

Whose bunk will I share tonight? Upper or lower? Not that either made any difference. The lower bunks were infected with the dirt and dust from the pallets above. The ones sleeping below were sure to get a mouthful at the slightest movement from someone above.

But those who bunked above had to clamber over the others. This was not easy after a day packed with work and a night filled with musical practice. Even worse, at reveille—which began at the ringing of the bell at the gate—the men on the top bunks received the brunt of the hits from the kapos, prisoner-guards, who assisted with the wake-up call.

Although he appreciated the help from the orchestra members, Jakub's body ached from exhaustion. He didn't care whether he was in a lower bunk or upper tonight, as long as he had a chance to sleep.

"What do I need to do? Grab your hands and guide the notes myself?" Alexi interrupted the flow of music as he yelled again.

Jakub's eyes flashed open. The tall conductor strode back in front of the orchestra members like a caged leopard Jakub had once seen at the circus.

"Do you want to live?" Alexi shouted. "You play as if you were about to perform at a children's musical, not as if your life depended on your music—which it does."

"I'm sorry." Stein rose and bowed before Alexi. "I've been driving tent pegs into the hard ground all day long. My fingers are crinkled tighter than the curls that used to grow on my head."

"Yes, but you have to move beyond your pain." Alexi took a deep breath. "It's not just your own little melody that suffers. The whole orchestra is not as good when one person does not do his part."

"I just don't understand," a musician from the Warsaw Philharmonic interrupted. "How can they expect us to put something together with such short notice? To have a new arrangement ready by tomorrow is nearly impossible. If we had a complete orchestra, it might be possible. But there is too much percussion, not enough flutes. Our members are coming and going. They get sick or hurt. They don't all know the same melodies!"

Alexi finished pacing. He lowered his voice. "I'm sorry. It's been a difficult day. I heard over a dozen died in the quarry today, including one of my old friends. I suppose even brutality becomes tedious after a while. It is on hard days like this that the SS guards need music to distract them, to get their minds off the death. And as long as it means our lives are safe, we will do just that."

Jakub curled up in a ball on the muddy floor and drifted off to the sound of world-renowned performers, now near skeletons, coaxing music from their instruments in hopes that their music would grant them one more day.

Evie pushed the wooden cart stacked with loaves of dark bread up the steep hillside. The narrow path was lined with trees, giving the path a tunnel effect. The ground was smooth and even, trampled flat by thousands of prisoners as they made their way toward the death camp. Sweat formed on her brow.

After twenty minutes, the camp appeared through a break in the trees. The gray fortress, built during Franz Josef's reign, covered the hillside like a walled citadel. As she cleared the trees, Evie took a labored breath and continued forward, ignoring the trembling of her shoulders.

She could see the side door up ahead and steered the cart in that direction. The sweet scent of burning flesh that often swept down to the valley below was overpowering this close, and it swallowed the yeasty fragrance of the bread. Her throat thickened, and she willed herself not to run down the hillside in search of fresh air.

A guard waited outside the door, just as the baker said he would. His eyes locked on Evie like those of a hungry wolf spotting his prey. Her light cotton dress made her feel bare, and she wished for the farmer's overalls and wool cap that had been her companions for so long.

She stopped the cart before him.

"Tasty looking bread." He stepped closer, his gaze moving up her body to her neck, pausing just briefly on her chin, then meeting her eyes.

Evie opened her mouth, then closed it again. What had the baker told her to say? The wind shifted, and a tendril of white smoke drifted over the wall. One wrong move and *she* would be smoke. Panic scratched at Evie's chest like a trapped animal.

The guard placed a hand on her shoulder. Then he cracked a smile. "The cigarettes are hidden, correct?"

"Yes, beneath the bread."

"And the package you wish for me to deliver. It's also hidden?"

She nodded and dared to look into his eyes.

"Good, good." He took the cart handle from her grasp. His face softened. "Do not worry, my little lamb; I will not bite. Go now and tell your friends that the package will be delivered as asked."

"Thank you, sir. Heil Hitler." Evie didn't need to act the fool. She was one. With her arms crossed over her floral print dress, she fled like a sinner from the gates of hell.

♫   ♫   ♫

Alexi walked toward Jakub, with hands behind his back and a gentle smile. He was different from the man who'd screamed at the musicians the evening before. "I have something for you. Something very special. But first we must talk."

Alexi leaned close as Jakub slurped down the remainder of his lunch. The conductor had called him alone into the barracks. Jakub knew it must be important.

"I have put up with the charade long enough . . . Jakub," Alexi said, his eyes intent.

Jakub lowered his head.

"I called you by your real name the first day, remember? I've known both of you boys since you were small children. I saw the talent God granted you both."

Jakub lowered his gaze.

"It's been a while, and we've both faced many hard things. You are unsure about the fate of your father—your mother too. It may seem like you have no one, but I have not forgotten you. And I have not forgotten the promise I made to your mother. When I came for the violin that day, I said that I would try to help you and your brother. I was arrested before I had a chance. Helping you in this camp is not what I would have planned. But the good Lord knew. He remembered how I hoped to assist your family, tried to protect your inheritance. And He brought you to me."

Jakub didn't understand his talk of "inheritance," but he realized he could no longer live under Daniel's fame. He removed his striped cap from his head and fingered it in his hands. "Are you angry that I lied?"

"Mainly confused. But I thought that if saying you were Daniel could help, if it increased your confidence . . . well, that's why I allowed it to happen."

Jakub lifted the bottom of his shirt and blotted his eyes.

"Son, I know you need to remember your brother." Alexi stroked Jakub's head. "But you cannot forget yourself in the process. Someday, Jakub, when the end of your life comes, God isn't going to ask, 'Why were you not more like Daniel?' He will ask, 'Why were you not more like Jakub?' It's true your brother was a wonderful musician, and he played from the music stored in his soul. But what about you? Are you willing to die with your own songs unsung?

"I want you to think about what's inside you. Think about the songs God whispered into your soul before you were born. And I want you to let that music out— to play as Jakub would play, and no one else."

Jakub had never thought about it that way before. *Was it true God believed he was just as special as Daniel had been?*

"Now, for my gift." With a sweep of his arm, Alexi produced a battered case.

Jakub leaned forward as the older man unfastened the latches. At the sight of the amber violin, he sucked in a breath. "This looks like the violin you picked up from my house. But where . . . how did it get here?"

"I sent it into hiding with a friend, then I asked it to be brought in . . . for you. It belonged to your father. It was given to him before he was taken away. It was to be your inheritance. But what good is an inheritance if the heir does not live?"

"But it's so valuable. What if the guards find out?"

"There is no one here who will realize its worth. These men may enjoy music, but they have no concept of instruments and such."

Jakub looked down. "I'm not worthy of such a violin."

"Son, didn't your father teach you that an instrument is simply a tool? The music comes from the player; the instrument can do nothing on its own. You are the important part."

Alexi placed his hands on Jakub's shoulders, kissed both of his cheeks, and hurried away.

Jakub picked up the violin, remembering when his father held it in his hands. Tears rolled down his cheeks. "I will try to be worthy of this gift, Father. I will try."

Thirty-Three

Jakub adjusted his position in the high-backed chair. His finger ran along the collar of his white, starched shirt, and he readjusted the man's necktie and jacket he'd been given to wear. The amber violin was perched on his trembling knees, and he took a deep breath, wishing for fresh air. The room felt stuffy with the presence of SS soldiers and their dates. At intricately decorated tables, dozens of guards in dress uniforms reclined with legs crossed. Watching them, knowing what he must do, made everything seem drastically important and unimportant all at once.

Yet one part of him remained unshaken despite the inner chaos—an unexplainable peace that radiated from Alexi's words whispered to him just moments before. "You have to believe the sun shines, somewhere beyond the clouds. You have to know God gave you the exact talent you need for this moment. Not Daniel's talent but your own."

After getting a signal from the front of the room, Jakub marched through the small restaurant and took his place in front. The conversation slowly died down until a hush settled over the room. Warmth seemed to radiate from the instrument in Jakub's hands. He squared his shoulders and stretched his back until he rose to his full height. Ever so slowly, he closed his eyes and lifted the violin to his shoulder.

Despite his pounding heart, the quiet anticipation in the room caused a slight smile to curve on Jakub's lips. "Bombs could be falling around them," Janos had said, "but true Germans stop everything for good music."

Jakub blew out a breath, and a sharp, perfect note burst forth with the bow's first slice. The music played in his mind, formed into a ball of heat in the pit of his stomach, and then streamed to his limbs. He concentrated on the notes and could almost feel the touch of Alexi's fingers upon his own, just as they had been the previous day during practice.

As he played, Jakub heard the music within and without as clearly as Alexi's encouragement had sounded in his ear. Then, as the last note hung in the air, the room filled with thunderous applause. Jakub bowed low, as he'd seen his brother do a thousand times.

Mueller, the guard who had beaten Jakub on that day he'd planned to die, came toward him with quick steps. His face was flushed, and his breath smelled acidic with beer. He lifted a hand.

Jakub winced, drawing back.

"Easy, boy," Mueller slurred. "I was just coming to pat your shoulder. Fine job. I knew you could do it." He pointed across the room. "Come. There is someone I would like you to meet."

Jakub expected to be led to Mueller's blonde bride, who was drinking and laughing with her friends. Instead, the guard led him to a small man in the back. The officer wore a Nazi uniform, but it was different from the others—decorated with all types of symbols and ribbons. Jakub noticed a musical note on the man's collar. His eyes moved from the man's jacket to his large eyes that seemed even bigger through his thick glasses.

"Herr Doktor Viktor Michitsch, this is the boy I was telling you about. See, aren't you glad I persuaded you to come earlier than planned? A concert such as this is far more interesting than searching through dusty camp warehouses, is it not?"

Viktor didn't seem interested in Jakub. Instead, he eyed the violin, then reached out his hands for it.

"Do you mind?" he asked.

Jakub had no choice but to obey. Shuddering inwardly, he handed over the violin, then scanned the room, hoping Alexi had sneaked in to retrieve him. But Jakub saw he was alone in a blur of uniformed officers and guards.

"Isn't he a great find?" Mueller asked, puffing out his chest. "Just think—so much talent in a scrawny boy."

"Yes." Viktor's voice held a hint of excitement. "I'm amazed by what one can find in the most unexpected places."

A female voice called out to Mueller, who waved in response.

"My bride beckons. Will you excuse me, Viktor?"

He scurried away, leaving Jakub wondering what to do next.

Viktor peered over the top of his glasses at Jakub. "What can you tell me about this violin?"

"I—I don't know much. It was just given to me to play, by my conductor."

"Your conductor, you say? What is his name?"

Black uniforms brushed past Jakub. The men laughed and joked around him. Seeing them this way was even worse than in the camp with their dogs in tow. There, it was easy to consider them animals in uniform, but here . . .

"Did you hear me, boy? I asked the name of your conductor."

"Alexi Hořký, sir," Jakub answered.

The man's eyes flashed with recognition.

"Here you go, boy. Take your instrument and leave . . . you have made my trip worthwhile."

🎕   🎕   🎕

Evie entered the house after a long day at the bakery. "Uncle, I'm home!" she called, entering the front door. She heard a noise in the kitchen and moved that direction.

"Uncle?" She rounded the corner and found herself face-to-face with the dark-haired officer, Seidler.

Something inside told her to run, but she ignored that urge. *I am simply a girl visiting my uncle. I have nothing to hide.*

"Officer Seidler, it's so good to see you. How is your search for a house closer to the camp?" She quickly moved to the closest chair and scooted into the table. "I should offer you some ersatz coffee, but the last time I looked, my uncle had none. Do you know where he is?"

Seidler took the chair nearest to Evie and scooted it even closer.

Evie rose from the chair and moved toward the stove. "Maybe I'll begin by heating the water. It does take a while. Now where are those matches?"

The officer followed her. "I know this might be too soon for me to confess my interest. Your uncle told me that you've recently lost your lifelong love on the Western Front." He took the matches from her hand.

"He told you that? Yes, he's right. It very nearly killed me."

She tried to move past him, but Seidler stepped in her way. "You are a pretty little thing."

The door slammed open, and Evie jumped. She turned to find the old man at the door. Seidler dropped his hands.

"Uncle!" She rushed toward him.

Uncle Katz tucked her under his arm, ignoring the SS guard in his kitchen. "Theresa, I have good news. I found you a place to stay at a farmhouse closer to your work. It will be safer without you having to take the train from St. Georgen to Mauthausen every day."

"Are they friends of yours?" Evie asked, glancing at Seidler out of the corner of her eye.

"Yes, dear friends I've known for years. But there is one problem. The farmer's family is very devout in their religion, and they don't want a boarder who is too casual with the opposite sex. Going on dates will be off limits for a while."

Evie glanced at Seidler, rummaging around for a rueful smile to cast his way. "I'm sorry to hear that, but I totally understand. Maybe once I live there for a while and they get to know me, they'll welcome the occasional suitor."

Seidler brightened visibly.

Uncle Katz squeezed her shoulder. "I'm sure you're right, my dear. But give it time."

꒜   ꒜   ꒜

Evie unpacked her things in the small bureau and looked out the window at the rolling hills behind the farmhouse. It had been over three weeks since she'd left Baden, and she wondered how long they'd have to wait until her "guardians" would think it safe enough for her to return. She thought of Felix. What would he think of her new arrangements? Uncle Katz had assured her that he had been contacted; the only word she'd received was a short note telling her to keep up the good work.

Then she thought of Nick. What would he think of where she was and what she was up to? She thought of him most—and was rewarded with his ever-present visits in her dreams. *If those dreams would only come true.*

She had been pleasantly surprised by the outspoken attitude of Frau Stoltz, the farmer's wife. As a dozen kids busily scampered in and out of the house, the woman grilled Evie about the latest news from Vienna.

"I'm sorry, I haven't been there for a while."

Frau Stoltz frowned, then hurriedly moved on to the next subject—obviously, there was no room for small talk at this table.

"You'll never guess what I heard." She lifted a baby boy dressed in red-checkered print from under the table and plunked him on her knee. "They're looking for a new assistant secretary at the main camp. They're sending every available soldier to the Western Front, so they're hiring townspeople to help with administration. Can you imagine all the information we could smuggle out if one of us worked inside?"

Frau Stoltz licked her thumb, wiped the baby's jam-caked cheek, and continued. "We have an underground route that delivers messages to our contacts in Switzerland. The Allies are mainly interested in British soldiers inside the camp. We've come up with some evidence that there are eleven British special agents locked in solitary confinement, but that news was a month old when we received it. The poor chaps could all be dead by now. Too bad we don't know someone who could go inside for us."

Evie knew what Frau Stoltz was asking. She also knew this could be the opportunity she'd been waiting for. "Frau Stoltz, if I agree to work in the camp, would there be any way I could get my own letters smuggled out as well?"

"You're interested in writing someone out of the country?"

"Yes, a friend in the States."

Frau Stoltz leaned closer, nearly smothering the infant between her ample bosom and the scarred wooden table. "A lost love perhaps?"

The baby let out a squeal, and she moved him to her shoulder, patting his back.

"Yes, how did you know?"

Frau Stoltz laughed. "If you'd been around as long as I have, you'd know the look of someone missing her true love. Yes, I can ask."

Evie's heartbeat quickened. She pictured Nick's face, his smile. The way he watched her in the dim light of a theater, instead of watching the movie. She had so much to say to Nick after all these years—to tell him she still loved him and longed to be with him. She'd have to begin her letter writing again to make up for the ones left behind in Vienna.

"Yes, please see what you can do," she told Frau Stoltz. "It's something I'd be very interested in doing for my country." She closed her eyes. *And for my heart.*

The long hike up to Mauthausen was the easiest part, Evie soon discovered. Nearing the gates, she lowered her head and passed by the rows of prisoners, lined up for roll call like thin pegs on a board.

How did I get myself into this? she wondered with each step she took—past the large tents encased in rows of barbed wire, past a water reservoir that oddly resembled a swimming pool, and into the SS garage yard.

With each step, Evie felt a heavy oppression bearing down on her, almost like a physical weight pressing against her chest.

To get to the central administration offices, Evie had to walk through the yard, then up a staircase to the gate towers. On her right was the administrative building. Although the day was bright, a darkness seemed to ooze from the granite walls around her.

She paused before knocking at the wooden door. A female secretary opened it.

"You must be Theresa. Come with me."

Evie sucked in a breath and followed her down the short hall to an open door at the end. A man with dark hair sat at the desk. Evie recognized him immediately.

"So, Theresa, we meet again." Seidler stood and took her hand.

Evie willed herself not to jerk it away.

"As soon as I saw your application come across my desk, I knew we were meant to be." He winked at her. "So, are things working out well with the devout farmers?"

"Yes, I like it there. Frau Stoltz is very nice."

"Good. I'm just so glad you've chosen to stay in our area. Come, let me give you a short tour of our office."

Evie followed Seidler down the hall as he pointed out each of the three small offices.

"These are the administrative offices. This is where we oversee the camp's economic and bureaucratic affairs. There are various positions held by junior officers, such as myself." He led her back to the first room. "This is where you will work."

She pulled her arms tight to her chest, noticing that her window looked directly into the camp's main square.

"You will be an assistant for all of the officers in this group. Some deal with supply, some construction. I deal with inmate properties."

"Properties?"

Seidler smiled. "Yes, the personal items turned in by the prisoners when they arrive. Or even those things they are allowed to keep—such as musical instruments. An officer from the Musik Aktion team just left today. He was searching for valuable musical instruments that may, by accident, have been allowed to enter the camp."

"Interesting." Evie walked to the window and placed a hand over her uneasy stomach. "And did he find anything?"

Seidler laughed. "Theresa, you are different from any secretary I've known. The first day on the job, and you're already asking about classified information." He placed a hand on her shoulder. "I like your curiosity, but you'll have to take care. And, no, we don't currently have any instruments of value in this camp."

Seidler gestured toward the hall. "Of course, we have many, many items of lesser value, which help support the war effort. You will keep track of the items collected by transports. I hope you enjoy typing long lists."

"A job's a job." Evie followed. "No matter what the challenge, I will do my best."

Evie worked throughout the day, putting her typing skills to use. Seidler visited often, offering a cup of real coffee or filling her in on the latest radio reports.

Once he entered the room and walked to a microphone mounted on the desk. "I have just received the transcripts of our great leader Goebbels's speech given at the *Sportpalast* on June 5."

Evie heard his words echoing around the camp a few seconds after he spoke them into the microphone. She watched the soldiers and prisoners moving in the *Appellplatz* outside. Only the guards, it seemed, cocked their heads to listen.

"Listen to the confidence of our leader," Seidler said. "'Germany and its allies are facing the most infernal plot against the freedom of humanity that history has ever known. We need not fear its threats. We face it with our heads held high. It will fall under the blows of the German sword, as often as it may be necessary. The enemy will receive no mercy. Let us eliminate all weakness of heart, all pity, all good-natured gullibility. The

German nation is forced to defend its very life. It will fight wherever there is opportunity. Victory is waiting at the end.

"'Heil Hitler. Victory in Germany.'"

Evie pressed a smile onto her face as Seidler glanced over at her. "Good news," she spouted.

"Yes, I like to announce such news whenever it comes. It does the morale of my workers good."

"I'm sure it does," she commented, returning to her typing.

At the end of the day Evie staggered out, exhausted. She'd typed dozens of lists of watches, eyeglasses, and shoes. Items to be sent away from the camp to be put to use by "worthy Nazi supporters."

As she walked in the warm summer evening back to the farm, Evie knew one thing. While death could be viewed outside her office window and breathed in through the contaminated air, it also lurked in hundreds of documents. In signatures, abbreviations, initials, and rubber stamps, death could be charted and graphed.

Death could be perfectly typed.

Thirty-Four

Otto finished filling out the last of the paperwork and shuffled it into a neat pile. While the Nazi occupational forces always enjoyed full authority to confiscate musical instruments and artwork for the good of the Reich, Otto's superiors still liked their paperwork in order. Rubber-stamped invoices with detailed lists of inventory were created for each location visited—unless a valuable item simply "disappeared," such as in the case of the Stradivarius.

Otto had never thought much about these forms until the Musik Aktion team's clerks were pulled from their posts and shipped to the front lines. Then he thought of nothing else.

He gathered his paperwork together and sauntered down to Viktor's office for his needed signatures.

They'd hardly spoken since Viktor had returned a few days prior. Obviously nothing of value had been discovered. Then again, maybe something had, which Viktor did not disclose.

Otto knocked once on the open door, then entered the room. "Your reports." He placed them on Viktor's desk.

"Thank you, that will be all," Viktor muttered as his pen swept across a page. Then he lifted his head, as if noticing Otto for the first time. "Oh, wait. I've been wanting to talk to you." He placed his pen on the table and folded his hands on his desk. "I see you've been handling things well in my absence."

He removed his glasses and wiped them with his handkerchief. "Who would have known that the cocky SS guard who discovered the legendary 'rare violin' at Nelahozeves would end up being such an asset to our team?" Viktor returned his glasses to his face. "Think of this now: What are the odds that you would just 'happen' to recognize a priceless violin? And just think, it had been right under my nose. You've done well."

"I'm sure the odds are very small." Otto shifted his weight from foot to foot, remembering that he'd promised Maddalena to meet her for dinner. "Will that be all?"

"No." Viktor seemed to sense Otto's eagerness and pointed to a chair.

Otto perched on its edge.

"Speaking of rare finds, I discovered an acquaintance of yours at Mauthausen."

"Someone from SS training?"

"No, a prisoner. While I was there, I attended a performance of a young Jew. The boy told me the camp conductor's name was Alexi Hořký. I knew it sounded familiar, then I remembered. Isn't that the fellow you knew from Prague?"

"Yes." Otto crossed his arms over his chest. "In fact, he's the man responsible for ending my musical career, thus forcing my current career choice."

Viktor pawed his unruly hair. "Oh yes, the one who refused to give you a chair in the Prague Philharmonic. I remember now."

Otto scoffed. "Thank you for putting it so bluntly. I'm glad to hear the Jew is where he belongs."

Viktor clicked his tongue and slowly shook his head from side to side. "Officer Akeman, you surprise me. I would've expected you to be on the first train to Mauthausen."

"What's the point? I know Hořký will have his day."

"If I were you, I would already be plotting my revenge. Have him tortured, hurt those he loves, have him killed. So many choices . . ."

"But I have work here. It's not as if I can simply hop on the next train."

Viktor rose and strode to his filing cabinet, pulling out a file from the top drawer. "Actually, I've just received some paperwork from Mauthausen, and it hasn't been correctly prepared. There must be a new person working in the administration office. And, personally, I

409

don't feel comfortable submitting *my* reports with these in such disarray."

"Are you inviting me to visit my 'friend'?"

"I'm inviting you to help get my files in order—it's only a day trip, after all."

Otto rose, smiling. "I'd love to see Herr Hořký again. I wonder how I should approach him."

"There are a million ways. Half the fun of revenge is planning it."

"And the other half?"

"Why, watching the scoundrel suffer, of course."

Otto turned, his mind already flooding with possibilities. He walked toward the door.

"Oh, and Herr Akeman?"

Otto paused and waited.

"While you are there, make sure you hear the young Jew, Jakub, play. He is quite a musician."

Jakub? The name stirred an image in Otto's mind of a lanky, awkward teen nearly falling into a bonfire for lack of confidence. *Look for a boy such as this.*

"I will do that, thank you."

Otto rubbed his hands together as he hurried to his desk and grabbed his jacket from the chair. He might have put his seeking aside for a time, but obviously the Ancients had not given up on him.

꧁   ꧁   ꧁

As the chauffeured car parked in the garage yard of Mauthausen, Otto knew Viktor was right about revenge. Otto had come up with dozens of ways to get back at Alexi. The hard part was choosing one.

He climbed from the car and let his eyes wander to the massive stone walls that jutted into the air, defying any attempt to bring them down.

The driver pointed to a flight of stairs. "Up those steps are the administration offices. From there you can get a great view of the 'final dead end' for enemies of the Reich."

"What did you call it?"

"The final dead end. I came up with the name myself." The driver laughed, slashing his throat with a finger. "For everyone who enters, this is the end of the road."

"Dead end. I'll remember that." Otto took the stairs two at a time and knocked at the door.

A young, pretty girl with soft brown eyes opened it, welcoming him in. Her face was pale. "Officer Akeman, we've been expecting you." She led him to the farthest office, motioned him inside, then scurried away.

The dark-haired man at the desk rose. "Welcome, and please accept my apologies. We have the paperwork prepared correctly this time. I'm so sorry for the wasted trip." He handed Otto a thick file.

"Thank you, but I have come for another purpose. I hear you have a fine orchestra, and being part of the Musik Aktion team, I was hoping to hear them play."

"Of course, they play on a daily basis as the prisoners march to and from work. But if you'd like a special concert, I'm sure we can arrange that too."

"I'm leaving in the morning. Is there any way I can

simply peek in on one of their practices? I don't require anything special."

"Yes, I'm sure I could find someone to help you." Seidler stroked his chin. "In fact, I could have Fraulein Bradl do it. I often catch her watching the orchestra as they play in the main square. I'm sure she'd enjoy joining you in a private concert. And who knows, it might even win me favor with the pretty little thing."

꩜   ꩜   ꩜

As soon as she walked through the gates, Evie was sure she'd lose her dinner all over her shoes. She'd watched the prisoners in the *Appellplatz* from a distance but to walk amongst them, to smell the stench of body odor, to brush past guards with guns and dogs, was a different thing entirely. The heaviness was even stronger here, within the gates.

She led the handsome blond SS officer toward the barracks where the orchestra lived and practiced.

"You move quickly for such a petite lady," the officer said with a smile.

She offered him no response but instead motioned to the door. "Here we are."

They entered, and Evie was sickened by the dank smell in the room. Her eyes widened as she noticed the three-tiered bunks made of wood, a few meager possessions, random musical instruments scattered about, and nothing else—except dirt, grime, and filth.

She observed the emaciated men seated around the

room. They all waited and watched as the tall conductor wrapped his arms around the youngest member and helped him play a challenging measure.

The boy looked up at the conductor and smiled as he hit the right notes. Even though they appeared as walking skeletons and wore nothing more than rags, Evie could clearly see the care between the two . . . like the love between a father and son.

The conductor glanced up, noticed his guests, and offered them a welcoming sweep of his hand. But when the conductor's eyes met the officer's, the smile quickly faded.

Evie eyed the officer for an explanation. He simply strode into the room and stood wide legged with his hands behind his back, chin cocked forward.

"Hello, Herr Hořký."

The conductor placed a protective arm around the boy's shoulders, then bowed low.

"I've come to hear the boy. His fame as a musician has spread. And to see your obvious care, he must be even more than I'd imagined."

Evie watched as the officer took a seat on an empty stool.

"Go ahead, boy. Play. Show me what has caused your conductor to love you so."

🍂   🍂   🍂

Jakub took a step forward, feeling the pressure of Alexi's hand on his shoulder. Finally Alexi released his grip, and Jakub bowed low before the officer.

"Do you have a special request, sir?"

"Jakub, is it?" the officer asked.

"Yes, sir."

The officer's eyes moved to the violin, and before the man could hide it, Jakub noticed a spark of recognition.

"Please, play anything you like."

Jakub closed his eyes and lifted his instrument. His fingers quivered more than they had in months.

"How about the Andante?" Alexi offered. "You play that so well."

Jakub heard concern in his friend's voice.

He lifted the bow and began to play, swaying his body back and forth in an effort to hide his trembling.

॰   ॰   ॰

The next day Jakub hurried out of the barracks, tin cup in hand, to join the others for breakfast.

A fierce-looking guard stopped him at the door. "Halt!" The wooden truncheon slammed into Jakub's stomach. Jakub doubled over, sinking to his knees in pain.

"By request of the administration office, you are ordered to stay in your barracks during all meals!"

Jakub looked to Alexi and the other orchestra members for help, but two more guards hustled them away in the direction of the soup caldron.

"If you are caught attempting to have your tin filled, you will be executed immediately! If anyone else is seen offering you food, he too will be hanged." The guard grabbed Jakub's tin and threw it across the room. His face pressed in on Jakub until their noses nearly touched. With brute force he pushed Jakub backward until he sprawled spread eagle on the floor.

Jakub walked back to his bunk, his arms wrapped around his aching stomach. Their food was hardly enough to keep one alive, but still it was something.

"What did I do to deserve this punishment?" he cried, overwhelmed by hunger. "What did I do wrong?"

    🍂   🍂   🍂

Otto stood near the place referred to as the Wailing Wall. From there he'd had a perfect view of Alexi's barracks—a perfect view of the look on Alexi's face as the boy was pushed back inside.

After a few minutes, the guard strode out of the barracks and nodded to Otto. "I've done as you asked. My pleasure."

"Good. Now there's just one more thing." Otto stroked his fingers along his chin. "Hang anyone attempting to give the young boy food—except the conductor. If you see him smuggling something in, do not stop him. But make sure he only has access to his own rations. I want the man to choose. His life or the boy's. I want him to know what it's like to attempt to save what you love most . . . and not be able to do so."

Thirty-Five

Otto slowly climbed the steps to his apartment. The questions that had haunted him during the train ride hounded him still. *Was seeing Alexi, plotting my revenge, Viktor's only motive for getting me to Mauthausen? Why hadn't Viktor discovered the boy's violin himself?*

He reached the landing, unlocked the door, and found Maddalena waiting on the sofa, drink in hand. She placed her glass on the coffee table and rose to greet him.

"How did you get in?" Otto attempted to clear his mind of his questions about Viktor.

"Is that any way to greet your girlfriend?" She embraced him, snuggling her head under his chin. "I missed you."

"You didn't answer my question."

"I convinced the locksmith that I had locked myself out of my apartment. There—does that make you happy? I figured if you weren't going to take the next step in this relationship, I was."

"Relationship?" Otto dropped his overnight case onto the floor, then slid off his jacket. "Who said anything about a relationship?"

Maddalena placed a hand on her hip. "I refuse to let you ruin your first night back with a sour attitude. Come see what I have for you."

She took Otto by the hand and led him into the bedroom. A framed print hung on an otherwise blank wall.

"Where did you find it?" Otto traced his fingers over the idealized drawing of a youthful Hitler. The Führer stood tall, an iron cross in one hand, in the other a waving swastika banner. "It's the one I wanted."

Maddalena pointed to the top edge of the print. "I know. Do you see the eagle descending from the sky above his head, hovering against the light of heaven?"

Otto pulled the blonde beauty into his arms. "Will you forgive me for being in such a bad mood? We should be celebrating." He lifted her hair from her neck, then placed one soft kiss near her ear. "I found it," he whispered.

She took a step back and looked up into his face. "Are you serious? You found a violin!"

Otto nodded. She slid into his arms, embracing his neck.

"This is all we've ever wanted! Do you think it will

be safe to travel to Switzerland this time of year? What do you think about crossing the border?"

"Switzerland? What are you talking about?"

"The violin, of course. It needs to be delivered across the border—keeping it in Austria wouldn't be safe. That is the one request our buyer made. I told you all this, remember?"

"No, you didn't tell me." Otto sank onto the bed.

"Surely, I did. I remember clearly, our first meeting. When can we leave? Do you already have a plan on how to take it from the boy?"

Otto sat straighter, catching Maddalena by the arm. "I never told you about a boy."

Her eyes widened, and she struggled against him. "Stop, you're hurting me. You did tell me, I swear!"

Otto stood. "No. I didn't say where I was going, or who I was to see. In fact, I remember leaving so quickly that I only had time for a short note." He grabbed her other arm and pressed her against the wall. "How do you know these things? How could you possibly know about the boy, unless—"

"Please, Otto, stop. You're hurting me."

"—unless Viktor is your contact."

Maddalena looked away.

"Of course. He wants the violin but doesn't want the risk of stealing and smuggling it out of the country. But why did he send you? Why didn't he just talk to me himself?"

Maddalena still struggled, but Otto kept her pinned.

"I don't know what you're talking about, Otto. Let me go!"

Otto pulled her from the wall and threw her onto the bed. Viktor's words replayed in his mind.

"Half the fun of revenge is planning the perfect scheme."

"And the other half?" Otto had asked.

"Watching the scoundrel suffer, of course."

Otto glared at Maddalena, curled next to the wall crying. She'd been created to pull off the perfect scheme.

"So let me guess." He walked to his closet and took a length of rope from his SS-issued duffel bag. "You have no interest in the occult, and you've never been to Tibet." He wrapped the rope around his hands and snapped it in the middle.

"No. I've never even been out of Austria. Viktor gave me the travel journals of the SS officers who went for Himmler. Really, Otto, it was all Viktor's idea. Please don't hurt me."

Otto leaned over her. "There's only one thing I don't understand. How were you going to kill me?"

Maddalena's breathing quickened, and she clawed the wall, scooting backward. "I would never have—"

"Viktor wouldn't pay for what he could take for free." Otto thought back to their first meeting at Nelahozeves. He clearly remembered the look of rage in Viktor's eyes when Otto pointed out the Stradivarius. Had Viktor planned to keep that instrument for himself? Is that why he'd denied knowing its worth?

"It's Viktor's perfect revenge. I made him appear

like a fool in front of his superiors. I also pointed out the violin he hoped to keep for his own. Am I right?"

She cried harder.

"Fine! Don't talk." Otto flipped Maddalena to her stomach, straddled her, and yanked her arms back, tying up her wrists.

"What are you going to do?" she asked, sobs erupting from her chest. "You're going to kill me, aren't you?"

"That depends. What was in it for you, my darling? Money, power?"

Maddalena shook her head, tears covering her face. "My young son. He's in hiding. Viktor swore he'd turn us in."

"Turn you in?"

Suddenly Otto understood. Viktor's revenge was meant not only to ruin Otto but to *defile* him as well.

🦋   🦋   🦋

AUGUST 3, 1944

Maddalena had wept, crying out for her son, most of the night. Otto would have felt a bit sorry for her, if she weren't a Jew who'd planned on killing him. Finally, as dawn neared, he devised a plan that would let him maintain his contacts with the Musik Aktion team, while at the same time taking Viktor out of action.

Maddalena had confessed she had no plans to meet with Viktor again until after they were due to return from Switzerland. With that news, he'd left her tied up at home, gagged and whimpering in the closet. He'd take care of that headache later.

He arrived at work early and took two blank forms from his desk drawer. The first was an inventory sheet. Pulling out an official form from Nelahozeves, Otto copied all the items carefully. Sneering, Otto thought of Kametler—the officer whose wife *and* pregnant mistress had both benefited from his position. Then Otto typed in two very special items.

Stradivarius violin, rare
Baroque center hall/library table
Southern Germany, c.1750

On the second sheet, he typed a note on Viktor's personal stationery.

Dear SS Unterscharführer Kametler,
Payment to Reich Protectorate for items invoiced is due immediately. If you cannot pay these funds, we can, perhaps, make an arrangement. Contact me at once.
Heil Hitler!
Herr Dr. Viktor Michitsch

Otto scattered the sheets amongst the other forms Viktor had to sign. The newly revised paperwork from Mauthausen added to the thickness of the stack, and

Otto was certain his superior would not take the time to read each one.

Otto addressed two envelopes, one to the *Unter-scharführer*'s work address and the other to his private residence. He only hoped that Kametler worked quickly.

Then he made his way down to Viktor's office. Viktor lifted his head and pushed back his glasses as Otto approached.

Otto dropped the pile onto his superior's desk. "These await your signature."

"Thank you."

Otto turned to leave.

"Oh, Officer Akeman, you did not tell me about the trip."

Otto turned, leaning against the door. "My plan to torture my *friend* is under way. You're right, getting revenge does bring one much pleasure."

"And the boy?"

"A fine musician, worthy of the visit."

Otto turned to leave, then paused, walking back to the desk.

"Sir, I also remember that I wish to ask a favor. I wanted to take my girlfriend on a short vacation. I know things are busy here; I could wait—"

"Nonsense." Viktor steepled his fingertips and leaned forward. "We all need a break every once in a while. The paperwork can wait."

"Yes, sir. Thank you, sir." Otto turned to leave, forcing his lips to remain in a straight line. Yet it was hard to do, when one's superior promoted leisure over work, especially during these tumultuous days.

❧ ❧ ❧

A mere week after Otto mailed the letters, a troop of armed SS guards burst into the office of Herr Dr. Viktor Michitsch. Viktor's wide-eyed, opened-mouth look of surprise was almost comical, like a scene from a ridiculous American movie.

The two guards had dragged Viktor away so quickly, the man hadn't time to protest, let alone plead his case. When the police van had roared away, Otto sauntered down to Viktor's office.

Look who's the winner now, Otto thought as he sank into Viktor's high-backed leather chair—still warm from the officer's presence—and smiled. *One problem down, two more to go.*

❧ ❧ ❧

Jakub grasped the bread that Alexi offered him. He shoved it into his mouth with large bites before reaching for the soup.

"Where is your food?" Jakub asked, drinking straight from the bowl.

"I've already eaten it, outside with the others."

"I don't understand how you sneaked this in. If you're caught—"

"Hush, let's not worry about that. It's in my Lord's hands."

Jakub furrowed his brow. "Alexi, may I ask you a question? You always say things like that. The others read from their prayer books and secretly celebrate Yom Kippur, but you don't. There's something different about you."

"Their faith is a little different from mine. I believe that the Messiah has already come in Jesus Christ."

Jakub sucked in a breath. "You are Christian? But isn't that what the Nazis believe—in Jesus?"

Alexi shook his head. "They say they do, but their actions show otherwise. Jesus asks His followers to love God and love their neighbors as themselves. *All* neighbors of every race and religion."

"But why do you believe in Jesus? How do you know it's true?" Jakub placed his bowl on the floor and wiped his face with the back of his hand.

"Hmmm, let me put it to you this way. Do you know what today is?"

Jakub scrunched his face and thought back over the week's events. "Saturday?"

Alexi laughed. "Yes, that too. It's October 28, Independence Day. Do you remember why we celebrate?"

Jakub's mind swirled with images of Prague aglow with a myriad of lights and decorated with thousands of flags and streamers. It seemed like a different lifetime. "Not really. I just remember that it was like a fairy tale celebration."

"Well, twenty-six years ago—before you were born

—our country gained freedom after three hundred years of Hapsburg rule. That became our day of statehood."

Jakub scratched his head, feeling his scalp crawl. He tried to ignore it but couldn't. He scratched again. "But can you still consider it a celebration of our statehood if we no longer have a republic?"

Alexi looked at him and frowned. "Jakub, close your eyes."

Jakub obeyed, and felt Alexi's rail-thin body settle on the floor next to him. "Let your imagination take you back. Think of when you last visited Hradcany Castle. Try to imagine our kings and queens who once ruled all of Europe."

In his mind's eye, Jakub pictured himself walking through the large front doors of the castle. His father and mother were at his side, Daniel too. "I can see the high ceilings with the curved beams. It's like being inside a whale's belly. I can feel the smoothness of the floor, even through the soles of my shoes, and I think about the great balls that used to take place in that very room."

"Good. Very good. Now imagine yourself wandering through the Old Town Square. You pause and glance up at the clock that has been keeping the townspeople on schedule for hundreds of years. Imagine walking past the Old Town Hall to Mala Strana with its crooked, quaint houses. Now you're crossing the Charles Bridge, taking time to study each of the medieval statues of the saints. The bridge has stood since the fourteenth century—"

"Built by Emperor Charles IV," Jakub interrupted.

Alexi chuckled. "Very good indeed. Now. Open your eyes."

Jakub looked into Alexi's deep brown gaze.

"Even though a different flag now waves over the city, it doesn't mean all is lost. The city still stands, even though we can't see it with our own eyes. The hope of our one day returning is something we must keep alive." Alexi patted Jakub's scrawny leg.

"Knowing that our beautiful city still stands, even when we cannot see it, that is faith." A serene peace shone from Alexi's eyes as if he were thinking of a dear friend. "And that's why I believe in Jesus. He gives me faith."

Jakub thought about all he'd learned in Home 1 about their ancient heritage. He'd found comfort in the stories of God's deliverance of His chosen people . . . but Jesus? It was all too confusing.

Alexi smiled. "I see that look on your face. I understand these things are sometimes hard to understand. Ah, Jakub, faith is believing that Good will triumph over Evil—in this dark hour and those still to come. I may not live to see it, but I trust that it will happen."

ॐ   ॐ   ॐ

CAMP CARLISLE, PENNSYLVANIA
AUGUST 31, 1944

Nick stacked his papers from the podium, then placed them in his briefcase, closing it with a click. The windows of the large classroom were cranked open, letting in summer sunshine along with a warm breeze. Jazz music drifted out the window of a neighboring building. Nick joined in, whistling along with the tune as he headed into the hall.

"Doc Fletcher? Do you have a second?" A young medic waited outside the door, medical handbook in hand. He glanced up at Nick with eager eyes, then threw him a salute.

Nick paused and his lips curled in a smile. Even though he couldn't officially put M.D. behind his name, all the new recruits called the old veterans "Doc." He returned the salute, then leaned against the corridor wall. "Sure, what can I do for you?"

"You mentioned the uses of penicillin to fight infection, and I—"

"Nick! Nick, you're not going to believe this!" The voice echoed through the tiled corridor.

Nick glanced up to see Twitch jogging toward him, waving a small stack of envelopes in his hand. Nick raised his hand, motioning for Twitch to be patient.

He'd been reunited with his friend after they'd both been sent back to Camp Carlisle to train the new troops. Their reunion had been kicked off by weekend leave in New York City. Nick had taken Twitch home, where the two had been treated like royalty. The only problem was that Twitch hadn't seemed to notice. He'd been too busy reading and rereading his letters from his girlfriend, Nancy—a nurse with the 48th Surgical Hospital—to anyone who'd listen.

Twitch stopped before Nick, panting, with his hands on his knees.

"I'll be right with you," Nick said, casting a glance at the envelopes in Twitch's hand. They read "Airmail." More letters from Nancy, no doubt.

"Now, you asked about penicillin." Nick turned back to his student, but Twitch wasn't about to wait. His hand grasped Nick's shoulder and swung him around. "You don't understand," Twitch panted. "These letters are for you. *From Europe.*"

Nick snatched them from Twitch's hand and ripped the first envelope open. It was her handwriting all right. With trembling hands, he unfolded the first sheet and glanced at the date. July 4, 1944. Just one month ago. Evie was alive!

> *Dear Nick,*
>
> *Darling, if you've heard a horrible rumor that I'm dead, don't believe it. I'm hiding with friends, hoping to make a difference in this war. Know that I love you. . . .*

Nick wiped his eyes with the back of his hand and barely realized that Twitch had taken over answering the student's question.

> *I'm still in Austria, and I wonder where you are, my love. Are you finished with school and working as a doctor now? Have you joined the service and are working to save lives on the field? Enclosed is an*

address where you can write, although I was warned that delivering letters from you will not be a Number 1 priority. How could they say that—hearing from you is my Number 1 desire. Just to know that you're thinking of me, loving me as I love you . . .

Nick pressed his head back against the wall and closed his eyes. *Oh, Evie, girl, I do love you. Couldn't stop.*

"Nick?" Twitch's voice interrupted his thoughts. "Is it really her; is she alive?"

"Yeah." Nick's voice caught in his throat. "She's alive." He gulped down his emotion. "She really is."

He opened his eyes and glanced at his friend with new determination. "I have to go back, buddy. I need to get back to Europe and find her."

Thirty-Six

Otto rubbed his face beside his ear and wondered if he'd done the right thing. After a week of being tied up as a prisoner, Maddalena swore she had no lasting ties to Viktor. Instead, she promised to remain with Otto, caring for him, loving him.

Still, every time he looked at the beautiful blonde, he could only think of one thing. *She's a Jew.*

He had debated what to do with her. Kill her himself? No, that would be too messy. Take her down to gestapo headquarters and turn her in? That was a possibility, but then he'd have to admit that he'd been intimate with a Jewess—putting his own reputation on the line.

He'd finally decided on the quickest, easiest way. He shaved off her blonde hair, burnt her identification papers, and dropped her on the outskirts of Vienna. It was only a matter of time before she would be caught and hauled off to a work camp.

One less problem to deal with.

Otto glanced out his office window to the hustling streets below, wondering if the woman was already headed away from Vienna in a cattle car. With Maddalena out of the way, his attention again turned to the violin.

He wanted to journey to Mauthausen to discover how things were developing. Was the young musician dying of starvation? Or was Alexi sacrificing himself for his prized pupil? He longed to see them growing thinner by the day.

But he'd have to wait. There would be opportunity in the future to see the fruit of his revenge. Either way, he knew the instrument wasn't going anywhere. Even if the boy died of starvation, another orchestra member would use the Guarneri. It would wait for him.

Otto leaned forward onto his desk, touching the tips of his fingers together like a steeple. *How can I get it out on my own, without the Musik Aktion team? No doubt this department is being watched even closer now. When I do get it out, where can I hide it? And what powers can I use to assist my efforts?*

♪   ♪   ♪

MAUTHAUSEN, AUSTRIA
NOVEMBER 23, 1944

Evie hurried down the granite stairs leading away from the camp administration building. She pulled her

432

jacket tight around her, blocking the cold and ensuring that the forms she'd copied would not slide from their hiding place in the waistband of her skirt.

She'd uncovered the information that their contacts in Switzerland were looking for. On the 6th and 7th of September 1944, forty Dutch and seven British special agents had been put to death. They'd been dropped above German occupied territory, in hopes of assisting the Resistance, but instead were turned to ash in Mauthausen's crematorium. *While I was typing endless lists of papers, they were being tortured and killed not far beyond my window.*

A cold winter wind scattered snow flurries into Evie's face, and she quickened her steps.

"Fraulein Bradl!" a voice called.

Evie turned and saw Officer Seidler stepping out of a parked car. "Surely, you're not going to walk home in this weather. Come, let me give you a ride."

Evie dared not protest. She ran around the side and climbed in, eager to get out of the frosty wind.

Seidler started the engine, then drove down the steep, icy road to town. "How about some dinner? The hotel serves a fine goulash."

Evie looked down at her coat, sure the wrinkle of hidden papers could be seen right through the fabric. "Perhaps not tonight."

"Fraulein Bradl, you should know I won't take no for an answer."

She cast him a smile and crossed her arms over her waist. "All right, then, sure. Why not?"

They drove to the main hotel in Mauthausen, and Evie excused herself to use the powder room. Pulling out the papers from her skirt, she looked around and wondered what to do next. Her coat had no pockets. The toilet would get clogged. Evie knew she couldn't walk around all evening with them tucked inside her slim skirt. She suddenly snapped her fingers and returned the papers to her skirt. Strolling back into the foyer, she approached Officer Seidler.

"Excuse me, do you have a cigarette and a light?"

Seilder cocked one eyebrow, pulling both from his jacket. "May I join you?"

She snatched the cigarette and silver lighter from his hand, then ran a finger down his sleeve. "No need. I'll just be a minute."

His mouth widened to a full grin. "Yes, please hurry. I'll procure a table."

Evie rushed outside and around to the back of the building. She quickly scanned the first page, committing the important parts to memory, then she dropped the papers to the ground, securing them to the thin layer of snow with her booted foot.

She tried the lighter, attempting to block the wind with her cupped hand. Once, twice, three times. It was no use. Every time the smallest flame flickered, a gust of wind blew it out.

"Come on—light, will you?"

Suddenly a black leather boot planted itself next to hers.

"I'll take those," a male voice said.

Evie jumped, then covered her pounding heart with her hand. A bearded face smiled at her.

"Felix!" She moved to offer him a hug, then thought better of it.

Remember Nick. Over the few months she'd lived at the farmhouse, she'd written and mailed over a dozen letters to Nick with the help of the Resistance. *He's the one I love.* Still, she felt happiness at the sight of Felix.

"What you are you doing here? What if someone sees us?"

"That was a long overnight stay, Theresa. I had to check to see how you were. I saw you inside, and it seems like you're doing *too* well at your job."

"I'm doing what the Resistance asks of me. Nothing more."

Felix took a step back. "You are doing wonderfully. I just . . . miss you."

"You come all the way here and risk speaking to me in public to tell me that? Anyone could waltz around the corner and see us. In fact, my boss, Seidler, is probably wondering where I am."

"I've asked Korina to keep him occupied for a few minutes. Listen. When I heard you were working in the camp—it's so dangerous. I was afraid we'd lose you. We've lost so many, and I never told you . . ." He cleared his throat. "I just wanted to check on you, that's all. And to let you know that we've found more inside the angel."

Evie pressed the papers to her chest. "In the angel?"

The armored car in front of Nick's jeep snowplowed to the side of the road, and Nick's driver, PFC Will Greer, followed suit. Four months ago it had taken a bit of convincing for Nick to talk his superior officer into transferring him back to Europe.

"Why would anyone want to go back?" he was questioned.

Nick had given one hundred reasons, except the real one. *To be closer to Evie. To find her,* his heart urged. After it was finally agreed that he could join a new division soon to ship out, it hardly took much more convincing for Twitch to join him. Soon the emblem of the 11th Armored Division was sewn onto their uniform jackets, and without even a short visit home, the two sailed to England, then a few months later found themselves on French soil.

"Ten-minute break!" echoed down the line.

Nick thankfully climbed from the jeep, stretched, and wondered how far ahead Twitch was. Two days ago, they'd been put into different units before their uneventful trip across the channel. Then, as a group, they'd begun to move toward Lorient, where the Nazis still had a stronghold along the coast. That—of course—had been the plan.

Yesterday, orders came down that the division

436

would instead move to the Ardennes as fast as possible. Hitler had pushed his army through the thick forests in Belgium, making one last attempt to regain control of France. The Allies hadn't expected the Führer's strike, and some of their soldiers, including the 101st, were stuck in Bastogne, pinned down by the Nazi midwinter offensive.

Nick stepped from the jeep and shielded his eyes from the sunlight glaring off the snow. "Hey, Greer, I think I see the Eiffel Tower."

"What a coincidence." The driver hopped onto the ice-slick road. "A break at the same moment the Eiffel Tower comes into view. Are you sure that tiny, pointy thing is it?" He pulled his shiny black camera from his duffel and shot a picture.

"I'm not sure, but hey, we can use it as bragging rights back home."

Greer turned and shot some photos of the other buildings. "Don't have many buildings that old in Illinois. Nope, sure don't."

Two French men walked by, talking animatedly — their words a jumble of sounds that made no sense to Nick's ears.

"Monsieur! Monseiur!" a voice called from behind.

Now, that I understand. Nick turned and spotted a small, white-haired Frenchman hurrying up the lane.

In his two hands, pieces of white fabric fluttered. The man paused before them, panting, and held out what Nick now realized were handkerchiefs. The edges had been embroidered with fine red and blue threads.

"For you," the man proclaimed with a roll of his tongue.

"Why, thank you." Nick took a handkerchief and nodded. He patted his pocket and pulled out his ration of Lucky Strikes, handing the whole package to the man.

The gentleman's mouth widened in a smile, revealing toothless gums. He grabbed Nick's hand and kissed it soundly, then turned and hurried off in the direction he had come.

"You know that pack you just handed him is like gold around here? You coulda got a lot more."

"Yeah, but I don't smoke." Nick shrugged. "It was obvious the war has been hard on the guy. Besides, we're their heroes now, remember?"

"We still have one more job to claim that title . . . and it's waiting for us at the end of this long push."

*   *   *

A thick cough racked Jakub's body. He stood in the line with the others, ready to play, shivering. Many of the orchestra members did not have coats or sweaters. Some stood with bare feet in the snow. Still, they remained poised and ready. Only one thing stopped them.

"Where is Alexi?" the SS guard Mueller shouted. "Where is the imbecile?"

"He is not feeling well," Janos stammered. "He's down with a fever and—"

"I'll go take care of him then." Mueller took a step

toward their barracks. "I'll show him what sick really is!"

"No!" Jakub cried out, surprising even himself.

Mueller paused and then laughed. "Oh, so this young man is going to stand up for his friend, is he?"

Mueller pushed against Jakub's chest and sent him sprawling on the icy granite. Jakub's tailbone hit the packed ice with a thud. His violin flew across the *Appellplatz,* nearly sliding under the feet of workers marching past.

"Don't you realize, boy, that you are the one responsible? What you've already done!" Mueller sneered, and he moved back toward the orchestra members.

"I don't care who takes over, but somebody must lead the music!" Mueller swung his arm in a large circle. "Play. Play!"

Janos hobbled to the front and led the players in a simple marching song.

Mueller peered down at Jakub. "As for you, boy, pick up your violin and get back in line. You're lucky my wife favors you. Otherwise, I'd take care of you myself."

Jakub retrieved his violin and scurried back in place. He joined the happy tune, but the guard's sharp words haunted him. How was *he* responsible for Alexi's illness?

⁊⁊⁊   ⁊⁊⁊   ⁊⁊⁊

Evie watched the orchestra members from her window and gasped as a beefy guard shoved the young boy to the ground.

She heard Seidler's chair scrape across the floor. His footsteps neared. She quickly returned to her desk and resumed typing.

"You're quite fascinated with the orchestra, aren't you?" Seidler plopped onto the corner of her desk. "Every time they come out to play, your typing stops."

Evie's face reddened. "I'm sorry. I won't do it again, Officer Seidler."

Seidler reached over and ran his thumb across Evie's fingers. "How many times have I told you, Theresa? I want you to call me Kurt."

"Yes, Kurt. Thank you. It won't happen again."

She resumed typing, but he didn't budge.

"It is an odd thing, I suppose—an orchestra of the finest musicians playing for half-dead prisoners." He drummed his fingers next to Evie's typewriter. "I mean, any aspiring musician would love to learn from such talented men. Don't you think?"

Evie paused again from her typing. "I'm sorry, what was that?"

"Okay, I'll just say it—would you like to have some free music lessons?"

"From the prisoners?" Evie's face brightened. "Could I?"

Seidler patted her hand. "Now that's the face I like to see. Consider it a late Christmas present. I'll see what I can do."

PART FOUR

The people that walked in darkness have seen a great light:
they that dwell in the land of the shadow of death,
upon them hath the light shined.

Isaiah 9:2

Thirty-Seven

NEUFCHATEAU, BELGIUM
DECEMBER 30, 1944

Large snowflakes dropped straight from the sky, and a thick layer of white had risen steadily through the night. Still, Nick's driver had ventured on, closer to the front. Word was, they'd be hitting action soon.

They passed supply trucks heading the opposite direction, empty and ready for another cache. More significantly, Nick counted twenty-one ambulances evacuating the wounded.

When they finally reached their destination, Nick stepped from the jeep and blew into his hands.

"See that?" Greer asked.

Nick squinted and followed the direction of the man's finger. Ahead, a line of artillery waited with flag-pole-sized muzzles pointed toward the German lines that were out of view, but within range of the large guns.

As they watched, the guns coughed and spit, belching their flame, then finally relaxed. Their blasts shook the forest, causing snow to sift off tree limbs. Even from this distance, the smell of smoke and gunpowder hung in the air.

"So that's what we've been hearing." The muscular driver covered his ears, raising his voice. "Must mean we're pretty close to the front."

"Not too close." Nick rubbed his hands together. "Those are the big boys, the long Toms. I'd be more worried if they had us up by the 105-mms."

"Fletcher, get a load of this."

Nick walked to where the younger medic, Benson, was looking up at the wreckage of a downed airplane in the trees. The plane hung suspended in the limbs as if it had been gently laid there by a passing giant.

"I wonder how long it's been there." Nick gazed up at the plane.

"Who knows, but it looks like *he's* been given the once-over."

Nick followed Benson's gaze to the base of the trees. A German pilot was sprawled, frozen in the snow. The pilot's face was bloated. His open, lifeless eyes were fixed on the suspended plane. The man's broken legs folded under him, and someone had nabbed his boots.

"Looks like he's been coated with melted sugar." Nick took a step closer, noticing his pockets turned inside out. "Man, he's been picked clean."

"That's a horrible way to treat a dead body. Did you see his finger?"

The man's finger was cut to a jagged stump.

Benson leaned close for a better look. "Someone chopped it off to get his ring, I bet!"

Nick heard feet shuffling behind him. He turned to find gray-haired Surgeon O'Conner, arms clasped behind his back. "Come with me, Fletcher. I need you for a moment."

Nick stumbled through the snow with a hollow, sickened feeling. Even though he'd seen plenty of dead bodies in North Africa, it wasn't something one could get used to.

O'Conner paused on the road, rocking back and forth on the balls of his feet. "It seems things are worse than we thought. The battalion headquarters needs additional help at the aid stations up front. The line units are receiving more casualties than they can handle."

"Do you need me to head up now?"

"Not yet. You'll be notified when they need you, and where. We'll give you a map and a driver. Depending on how the battles turn, you might stay only a day or two at each spot. When it eases up, you'll return to C Company and resume your regular duties."

Nick nodded. "Yes, sir."

"Now, part two. Did you see that guy?" O'Conner turned his attention to a ditch at the side of the road.

Another body, bloated by death, lay shrouded with a thin layer of snow.

"Some of these medics are green. They've never worked with a real body before. All that's in their head is photos and lecture."

"I imagine you're right, sir."

O'Conner placed a hand on Nick's shoulder. "Bodies will be showing up soon. Live ones. Gather the new medics up and have them take a look at this fellow. I expect a full report from each one listing the extent of his injuries and what killed him."

Nick hesitated, then walked over and hunkered down beside the man. With a soft hand he brushed snow from the guy's chest.

"I'll make sure it's taken care of."

"Good. I expect their reports in ten minutes."

ॐ   ॐ   ॐ

KZ MAUTHAUSEN, AUSTRIA
JANUARY 1, 1945

Evie waited, violin in hand, as the prisoners finished their evening drills.

They stood in long rows in the ankle-deep snow, working on their saluting with the kapos.

"*Mützen!*" the prisoner-guard called.

In unison, the prisoners' right hands rose to their caps and waited motionlessly.

"*Ab!*"

Thin hands snatched off the caps and, with a synchronous clap, slapped them against right thighs.

"*Mützen!*"

The hands went up again and clumsily set caps on heads.

"Auf!"

Hands went down, this time without the caps. Palms slapped against right thighs with the same synchronous slap. After a dozen repetitions of the same drill, the prisoners were finally allowed to bustle back to their barracks.

Evie noticed their "shoes"—some had wrapped their bluish feet in paper, others in rags from torn blankets. She followed the group into the barracks. Inside it was barely warmer than out. All eyes turned as she entered, gazing with curiosity.

A small group was huddled around a man lying on the lower bunk. It was the conductor. His paper-thin eyelids were half shut and his breathing labored.

"Will he be okay?" Evie asked.

A young man rose and shrugged his shoulders. "I don't know. But it doesn't look good. He'd been giving me his food . . . but he told me he was eating too. I never thought . . ." The boy's voice trailed off.

Evie didn't know what to say. "I—I'm here for a violin lesson." She raised her case as proof. "And as a thank-you, I brought you this." She pulled a small bag from the pocket of her oversized coat. "It's the lunch my landlord made for me."

Hunger radiated from the eyes of every man in the room, and Evie wished she had more to offer. "If—if I'm caught, I'll tell them it's my lunch. I don't have to lie." She offered it to the young man.

"Thank you. I'm Jakub." He pointed to the left

toward a man with a peg leg. "This is Janos. He will be your tutor."

Evie watched as Jakub carefully opened the paper bag. He held it up to his nose, taking a large whiff. Jakub blew out his breath and then held the bag out for others to do the same.

"It's only bread and butter, and an apple from the cellar." Evie placed a hand to her heart.

Jakub took the bread from the waxed paper, then lifted it to the conductor's lips. "Alexi, look."

Alexi's eyes opened wider. He lifted his head, took a bite, then motioned for Jakub to have some.

Jakub took a bite, his lips turning up into a soft smile. "Thank you again. I've never tasted anything so wonderful."

Alexi took a few more bites, then sealed his lips and shook his head. "No more. I don't want to overdo it," he whispered. "Please share with the others."

Jakub handed the group on the right one piece of the bread. To the group on his left, he handed the apple. Evie lowered her head and watched as the men each took a small nibble, then passed it on, each bite like a treasure.

When the last bite was taken, Janos touched Evie's arm. "Are we ready to begin?"

Evie lifted her old, beat-up violin and nodded. "Yes. I'm ready anytime you are, sir."

The man rose to his full frame and jutted out his chin. Evie could see that her respectful words were like water to a wilting plant.

Nick hadn't been settled in for an hour when the call came for him to move to the front. His driver maneuvered the jeep through the snow, getting him as close to the aid station as possible. When it was impossible to go any farther for fear of getting stuck in the snow, Nick climbed out and hiked up the road toward the sound of gunfire.

Groups of infantrymen struggled down the road toward him. Rifles were slung over their shoulders, and a dark growth of beard showed on many faces. The men didn't meet his gaze when they passed.

As he walked, Nick's eyes darted to the woods, expecting to see German infantrymen in pursuit. Instead, it was quiet as he found his way to the aid station. In the distance he watched as light tanks scooted across the snow toward the woods, bucking up clouds of white. Then he ducked into the aid tent, his eyes widening at the sight of a room packed tight with injured men. *Here we go again.*

A medic strode toward him, his frock stained red from blood. Large bags sagged under his bloodshot eyes. "You must be Fletcher. I'm glad you made it."

Nick nodded.

"I need you to perform triage over there."

"Got it." Nick walked through the rows, assessing who needed help first. He was drawn to a man with a large, gaping chest wound. Hastily Nick applied a bandage and took a fresh one from the supply shelf. *First, stop the bleeding.* His training, his experience came back as if it hadn't been a year and a half since he had worked on a live person. As Nick hovered over the soldier, he felt a tug on his frock.

A baby-faced GI lay on a litter, looking up at him. "I feel wet," he moaned.

"I'll be with you next."

Nick stopped the bleeding on the chest wound, then applied sulfa powder to guard against infection.

"I feel wet," the guy said louder.

Nick continued on, bandaging the wound and giving the soldier a shot of morphine. Then he motioned to two litter bearers who'd just entered. "This one's ready to go to the next aid station." Nick patted the guy's shoulder as he was whisked away.

"Okay, your turn." Nick reached under the baby-faced soldier to slide him off the litter and onto the table. The litter was filled with blood. *No. Dear God, help.*

The man's face was pale. His lips moved but emitted no sound.

"Stay with me, buddy." Nick worked quickly, applying pressure to stop the bleeding from a huge shrapnel wound on his back . . . but it was no use. In minutes he was gone. He swept his hand over the kid's eyes. Swallowing back his emotion, he turned to the next in line.

Nick curled himself into the corner of the aid tent under a dirty blanket. His stomach growled, and he realized he'd eaten nothing except a K ration that morning. It had been dark for hours, and he needed sleep before things picked up again. Images flashed through his mind: injured men and filthy litter bearers journeying into the front lines for more wounded. What were the names of his fellow medics, and how many guys had he patched up? Thirty? Forty? Mainly he saw the face of the kid he didn't get to soon enough.

Suddenly, Nick heard a familiar voice. He sat up and gawked as Twitch hurried toward him. His buddy's uniform was plastered with a mixture of dirt and blood. When Twitch slipped off his helmet, his white-blond hair was also caked with filth. "I heard you were here. Just had to see if it was true."

Nick jumped to his feet and embraced his friend. "Good to see you, buddy. Looks like they've got you in the front. I can't imagine how scary that is."

"Yeah, but you know what? I helped lots of guys today—probably saved their lives. I'm glad I'm back."

Nick sighed. "Me too. I just hate seeing so many guys injured, killed."

"It's a baptism by fire, that's for sure. But I'm glad I found you. I have a letter I want to read." Twitch's eyes flashed eagerness.

Nick placed a hand over his throbbing head. "Look, Twitch, I'm really exhausted. I just don't think I can handle it right now. I've just worked ten hours straight."

"No, I really think—"

"Keeting!" A shout interrupted Twitch's plea.

He glanced over his shoulder. "Never mind. I gotta go." Twitch took a step, then paused. He took the metal-plated Bible from his shirt pocket and pulled out a piece of paper tucked inside. "It's a letter to my parents. I'll just leave it and let you read it when you have time. I'll grab it from you tomorrow so I can mail it."

Nick took the paper and slid it into his pocket. "Sure, buddy, I'll read it after I get some shut-eye."

"Keeting!" The voice called again.

Twitch turned to go. "I'm glad we'll be working together. At least for a few days." He gave one final wave as he jogged out the door.

❧   ❧   ❧

After Twitch left, Nick gave up trying to sleep. Instead, he got up and began helping out with a new passel of wounded. He couldn't sleep, knowing that minutes made the difference between life and death for some.

An hour later, he moved to help a guy with a bullet to the leg. He glanced up at the guy's wincing face and recognized him.

"Hey, Jones, we were bunk mates on the ship, weren't we?"

The guy nodded and moaned. "I guess."

"Just a leg wound—you're doing good." Nick patted his shoulder. "Who knows? This might be the million-dollar wound, sending you home."

Nick sprinkled sulfa powder on the wound, bandaged it quickly, and signaled that Jones was ready for transport.

Jones opened his eyes, then rolled them closed again. "Hey, didn't you hang around with Frank Keeting?"

"Yeah, that was me. In fact, I just saw Twitch; he's in the area—"

Jones moaned louder as the two litter bearers picked up his stretcher. "No, wait!" He reached for Nick. "Fletcher, I have to tell you . . ."

Nick motioned for the litter bearers to stop.

The man looked into Nick's face with tear-rimmed eyes. "I don't know how to say it—it's Frank. He's dead."

The bearers set Jones down. Nick's air escaped from his lungs as if he'd just been punched in the stomach. "That's not possible. He was just here, not an hour ago." Nick looked to the corner where they'd talked.

"It just happened. Right before I was hit. Fletcher, you would have been so proud—"

Nick sank to his haunches, shaking his head in disbelief. "There must be a mistake. I just saw him. He's not dead."

The sorrowful look in Jones's eyes told him this was no mistake.

"What happened?"

"You should have seen him," Jones grimaced, holding his leg.

Nick took a vile of morphine, removed the cap, and plunged it in six inches from the wound. "Go on."

"We heard shots on the left, then everything opened up. Bullets buzzed by our heads. It stopped suddenly, and I turned to my buddy Montgomery. He sat there just looking at the big hole in his chest. I screamed 'Medic,' and . . ." Jones gasped, closing his eyes.

Jones's face was growing blurry as Nick wiped his eyes. "It's okay, slow down."

Jones took a breath. "I saw Frank running toward us, crouched below the waves of the tracers. He didn't even look scared. He bandaged up Monty, while I was too terrified watching the tracers flying overhead. Fletcher, he didn't look up once. He just kept doing his work. Together, we carried Monty back to the jeep and strapped the litter to the front. On his way toward another wounded soldier, Frank was hit. They had to have seen the Red Cross on his helmet and armband, and they shot anyway. When I got to him, he was already dead, at least five bullets in his head and chest. I'm sorry, man. I got hit trying to pull his body out."

Nick stood in silence as Jones was whisked away.

It was a gray sort of dawn. Nick had kept Twitch's letter tucked in his pocket, waiting for a quiet moment. It had been a busy night, filled with casualties. With each man brought in, Nick scanned the faces, hoping Jones had been mistaken. Yet a few more injured soldiers came through who had witnessed it too—Twitch was gone.

Hunched down in the snow, his back against a tree, Nick opened the envelope. A fresh wave of tears washed over him when he recognized Twitch's handwriting.

Dear Mom and Dad,

It's just a short note, because believe it or not, I'm on my way to the front lines. This is beautiful country, Dad. Perfect for hunting. Only here, I'm afraid we're the game.

I'm not scared, though. In fact, I have a new sense of peace. I never thought much about religion before I met Nick. He doesn't talk about God much with his words. But I can see a difference in him. He gave me a Bible a while ago, and he doesn't know I've been reading it every night. Last night, I read by my dim flashlight under an unfamiliar sky, and I thought of the light of God.

Sometimes it's hard to see God working when everything's going good. His light doesn't seem so bright when everything else is lighted too. Like a flashlight on a sunny day. It's easy to miss God sometimes. But in places where it's dark, like this place, I can see God better than ever, and I've started on that relationship.

Okay, don't get creeped out because this letter is all philosophical. It's still me, just trying to make sense of this big war. I'll write again soon and let you know what battle is like this time around. I'm dreading it and sort of excited at the same time. Excited to know that I may again be some help.

Give a hug to each other for me . . . until I can do it for myself. Thanks for being such great parents.

Love,

Frank

Thirty-Eight

Otto spread the maps out before him, finalizing his plan. The Reich was crumbling around him like a sandcastle, but he was determined not to be swept away by the incoming tide of Allied troops.

His finger followed the red-lined trail he'd marked off in the area surrounding Mauthausen—through the camp gates, around the backside of the mountain that the work camp sat on, and deep into the armament tunnels, which he had discovered in Reich maps of the area. Records indicated six kilometers of tunnels stretched in one mountain alone—enough to hide him until he felt safe to move south toward Switzerland.

The key was not to be hasty. He had to prepare, to hide away enough food and water to last months if need be. Just as the Ancient power had led Otto toward the truth he sought, so too he trusted it would guide his current plans. The Presence, which warmed his chest and whispered to his thoughts, had not steered him wrong yet. It had led him to the boy, Jakub. It had guided him to the treasure found at the place some called a "dead end."

Otto remembered the rest of Weber's prophecy, and a new confidence sprouted. *Along this path you will discover a treasure. . . . It will be yours until the day you breathe your last.* Otto had no doubt this would come true, and he looked forward to an enlightened future to use, and be used by, this Power.

But first, he must trust and take the next step. Otto stood and looked into the mirror. "Good-bye, Otto Akeman—at least for now."

He stroked his blond hair and newly grown beard, studying his profile in the mirror. Then he took a bottle of black dye from the cupboard and unbuttoned his shirt. *Tomorrow an officer in the Musik Aktion team will mysteriously disappear . . . on the same day the town of Mauthausen will acquire a new resident.*

"Hans is a good name," Otto said, camouflaging his Viennese resonance with the thick accent of a German farmer. "Hans Gutman."

          Ro   *Ro*   *Ro*

Evie rose from her bed and scanned the items laid out on the bureau—items brought to her by Felix on his last visit. The hymn sheet. Her miniature Statue of Liberty. The photo of her and Nick.

And then there were the items most recently found in the angel statue. First, a letter from Nick's parents offering sympathy for Evie's death. The English words on the page stirred happy memories of the laughing, boisterous family. She read the familiar words again.

We cannot stop crying over the loss of Evie. Nick's trying to move on, but she is forever on his mind. Nick is serving with the 81st Medical Battalion, attached to the 11th Armored Division. He's serving as a battalion surgeon, which means he'll be safe away from the front lines once they arrive in Europe.

Evie had worried about that. Afraid that word of her "death" would get to Nick. *Poor Nick.* Would he move on? Could he? He loved her intensely, she had no doubt. But if he thought she was dead . . .

Evie tried to consider what would happen if she believed the opposite was true. What if she'd received news of Nick's death? It would hurt more than she could imagine, but would she be able to live again? To move past the pain?

A face stirred in her thoughts. It was the look of Felix's pained eyes the last time she saw him. Evie had hurried inside the inn before Seidler grew suspicious, and they'd parted with few words. That had been nearly two months ago, and she hadn't heard from Felix since. Evie had to admit she missed seeing him, missed his gentle manner yet dedicated spirit.

Was she making the right decision? She lifted the photo and looked into Nick's face. It was so familiar, yet also distant, like the memory of a pleasant dream.

No, she loved Nick. He was the one she wanted to spend her life with, fairy tale or not. And until she knew for sure that all hope for their reunion was gone, she'd keep loving him, longing for him.

Evie reread the note. *He'll be safe away from the front lines once they arrive in Europe.*

Nick in Europe! He could be anywhere, assigned to numerous fronts, but he was nearer. And that renewed her hope.

She reread it yet again. *Once they arrive?* When is that? The letter was undated and had been tucked inside the angel in a simple white envelope. There was no indication of when it had been written or how it had been smuggled into Austria.

Evie glanced at the second letter. This one was just as surprising. It was from Isak, discussing his work in the Resistance. She smiled to herself. The mystery was finally solved, and she wondered how she could ever have believed her dear brother was a true Nazi.

I should have known, Evie thought. *He and Ilse were both involved, and Isak was just trying to protect me. He was the one on the inside who, for my own safety, made sure everyone believed I was dead. Well, almost everyone.*

She looked down at the letter. Nothing in it would

reveal Isak's identity if the wrong hands accidentally acquired the letter.

Dear One,

I'm so glad you are safe. I've helped your friends for many years from the inside. I knew immediately the true story of what happened that fateful night. I helped confirm the lie, but I couldn't keep the secret from Mother. The news would have taken her to the grave. She's the one who told me about the angel. Just like when we were kids, you keep my secrets, and I'll keep yours, yes?

Know that we love you and long to be reunited.

With all my love . . .

P.S. I will use my connections to let our friends across the sea know about the misunderstanding. Father sent them word of the accident without my knowledge.

Evie pressed the letter to her chest and considered Isak's closing comments. *Long to be reunited . . .* It was no wonder that Isak had been distant in past years—she now understood the tension and loneliness of living a secret life.

Evie also thought about her mother. Distance and longing for family helped her to see things differently. Looking back, Evie realized that most of her mother's actions were based on fear: fear of Evie getting hurt by people, by circumstances. Fear of the unknown in this changing world, so different from the one Mother had grown up in.

I'll let her know I understand better now. I'll let Isak know too—once we're reunited.

Evie only hoped her next plan wouldn't jeopardize that.

She hurried to the corner of the room and removed the violin from its case, tucking it away in her closet. Then she tiptoed through the quiet house toward the kitchen.

🎵　　　🎵　　　🎵

Evie nodded thanks to the guard who opened the front gate for her. A second SS man, Heinz, stalked over, escorting her to the barracks where the orchestra players were housed. *Breathe. Look in his eyes. Smile. Do not give yourself away.*

"Is this winter ever going to end? It's been a long one already, don't you think?" Evie pulled her wool scarf tight around her chin.

"It's a cold one, all right." Heinz walked with quickened steps. "I'm surprised you're out on a night such as this."

Evie shrugged. "I'm a dedicated violin student—who gets free lessons. How can I go wrong?"

Heinz opened the barracks door and led her inside. He scanned the room, then leaned against the nearest wall, blowing into his cupped hands to warm them. Sometimes Heinz stayed during the lessons; sometimes he left. Even though the room wasn't heated, "watching out for" the female violinist was a good way to get out of the wind.

Except for especially cold days. Then the guard left for a warmer spot in the kitchen. Evie hoped today he would do the latter. In fact, her life depended on it. *Lord, please make him go.*

She walked to the music stand and set down her violin case with a thud. Around her, the musicians were in various modes of rehearsal, their mismatched sounds growing in volume and clamor.

The guard shook his head and covered his ears. He called out to Evie. "I'll be keeping warm in the kitchen and will return in an hour."

Thank You, Lord. Evie nodded and released the breath she'd been holding.

As soon as the door slammed shut, the music began to fade. Alexi labored to his feet, taking wobbly steps toward Evie. "No! Keep it up." He waved his hands to the musicians. "Our plan has worked."

The orchestra continued on, making so much noise Evie was sure she'd hear it in her dreams that night. Then she snapped open the clasps on her case and held out her offering to Alexi.

The case was stuffed with bread, sausage, and boiled eggs. The men's eyes brightened, but still Evie knew it was a small amount of food for so many.

"Felix has chosen well." Alexi placed his hand on her shoulder. "You are like a ray of sunshine in this dark place."

Evie touched his frail hand. "You know Felix? Of course, what am I thinking? He was the one hiding your violin."

"Jakub's violin," Alexi corrected, taking a bite of bread.

When each man had enjoyed a few bites of their special meal, Evie placed her hands on her hips. "Now I need a violin—to practice."

Jakub did not hesitate. He pulled the amber violin from the case. "Here, try this."

Evie lifted it to her shoulder. Her eyes brightened at the clarity of the notes that flowed from the instrument. She paused, looking to Alexi. "I know this must be a valuable piece, but what makes it so?"

He settled onto a bench beside her. "First, this is a very rare instrument. Jakub doesn't even realize its true value."

Jakub stepped closer and lifted his eyes to Alexi. The others continued to "tune up" but at a much softer level.

"It's the crown jewel of fiddles. Made in 1742 by Guarneri del Gesu. Stradivari is known for superior violins, but because Guarneri made so few, his violins are worth more. Stradivari crafted six hundred instruments, Guarneri only two hundred."

Alexi stroked the amber violin in Evie's hands. "Guarneri also lived after Stradivari. He studied the master's work and enhanced it. This Guarneri produces a sound deeper and more penetrating in tone than any violin I've ever known."

"That's amazing." Evie ran her fingers over its surface. "Who would have known?"

"Also, during the time of its construction, the church paid craftsmen well for instruments with a powerful and deep resonance that could keep up with their organs and choirs." He closed his eyes and tipped his head as if hearing the age-old notes. "The great expanses of the cathedrals needed strong sound, and numerous quality instruments can still be found in churches and monasteries."

"You should say 'used to be found,'" Evie interrupted, raising her voice. "Who knows what the Nazis have done with them? But not for long. I've heard the Americans are pushing through Germany and have already gotten as far as Houffalize!"

The room erupted in cheers and cries of joy from the musicians.

"We might make it." Jakub grasped Alexi's hands. "We may live to see Prague's independence celebration once more!"

"Of course. Unless we do not practice and are no longer found worthy!" Alexi carefully rose to full height. "Come, let us get to work. We have a lot yet to do tonight."

Evie lifted the violin to her shoulder once more and scanned the room. Yes, she was certain of it. The news of the American advance had rallied the orchestra members even more than the food had. The news had provided the same encouragement for her. *Could Nick be as near as Houffalize?*

The farmhouse was void of children's voices and pattering feet when Evie slipped in that evening. A light glowed from the kitchen, and she wondered if Frau Stoltz was still up. Evie had no doubt the woman would enjoy hearing about the prisoners' response to the food—and the news.

Evie hurried down the hall and into the kitchen, but her footsteps stopped short at the doorway. A man with dark hair and beard sat at the table, shoveling down a large plate of fried potatoes.

Felix?

The man glanced up, and while he looked familiar, he was not Felix.

Frau Stoltz's voice near her ear caused Evie to jump. "His name is Hans, and he needs a place to stay."

"Oh, welcome."

"He lost his family from the bombings in Germany, and he's looking for work. I told him he could sleep in the barn. The heat of the animals will keep him warm."

"Yes, of course." Evie stepped out of the doorway and allowed Frau Stoltz to pass. She cocked her head and studied the man's features again, certain that she had seen him before. But where?

Thirty-Nine

Evie opened her bedroom window a crack, freeing a thin moonbeam to sliver in. Then she slid between the sheets overlaying her feather bed. Outside, warm breezes hinted of spring, of hope. She drifted off to sleep with thoughts of Nick somewhere in Europe, possibly moving closer by the day.

Sometime in the night, the sounds of gunshots and sirens exploded from the camp, waking her. In the past, voices from the loudspeakers sometimes traveled down to their farmhouse, but never a clamor like this.

She vaulted out of bed and raced into the front room. From the light of the moon, she read the Swiss cuckoo clock on the mantel. It was after 2:00 A.M. She peered out the window, wishing she had a better view of the rock fortress on the hill.

The sound of bare feet pattered on the farmhouse's wooden floors, and Herr and Frau Stoltz wandered in, sleepy eyed, wearing nightclothes.

"What do you think?" Evie whispered in the dark. "Could it be a revolt or some type of escape? Listen to that."

Even in the cozy house, shut up tight for the night, the sounds of automatic gunfire seeped in.

Herr Stoltz made the sign of the cross and perched his thin frame on the edge of a chair. "Please, Lord, no. For the prisoners to attempt such a thing in their condition . . ." His forehead creased in worry.

"You never know." Frau Stoltz wrapped her arms around herself as she gazed out. "You never know."

A few minutes later, the sound of a vehicle, with loudspeaker, overpowered even the gunshots. A man's voice sliced through the obscurity, speaking sharply. "Several hundred dangerous criminals have fled from the Mauthausen Concentration Camp. They pose a great danger for the population and must be rendered harmless. No captives. All are to be killed on the spot. Anyone caught harboring a criminal will also be liquidated!"

Evie's mind flashed to the members of the orchestra, and their excitement over news of the American advance. *Are they involved in this? Could I have encouraged an uprising? Please, God, keep them safe.*

Herr Stoltz moved to his bedroom, while his wife watched knowingly. A few minutes later, he emerged clothed. "This madness shall not continue. I'll be back."

"Luther, where are you going?" Frau Stoltz moved toward him.

"If even one has made it this far, he'll need help." He set a wide-brimmed hat on his graying head. "We have the barn or the attic. We'll make it work."

A nod of her head was her simple response.

Thirty minutes later, Evie attempted to lay back down, when Frau Stoltz's cry echoed from the front room. "He's back!"

Evie rushed to the living room and recognized the stench even before she saw the two men. Though she'd thought the men in the orchestra were in bad shape, these fellows were no more than flesh stretched over bones. Their pants were threadbare, shirts nonexistent, flesh covered with sores. Even their eyes held a hazy gaze as if their minds were half wasted as well.

"Russians," Herr Stoltz commented. "Fenced in and left to starve."

"Good clothes, a little food will work wonders," Frau Stoltz commented. Neither mentioned the scouring by the SS, which Evie knew would follow.

Herr Stoltz immediately hustled the men out the back door to the barn. Even after they'd left, the stench of disease and death lingered in the living room. Evie moved to the front door and opened it wide, shivering in air that had turned icy cold over the past few hours. Frau Stoltz said nothing as she swept up the muddied footprints left on the floor. Then she moved into the kitchen to light the cookstove.

Evie opened the back door, cocking her ear for any

noise of movement from the barn. Then a figure emerged. A silhouette of neither a thin or sick man rushed toward her. Would Hans tell? Give them away? She'd known many who'd betrayed even friends and relatives for the smallest gain. The Stoltzes were neither to Hans.

"Do you know what he's doing?" Hans spoke brusquely.

"Lower your voice," Evie whispered. "You'll wake the children."

"Wake them? With this nonsense they'll be dead by morning." Hans's wild eyes glowed in the moonlight. "Do they realize those men are from the camp? How can you allow this to happen?"

Evie took a step back. "It's not my house or my place to decide. Of all people, you should understand the need. They've lost everything, everyone." Evie studied the man's face. She'd seen him somewhere; she was certain.

Hans turned his head.

"Have you ever been in Vienna?" she asked.

"*Nein.* I've lived in Germany my whole life, until now."

He's lying. He won't even look at me.

She strode back into the house.

I have to remember. Where do I know him from? While she couldn't recall, she knew he couldn't be trusted. She chastised herself for not warning the Stoltzes sooner.

A bird's song welcomed the morning, stirring Evie from her sleep. She decided to stay home from work, knowing she could claim that fear had caused her to remain inside their locked home. Herr Stoltz stayed home also, and they all awkwardly moved around the house —doing nothing in particular except waiting for a knock on the door.

They arrived near dinnertime—three SS guards with bags under their eyes and rage radiating from their gaze.

Herr Stoltz opened the door wide. "Come in. How can we help you?"

"Everyone outside! Now."

They did as they were told, and two of the guards stormed inside. From her place in the yard, Evie could hear the soldiers rummaging through cupboards, under furniture, behind closed doors.

The third guard looked over their identity papers quickly, including Evie's and those of the German man, Hans Gutman. Then he turned to Herr Stoltz as his friends pounded the floor with the butts of their rifles. "You, come with me." They moved in the direction of the barn.

Frau Stoltz stood tall. Her children huddled around her and wept in fear.

Not five minutes had passed when two gunshots split the air.

"They found them," Frau Stoltz mouthed, her face drained of color.

Evie motioned for the older woman to stay where

she was. Then she ran around the corner of the farm-house to the barn. She cried out, stopping suddenly.

Only one prisoner had been found. Blood gurgled from the hole in his chest. By his side, Herr Stoltz also lay dead.

"If we discover any more prisoners on this property," the SS officer spat, "we'll line you all up."

The officers stalked down the road, not even glancing back at their victims sprawled on the frosty ground. Before long a horse and wagon arrived to take the body of the Russian back to the camp. With the help of a neighbor, they buried Herr Stoltz that very day.

When darkness came again, Evie and a weeping Frau Stoltz moved to the barn. They found the second prisoner shivering, hidden under a tower of hay. Frau Stoltz helped him from the hiding place. Tears ran down her cheeks, and with faltering steps, she led him into the house.

"Come, they will not be back. We'll create a safe place for you in the attic."

Hans ran his fingers through his hair and paced the front room. He turned to Evie. "This is foolish! Why would she put the rest of her family in danger? Who would sacrifice themselves for such vermin, for such—" His words slipped back into a familiar Viennese accent —and he halted as his eyes met Evie's.

"These are good people, just trying to make a difference." Evie pointed to the door. "*You* should go now. We have enough trauma in this home without your help."

The German—Austrian, perhaps—threw up his hands and stalked out, leaving just as he'd arrived, empty-handed.

❧ ❧ ❧

The next day, heightened security after the breakout made Evie fearful of smuggling any more food into the camp. When she returned to work, she heard a full report of the escape from Officer Seidler.

"Four hundred and ninety-five Russian prisoners pelted the guards with floorboards, wooden shoes, rocks, fire extinguishers—anything they could find—until they overpowered the guards."

The man hadn't been himself lately. Hurried and distant, he only spoke to Evie when spoken to. Outwardly, Evie feigned her shock. Inwardly she cheered the prisoners' ingenuity.

"Most of them have been recaptured or killed. Only a few dozen remain. I don't know what we're going to do. More prisoners are flooding into the camp every day. It is hard enough to process them all, let alone feed and care for them." He ran his hand through his dark hair and moved to the window. "They're like caged animals, hungry and desperate. I suggest you don't go in the gates anymore. As of now, your lessons are over."

"But I just started. I—"

Seidler jerked around, his jaw tense.

Evie took a step back. "Yes, of course. I don't know what I was thinking." She returned to her seat and began

473

to type the reports that had seemed to multiply ten times on her desk overnight.

Evie thought of the men of the orchestra—Alexi, Jakub, and all the others. *How are they holding up?* The guard who'd refused rations for Jakub had left weeks ago for the front lines, but she wondered if Alexi's health could be restored. He hung on the edge of death, and she knew the only thing keeping him alive were Jakub's prayers to the Savior he now believed in.

🍂   🍂   🍂

AUSTRIAN BORDER
APRIL 26, 1945

"Hold up; you've gotta stop here," Nick called to his driver. The driver pulled the jeep over. Nick jumped out of the vehicle and jogged back to the road sign. *Österreich*. He stared at the word, realizing he'd finally made it to Austria.

After all this time. Hey, Evie, I'm here! I've come to you.

The Battle of the Bulge, as the Ardennes conflict was now referred to, had been the worst of their fighting. Other battles, scattered across Belgium and Germany, had cost them equipment and lives, but nothing stood out stronger in Nick's mind than the first day during the Bulge when so many lives, including Twitch's, were lost.

Nick still regretted not taking a few minutes to listen to Twitch when he needed it most—yet every time he mourned for his closest friend, one hope shined bright. Twitch had met his Savior. First on earth, then face-to-face. *God be with you 'til we meet again* echoed in Nick's mind.

Nick could have used Twitch by his side more than once. Not only for friendship, but because once the 11th Armored Division pushed into Germany, Nick had found himself overwhelmed with treating more civilians than soldiers. Thousands of them—hungry, shivering masses.

Their aid stations leapfrogged through Germany, attempting to keep up with the tanks and armored vehicles. Groups of citizens wandered into their camps at night, seeking help. The war would be over soon. Of that Nick had no doubt. The height of Germany's power was now matched only by its destruction.

Nick hustled back to the jeep and climbed in. "Okay, head out. I just had to take another look so I could believe we're here."

Nick whistled as he looked out at the mountainous countryside. Joy filled his heart as it had that last evening with Evie—before her father had arrived with his devastating news. Nick slid his hand into his pocket and pulled out the letters that continued to arrive with postmarks from Switzerland.

Dear Nick,

Day and night I think of you. I received a note that you are in Europe. Are you coming for me? Do you still think of me as I think of you?

I haven't heard word from you. I hope it's because my friends have not considered it a priority to deliver them. Please tell me that is the reason.

I can't tell you of my work, except that I'm trying to help even in the most horrible place imaginable. Come for me soon, darling.

                          Forever in love with you,
                          Lady Liberty

"How many times you gonna read that?" the driver asked.

"As many as it takes for my heart to trust she's really alive and thinking about me." Nick grinned. "We made it." He slapped the seat. "I'm here."

"Yeah, well, the war isn't over yet."

"No, but it will be soon. And as soon as I get a chance, I'm headed to Vienna." He kicked a booted foot onto the dashboard.

I'm just glad I never got around to writing that letter to Barbara. . . .

        🕊   🕊   🕊

MAUTHAUSEN, AUSTRIA
APRIL 28, 1945

Evie had no doubt that the end of the war was near. From the window of the farmhouse, she watched as the forlorn band of stragglers limped up the street. Eyeing the tired, dirty, and hungry soldiers, it was hard to believe these were the same men who'd so confidently and arrogantly marched through Vienna under the flapping swastika banners of Hitler's regime. The same men who ruled the camp with whips and bludgeons.

Days ago, all civilian workers had been let go from the camp. Evie's hands kept busy helping Frau Stoltz care for her household while they grieved for their husband and father.

Then there was the Russian soldier to consider. Evie helped to care for him too. Some days he seemed stronger, but other days fever and sickness racked his thin frame. It was as if his body swung like a pendulum between fighting to hold on and wanting to let go.

Seeing him made Evie's mind turn to the other camp prisoners. *How are they?* She only wished she could do more for those left behind. On her last day of work, Seidler had been frantic, enlisting teams of prisoners to help carry the boxes of documents to a far courtyard to be burnt.

They're going up in ashes a second time, Evie thought as she hurried down the granite steps one last time. First their bodies, then their memory. Now only those who still breathed were left as a testimony of what had taken place within those walls.

Evie longed to find a way in—or find a way to get her dear friends out. She hadn't seen the members of the orchestra in weeks. The music had stopped playing once the work crews had ceased. The quarry waited in silence, as did the other industries and underground factories that had been worked with labor from the camp.

Liberation was as evident as the coming of spring. American bombers roared overhead. Every once in a while an announcement from the loudspeakers around the camp carried down the hillside, but for the most part the camp was silent.

The busiest workers were at the train stations. Huge transports of half-dead, ghostlike prisoners continued to pour in by the day. Evie wondered how the camp could hold such masses. Surely the trains would stop soon. They had to. Where did all these poor people come from?

Evie's stomach lurched. How on earth would they be fed? Or were they just being locked in and left to die as the Russians had been?

When she'd seen Uncle Katz at the bakery the previous day, he'd whispered that SS guards were running away, leaving the camp in the hands of the Viennese fire brigade and members of the Linz orchestra.

What good will old firefighters and professional musicians do? she wondered.

He'd also said the Americans were making ground from the west, as the Russians advanced from the north. Who would arrive first? And would it be soon enough to save the tens of thousands of prisoners barely clinging to life?

God, bring the Americans. Quick.

She thought again of the hymn she'd carried around for so long, and the stanza Nick had whispered in her ear so long ago.

Mighty Spirit, dwell with me.
I myself would mighty be;
Mighty so as to prevail,
Where unaided man must fail.

Unaided, we will fail, she thought. *But we are not unaided. I have to remind myself of that.*

Forty

They're coming!" Stein pushed open the barracks door, allowing rays of light to beam into the dark room. Many of the orchestra members flung emaciated legs over the edges of scarred and splintered wood. A few had become too ill to rise. Two didn't move at all.

Jakub rubbed his eyes with chapped knuckles and attempted to focus his muddled mind. "What do you mean? Who are coming?"

"The Americans! Driving up the hill. The remaining guards are on the run, fleeing for their lives. Many wave white flags."

"How do you know?" the trombone player called from the back of the room.

"I saw it myself. Mueller's body lies on the *Appelplatz*,

practically torn apart. He'd found a prisoner's uniform and tried to mix in."

Jakub shuffled to the dusty window. "Look! The barracks are emptying out."

"Get your instruments." Janos hurriedly grabbed up his violin. "If we hurry, we can greet the Americans as they arrive!"

Jakub found his violin and hurried to Alexi's bunk. The songs of their freedom rang in his head. In the night Janos, Stein, and others had sung the melodies over and over.

Alexi lifted his head and attempted a smile.

"Can you come?" Jakub grasped Alexi's hands in his own, rubbing his thumbs over the paper-thin skin and bony knuckles. "Please, Alexi, do you have strength?"

"No, son. My legs refuse." Alexi's face was pale. He forced his cracked lips into a smile. "But go for me. The music I love now lives in you. I will be listening. Hurry and witness our freedom." His breathing grew raspy. "Witness what our hearts have hoped for."

"Jakub, come!" It was Janos's voice.

Jakub kissed Alexi's hands. "I'll be right back. I'll play beautifully. Perfectly, just for you."

Alexi nodded, and Jakub carried his violin out the door.

The warm air surprised Jakub. He lifted his eyes, looking beyond the walls and noting green grass cloaking the hillsides. Puffy white clouds played hide-and-seek with the sun.

Jakub clutched his father's violin, his inheritance, to his chest and hurried to the front gates. The other prisoners stepped back, making room for the orchestra. To their side, a group of haggard-looking women stretched out a small American flag, stitched from small scraps of dirty and torn fabric.

Prisoners had overrun the lookout towers. "Step back," one called down in German. "They're opening the gates." The cry was repeated in a half-dozen other languages.

A hush settled over the crowd, and Jakub's ears were tuned to the unlatching of their captivity.

"Now!" Janos called out.

The orchestra struck up the first strains of the national anthem of the United States. Jakub watched as the heavy, wooden doors slowly swung open, being pushed by a trucklike object. Jakub's soul soared with the strains of the music.

Five tall, healthy GIs entered, eyes wide. One soldier with red hair tilted his helmet and began to cry, his shoulders shaking.

Even before the last strain of their song ended, cheers rose from the crowd. Gaunt arms stretched into the air. Men and women staggered forward. Some crawled in tears, reaching trembling hands toward their liberators, forcing weak limbs to carry them to freedom.

The last strain faded, and Jakub lowered his head. His chest heaved as he thought of Daniel, Mother, and Father. Why couldn't they enjoy this moment together? Where were his parents? Had they survived?

Will I ever find them? I don't know if I can go on without—

Alexi's words from a few nights before interrupted his own thoughts. *Jesus is our salvation. Our Lord God, He is mighty to save. He will quiet you with His love. He will rejoice over you with singing.*

Jakub's shoulders straightened.

The cheers of the crowd rose in fervor, and Jakub's own heart lifted in a strange entanglement of sadness and gratitude. For what he had lost, for what he gained.

જ   જ   જ

Evie's heart pounded as she hurried up the hill. The gates were open, but armed Americans guarded them, not allowing the prisoners to leave.

"Excuse me, do you know a Nick Fletcher?" she asked one American by the gates. His eyes widened at her English. "I'm sorry, ma'am. I have to ask you to step back. This area's not secure."

"But do you know him? Nick Fletcher. He's with a medical unit."

Men in striped uniforms stumbled forward, grasping the soldier's legs.

"Ma'am, you have to leave. You can check with our commander later, but please, I have too much to think of right now."

"At least, can I go inside? To check on friends?"

The soldier's eyes narrowed. He struggled to push a prisoner aside gently so the frail man wouldn't tumble.

The soldier's eyes radiated sadness, and also fear. Fear at being overrun by joyful prisoners.

"Never mind. I'll be back." Evie wrapped her arms around herself and turned away.

꽃　　　꽃　　　꽃

KATSDORF, AUSTRIA
MAY 5, 1945

The uneven marching of thousands of feet stirred Nick from his sleep. He peered out the window of the cottage they'd occupied for the night. Through the pouring rain shapes emerged—an endless trail of men trudged up the road.

"Look at their uniforms." His driver, Will, stepped toward him through the dark. "They're German soldiers —no wait, Nazi SS."

"Where from?" Nick hopped on one foot, slipping on one boot, then the other. *Does this mean the Germans have surrendered?* He threw on his rain slicker and rushed to the command post. He burst through the door and spotted recon scouts wearily giving a verbal report to their company commander.

Nick saluted, then took a step back. "Sorry to interrupt."

"No, Fletcher, step closer. You'll need to hear this."

Nick neared the table where a map was spread out.

"To catch you up, two concentration camps have been found approximately twenty-five miles away. In this area"—the commander circled with his finger—"along the Danube. The victims are estimated to number in the tens of thousands. They're sick and starving and in need of immediate medical attention."

"*Tens* of thousands? How can we possibly handle that? We'll need more men, more supplies."

"I agree. I'll see what I can do. Until then, we do the best we can."

A haggard and weary recon scout turned to Nick. "I've never seen humans in worse shape. They were sleeping in their own waste—eating whatever scraps they could find. They need medical help as soon as possible, Doc. Some crawled toward us. Others tried to walk and collapsed. I didn't know better and gave one guy a K ration." The man's voice caught in his throat. "He ate it, then fell over dead."

Nick blew out a breath and rubbed the back of his head. "I'll get my medics and head out. We'll need someone to lead the way. Let's hope they can hold out just a little longer."

≈   ≈   ≈

BERKINSTALL TUNNELS
MAY 6, 1945

Our time has come. Otto shielded his eyes and staggered out of the tunnel. It had been the perfect hiding place, except that it had nearly been destroyed—with him inside.

When he first entered the tunnel, gun pieces and airplane parts lay scattered on long tables, half-assembled. The underground rooms were like a miniature factory within the hillside. He would take advantage of its expansive rooms and corridors.

Otto knew from reports that the Americans had already spread through Germany and into Austria. Like fingers of destruction, the plague took control of all in their path. Then there were the Russians moving in from the north. Roads were guarded, cities purged. The underground caves would provide a place of hiding until things settled down. And thanks to the bounty of the Stoltzes' farm, Otto had stored enough food and water to last months.

He'd assumed the tunnels had been abandoned until hasty groups of soldiers entered, stringing out lines and explosives. Moving with swiftness, they began wiring the tunnels. From his hiding place behind a stack of airplane wings, Otto heard their discussion of "orders from Berlin" to destroy all evidence—both the factories that produced goods for the Reich and the worthless prisoners who had worked them.

Yet before their task was complete, the sound of American bombers droned overhead, and the soldiers fled, leaving their work unfinished. Otto was alone once more.

He took a deep breath of fresh air as his eyes adjusted to the light. Then he set his focus on the camp and strode forward.

Now is the time to obtain the treasure prepared for me.

MAUTHAUSEN, AUSTRIA
MAY 6, 1945

Evie waited a full day before again facing the camp gates. She hurried up the hill, excited to see more American vehicles driving toward Mauthausen. She also noted thin waifs, who had somehow escaped, staggering down the hill. Even though she'd witnessed the prisoners in the camp, the reality of their situation seemed even more desperate as they tottered into a world, into a freedom, they'd been denied so long.

Evie sucked in a deep breath as she paused near the garage yard. Parked in spaces that SS vehicles had previously occupied, a dozen brown jeeps with white stars and Red Cross ambulances waited. Men in uniforms with white armbands hustled to and from the camp. Evie scanned their faces, her hands clasped to her chest, daring to hope for the one she longed to see.

"Son, you must let go." Janos tried to pry Jakub's fingers loose. "I'm sorry, but he is gone."

"No. They are here. The Americans have come. We have to go back to Prague. He promised."

"Jakub, listen. You must release Alexi's hand. He is gone to a better place—someplace even more beautiful than your beloved Prague."

Jakub dropped the lifeless fingers of his dearest friend and watched as two of the orchestra members carried Alexi away. The last few orchestra members who'd remained by the conductor's side also filed away, until only Janos and Jakub remained seated at the now-empty bunk. Jakub touched the straw where his dear friend had lain. The heat from his body was already beginning to fade.

"Where are they taking him?" Jakub's hands covered his face.

"To the . . . to the graves," Janos whispered.

"It's all my fault. Alexi gave me all he had. I had no idea, and by the time I knew he wasn't eating, it was too late."

Janos stroked Jakub's hair. "Listen to me. It was not your choice. It was his."

Suddenly Janos's hand stopped midstroke. Jakub wiped his tears and looked up. A man stood in the doorway with eyes intent on Jakub. He was dressed in the attire of a local farmer but walked with the stride of an SS guard.

Jakub recognized him immediately. Despite the darkened hair and farmer's clothing, he knew it was the officer who had visited the barracks and had asked him to play. The evil in the man's gaze was the same.

The man rushed to the violin cases. He opened them, throwing them to the side, until finally coming to the case of the amber violin.

"No!" Jakub overcame his fear and rose. The violin

was all that remained of his father, of Alexi. He moved to block the man's escape. "You cannot take that."

"And you will stop me?" With a strong sweep of his arm, the Nazi officer shoved Jakub to the floor.

Jakub hit the ground. His head slammed against the wooden floor. He bit his tongue, and the taste of blood filled his mouth. The man rushed from the barracks, and Janos hobbled to Jakub's side.

"Are you okay? You're bleeding."

Jakub nodded, struggling for a breath. He wiped at his mouth. "We must go after him."

"Don't be foolish." Janos attempted to hold Jakub's shoulders down. "It is too dangerous. You are too weak."

Jakub struggled to his feet, pushing Janos to the side. "This cannot happen. I will not let it!" He struggled forward, out of the barracks, and hobbled toward the gates.

It took all of his strength to make his way through the crowds of prisoners. By the time he exited the gates, Jakub was out of breath. He bent over to catch some air in his lungs, then scanned the road into town and the steps to the quarry, but there was no sign of the man. He sank to the ground. *What use is it? To be free but have nothing?*

Suddenly he felt a soft hand on his shoulder. He lifted his head and noticed the young woman, Theresa, who'd often brought food to their barracks.

"Are you okay?" Her tender gaze fell upon him. Jakub opened his mouth to tell her about Alexi, about the man in their barracks, but only sobs emerged.

"His violin. A man came in and stole it." It was Janos's voice.

"Stole the amber violin?" Theresa straightened. "Who?"

"A civilian, a farmer maybe," Janos said.

"He wasn't a farmer," Jakub cut in. "He was an SS officer, the one who came to watch me play."

"That's it!" Theresa slapped her forehead. "That's where I knew him from." She glanced around. "Did you see where he went?"

"He ran away. I'm sure he's long gone by now." Janos sighed.

"Maybe I can help. That violin—we have to get it back."

Jakub watched as the woman hurried to a few of the American soldiers. They brushed her aside with a shake of their heads. She returned a few minutes later and hunkered down before Janos.

"Do you have any idea where he could have gone? The roads are packed with American soldiers. Where could he hide?"

Janos shook his head. "I don't know. I've spent most of my time inside the camp. I . . ." He paused.

"What?"

"The caves. That would be a good place to hide. The Germans made weapons and airplane parts underground. I've heard others speak of the place. That's where I'd go."

Theresa stood, wiping her palms on her pant legs. "Tell me. What direction?"

Janos pointed down the hill. "Down there. See those large piles of rock over the rise? Those are the rocks they pulled from the mountain. The caves should be nearby."

Theresa started to jog in that direction, her auburn hair bouncing with each stride.

"But wait!" Janos called. "You can't go alone."

She glanced back over her shoulder. "I don't think we have a choice!"

🎔   🎔   🎔

Evie moved toward the hillside, then stopped. A sense of uneasiness told her not to do this, not to go alone. The last time she ran ahead, tried to go on her own strength, two people had ended up dead.

God, grant me favor, bring someone to help, she prayed, running back toward the main gates.

She approached a soldier not much taller than herself. A rifle was hung over his shoulder, and a silver cross hung around his neck.

"Excuse me," Evie called as she neared. "Can you help me? There is a man—an SS who has stolen a violin from one of the prisoners. I believe I know where he's gone, and it's not far."

The GI scratched his head beneath his helmet. "You speak English?"

"I lived in New York for many years, but now—now we need to go after this SS man."

"An SS hunt." The man fingered his weapon. "I'm

with you." He turned and called back over his shoulder. "Hey, Arthur, didja hear that? An SS is trying to get away."

The other soldier jogged over. "I'm with you, LeRoy. I'm with you, buddy."

LeRoy turned to Evie. "Go ahead, lead the way."

"Wait," a voice called from behind. "I'm coming too."

Evie glanced back to see Jakub shaking off Janos's grasp. The look in his eyes was desperate.

She didn't have time to argue. "If you can keep up, you can come."

The four of them half ran, half slid down the brush-covered hillside. It wasn't until she was halfway down that Evie realized she hadn't even thought about the height of the hillside.

Evie paused, looking toward the tunnels in the distance. "There he is!" She recognized the farmer's overalls Frau Stoltz had shared with the man who'd called himself Hans. She watched as he entered what appeared to be a cave in the side of the mountain. "We have to hurry!"

℗   ℗   ℗

Nick ran a hand down his face. His shoulders sank as he viewed the stack of corpses. As a medic he'd dealt with all types of injuries. He knew how to extract bullets from wounds, how to amputate legs shattered by mines, how to scrape away skin burnt by flames. But what could he do here?

As he'd entered the gates earlier that day, an indescribable darkness bore down on his chest. Like a shroud of oppression, it hung over the camp, not to be shaken. And the overwhelming stench. His stomach wretched at the odor of decaying and burnt flesh.

Weak prisoners rushed their medical group as they entered, their skeletal hands reaching, begging for food and cigarettes, seeking help for sick friends. Farther into the camp, they discovered barracks lined with squalid bunks. On them, the living looked dead, and the dead stared back.

Finally the bodies. Piles of bodies stretched across the camp like massive heaps of logs, white arms and legs entwined. Matted hair. Distorted faces.

Out of all the prisoners Nick had tried to treat this morning, only half could be helped. Most were too far gone for him to offer much assistance. Those still able to stand were given food, but only in small amounts.

Nick and the other medics then washed the frail bodies and helped to prepare them for transport to a tent hospital being set up in St. Georgen. He knew it would be months before their bodies fully healed. And their spirits? Nick wondered if they'd ever recover. *How could one live a normal life after this?*

He thought he'd seen it all, yet he let out a slow breath as he walked through the camp and discovered yet another pile of bodies. This one had been recently stacked since the last time he'd passed.

He turned to walk back to the former administration building, when his eyes caught the slightest movement coming from the pile of corpses. *Must be a rat.* He looked away, then paused. Something told him to look again. A chill swept down his spine as he inspected the tangle of limbs.

There! One thin white hand moved ever so slightly. Nick rushed over, looking down at the man who lay on top. *My dear Lord,* Nick prayed, *he's alive!*

Gingerly, Nick lifted the man and hurried toward the nearest aid station. The man's chest barely moved, but barely was enough.

※   ※   ※

It took five minutes for Evie, Jakub, and the two soldiers to make their way to the tunnel. Evie walked to the entrance and paused. She turned to the other men. "Maybe I should just sneak in and get a peek."

"No, let us." LeRoy entered the mouth of the cave. "Come on, Arthur."

The taller soldier followed, gun pointed, eyes intent on the tunnel ahead.

Evie motioned to Jakub to stay put and cautiously took a step into the mouth of the cave. She caught her breath, noticing that about twenty yards in, the rough rocks opened up to arched concrete walls. Swinging, metal lights hung from the ceiling. A soft glow radiated from what appeared to be safety lights mounted to the walls.

Before she'd taken another step, the ground shook, and an explosion filled the air. The air was knocked out of Evie's lungs as she was thrown into the concrete wall. A flash of light filled the entrance. She struggled to her hands and knees as coughing overtook her.

The Americans! I have to see if they're okay. But first I need air.

⁊ ⁊ ⁊

Jakub watched Theresa stumble out of the mouth of the cave. Coughs racked her body as her lungs attempted to expel the dust.

He rushed forward. "Are you hurt?"

"No, I'm fine. Do you see the Americans?" She glanced behind her, wiping her face.

"Yes, look. There!" Jakub pointed down the tunnel where the two American soldiers staggered out. A layer of dust covered them. They hurriedly spoke to Theresa.

"What are they saying?" Jakub asked.

Theresa turned to him. "The SS man. He must have rigged explosives. They tripped the wire, but thankfully it blew up farther down the tunnel. They say he's hurt; they heard him cry out just after the explosion."

Theresa turned to Jakub. "You stay here. We're going in."

"No, I want to go. It's my violin."

Her eyes narrowed. "Jakub, please. You're shaking as it is."

He looked down at his hands. Sure enough, they

were trembling. His knees too felt weak. "Fine, I'll stay."

Theresa ran into the tunnel behind the soldiers.

"I'll pray for you," he called after her, sitting down upon a nearby rock. "I will pray!"

By the time they entered the first large, warehouse-type room, the dust had already begun to settle. A thick layer covered the tables of machine parts. The room itself appeared secure, but the walls and ceiling of the tunnel beyond had crumbled. Chunks of concrete formed a small mound, and beyond, flames boiled from a large crater in the earth—obviously the point of explosion.

"Some type of fuel over there is feeding this fire." LeRoy coughed, covering his mouth with his sleeve.

Evie paused, hearing a human sound coming from near the flames.

"Hear that?" Arthur glanced at Evie. "Sounds like a man's cries."

"Sounds more like chants to me," LeRoy said.

"We have to get to him. We need that violin." Evie crossed the room.

LeRoy wiped his face. "I'm more concerned about that German right now. He's got to be stopped."

"Oh, if you knew about the violin," she whispered to herself, "you'd be worried about that too."

Otto wiped his eyes, attempting to focus. The walls had crumbled around him. The fire glowed, boiling from a crater that separated him from the first room.

He tossed chunks of rock off his torso. Pain shot up his leg, and a dull ache radiated from his head. Moisture trickled down the side of his face. He touched it. Blood. Then he remembered . . .

The violin. Otto searched the rubble around him. It was gone. His hands climbed the wall, pulling him to his feet. He took a step, and his right leg nearly gave.

There. The violin had been thrown in the blast. It rested on the other side of the pit of flames, which stretched from wall to wall. *There's no way around.*

Just as real as his own thoughts, a voice filled his mind. *Don't be fearful. Jump.*

The image of the Nazi youths gathered around the bonfire flashed through Otto's mind. The voice had been right about the boy named Jakub. It had been right leading him to this place, to this prize. Surely it was right now.

♪   ♪   ♪

Evie ignored the pounding of her heart and scrambled up the jagged pieces, following the two soldiers. A sharp incline of loose rock tumbled toward the flames. On the other side of the pit, the tunnel continued on, untouched.

The crumbled passage glowed and burnt with heat. The acid smell grew stronger. Evie began to crawl back, nearly overwhelmed with fumes, when she spotted him.

"Lookie there," LeRoy called, pointing. The SS

guard, Hans, or whoever he was, stood at the edge of the pit. Blood streamed down his face. He limped, and Evie saw that part of his bone protruded from his flesh.

Hans stretched a hand forward, over the flames. He eyed the pit and scrunched his body down.

"Stop!" Evie shouted. "Don't do it!'

🝔   🝔   🝔

Otto stepped nearer to the pit of flames. It was no more than six feet across.

The voice came again. *Don't be timid. The Power is in you. The Power will carry you.*

Quickly he touched his forehead. He knew it was time to put his trust in what he knew to be true. With his own blood, Otto touched the rock wall and drew a swastika in red. *The symbol of the life force. The symbol has the power.* He lifted his arms and warmth radiated outside and within. He felt the Presence.

The chants he had heard long ago in the bunker came back to him. He cried them as his mantra.

Jump. The voice spoke to his thoughts again.

Otto staggered forward. He remembered the fear in the boy's eyes as the lad had gazed at the fire. The boy had stumbled, nearly falling into the flames. But Otto swore he would not.

Jump. The Power will carry you.

The voice echoed in his ears. From atop the precipice of rocks on the other side, three human forms materialized. They waved to him, calling him.

499

Jump.

Otto launched his body, but his wounded leg failed, shooting pain upward, causing his eyes to dim. Otto stretched, reached for the violin, grasping for the rocks on the other side. But as his body tumbled, he found only scorching, blinding flame.

℘   ℘   ℘

"No," Evie whispered. She turned her head, quickly looking away.

LeRoy grasped Evie's arm. "Let's get out of here."

The flames roared louder, as if hungrily consuming their prize.

Evie looked back one last time and spotted something that appeared different from the rock around it. "Wait, look. The violin!" She pointed to the brown shape near the crater's edge. "It's going to catch on fire if we don't get to it."

"Are you crazy?" Arthur called. "It's too dangerous. We need to go before this whole place goes up."

"I have to do this." As Evie scooted down toward the case, the loose rock slid beneath her.

"No, you're going to fall in." LeRoy stretched his hand to her. "Give me your hand; I'll hold you."

She did as she was told.

LeRoy's grasp was strong. "Arthur, grab my legs," he called over the roar of the fire.

Evie stretched downward, ignoring the fear that urged her to turn, to climb back. The heat made it hard to breathe. She stretched her fingers, then pulled against LeRoy, needing just a few more inches. *Almost there.* He gave her slack, and she sucked in a hot breath, feeling the loose rock shift beneath her. "Dear God, I need Your help now!" she cried into the flames.

"I've got you, just a bit more," LeRoy called.

Evie's fingers wrapped around the handle. It scalded her but she refused to let go.

"Got it!" she cried. "Pull me up!"

～   *～*   *～*

Evie felt herself being led into the sunlight. She shielded her eyes, then squinted and found herself looking into Jakub's face.

"You did it." Jakub embraced her, tears streaming down his gaunt cheeks. "The violin."

Evie set the violin on the ground and stretched her arms around the young boy. Her chin rested on his shoulder. "Your prayers worked," she whispered in his ear. "They worked. Now, let's go show Alexi."

More tears came, washing over Jakub's dusty face. He shook his head. "No, Theresa. There's something I have to tell you."

～   *～*   *～*

The four of them staggered back to camp. Jakub clutched the violin to his chest and allowed the soldiers to help him along. Evie followed behind, wondering how long the boy's strength would last, especially now that Alexi was gone.

They soon entered the front gate, and the two soldiers led Jakub toward the medical barracks. Evie followed. Her head ached from the experience in the tunnels. Yet her stomach also flipped at the thought that one of these men might know Nick. She didn't dare hope that he'd be amongst them.

But what if? She bit her lower lip. *I should have brought the picture. I could have shown it around.*

She walked into the medical barracks, noticing it smelled of alcohol and soap—a sharp contrast to the rest of the camp. Instead of looking at the faces of the patients in the bed, she scoured those of the medics.

"Nick Fletcher, he's a surgeon, do you know him?" she asked one medic. He too seemed surprised she spoke English.

"Uh, no," he stuttered. "He's not with our unit. I just got here today."

Evie moved through one hospital barrack, then the next. Her shoulders fell when there was no sign of Nick. She exited, deciding she'd continue to look in all the buildings, when a hand touched her shoulder. She spun around.

It was LeRoy. The man's blue eyes were rimmed with tears. "It's the boy. You need to come. Quick."

Evie hurried after the soldier, back into the first hospital unit. *There.* A crowd had formed at the foot of one cot, Jakub's form stretched over the form of another. Evie rushed forward, looking to the face of the man on the bed. Her hands covered her mouth. "Alexi! He's alive. Jakub, he lives!"

Jakub's cries of joy continued, and he merely nodded his head.

Evie kneeled before them. Alexi's eyes were still closed. An IV was attached to his arm. Color seemed to be returning to his cheeks, and his breathing was strong.

"They say he's receiving blood from the medical officer who discovered him on the pile of dead corpses," LeRoy explained. "It's a miracle."

"Yes, a miracle," Evie repeated. And more than anything she longed for one of her own.

⁊   ⁊   ⁊

It was nearly dark when Evie made her way back toward the gates. She'd stayed by Jakub's side, while also searching the face of every GI who passed by. It was no use. The camp stretched in all directions; the Americans were constantly in motion. How long would it take to cover all the ground? Even then, the idea of Nick being at this very place seemed remote. Should she go back to Vienna? Wait for him to find her there?

Lord, help me to know what to do. Guide my steps.

A soldier led Evie through the masses of humanity to the gates. He turned to say something, but then the loudspeakers that barked to life drowned his words out.

"Hitler has committed suicide. His body was found

in the garden of the chancellery of Berlin." The announcement was repeated in various languages. Evie paused,
recognizing French, German, Polish, and Hungarian.
She imagined the small group of liberators and former
prisoners packed in the little room that once was her office, happily giving the report.

The American's announcements continued. "*Lager-
kommandant* of Mauthausen, SS *Standartenführer*
Franz Ziereis, was mortally wounded during his attempt to escape from members of the American Military Police. This took place at Phrym, in the Alps."

The voices began again, one language following another, their voices covering every inch of the camp.

"That's it!" Evie snapped her fingers. "I need to get
back into that office!"

She moved to the granite staircase leading to the administration offices and waited for the delegation of
men to exit. Then she jogged up the steps and made her
way to the door. Evie touched the knob and found it
unlocked.

"Thank You," she whispered. She slipped inside
and shut the door behind her, then made her way to the
microphone. She sucked in a deep breath and pushed
the button to turn it on.

"Excuse me, Americans. If anyone knows a medic
named Nick Fletcher, would you please meet me at the
front gates? My name is Evie Kreig, and I repeat again,
if anyone knows a doctor named Nick Fletcher, would
you—"

The door behind Evie burst open, cutting off her

words. An American soldier grasped her arm. "I don't know what you're up to, miss, but we need you to leave."

"Please, I'm looking for an American. A man—"

The soldier scoffed, pulling her along. "Aren't they all, doll. Aren't they all."

Evie ignored the comment and pulled against his hand. "Please, if you just let me go, I'll wait by the gate."

"I'm sorry, ma'am." The soldier shook his head. "We're securing the whole area. No arguments; you have to head back to town."

Evie's feet pounded down the granite steps. "Just fifteen minutes at the gate, please!"

They reached the bottom step. "I'm sorry. You have to—"

Suddenly another GI stepped before him, panting. A Red Cross armband was wrapped around his arm. A surgical mask covered his face. He lowered the mask. "Excuse me, soldier. I'll take it from here."

Evie froze in her steps. "Nick?" She looked to his eyes in disbelief. "Nick!" Evie stepped into his embrace, and he pulled her close. She closed her eyes and squeezed tighter. "It's you. It's really you."

She knew everything would be okay when he started placing a hundred kisses upon her head.

"Evie," he whispered. "My love."

"Say my name again, Nick. Say 'Evie,' please."

℞   ℞   ℞

505

Darkness had nearly settled over the countryside when Evie heard the American jeep pull up the drive to the farmhouse. She quickly removed her apron, smoothed her skirt, and hurried out.

"Nick!" She rushed toward him and was rewarded when he lifted her in his arms.

Nick gave her a warm kiss, then planted her on the ground. "So, my lady." He stroked her cheek with his hand. "What's the surprise?"

Evie took his hand. "Come with me, around back. Everything is ready."

🐦   🐦   🐦

A large summer sun hung in the sky, but Nick's heart was even brighter. It was really her, the love of his life. He studied her flushed excitement as she pulled him along. *She's beautiful. She's mine.*

Evie led him around the house where a small table was set up, lit by a dozen candles. A man with a peg leg was dressed in lederhosen. The man said something in German, then pointed to the table. Nick understood and held out the seat for Evie, then he settled into the chair across from her.

Evie smiled and waved toward the kitchen. A large, round woman approached with two plates in hand.

"Goulash." Evie clapped her hands together. "And Sacher torte for dessert. And you can't see it now, but" —she pointed across the field—"the Danube River."

Nick grinned. "Darling, you've re-created our night in New York." He took up her hand and kissed it.

"Well." She tipped her head and cast him a knowing grin. "I've done my part."

"Yes, of course." Nick stood, then sank down on one knee. "Evie Kreig, will you marry me?"

Evie pushed back her chair and sank on her knees, wrapping her arms around him. Nick pulled her close, taking in her scent of sunshine and cooking spices.

"Yes, Nick," she whispered in his ear. "I've been waiting years to answer that question. Yes."

Nick kissed her once more, and then he stood and pulled her to his feet.

Evie straightened her skirt. "Now, one more surprise. My first gift to my fiancé." She stretched out her hand, and a teenage boy walked from the shadows of the house with violin in hand.

Nick recognized him from the camp. He pulled out Evie's seat for her, then returned to his own.

"This is Jakub. I can't wait to tell you his story. But first, listen to him play."

The boy closed his eyes, then his bow made its first slice and music flowed from the instrument. Melody filled the air and drifted on the Austrian breeze. Nick was sure it was the most beautiful music he'd ever heard. The most beautiful place. The most beautiful bride-to-be.

Epilogue

Evie twirled a strand of her hair around her finger and gazed at her mother, who stood near Evie's bed folding another set of sheets.

"Mother, really. Do you think I'll need all this? The house we're getting is really small."

Her mother placed the lace-trimmed sheet set on the bed and pulled Evie into a tight embrace. "I'm sorry. I know I'm overdoing it. But it's not every day a mother helps prepare for her only daughter's wedding. How can I help but spoil you? You're starting a new life. What if you need something? Soldiers don't make that much money."

Evie kissed her mother's cheek. "Mom, Nick will only be stationed with the occupational forces across town. We'll just be a trolley ride away . . . at least for a little while."

Violin music drifted up the stairs. A piano joined in.

"I still find it amazing how you found each other again." Mother released her embrace and took a step back.

Evie tapped her lip. "You haven't heard even half of the story. I didn't want to scare you. Dad and Isak, you should have seen their faces when I told them—"

An army jeep rumbled into the driveway, interrupting their conversation.

Evie rushed to the window. "Hurry, it's them! Jakub will be so surprised!"

She ran down the steps, hearing her mother's high heels demurely clicking behind her. Evie opened the door and lunged into Nick's arms.

"Ah, there's my girl. I've missed you." He stroked her brown hair, then led her inside. A thin man followed, eyes wide.

Nick cleared his throat. "Evie, I have someone I want you to meet."

She turned to the man she'd heard so much about, then reached over and gently wrapped her arms around his frail frame. "Mr. Hanauer, I hope your trip from Germany was uneventful." She took a step back and looked into his face, realizing how much his son favored him. "I've heard so much about you. Jakub wept when he heard you were alive. But he doesn't know you are here. Follow me. After so long, let's not waste another moment."

Evie led the way down the hall, toward the large living room. The lively melody of the violin and piano grew louder with each step. Alexi sat at the piano, and Jakub stood next to it. Her brother and father sat nearby, rapt listeners.

Mr. Hanauer paused before the door. Tears overwhelmed him. "That is my Jakub playing?" His hand covered his heart.

Evie nodded.

"Oh, my sweet boy." He peered into the room. "My, he's gotten so tall," he whispered. "He's practically a man. And look, the violin, it still plays beautifully. And my friend Alexi on the piano . . ."

Evie gently patted the man's frail back. Nick squeezed her shoulder.

Jakub's eyes were closed as he played.

"It was Daniel's favorite song," Samuel Hanauer commented. Tears trickled down his cheeks.

"Now it's Jakub's favorite too," Nick whispered.

Evie cleared her throat.

Alexi turned, and his eyes widened when he spied them standing in the doorway. The piano stopped abruptly.

Jakub paused, casting a questioning look at Alexi, then he followed his friend's eyes toward the small group huddled in the doorway. A gasp arose from Jakub's chest.

"Papa?" he mouthed, his face scrunched in sobs. "Papa?" He placed the violin on the side table and rushed forward, arms wide.

"Papa!" he cried. "Oh, Papa."

"My boy." Samuel's bony arms enfolded his son. "Every day, I thought of my family." He wiped his quivering chin with the back of his hand, then tenderly wiped Jakub's tears. "It gave me the strength to go on." He took a deep, shuddering breath. "Come. I want to hear you play. It's such beautiful music."

Jakub helped his father to the couch, then he turned and placed a hand on Alexi's shoulder. "He taught me, Father. Gave me life and music. He and his friends, in the darkest of places . . . they gave me songs in the night."

Acknowledgments

Thank you to my family and friends who have made this novel possible. John, my true love, and our three great kids Cory, Leslie, and Nathan. Mom loves you! My in-laws, John and Darlyne Goyer, and my family Billy and Linda Martin, Ron Waddell, and Dolores Coulter for your love, support and prayers. big thanks to Tim and Sandy Goyer for all the work on my Web site. Thank you for helping me to share the true stories of my research and writing!

Thanks to all my friends who offer love and suport, especially those who pray: OH and BH sisters, AWSA, ACRW and FCW buddies, and writer-friends Cindy Martinusen, Anne de Graaf, Robin Gunn, and Judy Gann. Also my face-to-face friends who always brighten my life: Twyla Klundt, Tara Norick, Sandy McCollam, Joanna Weaver, Erica Faraone, and Rebecca Blasing. Also my friends at Hope Pregnancy Center and Teen

MOPS. Tanya Flores, Jeannie Schelling, Jamie Spaulding, Jessica Meadows, and all the rest. You guys are the best cheerleaers!

Thanks to my agent and friend, Janet Kobobel Grant. I'm so thankful for you.

The book was truly transformed with the wonderful guidance of my editors, LB Norton and Lisa Bergren. Also, I greatly apreciate the whole Moody Publishers staff who believes in me and shows it! Dave, John, Janis, Lori, and Amy—Thanks!

This story is inspired by the stories of the veterans of the 11th Armored Division. The following men helped with research and so much more: Kenneth Aran, Gerald Arndt, Joseph Barbella, Ray Buch, George Crowley, Al D. Dunn, John Fague, Roy Ferlazzo, Scott Foster Jr., Sidney Friedl, Howard Greinetz, Bert Heinold (medic), Shelby Keeton, Robert Kenney, Leonard Kyle, Orville Larson, Robert Linley, Alvin Marske, Duane Mahlen, Wilfred McCarty, Tony Petrelli, LeRoy Petersohn (medic), Patsy Potente, Richard Robertson, Darrell E. Romjue, Harry Saunders, John Slatton, Ross Snowdon, Ralph Storm, Charles Torluccio, Charlie White. Additional help came from Bob Pfieffer and Dan O'Brien from the 11th Armored Division Association.

I'm appreciative of research help given by Martha Gammer, Gusen and Mauthausen Historian, who first told me about the orchestra in the Mauthausen camp, and Philip Beckman, Mauthausen survivor. Thanks to Dr. Lee D. Joiner for suggestions concerning violinists and their music. And to Skylar Norick who gave me the inside scoop on German weapons. Also thanks to Vienna resident Anita Zornig for help with German phrases,

I'm forever grateful to writer friends who read all stages of this manuscript, gave me ideas, and offered suggestions: Ocieanna Fleiss, Cindy Martinusen, Amy Lathrop, Mike Yorkey, Marlo Schalesky, Randy Ingermanson, and Joanna Weaver. And thanks go to my friends at Christian Book Supply in Kalispell, MT, Ray and Mary Lodien. Thanks for talking "book stuff" with me!

I also have special memories of those who shared their stories and their love, yet are no longer with us: Arthur Jacobson (11th Armored Division), Earl Lovelace (2nd Infantry Division Medic), Vera Zanardelli (Former Secretary 11th Armored Division). May your memory live on through these pages!

A Story of Liberation

Nazis flee under cover of darkness as American troops near the town of St. Georgen. A terrible surprise awaits the unsuspecting GIs. And three people—the wife of an SS guard, an American soldier, and a concentration camp survivor—will never be the same. Inspired by actual events surrounding the liberation of a Nazi concentration camp.

From Dust and Ashes
ISBN: 0-8024-1554-7

MOODY
PUBLISHERS

THE NAME YOU CAN TRUST.

1-800-678-6928 www.MoodyPublishers.com

Night Song Team

Acquiring Editor
Andy McGuire

Copy Editor
LB Norton

Back Cover Copy
Laura Pokrzywa

Cover Design
LeVan Fisher Design

Cover Photo
Nonstock, Michael McGovern and Bettmann/Corbis

Interior Design
Ragont Design

Printing and Binding
Dickinson Press Inc.

The typeface for the text of this book is
Sabon